CW01212373

MASTERMIND

MITCHELL PARKER CRIME THRILLERS BOOK 1

HELEN GOLTZ

Copyright (C) 2020 Helen Goltz

Layout design and Copyright (C) 2020 by Next Chapter

Published 2020 by Gumshoe – A Next Chapter Imprint

Cover art by Cover Mint

This book is a work of fiction. Names, characters, places, and incidents are the product of the author's imagination or are used fictitiously. Any resemblance to actual events, locales, or persons, living or dead, is purely coincidental.

All rights reserved. No part of this book may be reproduced or transmitted in any form or by any means, electronic or mechanical, including photocopying, recording, or by any information storage and retrieval system, without the author's permission.

ALSO IN THE MITCHELL PARKER SERIES

Mastermind

Graveyard of the Atlantic

The Fourth Reich

Dedicated to my mother
And with sincere gratitude to Francis Price for the ideas, research and inspiration

1

Special Agent Mitchell Parker had a clear plan – get the security tapes, get out of there, and get home in time for Inspector Morse on television at eight. Crouching on a hanging bridge spanning the middle floor of the university's science block, Mitch silently cursed the architects who thought suspended walkways and wire railings would be 'arty' in the new science wing. It left nothing to hide behind and exposed him and his partner, Jack Jameson, to the lab entrances and thoroughfares.

Mitch flattened himself against the railing in the shadows on the bridge. At six-foot-two, with dark hair and an athletic build, he was a man who didn't spend much time in the shadows. His sharp blue eyes swept the area, landing on J.J.

"J.J., nothing here. Try the next level up," he whispered into his throat microphone.

The stocky J.J., five-years older and a stone heavier, nodded and crawled out of sight.

Mitch looked between the wire railings to the hallway entrance below. He saw one security guard at the front desk. His eyes traveled above the guard, finding the security camera that broadcast images to the desk monitor while recording them somewhere in the building.

I want those recordings!

Mitch glanced at his watch. It was nearing seven o'clock; the night-shift security officer was due.

"Mitch?" J.J.'s voice broke his concentration.

"Yeah?" Mitch whispered into the headset.

"Are you sure this is going to work? There'll be two guards to deal with during the changeover."

"I know," he whispered back, "but they'll be talking, not watching the monitor. It's our best shot. Just find the room where the tapes are – I need them and we're running out of time!"

Mitch took in the area. The walkways reminded him of the modern shopping centers designed to make you walk one hundred and eighty degrees to get to each level.

A pain in the ass, he thought. OK, walk around or straight up?

Mitch jumped up, missed and tried again. Grabbing onto the overhead landing he heaved himself up, squatted, and did a quick reconnaissance. He saw lights on in one of the rooms.

"J.J., the large room with the lights on, that's got to be the main lab – and bet the small room next to it is our tape room," he whispered into the mic.

J.J. came into sight from the opposite direction. He glanced through the glass strip on the door of the small room.

"Yeah, we've found it," J.J. confirmed. "You'll have to pass the main lab or drop back down below again and work in reverse."

"Too hard; main lab it is. Head count?" Mitch watched J.J. move closer to the main lab, glance in and move back.

"Three. Two males at the back, one female near the door."

Mitch checked the coast was clear and increased his pace, sidling alongside the lab wall. He looked through the glass strip and saw a diminutive female with long dark hair working inside. No one else was in view. He ducked underneath the glass and moved to the taping room. With a silent prayer, he swiped a pre-programmed access card in the slot on the door. The access light flicked to green and he exchanged a quick look of relief with J.J.

Mitch pushed open the door and entered the pitch-black room.

He reached into his vest for a small penlight, flicked it on, surveyed the room and headed straight for a glass cabinet that housed numerous tapes, all dated. It opened first try. He found the previous week's tape and set it aside. He stopped, listened and followed the whirring noise to locate the tape machine.

"Shit!"

"What's wrong?" J.J.'s voice came through his earpiece.

"Tape recorder's a hundred years old! Our blanks won't fit."

He glanced around and spotted some blank tapes still in their plastic wrappings on the counter.

"Make my day."

"Come again?"

"Nothing, problem solved. Let's cut the chatter."

Mitch fished around in his black vest for a glove and put it on, being careful not to leave fingerprints. He grabbed a tape and unwrapped it, trying to minimize the noise from the plastic wrapping.

"What the hell's that?" J.J. cut in.

"Plastic wrapper."

"Nightshift's arrived," J.J. said. "I can hear them talking. Hurry up, you've got about five minutes."

"Don't sweat, I'm almost done."

Mitch moved back to the tape machine.

"Just had a thought ..."

"What?" Mitch asked frustrated.

"Old technology ... what if their monitors go to black instead of relaying the hallway feed live?"

"Security'll head straight to the tape room."

"Great."

Mitch positioned himself next to the recorder.

"Hurry up! What's taking so long?"

"Shut up for chrissake, I'm working here." Mitch took a deep breath. "OK, here goes. Stopped recording ... eject ... tape out ... new one in ... recording ... done!"

They waited a beat.

"All clear. Didn't even notice," J.J. proclaimed.

"Excellent," Mitch stuffed the tape and plastic in his vest, picked up the tape he had set aside and pried open the door. He spotted J.J. who gave him the 'all clear' thumbs up.

Mitch closed the tape room door behind him.

Less than three feet away, the main lab door began to open.

2

Mitch flattened himself against the wall as the dark-haired female walked out of the lab and turned right. She headed straight for J.J.

"The bins," Mitch whispered into his microphone. He watched J.J. grab the nearest garbage bin, pull out its lining, and with the bin under his arm and a bag of rubbish in the other, he nodded to her as she passed. She returned his nod and walked on. As she rounded the corner, he bolted behind Mitch.

"Man, now I'm the janitor. Step up from my current job," J.J. muttered.

"Yeah?" Mitch frowned. "Close call, let's go." He led the way to the bridge. He heard the security guard's footsteps approaching from the same direction.

"Too late, this way." He tried the access card on the door marked Lab G and it opened with a click. They slid in and the door locked behind them. They squatted beneath the bench in complete darkness.

"Smells like the dentist," J.J. sniffed.

"Shh! Stay down, he might not come in."

They waited, immobilized. Mitch wiped a thin layer of sweat from his forehead. The security officer's footsteps drew closer. He stopped at their door, rattled it as if testing the lock and then continued on.

Mitch heard the security officer stop at the next lab and exchange greetings with the inhabitants – then the footsteps began again, moving away. Mitch rose, pushed the lab door open a few inches and glanced up and down the hallway.

"Clear! Come on."

He sprinted for the wire bridge and swung through the rails to the walkway. He landed with a soft thud, turned and waited for J.J.

Remaining low, Mitch led the way along the length of hanging walkway to the emergency exit door less than ten feet away. They made it out. Mitch scoped his new surrounds; it was a dark, confined area that was fenced.

"Clear the fence and we're safe." He heard a growl. "But then again …"

"Guard dog!" J.J. exclaimed. "Where is it?"

Mitch moved his head to the right and saw a sleek Doberman, no more than fifteen yards away.

"Four o'clock. When did they get that?"

"Five yards to the fence. Can he outrun us?" J.J. asked.

"Maybe. OK J.J., here's the plan. I'll drop a doggy snack to …"

"You're carrying a doggy snack?"

The Doberman growled.

"On the count of three, I'll drop a snack and we'll bolt for the fence."

"Security'll hear."

"It's that or hope Rover's friendly."

"Count it," J.J. agreed. "One …"

The growling became louder.

"Two, three," Mitch snapped, throwing beef pellets towards the dog without sticking around to see if the distraction worked.

They hit the fence, found footing in the wire uprights and hurled themselves over. Mitch heard a car start up. A black sports utility came into sight and he led the way towards it. He could hear the dog barking maniacally now.

"You know," J.J. panted beside him, "you might get home in time to see Morse."

"Nah. You know what it's like, miss the first ten minutes and you never catch up."

Mitch reached the car and leapt into the front seat.

"Go," he yelled as he heard J.J. slam the back door. Agent Ellen Beetson took off and the sound of the dog's barking died away.

"Nice driving Ellie," Mitch collapsed back into the seat.

"Just once," J.J. complained, "I'd like to do a job without a dog, a security officer or some idiot in hot pursuit."

"Where's the fun in that?" Ellen flashed a smile at him in the rear view mirror.

"Why couldn't we get a warrant and confiscate the tapes?" J.J. puffed.

"We've acted on a tip off," Mitch turned to look at him. "If we confiscate the tapes at this stage, we close down anything that might be in progress. Plus, we don't know who we're dealing with. The guy on the front desk could be involved, or the guy who tipped us off. You're bleeding on the boss's seat."

"Clipped the fence." J.J. pulled a handkerchief out of one of the vest pockets and wrapped it around his hand.

"Anyway, did you get it Mitch?" Ellen asked.

Mitch patted his vest. "Got it. Now, let's see who's on it."

3

Charlotte Curtis frowned at the black toast.

"Mitchell!" she muttered. "Why do you always have to fiddle with the settings?" she slapped jam over the burned toast and threw the knife in the sink.

The chime from the wall clock announced six o'clock.

An hour to read the file, get dressed and get to the office, she thought. Never going to happen.

She stopped to listen, heard the tap running and left Mitch's coffee cup unfilled. With her plate of toast, coffee and the file, she headed for the warmth of the lounge room, falling into the cushioned sofa. Charlotte opened the file from the Child and Family Services Agency on her new client, Bradley James Parnell, and sighed.

Counseling minors, not a great start to the day, she thought.

The bathroom door opened and she looked up as her roommate emerged in a smart black suit, crisp white shirt and in the process of doing up a blue patterned tie. "What?" she asked noticing his grin. "Have I got bed hair?"

"No, no, thy name is beauty," Mitch placed his hand over his heart.

Charlotte pulled her blue dressing gown around her and gave him a wry look. "The kettle's boiled." She returned to her file.

Absorbed in her paper shuffle, she inhaled Mitch's aftershave as he re-entered the room. She looked up. "Why are you up so early?"

"A seven o'clock meeting," he said as he sat next to her with his cereal and yesterday's newspaper.

Charlotte watched him as he read, his hand performing the reflex motion of cereal to mouth. Every now and then he frowned.

He looked up and stuffing another spoonful of Wheaties into his mouth mumbled, "What?"

"Your hair is starting to cover that scar. Did you really shave it for charity or just to look tough and pull girls with stories of gang fights?"

"Hey, I only used the gang fight story a few times. The shark-attack angle seemed to work better."

Charlotte snorted. "I've known you for three years and never seen you even fake a punch let alone wrestle a shark. Besides, your face is far too pretty to have led a street life."

"Handsome, not pretty. Anyway, I've been on the streets! My job is fraught with danger."

"When? I thought you told me your FBI unit took a few photos on location and ran office-based passport checks?"

"That's about it. But trust me, there is danger in the office! Those pencil sharpening machines ..." Mitch shuddered.

Charlotte laughed.

"So how many nut-cases are you seeing today?"

"They're not nuts; they're normal people with problems. This kid," she held up the file, "was a straight-A student right up to four months ago, and now he's gone off the rails big time; petty theft, absenteeism, bashing another student. He's hardly a nut-case ..." Charlotte stopped mid sentence. "You know, one day you may need someone to talk to and ..."

"Highly unlikely," Mitch interrupted. "I'm not into the put-it-out-there kind of therapy. Speaking of getting over it, Lachlan rang for you after you went to bed."

"Did he?" Charlotte chewed on her fingernail. "Why didn't you wake me? What time?"

"Not long after Morse. I stuck my head in but you were out of it. I thought it was over with him," he rose.

Charlotte followed him into the kitchen.

"It is over, but I'd speak to him."

"Well, he said he'd be stuck in meetings all day and he'd call back later."

"Anyway, what do you care if I get up to talk to him?"

"I don't. Whatever. I'm just the messenger."

"Did you talk for long?" she asked.

"No."

"So, what else did he say?"

"Nothing much."

"Honestly, you can be so exasperating!"

Mitch grabbed his coat, phone and keys. "Hmm, I know. Anyway, I'm off. Happy counseling."

She followed him to the front door.

"Have a good high-security day," she said locking the screen door behind him. Charlotte glanced around the neighborhood while she waited for his car to pull out of the garage. With a wave, she closed the door and headed to the bathroom. The phone rang and she retraced her steps.

"Hello."

"It's me ..."

"Mitch, sorry I snapped at ..."

"No big deal." Mitch cut her off. "Don't forget to turn the heater off."

"I won't. Will you be home for dinner?"

"Uh, don't know."

"Of course ... depends on the outcome of this morning's meeting?" she asked knowing he wouldn't answer.

Lawrence Hackett fidgeted; he wasn't one for small talk after sex. Earlier he had wined and dined her, put up with inane banter about a day in the life of a model and gotten what he wanted by the end of the night. It was a fair trade in his mind. Now he had to get rid of her. Lawrence excused himself to go to the bathroom, picked up the phone installed on the white tiled wall and called his Chief of Staff, Andrew Kenny. It was nearing midnight but Lawrence's staff worked twenty-four seven.

"Call me back, Andrew, will you?" He didn't bother to introduce himself. Within a few minutes the phone rang and Lawrence faked an emergency. He begged forgiveness from what's-her-name, called a taxi and hurried her along saying all the right things. He saw her off at the front door and headed for the shower, preferring to sleep clean and alone.

He let the hot water stream over him and watched as it pooled at his feet.

"Treading water," he muttered, "that's what it feels like; day in, day out."

He turned off the taps and reached for a towel. Stopping to look at his reflection, one question came to mind. When was the last time I was excited by anything? Lawrence thought. He remembered the rush when he took over his father's global media empire after his old man died. He also remembered bedding the hottest actress that same year and replacing everyone on his father's board with his own people. Buying his first Lamborghini Countach was up there too. He realized those thrills were almost two decades ago.

Done it. Milked every high that could be had ... except for Mastermind.

He walked from the bathroom, grabbed the Mastermind file from his bedside drawer and collapsed on the bed. He scanned the six entrants selected to play in this year's high-risk game; they were located in Munich, Tokyo, Monaco, Paris, Nevada and Washington D.C.

Bring it on! He smiled.

"White with none," J.J. handed Mitch a coffee.

"Thanks J.J., what's the latest?" He looked over at the Executive Director for the Trans-National Crime Unit's office. John Windsor was on the phone.

"Our tapes are back and the lab rats identified."

Mitch saw John hang up and signal them in. Looking around, he spotted the rest of his team, Ellen Beetson and Samantha Moore, walking towards him with cappuccinos from the canteen.

"I bought you a coffee, but if you've already got one …" Samantha held onto it.

"Thanks, Sam," Mitch grabbed it, looking for somewhere to toss J.J.'s strong brew.

"Ready for another day of official non-existence and denial?" Ellen greeted him.

Mitch laughed. "I like being deniable. Gives us scope." He followed his team into John's office and closed the door. "What've we got?"

"Good and bad news," John began. "The good news is we've identified the people on the tape. The bad news is, as a result, we've got one hell of a problem." John pressed a button that closed his office blinds and another to lower a screen from the ceiling. He logged into his laptop, opened the surveillance footage file and hit play. They watched as several figures came within sight of the university camera. He froze the video on a tall, gray-haired man in his late fifties.

"Johan Booysen," John announced. "Former Chief Executive Officer of a large Telco in South Africa."

"Former?" Mitch asked.

"Yes, he stepped down last year amidst a controversy about misused funds. Nothing was ever proven. He's here on a tourist visa."

Mitch scribbled down some notes. "Sightseeing around the university. That's a little different from most."

"Precisely. He's got his fingers into something. The universities are cash-strapped; they're contracting facilities out-of-hours in all faculties without any real security checks. The science lab is one of the most lucrative for private hire. I want to know what he's doing there." John continued the tape. "This guy ..." he froze it on an image of a tall, blonde man who looked to be in his mid-thirties.

"Nicholas Everett!" Mitch said, surprised.

"Yes. Nicholas Patrick Everett. You know him?"

"We were close friends at school and in the Air Force. He moved to the west coast and I haven't seen him for ... seven or eight years."

"He's flying for a courier company in Nevada. Don't know what he's doing in D.C.," John honed in on the female. "This is Maria Elena Diaz, a trader in antiques, jewelry and fine art. She's a celebrity in the Venezuelan community and well connected."

"She's a stunner," Samantha said.

"Yes, it hasn't set her back. She's had her deals well funded."

"She was at the lab last night," J.J. added.

John closed the program and opened the blinds.

"A South African with a shady past, a former Air Force pilot and a South American dealer meeting in a science lab at the university. What's the connection?" Mitch mused.

"You tell me," John replied. "Our source has been watching Johan since he entered the country. When he visited the university after-hours and met with your friend, Nicholas, we were alerted right away. That's it. It's all yours."

Mitch rose to depart, his team followed.

"Mitch," John said, stopping him. "Keep me in the loop."

───────

Mitch paced around his sparse, glass-walled office. He turned to his team who sat waiting for instructions.

"OK, Ellie and J.J., head to the university science department and find out what inter-country science programs are running, if any, between the U.S., South America and South Africa. Then start work on Johan. Get as much info as you can on him."

"Done," Ellen answered.

"Stay in touch. Sam and I will head to the university admin to book some lab space and find out when the main lab will next be available. We'll try and get a room as close as we can to it to watch coming and goings. Let's see what they're up to in there."

4

"Gentlemen, it's time to play," Lawrence Hackett said as he turned his back on the bleak London day and swiveled his chair to face the directors around the board table. "For the few of you that were not with us five years ago when we last played, let me remind you of the rules of the game. Contestants must mastermind and carry out the perfect crime. A prize pool of five million pound will be divided amongst the Mastermind entrants that succeed. So, the less who succeed, the better for the winners. Clear?"

The directors nodded in agreement.

"Rishi, another one?"

"Entry is by invitation and only six entries will be selected to play."

"Bravo. Richard?"

Richard cleared his throat. "I'm too old for a pop quiz, Lawrence."

Lawrence laughed. "Indulge me, Richard."

"For security reasons, one person only will represent each group. No other members of the group are to have contact with us or be aware of Mastermind. They are briefed on the job, not the competition. Should the team rep withdraw, the entry is disqualified," he rattled off.

Lawrence heard Daniel Reid shuffle in his seat. He turned to him. "Daniel, you haven't played before …"

"But I know the rules. Mastermind directors will be accessible one month prior to the event in the capital city of the entrant. This will be the contestants' only point of contact."

"Go on," Lawrence encouraged him.

"The Mastermind act cannot be a Mastermind that was performed in past events."

"Correct, and finally, when you are allocated a Mastermind entrant, get full security checks on all team members, and confirm everyone's timing is going to work. It must happen between November 1 and 30. If your group fails and keep their mouths shut, you can offer them legal help – otherwise pull out and disown them. Make sure the team reps know this. Anything else, Andrew?"

"Yes, if they succeed, they'll be paid on December 1. They also get to keep the spoils of their crime. I'll have Mastermind projects allocated to directors by tomorrow."

"Good," Lawrence concluded. "Let the fun begin! We've got some good ones this year."

"What's your all-time favorite, Lawrence?" Daniel Reid asked.

"Ah, there have been a few. I liked the Swiss Mastermind in the inaugural competition, before your time, Daniel. The entrants held up a bank, handcuffed and blindfolded the staff and customers, then transferred funds to untraceable accounts. After the transfer, they tied themselves up and joined the hostages. When the cops burst in, they were released with the hostages. It was beautiful. What was your favorite, Richard?"

"All bias aside, since I worked on it, I liked the New York print run in Mastermind-2."

"That was the thanksgiving weekend wasn't it?" Lawrence recalled.

"Exactly, a traditional busy time. The Mastermind entrants dispersed half a million worth of counterfeit notes across four U.S. borders that weekend. Simple, effective and by the time the notes were detected, the perpetrators were sunning themselves in the Cayman Islands."

"What was your favorite, Mike?" Lawrence turned to Michael Germaine.

"It would have to be another one in the Mastermind-2 competition – the selling of the Parisian apartment."

"Yes, the second round gave us some great ones," Lawrence agreed.

"It was classic," Michael continued. "The entrants sold that block of units while their landlord was out of the country. When he came back two months later, his units were being demolished and they were gone with a large wad of French francs and their Mastermind payout."

Lawrence laughed. "Yeah, that was great. So, we had three Masterminds succeed in our inaugural Mastermind and two in Mastermind-2. Let's see what this year brings us for Mastermind-3. Who do you think will take it out, Andrew? How about a bet?"

"OK, fifty pounds on Monaco," Andrew Kenny started the betting.

Lawrence turned to Alan Peasely.

"Tokyo," Alan answered.

"Ian?"

"Hmm, tough one. I'm going for Nevada."

"And you, Lawrence?" Richard put him on the spot.

Lawrence answered without hesitating. "My money's on Washington D.C."

Mitch rang the bell on the desk in the university's administration building. He looked over at Samantha.

"Sam, see if you can see what name the lab's booked under."

"Will do."

A young woman came out from behind a glazed partition.

"Faculty bookings? Yes I can help you," she responded to Mitch's request. "Where were you looking to book?"

"The main lab in the science faculty."

"I'll get the book," she looked under the counter and pulled out a large diary.

"Now ... the main lab ... hmm. It seems to be booked for a while. When did you want it?"

"As soon as it's available," Mitch attempted to read the book upside down.

"It's been booked for ..." she rifled through the calendar, "at least the next three months – and they have first right of extension."

"Must be a significant project?"

"Yes, science is a growth industry," she agreed.

Mitch waited, hoping she would elaborate.

"We might not need as much space as the main lab," Samantha said. "Is there a smaller lab we could access?"

"Let me see." She shuffled through the bookings. "For how long?"

"Three months, with an option for another three," Mitch confirmed.

"Yes, that won't be a problem. There are two small labs available."

"I'd like the one closest to the main lab. I'll have staff working late, so I'd rather other people were around ... just in case."

"Of course. We have campus security; you can ask them to escort your staff to their cars. Lab G is on the same level as the main lab."

Déjà vu, Mitch recalled squatting with J.J. on the Lab G floor.

"That will be fine. The booking's under the name of James Owen, company name of Innovation Enterprises," Mitch said using one of his issued and untraceable names.

"You'll need to fill out a booking form," she said, looking around the counter. "Sorry, I'm just temping, I'll have to go ask someone where they are."

Mitch waited until she was out of sight and spun the book around. Scanning down the list he found the entry. He frowned at its name.

"She's coming," Samantha nudged him.

He turned the book back.

"Here's the form, Mr. Owen," she smiled. Mitch read the signs.

I might get more information on that booking yet, he thought.

"It's this one," J.J. said indicating a building to Ellen as they made their way through campus. They mounted the stairs.

"Wait," Ellen grabbed his arm. She nodded towards reception. "The security guard's an older guy. Why don't you try the buddy system? I'll wait out here."

"Alright," J.J. agreed. He ran up the final few steps, entered and stopped at the desk.

"Can I help you?" the security officer looked up.

"Yeah buddy, thanks," J.J. began. "I'm with the Science Gazette. We're a web-magazine and we're doing a story on the rush for university facilities by independent medical and science teams."

"You'll need to talk to our media unit," the guard interrupted him, writing down the phone number on a card.

"OK, thanks. I hear you've got a few labs booked out after hours, including one booked for a huge research project?" J.J. slouched across the counter.

"That must be the main lab guys."

"Sounds exciting. What are they up to?"

"Good question, not sure myself. Something to do with ..." he looked over at the booking sheet, "yeah, the Aurum project. Got the lab booked for three months."

"Hmm. Interesting,"

"Yeah. They're not too hard at it though."

"Been knocking off early?" J.J. asked.

"Well, I finish here at seven and I hardly ever see them. Their booking's from five. Joe, he's night-shift, he never knows when to expect them. Some nights they're in for an hour, other nights for two hours, and then we won't see them for a few nights."

"Where do I get a job like that?" J.J. asked.

The security guard laughed.

"Big team?"

"No, three of them come regularly. The fourth one, a British guy, all swanky in his suit, briefcase, the whole bit; you know the type, he's only been here two or three times."

"Might be their bank manager," J.J. joked.

The security guard handed J.J. the card with the media unit's phone number written on it.

"Thanks. I'll give them a call."

"No problem."

"Have a good one," J.J. said with a wave. He headed out of the building, took the stairs two at a time down to the campus courtyard and found Ellen.

"The Aurum project, booked in for three months, four people all-up, including a Brit. How much damage can they do in that time?"

Ellen frowned. "Substantial."

5

Charlotte Curtis turned her red MG into the familiar surrounds of the juvenile detention center, finding a parking space between a news van and a motorcycle.

Late again, she cursed, then quickened her pace from the car to the building, racing up the stairs as fast as her fitted navy suit and heels would allow. She pulled up at the security desk.

"Hello Charlotte, you know the drill ... your bag and folder please," the guard instructed as he ran a scanner over her body looking for metal objects.

"Hi Roger, I suppose you want my knife collection?"

"Yes thanks, but the escape kit is fine to take in."

Charlotte laughed.

"You're here to see Bradley Parnell?"

"I am."

Roger shook his head.

"What is it?" Charlotte prompted him.

"Charlotte, that boy has had some terrible nightmares."

"Really? How often?"

"Several times a night. He wakes himself up yelling, poor kid."

"Do you know what about? Has he said anything?"

Roger paused. "Sometimes he will yell out words, you know, stop, no – once he called for his mother. Now that's one messed up kid."

"Mm, thanks Roger. He'll be out by tomorrow. They always give the new kids a few days in remand to scare the hell out of them." She gave him a wave and hurried down the hall to the counseling rooms, walking on her toes to reduce the echo on the tiles announcing "intruder" to the insiders.

Charlotte opened the door to room 7J. She glanced up at a flickering fluorescent light in the ceiling panel and shuddered at the sight of a huge spider web in prime position for moth catching. She did a quick scan of the room to ensure the owner wasn't in sight, then dropped into a deep, red vinyl chair that groaned beneath her.

I know how you feel, she thought. Right, a ten-minute wait till they bring Brad.

She turned off her phone and sat back with a sigh.

An inscription carved into the timber table caught her eye. Jason loves Samantha. Jason's probably long gone by now and has kids of his own, she thought. Samantha ... Mitch's colleague. I wonder what she's like, Charlotte thought, surprising herself at the tinge of jealousy she felt. Ellen and Samantha. The only two girls Mitch has mentioned for a while, since that last one slept over ... Lena, Leonie, Lana?

Ah, Lachlan. What are you doing, why are you calling me again?

Charlotte jumped as the door opened, bringing her back to reality. Security brought in a good-looking teenager in a regulation orange jumpsuit. She looked at her watch – she had exactly one hour.

"Ready, Lawrence?" Andrew Kenny asked.

"Fire away," Lawrence sat down and joined the directors.

"OK, gentlemen," Andrew began, "I have allocated each of you a Mastermind entrant and city. Your allocated team should already be on the ground and have started their project. It is your responsibility to be across their work. You will continue to manage your current portfolios as well as your new project and file a report via email every Friday by close of business U.K. time. An office has been booked in the capital city of each project for your exclusive use. As you may recall, the project does not always take place in the capital city, but for security purposes you will be located there. Any questions so far?"

Andrew looked around the room, seeing nods of understanding.

"Most of you were here five years ago for Mastermind-2, so you know the rules. You're to meet with one team representative only throughout the project. Reinforce the deadlines and your expectations. The projects must be concluded by November 30. As soon as the project is completed, whether it succeeds or fails, you are to return to the U.K. office."

Andrew read out the board members' assignments, allocating directors to Paris, Munich and Monaco. He glanced at Daniel Reid with disdain.

I know you want Tokyo, Daniel. Bad luck.

He continued to read from the list. "Richard, Tokyo." He suppressed a smile seeing Daniel' disappointment. "Your contact is Seika Tajimo. Now there are two Mastermind entrants in the U.S. Michael, your entrant is based in Washington D.C. and your contact is Paul Asher. Daniel, you will share office space with Michael in D.C., your project is based in Nevada and your contact is Johan Booysen."

Johan Booysen ran his hand through his gray hair, sweeping it back over to one side. He frowned at Nicholas Everett.

"We don't have the luxury of time. You know the timeframe – if we don't meet it, we forfeit."

"We'll meet it," Nick said, shuffling papers into his black leather compendium. "It's a little unpredictable because the locations for pick ups aren't booked until a week out, but it's manageable. You forget, I've done the route numerous times already."

"Then do whatever it takes to get the roster tightened," Johan ordered.

"It doesn't work like that," Nick snapped back. "They'll be suspicious if I push for it."

"We're still on schedule, so don't panic," Maria Diaz assured him. "Daniel is not due here until next week. It will be refined by then."

"It better be, we have no choice."

"Remember, this is supposed to be fun," Maria took his hand.

He pulled away from her.

"The fun is in the winning."

Mitchell Parker hurried in, last to arrive at his own meeting.

"You look pissed, what's up?" Samantha asked.

"That's putting it mildly," Mitch showed them the university lab booking form for the main lab.

"How did you get that?" J.J. asked.

"Good luck."

"How old was she?" Ellen asked.

Mitch smiled. "Legal age. I had to get rid of Sam so I could smooth talk it out of her."

"Yeah, nice to be dispensable," Samantha punched his arm.

"Ouch!" Mitch rubbed it dramatically. "Check this out. The lab's been booked for three months for a project called Aurum."

"Aurum. The security guy told J.J. the same thing," Ellen cut in. "That means gold."

"It does," Mitch agreed. "They've left a phone number that goes to a paging service and they've paid in cash, so there is no tracking them. Their signature is illegible ..."

Mitch looked up as John walked into his office finishing his sentence, "And their cover is as good as ours; all of their details are dead ends."

"We're not meant to know what's going on in that lab or, more to the point, what's going on outside it," Mitch concluded.

Charlotte raced up the front stairs to get out of the cold, opened the door and inhaled the scent of Thai food. She heard Mitch call a greeting from the kitchen. Passing through the lounge, she found him in his black suit pants and white business shirt, sleeves rolled up, and stirring a beef dish.

"Hi, did you get an early mark?"

"Hmm, for good behavior," he snacked on a wedge of carrot from the stir-fry. "What were you smiling about?"

"When?" Charlotte asked.

"Just then, when you walked into the kitchen. In love again?"

Charlotte groaned. "No. Actually, it was so nice coming into the warmth that I was recalling when I first saw this house, fell in love with it and bought it on the spot. I remember the day that you came over to talk about renting, I spent hours cleaning and making it look pretty. You walked in and all you wanted to know was which room to put your one suitcase and a box in."

Mitch grinned. "I'm not very territorial."

"I noticed. Has Lachlan called yet?"

"No, Princess, but he will."

She smirked at him. "Don't give me a hard time."

Mitch's phone rang.

"Go and change, dinner's ready," he ordered, stabbing at the stir-fry with a wooden spoon.

She reached over and stole a mushroom, noticing Mitch continued to let his phone ring until she had left the room. Moments later she heard him yell: "Got to go, Charlie."

"But …" Charlotte wandered out of her room and saw the front door closing behind him.

6

"I'm freezing my ass off," J.J. rubbed his hands together to keep the circulation going.

"Turn the heater on," Mitch stated the obvious.

"Are we going to be here much longer?"

"Another half hour or so. You know, I just finished cooking this great stir-fry."

J.J. reached over to the car dashboard and changed the settings to warm.

"Why can't we go into the lab we booked while we wait?"

"Because I need to work out what we're doing and who's doing it, and I don't want any of us recognized yet."

"So, what did John say when he called?"

"He said they've accounted for everyone on the tape except for one guy; probably their British partner. John's panicking. He wants us to lift whatever info we can to find out what's happening in there. So, an orchestrated evacuation has been scheduled for eight," Mitch read J.J.'s blank expression, "a fire drill."

"Right."

"We'll go in while they're coming out."

"He didn't waste any time getting that happening."

"The more impromptu the better; less chance it will leak. Plus, if we wait until after their shift, they'll take material with them. Johan's been carrying a case in all the video footage. Nick's the same. I'm hoping they'll leave it there during the raid."

"What if they don't all come out?" J.J. asked.

"That's the risk we take. That's why we're here early, to see how many arrive tonight. Only been two so far."

"The female and Johan?"

"Yeah."

J.J. pulled out a thermos.

"Coffee, decaf, tea or herbal tea?"

"Geez, what are you, a walking espresso bar? Coffee, white, thanks."

Mitch sat up straight and pointed to the building. "There's Nick. It's a full house unless they're expecting guests."

"Cream or plain cookie?"

Mitch surveyed the selection and reached for a chocolate cream.

"Thanks, you can come on surveillance anytime." He took the offered coffee and turned his attention back to the building.

Sitting in silence, they drank their coffees and waited. Mitch glanced at his watch, fifteen minutes had passed. J.J. slid down making himself comfortable. Another glance at the watch and across at J.J. who was drifting off to sleep in the warmth of the car.

Mitch jolted upright as the first alarm wailed.

"Let's go, J.J."

"Man! OK."

Mitch bolted from the car. He looked back to check J.J. was behind him. They strode to the side of the building as the fire alarm kicked into a full-on scream. The exit doors automatically unlocked and Mitch slipped in through the side door, holding it ajar for J.J. He waited for his eyes to adjust as the house lights went off and the generator floor lighting flickered on.

Crouching, Mitch and J.J. waited underneath the stairs. Mitch watched as the security guards hustled everyone out. He could hear a heavily-accented male voice complaining about having to leave.

Finally he saw the three from the main lab cross the walkway and exit through the door with the security guard behind them.

"We've got fifteen minutes so we want to be out in ten. The firemen are ours, but they can't stall forever," Mitch said leaping to his feet and hoisting himself up again to the landing in a repeat performance of the previous night. He moved out of the way as J.J. followed suit.

They arrived at the main lab and Mitch swiped his card in the slot. The door wouldn't open.

"Shit! It won't open with the building on emergency alert. OK, think!" The alarms continued to wail. "J.J., you're the expert ... what do you suggest?"

"It'll take a few minutes to pick, or we can break the glass window."

"We don't have a few minutes and we can't break the glass; they'll get suspicious and relocate. I can't lose them. We need a master key."

"Hang on."

Mitch watched as J.J. headed to the tape room and swiped his card. The green light flashed, the lock clicked opened.

"What the ...? Gloves!" Mitch snapped before J.J. put his hand on the door. They both slipped them on.

"The security area should override all areas ... makes sense," J.J. explained. "I can override it in here if you want to head out and tell me when it flashes green?"

Mitch headed to the main lab and waited for the green light to flash on.

"Green!" he called to J.J. above the alarms and pushed the main lab door open. He went straight to the microscope.

He heard J.J. enter behind him.

"Get set up," Mitch ordered, "we need to bag some samples."

"Seven minutes," J.J. stood beside him and pulled compact storage containers from his vest, setting them up on the counter.

Peering through the microscope, Mitch saw a slide with several cells.

"Taking that one?" J.J. asked.

"Too risky." Mitch eyed a stand with a dozen tubes half filled with some fluid. J.J. handed him two empty tubes. Mitch filled them with water and selecting two from the stand, swapped them, handing them back. He moved to the refrigerator.

"Six minutes," J.J. called.

"Petri dish," Mitch gestured to him.

J.J. handed him the dish. Mitch opened his vest and withdrew a sealed syringe with a liquid substance in it. He placed a few droplets into a new petri dish, sealed the syringe, selected a similar sample and swapped them. Grabbing a swab from his jacket, Mitch immersed it in two other foreign fluids and bagged the swabs, passing it to J.J. for storage. He pulled a mini camera from his vest and looked around.

"Beautiful," he whispered seeing the brief case. With his gloved hand he opened the lid, pushed aside a selection of Mont Blanc pens and pulled out three manila folders. He opened the first file and found a list of names next to a column of dollar amounts. He snapped photos of the first few pages.

"Five minutes," J.J. announced. Joining Mitch, he whipped out his camera, removed the second file and began to take photos. Mitch opened the third folder, finding profiles on Nick, Diaz, two security personal and three people listed as scientists and a pilot.

Finishing, he took J.J.'s file and returned them to the case in the correct order.

"Four minutes," J.J. counted down.

Mitch looked around; there was no sign of Nick's folders.

Damn. He handed J.J. his camera, storing the evidence together.

J.J. zipped up the pack.

"I'm going to wipe the area for prints and hair. You move out, I'm right behind you," Mitch instructed.

"OK, you've got three minutes."

Mitch heard the door close as J.J. departed. He pulled a soft cloth out of his vest and wiped the area carefully; the magnetic cloth picked up everything. Another glance at his watch.

Two minutes, thirty seconds – what the heck? He unzipped a

small section of his vest and pulled out a tiny magnetic microphone and receiver, no larger than a half dollar. He felt under the table; no metal. Mitch glanced around the room looking for something metal that would hold the magnet.

Top of the refrigerator? Too visible. Back? No, the hum may interfere with recording audio. Two minutes. Hurry, where can I put this?

He looked up.

The air conditioning duct; nicely centered to capture conversations.

He leapt up on the counter, pushed a ceiling panel upwards and felt around for a suitable spot. The alarm bells stopped.

I've got to get out of here!

He pulled himself up into the ceiling, locked his feet into a beam, swung upside down and wiped his tread marks off the counter. The house lights flickered on and he hurled himself up hearing footsteps on the walkways. Mitch placed the microphone in the tread of the ceiling air conditioner vent and lowered the panel back into place as the lab door swung open. He froze behind the grate and watched Johan enter, stop, pat down his pockets as if looking for his cigarettes and head out again.

Move! Mitch hurried towards the outlet at the side of the building.

———

J.J. waited, watching everyone enter the building via the walkway above him. Security was the last to pass. He rose slowly, checked the coast was clear and raised himself up to the walkway. He heard footsteps and ducked back under the stairs, looking up to see who was passing.

Johan! Why is he going out? Is he coming back?

He waited a few seconds, pulled himself up again and headed to the fire exit. As he reached for the door, it opened. J.J. found himself face-to-face with Johan.

———

Mitch crawled along the inside of the ceiling. Coming to the end, he pushed open the vent and looked out, then down at the side of the building.

Great, no dog. He studied the drop. Not so great ... it must be at least twenty-five feet to the ground! Shit.

He glanced around.

Nope, nothing. No pipes, no tree branches, he thought. He strained forward to see the car. No one in the driver's seat. Where the hell is J.J.? Just get on with it. He lowered himself full length from the vent.

That cuts about six feet off the fall, he thought glumly. On the count of three. What am I saying?

He let go, hit the ground with a thud, rolled, then squatted to assess the damage.

Sprained ankle, all else intact. Where the hell is J.J?

———

"All clear in there," J.J. nodded to Johan. "Thanks for your co-operation."

Johan ignored him, and pushed past.

"Yeah, you're welcome," he muttered under his breath and exited the building. "Cover blown! Mitch is going to be pissed off."

He bolted to the car; it was empty.

Where the hell are you, Mitch?

J.J. tried the car door; it was open and he slid into the driver's seat and dialed John Windsor.

"What's happening? I haven't heard from Mitch," John answered.

"Me either. We split ways. The drill's over and I'm outside."

"Who's got the samples?"

"I have; plus photos. Johan left his brief case in there."

"Excellent. Don't get caught sitting there with them. Give Mitch five minutes and then get those into the lab. You can go back and pick him up. Understand?"

"Yessir!"

J.J. hung up and glanced at this watch.

Come on, Mitch, what the hell are you doing? He reached under the seat feeling for the spare key and found it. He put the key in the ignition, turned on the heater and waited.

Where are you?

He saw movement up ahead; someone with a slight limp was coming around the hedges.

"Shit," J.J. glanced at the samples from the lab in the back seat. He locked the doors and started to drive, swerving to miss the figure as it ran up the side of the car and banged on the window. J.J. recognized Mitch and slammed on the brakes, unlocking the doors. Mitch limped in.

"Take off."

"What happened to you?" J.J. floored the car.

"I took a scenic trip through the ceiling into the garden," Mitch put the seat back and stretched out his leg.

"Geez, you're ankle's swelling already." J.J.'s phone rang. "That'll be John," he handed it over.

"Chief, all OK, job done," Mitch hung up. "So where were you?"

"I've got good and bad news," J.J. said. "The good news is I got out alive with the samples intact."

Mitch grunted at the obvious.

"And the bad news?"

"Johan saw me."

Pulling up at J.J.'s apartment, Mitch limped around to the driver's side of his car.

"Thanks for the lift."

"Thanks for coming on the shift. See you tomorrow J.J."

He swung the car around and headed back to the office, pulling into his usual car space. He limped to the door, flashed his security pass to get in and took the samples to the lab, finally climbing the stairs to his floor.

"You're still here," Mitch said entering John's office.

"You're a mess, John greeted him.

"So I've heard," Mitch fell into a chair.

"You should've got the fire lads to hose you down. What have you done to your leg?"

"Just a sprain."

John picked up the phone and called for a medic to the fourth floor, then opened a cabinet and poured two scotches.

"Samples?"

"Delivered."

"Good. Any hitches?"

"J.J. was compromised; Johan saw him. Otherwise, no problems." He took the offered scotch and swallowed it fast, feeling it burn down the back of his throat. He fished the microphone remote from his pocket and handed it over.

"I didn't know you were going to get that into place," John jumped to his feet and attempted to patch it through the system, unable to pick up any noise.

"Could be working, they might not be saying anything. Or have left for the day."

A South African accent crackled on the line.

"Excellent," John listened in.

"Good. I was worried about where I stuck the mic but that's crisp."

John reached for the phone again and ordered transcript recording from the lab.

"Nice work. If your samples are good, you've earned a night off."

Mitch rolled his eyes. "Yeah, yeah, heard that before." He emptied the glass and turned to see the medic coming his way.

7

Mitch rang Charlotte's phone; she answered on the third ring.

"Mitchell Parker, what happened to you? One minute I'm waiting for my stir-fry, the next I'm on serving duty!"

Mitch laughed

"Sorry, emergency work call. Where are you? I can hardly hear you."

"At the hotel's new wine bar. Come down, I'm with Sally."

"Thanks, but I've sprained my ankle so I'm going to hobble home."

"Don't be such a wet blanket. Hobble on down. You'll feel better after a red wine or three."

"I would, but I'm covered in dirt."

"So dust off and stop making excuses. Hang on, Sally wants a word."

Mitch waited, listening to the girls pass the phone.

"Mitch some knight in shining armor you are. Where are you? We're getting hit on every minute. We need a man at the table."

"I bet you are, Sal. Well, don't complain if I don't look up to standard."

He swung the Audi around to head to the hotel. He found a park

Mastermind

and brushed down as he made his way into the bar. Mitch spotted them in the corner. He slipped into the booth beside Charlotte and noticed they both checked him out.

"You look alright," Sally told him, "except for ... is that grass? How do you get grass stains on a business shirt?"

"I fell on the grass!" Mitch answered.

Charlotte laughed.

"I hate these trendy bars," Mitch shuffled in his seat.

"Listen Happy, you hate these trendy bars because you're scared someone will think you're trendy," Charlotte waved to a waiter.

"I'm too old to be trendy."

Mitch ordered more wine and tapas.

"I'm starving, how was my stir-fry?" He sat back and observed the girls.

"Delicious!"

"What did you do to your ankle?" Sally stared at the strapping.

"For a person with a desk job, you've never seen so many injuries in your life," Charlotte interrupted. "Check out the scar above his ear. Not to mention ..."

"You're right, let's not mention it," Mitch cut her off as the waiter passed him the opened bottle of wine. He filled their glasses.

"So, Mitch, anyone on the scene this week?" Sally took the glass of red.

"Well, there is a new girl in the records management division ..."

"Woo-hoo, all the reference material you can handle," she nudged him.

"Listen Blondie, don't give me a hard time." Mitch smiled at her. "I'm sore, hungry and reading is not what I had in mind for records girl."

Sally laughed. "Look, why don't you and Charlie go out and be done with it?"

"Who, us two?" Mitch choked on his red wine.

"Why not? You can obviously live together, so economize and share a room."

Charlotte crinkled her nose.

"No offence, Mitch, but it would be like dating my brother ... I love my brother, but he's my brother. Same theory applies to you," she patted his hand.

He looked at Charlotte, "I'd go out with you."

She stopped, gazed at him, and then laughed.

"Nice try. You almost got me then. But we both know if I said I'd go out with you, Mitchell Parker, you would organize a stack of assignments and conveniently never be home."

"Not true. Anyway," he turned to Sally, "my rival's still on the scene."

"Are you serious?" Sally asked. "When ...?"

"Good one, tittle-tat! I was going to mention it."

"When were you going to mention it? We've been here twenty minutes!"

"Look, it's over with Lachlan; we're just tying up loose ends."

"Loose ends? You're addicted to good sex," Sally exclaimed.

Mitch looked away.

"If you want my advice," she continued, "I think you should burn him for good. He's a lovely guy, but it's a flogged horse. What do you think, Mitch?"

"Nothing to do with me," he shrugged. "Although, one of the girls in the office cooks a lot when she breaks up with a guy ... that could work out well if you were inclined."

"Or clean ... I've heard of people who clean a lot when heartbroken," Sally added. Mitch nodded.

"Ha, nice try you two but don't count on it." Charlotte tossed back her wine.

―――

Mitch carried Charlotte's belongings into her room.

"Stay and talk a while," she sat on the bed. "Please!"

"Charlie, you're pissed. You'll be asleep as soon as your head hits the pillow."

"Please, just for a while."

Mitch sat next to her as she curled up on the bed.

"Talk to me ..." she yawned.

"I'm all talked out," he covered her with the quilt.

"Mitch?"

"Yes?"

"I'm cold. Can't you lie here for a while?"

"I'll fall asleep and we'll scare each other in the morning. You'll think I took advantage of you. Might be safer to put your electric blanket on."

"No." She put her pillow in his lap and wrapped her arms around his waist. "You can set the record straight tomorrow. Besides, I'm used to your scary appearance."

Mitch kicked off his shoes and propped himself up in sitting position behind her. He stroked her hair, listening to her steady breathing.

He woke with a start twenty minutes later.

Shit! He swore, realizing where he was. He touched her hair again.

No! Got to go. I need that nightshift at the lab to start ASAP.

8

Mitch could see his team waiting for him. He grabbed the paperwork from John and limped towards them.

"All quiet on the Western Front?" J.J. asked as he neared.

"Too quiet. Budgets," Mitch answered.

"Aah! I thought you looked glum. We got any money left?"

"Not if those Cobra helicopter repairs come out of my budget."

"Geez, wasn't that last financial year? You told them it was an accident?" J.J. asked.

"Yeah, tried that one. OK, Ellie ..."

"I'm continuing with checks on inter-country grants and on Johan," Ellen cut in.

"Plus, I've started background checks on Maria and Nick," Samantha concluded.

"Good. J.J., let's see what the science department turned up from our lab raid." Mitch said. "John's meeting us there."

"Right, walk this way," J.J. walked beside Mitch with his own limp imitation.

"So, give me the heads-up, Henri, are we going to be happy with the lab findings?" John lowered himself onto a stool opposite Professor Henri Spalter in the science division.

"Depends, John, on whether you were hoping to find something incriminating or hoping not to. Ah, here's the boys now, excuse me a moment." Henri rose and walked through the department to let Mitch and J.J. in through the security door. He frowned noticing Mitch's limp.

"Mitch. What have you done to yourself?"

"Playing Superman again ... you know, leaping from tall buildings in a single bound."

"No cape?"

"Ah, that's what went wrong," Mitch grinned.

Henri chuckled and nodded a greeting to J.J. He led them past two young lab technicians arguing over a lab sample.

"Come, I've got something interesting to show you." They entered another lab where John was looking through a microscope. He moved away and Henri projected the microscope slide onto the wall.

"Your results from last night's raid are interesting. Here's a projection of what we found in the test tubes." He watched Mitch squint at the image of clear, small bubbles.

Mitch looked from Henri to John. "Nothing? You mean to say we've collected air and water?"

"Apparently so. The second sample," Henri called up another slide, "appears to be membrane-based. And this next one is water."

"What the hell is going on?" Mitch stared at the slides.

"My thoughts exactly. There is a ground swell of scientists pushing the government for tighter constraints on labs and to monitor work in progress," Henri said. "There are experiments going on under our noses that could be real threats to our society; this isn't one of them."

He put up another set of images.

"This is what was in your petri dishes. This batch has nanometer-sized gold particles in it, surrounded by a negative charge layer."

"Which means?" Mitch asked.

"It means it could be a test for any number of samples." Henri looked at the blank faces around him. "You've picked up a sample which forms the basis of a test because of its stability. Think of it as having a cup of hot water. You could add tea, coffee or chocolate and each will give you a pure representation of what you have added. Whereas, if you had a cup of cola and added tea, coffee or chocolate, the taste would be compromised by the flavor of the cola."

"So, give us an example of what they could use this exact type of testing for?" J.J. asked.

"They could be doing agricultural testing for plant and crop disease, or clinical testing for tumors or allergies; even biological testing for contamination. It means nothing really."

"So basically, what we've collected tells us they're doing what we're going to be doing; using a few fake props to look like lab work is going on?" J.J. asked.

"In essence, yes. The specimens in the tubes and the petri dish are as good as tap water. Sorry to disappoint you, boys."

"So, if the lab's a smokescreen, what would these three people be doing together and why meet at the university?" Mitch asked.

———

Friday night, Saturday night and now Sunday night. I need to get a life, Mitch thought as he glanced at his watch; eight p.m.

Two hours down and no sign of Johan, Nick or Maria in the lab.

He spread out the photographed material taken from Johan's brief case and revisited the material and the notes he'd made earlier. Shuffling through the papers, he found the list of investors' names. Mitch glanced through them; most were from South Africa and South America and the minimum amount donated was twenty thousand dollars. One investor had contributed a quarter of a million dollars to take the largest number of project shares. Mitch did the calculations: Johan was playing with a total of $845,000 worth of investors' money and must have pulled strings to get these on board. But what were they promising in return?

He read through the entire file, yawned and looked at the clock again; another hour had passed.

Where the hell are they? The job can't be too urgent ... unless the lab was hired to provide a fixed address, or to keep investors believing a project they were funding was underway.

He returned to the paperwork and found profiles on the three leaders, a couple of scientists, two security guards and a pilot.

Another pilot, he thought. Why do they need an additional pilot when they have Nicholas Everett? Mitch's eyes lit up at a page containing details of a science project.

This is it! A developmental drug for the prevention of Alzheimer's. Mitch let out a low whistle. Given the aging population, if this drug works, the investors could make billions. He stood up and paced around the room, stopping to pick up the profiles on the scientists again.

He thought it through: do these scientists exist or do the investors just think they do? Is anyone actually developing this drug or are the investors getting false reports? Mitch glanced at his watch again and began to pack up. I'm not going to find out tonight ... nine-thirty and no one's shown.

He stopped suddenly, hearing a noise in the main lab and grabbed the headset to listen in through the microphone in the ceiling. He recognized Nick's voice; he was talking on his cell phone. Mitch listened to the dialogue.

"I'm sorry I missed this afternoon's meeting, it was unavoidable," Nick was saying.

Shit! I'm not here for two hours and I miss their meeting.

Nick continued. "I'm not taking this project lightly ... Johan! ... fine, I'll be there."

Mitch could hear the frustration in Nick's voice as he hung up. He waited, hearing the sounds of paper shuffling, then the door opening and closing again. He waited a few minutes, put his head out the door and saw the main lab was in darkness. Mitch rushed out and made his way to the car park, ducking behind a light tower as car lights came towards him. He strained to get a glimpse of the driver.

Definitely Nicholas Everett! He must have gone in to collect something, but what? Did he see me?

He returned to the lab.

Will Johan and Maria make a guest appearance tonight as well?

―――

Mitch closed the front door behind him, wincing as it creaked. He shed his gear—shoes, jacket, backpack—throwing them in his room, then headed to the kitchen.

"Mitch?"

"Just me, Charlie," he answered in a whisper.

"It's after two ... have you been at work all that time?"

"Yes, go back to sleep."

He entered the kitchen, feeling his way without turning on the light. Mitch heard a sound and spun around. A figure emerged from the dark. He grabbed the intruder and slammed him against the wall. In a single move, he pinned him by the throat.

"Mitch, it's me," the voice choked.

"For chrissake," Mitch pushed Lachlan away. He could feel his heart pounding.

Lachlan Monterey put his hand to his throat and coughed dryly.

"Didn't you know I was staying?"

"Obviously not," Mitch said, hands on his hips.

Charlotte appeared in the doorway.

"What's going on?"

"Nothing," Lachlan rubbed his throat.

Cool down, Mitch told himself. "Sorry, are you OK?"

"Yeah, don't worry about it."

"I didn't know you were having a sleep over," Mitch looked at Charlotte.

"Forget it. Been out?" Lachlan asked.

"Working."

"After-hours shift, huh?"

"Yeah, night watch." Mitch reached around Lachlan to grab a

bottle of water from the refrigerator. He passed by them, running his eyes over Charlotte as she stood in the doorway in a pale blue slip.

"Mitch?" she called.

"See you in the morning," he snapped. Why am I pissed off? Because she's back with him? Because she's a sucker for punishment? Or because he's in there with her!

He dropped on to his bed and set the alarm to be up in four hours. He lay back.

"Got to get you out of my head, Charlie and focus," he muttered. "What is the Aurum project? Did they choose that name because an Alzheimer's drug would be a gold mine?"

———

Charlotte heard Mitch's car backing out of the garage. She looked at the bedside clock and rolled back over.

"Time?" Lachlan mumbled.

"Just after six."

"What's up?"

"Nothing," she sidled up to him.

Nothing that talking to Mitch won't fix, she thought. All weekend he's come home after midnight and bolted by six a.m. Which means he's either flat-out busy or busy avoiding me.

———

Mitch drove his car into his allocated car park and headed into the building. He stopped in his office, called and confirmed someone was in the Information Resource Division, and then detoured to the canteen before taking the stairs to the second floor.

"Morning, Marco," he ran an eye over the six-foot Caribbean from the I.T. Division. "Nice shirt."

"Mitch, my man, this shirt's from my Hawaiian collection."

"There's more?"

"Indeed. Ah, you've come bearing gifts." Marco took the offered coffee and toast. "That'll warm my fingers up for the keyboard. So, what have we got? I thought you were in the lab last night. How come you need the recorded material?"

"I was there all weekend except for a few hours Sunday afternoon."

"And that's when your subjects arrived?"

"There was a meeting, I believe. I'm dying to know what they said."

"Why didn't you call me in last night?"

"Budget. I'd have to justify it to John."

"Gotcha. How did you pick it up?"

"A microphone in the ceiling."

"OK," Marco sat at the computer. "Can you identify who's speaking?"

"Should do. One male with a South African accent, and one female. Not sure if anyone else was there."

Marco put the tape in the deck and turned to the computer, typing in the date and time as the tape began to roll. "Here we go."

Mitch finished his serve of toast and coffee before he heard a cough on the tape.

"Exciting so far," Marco said.

Mitch laughed. Finally, he heard a South African voice and followed Marco's prompts as the screen identified the voice as Male one.

Male one: "It's confirmed for six-thirty on Wednesday, here."

Mitch heard the female voice.

Female one: "OK. That gives us a few more nights to get it right."

Male one: "Nick and I, yes. You will stick to your plan and leave for the site on Tuesday afternoon; we need someone there. We'll depart as soon as we can after the meeting. I want to be gone before the investors' tour."

Female one: "Got it. Will that be the final meeting with Daniel?"

Mitch stood and began to pace. Daniel ... must be the British guy Ellen heard about.

Male one: "Yes. And remember, neither of you know about him or M.M. Only about the job. I'm trusting you with that information."

Mitch frowned. What the hell is M.M? The voice continued.

Female one: "We won't be saying anything to anyone."

"What are they talking about?" Marco asked.

"Damned if I know," Mitch shook his head.

Male one: "I'm worried about Nick."

Female one: "Why?"

Male one: "For starters, his roster's not locked in. Aren't you concerned?"

Female one: "Truthfully? Of course. I have my doubts about the project, but not about Nick or the location."

Male one: "You think this Eureka County is the best location?"

Female one: "If this site is as good as Nick says it is, it'll be fine. The nearby township is not so small that we'll stick out. It's normal for sites to be leased, so it shouldn't raise any suspicion – and it's close to the route. I think he did a good job securing it."

Male one: "After this is all over, you and I can find our own route for a while."

Female one: "Hmm, I'm counting on it."

Mitch and Marco exchanged looks.

"Smooth line, buddy," Marco raised his coffee cup in salute.

Male one: "I've gone through it a hundred times in my head. The real issues for me are in the cleanness of the swap and getting it across the border. The rest should go like clockwork."

Female one: "I'm worried about the investors. What if they try to find us?"

Male one: "Unlikely. Most of them won't want to reveal their company funds were allocated to a long shot like a cure for Alzheimer's. I want to win this. Imagine what we could do with that money! We'll be set for the rest of our lives."

Female one: "I know how important it is to you."

Male one: "Do you really trust Nicholas?"

Female one: "Implicitly. He's family."

Male one: "You mean he was almost family. Now, I'm your family!"

Mitch and Marco heard a click on the tape.

"Was that the sound of the door?" Mitch asked.

"The conversation has stopped, I'm guessing they've left the room," Marco said.

"Is that all?"

"Looks like it, Mitch," Marco spooled forward on the tape. "Does it help you at all?"

"Raises more questions than it answers," Mitch rubbed his hand over his chin. "But, Nicholas Everett's going to help me whether he likes it or not."

9

"Clearly the game is afoot," John said. "Johan says 'I want to win' but what?" he read from the printed transcript in front of him. "The 'cleanness of the swap'," he looked up at Mitch. "A swap in Eureka County; the Nevada desert to be exact."

"Low traffic area," Mitch agreed, "but what's being swapped and what are they using the investors' money for? Johan's meeting with Daniel may help us to turn up some answers."

"Good. What else, Mitch?" John asked.

"I'm sending J.J. and Sam to Nevada to follow Maria. According to the tape, she's leaving for Eureka County on Tuesday. Ellen and I will keep up the research and shifts in the lab, monitoring Johan, Nick and this Daniel meeting. Plus, I'm planning another lab raid to see if we can turn up anything on 'M.M.' God knows what that is."

"Do you need help with the raid?"

"No, thanks. Some nights they're only in for a few hours. I'll wait and slip in once they've left. Ellie can watch my back."

"OK," John studied Mitch's face. "Get some sleep. You're supposed to be on night shift, not night and morning shift. Don't come in until after ten. You look wasted."

"The trouble with you two is there's an underlying, seething passion, but you are both too scared to be the first one to admit it," Sally spooned the cappuccino froth from her cup.

"No," Charlotte disagreed, "definitely not."

"Come on," Sally argued. "Otherwise, why would you care if Mitch was mad at you and why do you think he would be bothered being mad?"

"I care because I hate having tension around the house. I have enough tension at work without adding to it."

"Charlie, I think you need to be careful with Mitch. There, I've said it, so you can tell me to shut up."

"What do you mean?"

"I've got a craving for lasagna," Sally eyed the blackboard menu.

"Don't change the subject Sal, what do you mean?"

"He's mad about you. Can't you tell?"

Charlotte snorted with laughter.

"Mitch's got a date this weekend with records department girl. So, I don't think he's too caught up on me."

"Don't be fooled. Records girl is a distraction. He's not going to make a move on you when you are going through the Lachlan rebound phase. But if you gave him any encouragement, he would drop records girl before you could say 'filed material', guarantee it."

―――

"I want to be ready to move by early next week, Nicholas, no later." Johan hung up and turned to Maria.

"Don't be too hard on Nick, he's been through a lot," she said, "and we need him."

"You're too soft on him. Besides, he's not going to pull out, he's doing this for you," Johan touched her cheek. "Do you like the timeline? I'm moving it forward."

"I love the new timeline. What girl wouldn't be happy at the prospect of escaping with the man of her dreams and riches beyond her wildest imagination sooner rather than later?"

Johan pulled his chair closer to Maria and kissed her.

Mitchell Parker watched their reflection in the window. He took his coffee order, thanked the waitress and hurried to Lab G.

"Well, it's confirmed, Johan and Maria are definitely a couple ... I just saw them locking lips in the university coffee shop," Mitch said entering the lab and placing a coffee in front of Ellen.

"Mm, I'd be a bit worried if I was Nicholas Everett," Ellen said.

"I suspect he knows all about it."

"What now?" Ellen asked.

"We wait and hope they're coming here to the lab after they finish kissing. Tell me what you've found out in your research, Ellie," Mitch sat down and pried the lid off his coffee.

"OK," Ellen grabbed her note pad. "We can't find any reference to M.M. It's eluding us. As for Nevada, we may be on a winner there. We found two sites in Eureka County leased in the last two months. The first one was formerly a gold mine. The name of the lessor is an alias and untraceable. They've paid cash for six months in advance, and have only a paging service contact number."

"It's unbelievable," Mitch muttered, "doesn't anyone do security checks anymore?"

"I imagine the parent company is ecstatic to lease it and don't care to whom."

"What's the name of the site they've leased?"

"Broad Arrow. It's about thirty-five miles north of Eureka; four hundred miles from Las Vegas."

"And the second one?"

"Yep," Ellen shuffled more papers. "The only other recently leased site is a warehouse in Crescent Valley, in the northern part of Eureka County. It's small, not really in a deserted area and attracts a bit of tourism. The name on the contract is for a local company, they check out."

"OK, so assuming it is Broad Arrow, what's there?" Mitch looked up as the door opened and Samantha came in with takeaway, filling the room with the scent of Indian spices. Mitch cleared the lab bench making way for her.

"Great, I'm starving," he took the offered Naan bread.

"Broad Arrow's a ghost town," Ellen mumbled with a mouth full of bread. "It used to be a successful gold mine with a little satellite city around it, now it's on the Abandoned Mine Lands list waiting to be secured. When it was thriving," she referred to her notes, "it had two hotels, a hospital and, believe it or not, its own stock exchange."

"So, when did it all dissolve?" Samantha asked handing Ellen and Mitch their curries.

"The gold dried up about the mid-1990s and everyone moved on. Most of the buildings were relocated," Ellen inhaled the aroma of her Beef Vindaloo and tried a mouthful. "Mm, this is great, try some."

"No, thanks, it's making my eyes water from over here," Mitch said.

"I was weaned on the hot stuff," Ellen boasted. "Anyway, the underground mine's still intact, there are a few houses, an office block and miles of nothing."

"What on earth would Johan, Maria and Nick be doing there?" Mitch frowned.

Ellen continued. "Now, for backgrounds for Johan, Maria and Nick."

Mitch motioned for her to stop. "Someone's coming." He sidled up to the rectangular window in the lab door and saw Johan and Maria walking into the main lab. He looked at his watch; it was eight-thirty.

"Took their time," he whispered and sat back down, putting one of the earphones in and continuing to eat.

"Only the two?" Samantha asked.

Mitch nodded. "So far."

He listened in via the microphone in their ceiling.

"He's flirting with her," Mitch whispered.

"Men, they're all the same!" Samantha helped herself to a forkfull of his Lamb Korma.

They looked up as a shadow passed their lab window.

"Nick!" Samantha whispered.

Mitch nodded as he heard the door open in the main lab; the conversation stopped. "They clammed up when he walked in. OK, talking again … Maria is going to Nevada tomorrow afternoon to meet a distributor the next day, whatever that means. Sam, you and J.J. are going to be on that flight. Call our travel department, find out what flight she's on and get on it, I want you on the ground following her."

Mitch continued to listen, relaying the conversation.

"Nick and Johan are staying to meet with Daniel."

"Any insight into the Nevada connection?" Samantha asked.

"Not yet," Mitch answered. "That's it … they're leaving."

Samantha moved to the door.

"Two gone," she reported.

"Nick's making a call," Mitch told them, still listening in. "It's a personal call." He listened as Nick greeted his father. "OK, he's hung up and is calling someone else. Here we go," he sat up. "He's talking about counties in Nevada … and a timeframe … between nine and midday. Damn! He's hung up. What the hell are they doing in there? Another night shift over and we're no further ahead."

Mitch reached over and turned off the alarm clock. He rose, showered and an hour later, he lowered himself behind his desk at work and logged on to his computer.

Sitting back, he threaded his fingers and looked at the ceiling.

"What are you thinking about?" John asked from the doorway making Mitch jump.

"Shit, you nearly gave me a heart attack."

John entered and sat down.

"I was thinking about Daniel Reid," Mitch showed John the profile on screen. "The report's back and it lists forty-five males by the name of Daniel in Washington D.C. who fit our profile. Three of them have British links but only one recently entered the country. He works for the media company Globalnet and is here for a conference; it's probably not the Daniel we're looking for. I'm going to try for a photo on Wednesday night when he meets with Johan, might help to pull an I.D."

"OK. Aren't you sleeping?"

"Yes," Mitch answered not looking at him, "sleeping fine."

"I've received the weekly security sheets; you've done four night shifts and come into the office after them, a weekend shift, plus beaten me in here every morning. It's eight a.m.! What's bothering you?"

"Nothing," Mitch shrugged. "Fired up; a head full of this project."

"Is that all?"

"That's it."

"Well, you're no use to me if you're not sharp. Go home, get some sleep and come back late this afternoon."

"I've got to ..."

"It can wait," John ordered

"John, if I need sleep I'll ..."

"It's not up for discussion," John cut him off and rose to leave.

Mitch gritted his teeth. "OK, give me an hour."

"Thirty minutes."

Mitch opened his mouth to say something.

"We'll talk this afternoon," John cut him off.

He swore under his breath.

———

Mitch's eyes widened as he opened the front door and found Charlotte sitting on the sofa covered in paperwork.

"Hi, what are you doing here?"

"I live here. My name's Charlotte, my friends call me Charlie."

"You're a bit messy Charlotte, or can I call you Charlie?"

"After that comment, you can call me Dr. Curtis."

He ducked as she threw a balled sheet of paper at him.

"So, you've decided to catch some sleep? You look wiped out."

"Yeah, I've been told. I've been on the night shift."

"Night or morning?"

"Both, maybe," Mitch diverted his eyes and lowered himself into a chair opposite her. "How's your young lad? The straight-A student up for assault?"

"OK. He's out of detention and back at home," she sighed. "He's been having these shocking nightmares before and since leaving detention. Bit like you of late," Charlotte said.

Mitch looked up surprised.

"His parents split up and they're fighting for custody. Both trying to win him over with bribery or guilt," she continued.

"Poor kid," Mitch sympathized. "Don't they get it?"

"They're too full of their own pain to see it. It manifests itself in his dreams and in outbreaks of anger – hence, his assault charges. He's a bit of a closed book though; doesn't give much away. I'm working on him."

"I'll bet you are," Mitch closed his eyes.

Thank God she can't see the dreams I've had lately; going over stuff I haven't thought about in years; seeing people from way back. It's just sleep deprivation, change of routine. Or ... maybe seeing Nick again.

He opened his eyes and saw Charlotte watching him.

"The whole nightmare scenario," she said, "could also be a reaction to a fear, or a sighting, maybe a memory from the past?"

"Are you telling me about the kid or asking about me?" he said irritated.

"Calm down, Mitch. I'm not analyzing you."

"Are you sure?"

Charlotte shrugged. "I'd like to. Who's Henry?"

Mitch paused.

"Henry?" she repeated. "Do you know a Henry?"

"Henri Spalter. He heads our science division at work," Mitch drew a deep breath. "He went out with my mother for five or six years when I was a teenager. He's a good guy."

"That's a coincidence ... that you'd end up working together."

Mitch shrugged. "He's a professor of science ... different trades, same organization. Why? Did he call? I didn't give out this number."

"You can, you know," Charlotte said. "No, he didn't call. You yelled out his name last night."

Mitch shuffled.

"Closed subject, hey? OK. So what's with all the night shifts? You haven't volunteered for it to get out of the house?"

"I'm on surveillance."

"Listen, Mitch, I know you were angry with me for not telling you Lachlan was sleeping over the other night," she started.

"Forget it, it's not a problem. I nearly choked him in the kitchen, but he seemed OK about that."

"You don't have to sneak in and bolt out first thing. Lachlan's ..."

"Charlie, its work, no other agenda," he interrupted her. "Whatever you guys are doing is fine by me. I mean, you're OK aren't you?"

"Sure, fine."

"Good, as long as you're happy," he rose departing for his room.

Mitch felt himself drifting to sleep as soon as he lay down. He could hear a South African voice and a female speaking with a Spanish accent, and then Ellen was calling his name. He saw Sally talking to J.J.

Do they know each other?

Lachlan appeared with his arm around Charlotte. He turned and found himself in the lab with Henri. Then Mitch saw his father, drunk again. Suddenly Henri was gone. Mitch called out to him.

"Henri! No, wait!"

He felt his skin prickle with fear; his heart was thumping. He tried to get away, but his father held his wrist. He looked down, it was a small wrist; his father's hand was much bigger and tightly gripped around him. He called to his brother.

"Get Mom, go. Now! Go!"

What's ringing. Stop ringing!

His father raised a leather strap and he felt the sting. He gasped in pain. Again, the strap struck him and again; his skin reddened and throbbed; blood came to the surface of the welts. He saw the red glow of the cigarette coming towards him.

"Dad, stop!"

The ringing noise cut into his dream. He yelled, feeling the burn – he couldn't see through his tears.

Mitch bolted upright, hearing his phone ringing. He fumbled for it.

"Hello?"

"Hi, Mitch, we've stopped over in Salt Lake City and got a few hours to kill. All's OK though."

"What?" Mitch rubbed his eyes.

"We're in Salt Lake City, having an hour-and-a-half stopover," J.J. explained. "Oh shit, did I wake you? Sorry, Mitch, I forgot you were on night shift. I'll call back …"

"No, that's fine," Mitch glanced at the clock. It was eleven o'clock. He looked down; no welts. His shirt was saturated with sweat.

"Mitch?"

"J.J., sorry. I'm glad you called," he leaned back. "So what's up, what time is it there?"

"It's just on eight, we're waiting for the connecting flight to Elko. Sam's gone to check our seating and I've got my eye on Maria … me and a million other guys, she's some looker."

"What's she doing?"

"Waiting in the airport departure lounge."

"OK, thanks J.J.; stay in touch. Don't go storming the joint, play it cool. We don't know what we're in for or if Broad Arrow is manned."

"Maybe those two security guys are located there, the one's we found profiles for," J.J. said.

"Yeah, maybe. The security guards might exist, but I'm pretty sure the scientists don't. I'll have a better idea after their meeting with Daniel, hopefully."

"Cool. We'll call you when we get there," J.J. assured him.

"Thanks and be careful, I don't want to come to Nevada if I can avoid it. Talk to you later."

Mitch hung up and swung his legs over the side of the bed.

I hope Charlie didn't hear me call out again. Anyway, that'll do you John. Two hours sleep ... mission accomplished. Back to work.

10

"We've just arrived in Elko and it's pouring down," Samantha reported to Mitch on speaker phone as she drove. "We've followed Maria's hire car the last one hundred and fifty miles, and she's turned off at Elko."

"Are you both OK?" Mitch asked.

"Fine, just tired, you know, five hours of hanging around airports, a couple of hours in the car driving ..."

J.J. cut in. "It's a shame they closed the Eureka airport to commercial flights. We'd have six miles to drive instead of a hundred and six!"

"Mitch, we'll call you back. Maria has just pulled into a fenced compound; looks like the former mining complex we were anticipating."

Samantha disconnected and drove past, keeping Maria's car in sight. "The gold rush is well and truly over," she said looking around. "Let's drive around the site; see what we can see from the back."

"I'll get a few shots," J.J. reached for the digital camera. "Then, all I want to see is a bar. Notice there is no security on the gates?"

"Would you need security? Let's face it, besides you and me, who in their right mind would come out here for a drive?"

Samantha pulled over to the side of the road; there was a clear view of the site.

"OK, she's getting out of the car; looks like she's here to stay. At least we found the site. Let's head to Eureka and get a hotel; see what we can find out in the bar. There must be a local or two who will talk after a few rounds."

"We'll send these shots through to Mitch as well," J.J. agreed.

"About a thirty minutes drive to Eureka," she said yawning and turning the car around. "But I hear it's a pretty little town."

"I think we should share a room, we need to look like a tourist couple. It'll raise suspicion otherwise."

"Probably best," she agreed.

Mitch and Ellen did their scientist impersonation as the security guard passed their lab.

"He's gone," Ellen announced.

Mitch grabbed the earpiece, offering one to Ellen. He could hear Johan talking.

"OK, let's visit this timeline," Johan said.

"Let me get my copy." Mitch recognized Nick's voice.

"Right," Nick continued. "The pick up will be on a Friday – the day with the most collections on the route. This one," he said pointing to something that Mitch couldn't see, "will be the biggest load; the smaller ones are still significant because it will be a couple of weeks' worth. After the last pick up, the cargo goes straight to Vegas. It's met on the tarmac by a security van, then the vaults, fully intact, are removed and not touched again until the next working day when they're opened for weighing."

"What time do they weigh the gold?"

"Usually around nine when the security staff arrive at work."

"So," Johan summarized, "if they remove the vaults from the plane, put them straight into the security van, store them, then transfer and open them the next morning, we've got a good ten or eleven hours to get our load out, and they won't find the substitute goods until after nine the next day."

"Precisely," Nick confirmed.

"Are you positive they don't open them beforehand?" Johan continued to prod.

"One hundred per cent sure, I've done this run a stack of times. Once the vaults are on board and the release is signed, no inspections are carried out. They are signed off as intact and they don't get opened until weigh-in the next morning."

"Excellent," Mitch heard Johan say.

Nick continued. "When I land, we'll square off the staff, refuel and then the three of us can head off within the hour."

"And the flight?"

"We're going from Elko to Atlanta in around five hours. We'll refuel there and then from Atlanta to Venezuela in four hours. We'll be long gone before the vaults are opened the next day."

"What if it has to be next Friday?"

Mitch heard the hesitation in Nick's voice.

"OK. It's do-able. I'm on duty for the next three Wednesdays and Fridays anyway."

"I'm not saying it will be next Friday. I want to be prepared should Daniel ask me. Are we ready for him?"

"We're fine" Nick assured him.

Mitch exchanged looks with Ellen as Johan continued.

"I'm meeting him at six tomorrow. You can come in once he leaves, just don't let him see you."

"I'll wait in the parking lot and come in after seven. You should be done by then."

"Yes, unless he finds a problem."

"If he's still here, I'll walk by and come back later. All going well, he'll be happy with it," Nick said.

———

Mitch swore. "Don't they ever speak in sentences? Half names,

HELEN GOLTZ

ambiguous locations. I've got a good mind to go in and shake it out of them," he spat out. He heard the lab door open and caught a glimpse of Johan departing.

"Ellie, you head home. I'll stay until Nick leaves in case he does anything exciting."

Checking the coast was clear, he walked Ellen to her car, then went back to Lab G and listened in as Nick continued to shuffle around. Mitch flicked between television channels, watching the picture while listening to the lab. He checked the time: an hour had passed.

What's he doing in there? Mitch wondered. He settled back, watching the football action; the Washington Redskins were whipping the New York Giants. He heard a noise; Nick had opened the door and was heading out. Mitch backed against the wall. Can't risk being seen now. He peered through the glass and saw Nick departing. He began to pack up.

———

Mitch and Ellen arrived early at the lab the next evening, keenly anticipating the meeting with Daniel.

"I've spent more time in this lab over the last week than I've spent in my own home," he said as he stretched.

"I know how you feel," Ellen poured them both a coffee from her thermos. "I'm looking forward to this meet with Daniel."

Mitch pulled a digital camera from his backpack.

"Me too. I don't think we'll be doing too many more shifts after tonight. If we're reading this right, Nick's got to be in Nevada for work next Wednesday. I think they'll be on the move ASAP."

"How are you going to get the shot of Daniel?" she asked.

"I'm going to leave you here with the headphones on and I'm going up and over." He indicated the ceiling. "Hopefully, we'll see his face clearly. After they all leave, wait ten minutes and then you go. Turn off the light so the lab looks empty. If Nick doesn't leave with

60

Johan, I'll stick around up above for a while. I want to photograph what he's doing in there."

"OK," Ellen agreed.

Mitch climbed up on the counter. Pushing aside a ceiling panel, he raised himself up effortlessly. Ellen passed him up the camera. He returned the panel and inched his way along, stopping once he was over the ceiling duct in the main lab.

Mitch hovered above the main lab, waiting. He rolled over and lay on his back staring above, thinking.

Six p.m. In fifteen minutes when Daniel arrives, I hope to crack this case.

His mind drifted to Charlotte. *Why can't she let Lachlan go? Maybe it's the sex, like Sally said ... ugh! Don't go there.*

Mitch glanced at his watch; it was five minutes past the last time he looked.

He heard the lab door below open and rolled over to see Johan Booysen enter. Mitch had him in perfect view through the ceiling grill. Johan spread out a number of documents across the lab benches and then walked around checking everything. Johan stepped back from the bench and consulted his watch. At exactly six-fifteen, a young man in a dark suit entered the room. Daniel!

The accent confirmed Daniel was British. Mitch adjusted his camera for low-light performance and checked the flash was off. He clicked a few photos and listened in.

"The timetable is tight but manageable," Johan explained.

Daniel looked over the documents moving from one to the next. Finally he looked up and smiled.

"I agree. Well done. I won't put the kiss of death on you by saying it looks foolproof, but you've covered it thoroughly. How will you get around the risk of being identified by the two pilots?"

"One pilot is contracted to do a specific job and has only dealt with Nicholas Everett by phone. On location, he'll deal with our hired security staff and won't be able to identify the three in our team. The other pilot is Nick, and he's one of our team."

"Excellent," Daniel said. "And you've got your insiders already in place?"

"Yes," Johan confirmed. "The security guards on the flight are the key players. They'll be paid handsomely for their roles. They have insider knowledge of the courier company's regular route and a basic knowledge of what our project is about. The money they will make buys their silence."

"Greed is a wonderful thing," Daniel agreed.

Johan continued. "We'll be finished with this lab late next week. Do you want to cancel it?"

"No, leave it. I've booked it for three months; let it run its course. Tell me about this route Nick will cover?" Daniel asked.

"It takes in a number of counties, depending on who books for a pick up. Nick has done it many times; he's been working with the courier company for a while now and they trust him.

"Excellent. You don't foresee any trouble getting the cargo out of the state?"

"None. We will be leaving with it within the hour, that day."

"Excellent, excellent."

Mitch watched Daniel as he continued to read the documents. He took some close up shots.

Daniel looked up at Johan. "Will you notify the investors of the failure of the project?"

"Yes, we're drafting a letter now to be sent the day we leave. It will explain how our tests showed the drug had too many side effects and thank them for their courage in investing in something with the potential to change lives, etc., etc." Johan waved his hands.

Daniel smiled. He read through the paperwork and looked at the maps for another thirty minutes. Mitch waited and watched as Daniel occasionally asked for an explanation.

Finally, Daniel seemed satisfied. "Well done, all seems to be in order. I'll speak to you on your way to Venezuela. Good luck."

The two men shook hands and Daniel departed the main lab.

Mitch kept perfectly still as Johan packed up the documents. Nick entered the lab.

"How did it go?" he asked Johan.

"Like clockwork. Go ahead and organize our flights out for Tuesday next week," Johan said.

Nick moved beside Johan and gathered the maps. Mitch squinted hard to see detail on them. Suddenly, he realized Nick was looking up at the ceiling.

Did I make a noise?

Mitch froze. A few seconds later, Nick looked away.

———

Ellen heard the main lab door open. She caught a glimpse of Johan Booysen as he went past. She glanced up to the vent, but Mitch wasn't in sight. Ellen packed up and gave Johan fifteen minutes lead time, then turned off the lights and departed.

Mitch heard Ellen leave. He watched Nick through the vent as he surrounded himself with the maps.

Flight maps! Counties in Nevada, Mitch noted.

He put the zoom on his digital camera, checked it was still on silent and took some shots. He moved the camera to take some close-ups of Nick.

Looking thinner, Nick. Why are you involved in all this?

Mitch jumped as Nick slammed his diary closed. He watched Nick fold and stuff the maps into a bag and log out of his laptop. Nick patted his pockets and pulled out his keys. He headed to the door, switching the lights off.

Mitch waited a few minutes, giving Nick time to be out of range, then shuffled backwards along the chute to Lab G. He lowered himself from the ceiling into the dark room. Placing the grate back in place, he jumped off the counter and reached for the light.

Nick beat him to it.

———

Mitch blinked as his eyes adjusted to full light.

They stood staring at each other. Neither spoke.

A grin spread across Nick's face. He saluted.

"Major Mitchell Parker, air conditioning contractor?"

"Captain Nicholas Everett, courier driver?"

"Not likely. What's on that?" he nodded at the camera in Mitch's hand.

"Exactly what you think," Mitch said not taking his eyes of Nick.

"Then, Major, you'll know exactly what I have to do," Nick drew his gun and pointed it straight at Mitch's head.

11

Mitch felt his anger rising close to the surface.

"What are you doing, Nick?"

Nick licked his lower lip.

"What I need to do."

The two men stared at each other. Eventually Mitch spoke.

"Not one of your brightest ideas," Mitch stared at him. "Shoot me, and security will be up here before you can get down the stairs."

"I'm not going to shoot you here. We're going for a drive. Move." Nick pushed his gun into Mitch's ribs. "And Major, don't do anything stupid."

Mitch moved slowly, but his mind raced ahead. He pushed open the exit door and felt a shove in his back as Nick directed him to a Land Rover.

"You're driving," Nick pushed Mitch towards the front door of the vehicle.

Mitch stiffened.

Push me one more time, Nick ...

"Get in," Nick ordered, coming around to the passenger door, he handed Mitch the keys. "Take Glover Road."

Mitch started the car.

Got to make a move, but I need an element of surprise.

He glanced over at Nick. *I can wait.*

Pulling out of the campus, he followed Nick's directions, feeling the barrel of the gun pushed into his side.

"Keep going," Nick barked.

Mitch glanced at the time; he had been driving for fifteen minutes. His phone rang.

"Answer it," Nick ordered.

Mitch looked over at him.

"You're on surveillance aren't you? If you don't check in what happens?"

Mitch shrugged.

"As I thought. Answer the phone and remember, I've got a gun pointed at you. Keep it short and sweet."

Mitch grabbed his phone answering it before it diverted to message bank. He recognized John's number.

"Mitch, I've been waiting for your call. What happened at the meeting?"

Mitch felt Nick push the gun into his ribs.

"Mitchell?"

"I'm on my way home, John. Nothing happened."

"What do you mean nothing happened? Didn't Daniel show?"

"I'll be in at seven in the morning for our meeting."

Come on John, catch on!

"What meeting?" There was a momentary silence. "OK ... can you put your tracker on? Are you OK?"

Mitch hung up, he slumped with relief.

"See, didn't hurt a bit," Nick said.

Mitch put the phone back in his pocket, hitting a button on the side of his watch that relayed his whereabouts to head office.

Traceable!

He kept driving waiting for instructions, feeling Nick's eyes boring into him.

What has happened to you, Nick, to make you do something this desperate? We've known each other since high school. We've flown together, crammed for exams together, graduated in the Air Force together.

"So, what are you going to do now hot shot? What plan's running through your head?" Nick asked.

"Something to cause you a degree of pain hopefully," Mitch snapped.

Nick laughed. "I can hear your mind working overtime. How do I get out of this? When can I jump him? I know you, Mitch; I know your moves too. I'm looking forward to seeing your next one. Any clues?"

Mitch looked over at him and frowned.

"Nick ... what's going on?"

Nick broke eye contact.

"Shut up and drive, Mitch."

You don't want to remember the good times because you're onto something big and we're close to closing it down.

John was in the office within fifteen minutes. He stood behind the computer operator who was tracking Mitch's signal.

"Where is he now?"

"He's heading out on Glover Road, sir. Looks like he's heading to Rock Creek Park."

"Plan, sir?" the team leader moved beside John.

"Assemble a squad now and get to him ASAP. I'll be on my phone following; call me if he changes directions."

"Yes, sir."

"And tell the squad there'll be no firing. I need everyone in that vehicle alive and functioning." John walked out of the room.

Mitch took a deep breath.

I need to get you talking, Nick. It's worth a shot.

"So where are we off to, Nick?" Mitch kept his voice calm.

"I thought you might like a walk. I hear the park's nice this time of year – cold, but refreshing. Take the next left."

Mitch steered the Land Rover onto a dirt track and took the steep incline.

Thank God for the tracker. It's a long walk back, he thought.

He continued to drive, heading further away from the main road, dense scrub and tall trees closing them in.

Where the hell are you John? His eyes flicked to the mirror. *No one.* He drove further into the woods.

It's pitch black and freezing, he thought. I could be out here for weeks without anyone stumbling on me. Great.

Mitch tensed.

"Got you worried now, huh?" Nick turned side on to watch him.

Calm down. It is Nicholas Everett after all. What is he capable of doing?

He struggled to keep the Land Rover steady in his hands up the rough dirt track.

I've got to get you talking, Nick.

"This drives like your dad's four-wheel drive," Mitch tried, working at keeping his voice casual. "Remember when we just got our licenses and your dad let us take it camping? We thrashed it that weekend."

"I hated that car; it was like a tank to drive," Nick answered. Mitch felt the gun in his side again.

"Shut the hell up. I know what you're doing. You must think I'm an idiot."

"I don't know who you are."

"I'm the one with the gun!"

Mitch continued to drive. He checked the rear-view mirror again.

Nothing. No sign of life. How long does it take?

He took a sharp corner, gripping the steering wheel with both hands.

"Pull over and get out," Nick ordered.

Mitch pulled the car over and cut the ignition. The lights remained on. He could hear his heart hammering in his chest.

"Nick ... don't do this," Mitch felt sweat trickling off him.

"Get out of the car," Nick ordered. He opened his passenger side door. Mitch felt a rush of cold air.

Where are you John? I can't wait. I'm going to get knocked out here. Damn you, Nick! It's not going to end this way.

Mitch got out of the car. As Nick came around from the passenger side, he cut the lights. It was pitch black. Mitch jumped from the driver's seat, losing his balance in the blackness. He grappled his way around the door, rolling in front of the Land Rover.

"I'll shoot Mitch! Don't think I won't," he heard Nick yell.

Mitch controlled his breathing, listening for Nick, and waiting for his night vision to kick in. He saw him. Mitch charged at him feeling the impact in his chest as they toppled to the ground. Mitch was on top. He saw the gun fly out of Nick's hand and land out of reach. He reeled backwards as Nick struck him in the face with a tight fist, spilling him on the ground. He felt his own blood spray from his mouth. Pain shot through him. Nick landed another jab and pinned him down.

Mitch gasped at the blinding pain in his eye and felt blood running down his face. His vision cleared and with a burst of anger, he pushed Nick off, punching him hard and fast to the face and ribs.

Nick landed a strong blow to Mitch's throat.

Gasping and trying to get a lungful of air, Mitch retaliated, his fist impacting with Nick's jaw. Nick pounded him again. Mitch hit back with equal force, as they took their frustrations out on each other.

Mitch saw the gun. He leapt for it, pulling away from Nick and crawling towards it on his hands and knees through the dirt. Struggling for air, he swallowed the pain in his throat and ribs and surged forward trying to reach the gun. Mitch felt the metal in his hand. Face-to-face on the ground, he raised the gun to Nick's chest.

Nick froze. They stared at each other, chests heaving and blood pouring down their faces.

"That was my next move. What'd you think of it?" Mitch gasped.

"You're not going to shoot me," Nick said.

"You're right," Mitch pulled Nick into sitting position and shoved him against the car. "What the hell is wrong with you?" Mitch wiped blood from his nose. "When did you start playing on the other side?"

Nick spat saliva and blood next to Mitch's feet.

"As if you'd understand, golden boy."

Mitch shook his head. He traced his teeth with his tongue, spitting out a fresh round of blood.

"Oh, get over it," Nick said, "I wasn't going to kill you; just make sure you were out of action for a while, until the job was done."

"How comforting," Mitch pulled out his phone to call John.

Before he finished dialing, he heard two squad cars racing up the dirt track and saw the lights blazing. A voice over a loud-hailer ordered him to drop the gun. He threw it as far as possible from Nick and raised his hands. The two squad vehicles pulled over and John was the first to alight. Two officers ran to detain Nick, cuffing his hands behind his back and dragging him to his feet. They patted him down to check if he was armed.

"Clear," one of them called.

Mitch turned to John.

"Two squads; impressive, John, thanks." Mitch smiled. He swayed with the pain.

John grabbed his arm. "Are you alright?"

Mitch nodded and pulled away.

"Can you tell them to take it easy? He's a friend of mine."

John passed him a handkerchief.

"Thanks," he released a long breath as he watched John walk over to the squad.

12

"You have two options," John walked around Nicholas Everett.

"I can't wait," Nick smirked, as he sat in the interview room covered in dried blood and dirt.

"You can continue working with this project on our side, or we'll charge you now and you won't see the light of day for quite a while."

"You haven't got anything to charge me with," Nick scoffed.

"Think again," John said. "We've been taping your conversations for weeks, including Johan's conversation with Daniel. So, unless you're confident about what's on those tapes, you might want to reassess that."

John gave Nick time to think before continuing.

"I suggest you make life easy on yourself and go for the self-preservation option. Continue doing what you were doing but as an informer, and you will get leniency."

"Leniency?" Nick exclaimed, and then winced with pain. "I want to be completely cleared if I'm going to be doing your dirty work – and I want immunity even if you stuff it up," he bartered.

"We won't be stuffing it up," Mitch joined in, grimacing as he lowered himself onto the edge of the desk. "We'll be watching you every minute of the day, so don't think you can play on both sides."

"Have we got a deal? John asked.

Nick looked away.

"If you don't play the game Nicholas, we'll arrest Maria and Johan now as well, on a charge of defrauding investors."

Nick put his head in his hands and groaned as he rubbed his temples. "Damn, my head hurts."

"Well you started it, dickhead," Mitch snapped.

Nick looked up at him. "How old are you? Twelve?"

John watched their interaction.

They've still got rapport, he thought. Got you, Nicholas.

Nick turned to John.

"Can I do a deal to get Maria out of this?"

John thought about it. "If you cooperate, any sentence she gets will be greatly reduced."

"I'll take that as a no," Nick frowned. "Fine, do I have a choice?"

"No, not really. So, tell us what the Aurum Project is all about?"

"And what's 'M.M.' stand for?" Mitch pushed him.

John noted Nick's look of surprise.

"I don't need to tell you a thing. I'll go in, play my part and you work it out from there."

John looked at Mitch.

"Can I kill him now?" Mitch asked.

———

Mitch dragged himself up the front stairs of his house. He attempted to silently unlock the front door, then crept in and made his way to his room, collapsing on top of the bed.

Can't shower, can't get up.

He felt himself drifting into sleep. He woke with a start.

Did I just yell out? No ... no sound from Charlotte. Can't have yelled too loudly. He sighed and fell back onto the mattress. Next thing he knew, he could hear Charlotte's alarm going off down the hallway.

Everything's aching. Got to get up. Can't ... ribs have melted into the mattress.

He pushed up, groaned and fell back down on the bed. He heard a knock on his door.

"Are you alright?" Charlotte's voice called.

"Uh-huh."

"Can I come in?"

Mitch hesitated. He heard the door open. He tried to turn his head the other way.

"Mitch!" He saw her eyes widen. "Oh, my God! What happened to you? You're covered in blood, your eye is black."

He tried to get up and find a comfortable position, but pain came from every inch of his body. "It's nothing. You know the story: you should see the other guy," he smiled at her, feeling the dry blood crack on his face.

Charlotte's mouth dropped open.

"Hey, it's OK," he struggled to a sitting position.

She moved closer and held him.

"Ah, thanks," he said. "I'm OK, really."

"Shut up, Mitch."

He dropped back on the mattress and accepted her embrace with a smile.

―――

"Sam! Where are you?" Mitch answered his phone as he entered his office.

"In the Best Western Hotel in Eureka," Samantha answered. "We had some luck at the bar last night. It only cost us three rounds of scotch and a few beers to find out the place was leased four months ago by a South African firm. Supposedly, there are only two staff members on site, both security officers; one on day shift, the other on night shift. They pretty much keep to themselves. A few of them remember someone matching Nick's description hanging around when it was first leased, but they haven't seen him for several months. They remember seeing lots of courier vehicles coming and going."

He heard Samantha stifle a yawn. Mitch looked at his watch.

"It's about six there isn't it? What are you doing up?"

"Couldn't sleep. All the fresh desert air, I guess. So, how do you want us to play it?"

"Surveillance," he instructed. "Set yourself up somewhere where you can't be seen and watch everything and everyone that goes in and out."

"I would love to get in …"

Mitch cut her off. "Not yet, Sam. Concentrate on who and what comes and goes. Find out which is the main building and if anyone else is on site, besides the two security guards. If and when they leave, find out where they are staying. Make sure no one is residing at the site. What's Maria up to?"

"We saw her car arrive in town about eight last night. She stayed up the road at the Sundown Lodge. No doubt she'll be back on site at Broad Arrow today."

"OK, keep in touch, Sam," he hung up and seeing Ellen waiting outside his office, motioned her in.

"Good grief, look at you!" Ellen announced. "You're going to scare small children."

Mitch laughed. "You mean more than before? I was just on my way to see Henri. You got plenty to keep you going?"

"You bet. I heard you had a biff with Nick. How's he looking?"

Mitch pushed himself up from his office chair and groaned. "Just as bad, I hope."

―――

Mitch leaned heavily on the rail as he took the stairs to the science department. He spotted Henri jotting notes on a pad beside a microscope.

"Henri!"

"Mitch!" Henri's smile faded. "My God, what's happened now?"

"Midnight ride. It's OK, looks worse than it is."

"It looks bad." Henri studied the bruising and cuts.

"OK, maybe it feels that way too."

Mitch fidgeted with the equipment.

"What's wrong, you want to talk about something?"

"Have you got time?" Mitch asked.

"Always." Henri put his pen down as Mitch pulled up a stool beside the bench.

They sat opposite each other in silence. Henri knew better than to rush Mitch.

"Can I ask you something?" Mitch said, not looking up at Henri.

"I suspected you had something on your mind. Ask away."

"I know it's a lifetime ago ..." Mitch shuffled in his seat.

"Ask me," Henri invited.

"In the time you were with Mom, did she ever say anything to you about my father?"

"Such as?"

Mitch heard the change in Henri's tone.

"Where he went?"

He felt Henri's eyes studying him.

"Mitch, I'm really proud of the man you've become; impressive given the start you had ..."

"Henri ..." Mitch said, embarrassed.

Henri continued. "Why do you want to dig this up after twenty years?"

Mitch looked away and shrugged. "I had a dream, several dreams. It triggered a thought process – and I guess running into Nick again."

"Nick?" Henri cut him off, "Nicholas Everett from school?"

"Yeah, that Nick."

"Well, that's great. You two were as thick as thieves."

"Yeah. So, back to my father. Do you know where he went?"

Henri cleared his throat. "After he cleared out, I heard he went south for a while and was working for the rail network. Then, when you were about fifteen, he sent your mother divorce papers. He said in the letter he wanted to remarry. The papers were postmarked from Dallas."

"He remarried," Mitch murmured.

Did he have another son?

Were my brother and I just replaced like that? Did this kid cop beatings too?

"Mitch ..."

Mitch looked up at the sound of Henri's voice.

"I hate to be the one to give you information about your own father."

"Did he have any other kids?" Mitch continued, not hearing Henri.

"I don't know."

"Tell me, it's OK."

"I honestly don't know." Henri continued. "I admit I didn't speak to your mother a great deal in the latter years, but ..."

"But what?"

"Mitch, maybe you should be talking to your mother."

"Tell me Henri ... please!"

"He came to your graduation."

Mitch looked shocked. His eyes widened.

"From school?"

"Air Force graduation," Henri finished. "I understand he was there in the crowd watching you; undeservedly proud, no doubt."

"Did you see him there yourself?"

"Yes. I hoped your mother didn't; I think she might have."

Mitch nodded.

"That's all I know," Henri concluded.

Mitch cleared his throat. "Thanks Henri."

"What's going on with you, Mitch?"

"Nothing. Don't worry. I was just curious."

"Why are you curious now? Just because of a couple of dreams?"

Mitch didn't answer. He stared off into the distance.

"Mitch, he doesn't deserve a minute of your thoughts. Think carefully if you're intending to seek him out."

"I've got no intention of seeking him out," Mitch cut him off. He subconsciously rubbed the scar on the side of his head.

"You know, he worked your mom over terribly, and you boys. You were so little, so young – you can't forget ..."

"Of course I haven't forgotten!" he faced Henri. "I lived it day-in day-out, always waiting for the next beating," Mitch spat out the words angrily.

He stopped, noticing everyone in the lab was looking at him. Mitch swallowed.

Neither of the men spoke.

Mitch rose and walked out of the lab. He heard Henri call his name.

Just go, now, you've said enough! He strode towards the stairs.

13

J.J. and Samantha slid into a booth and ordered a couple of beers from the waitress.

"That was the most boring day ever," J.J. rubbed his eyes. "Did I mention I hate surveillance?"

"Maybe, once or ten thousand times. We did get some good info on Maria's movements and some registration numbers from courier deliveries. I also got a good photo of that guy she met with."

"Whatever, but I'm not doing another day of it … I've got a plan."

"Uh-oh!" she took the beer from the waitress, sipped it and sat back with a sigh. "OK, give it to me."

"Today, a number of deliveries were made by Rightway Express Couriers. What if we were to make a few deliveries of our own?"

"What did you have in mind?" Samantha asked.

"Let's say one of the delivery drivers is removed from the equation and I step in, check out the delivery and make the drop. We get a closer view of the premises and see what's going in and what's going out …"

"Could work."

"Using a bit of chloroform – and by the time the driver is back on his feet, we're out of there."

"That worries me," Samantha said. "How will it play out?"

"OK, I'm thinking we'll set ourselves up about fifteen miles out of Eureka. I'm gambling on the courier driver stopping to help you out when you break down on the side of the road. They'll never see me when I come up from behind with a chloroform rag," he lowered his voice. "We'll put the driver in the van, check out what's being delivered, make the delivery and see how many people are on site. We'll be long gone by the time the driver wakes up, unharmed."

"What if he can identify us?" Samantha said.

"He'll get a brief glimpse of you with a hat and glasses on and he won't see me coming up from behind, we'll be fine."

"What if they don't have a delivery for Broad Arrow and we pull them over?"

"Come on, what else is out there? The only courier deliveries that came past today all stopped at Broad Arrow, then turned and headed back north to the junction."

"My instincts tell me we should run it by Mitch," Samantha suggested.

"Forget the whole idea, we'll do surveillance. You know he'll say no, that it's too risky."

Samantha looked at J.J. and frowned. "We should think it through a little more, walk me through it again."

"You sound like Mitch now. Surely every now and then he wants his agents to use their initiative? I mean, you've been with him a few years now; doesn't he encourage that or are we all drones?"

Samantha thought about it. "Can't remember him being big on surprises; he likes to know what's going on."

"Let's be impromptu, take advantage of the opportunity," J.J. continued. "We'll tell him it was something that came to us on the spur of the moment. He'll be pleased when we get the results."

Samantha squirmed. "For your sake, I hope you get to tell him the results on his message bank first, so he can warm to how you got them before we get home."

Samantha woke as the sun came through her hotel window.

I don't think we should be doing J.J.'s plan, she thought. Should I tell Mitch? If I do, then I lose J.J.'s trust ... if I don't and it goes wrong, I'll lose Mitch's confidence. A no-win situation.

She looked over at the sound of J.J. stirring in the bed next to her.

"Coffee?" he mumbled.

She rolled her eyes and rising, moved to the kitchenette to put the jug on.

"It's after seven, we need to get moving."

J.J. groaned and threw the covers off. He dragged his feet into the bathroom.

Samantha froze as her phone rang. She looked at the number.

"Mitch!"

———

Samantha parked their hire car on the side of the road about fifteen miles out of Broad Arrow.

"OK, it's now nine; that's twelve noon in Mitch's time zone. I've already bullshitted earlier that we're going to do surveillance all day, so you'd better pull this off J.J. – I don't feel right lying to him."

"Yeah, yeah, think of it as surveillance, but from within the truck. Besides, he won't call again now until this afternoon. It'll all be over by then. Pop the bonnet but don't raise it until you see a courier van coming, otherwise every car will stop to help," J.J. said. He got out of the car and Samantha watched as he walked around the car and hid amongst the scrub. She sat in the front seat, her eyes glued to the mirror. She yawned as the first hour passed.

Two cars in one hour. Ho-hum.

"Heads up," she heard J.J. call. Her eyes went to the review mirror. A courier van was approaching. Samantha leapt out of the car and began to lift the bonnet. She heard the van slowing down, the ignition being cut, and a door opening as she continued to gaze at the engine.

"Are you alright?" a male voice called.

Samantha buried her face under the bonnet.

"It started to splutter while I was driving, now it won't start at all." She heard a struggle.

"Clear," J.J. panted.

Samantha turned to find J.J. supporting the driver, a middle-aged man in blue overalls. She raced to the van and opened the rear doors. J.J. dragged the driver to the back. Jumping in first, she helped pulled the driver in.

"I feel terrible; he was being a good Samaritan."

"He'll be up again in no time doing more good deeds," J.J. assured her.

"How long have we got?" Samantha asked.

"He'll be out for about two hours. Thank God he's a small guy," J.J. grunted. "Let's get to it so we can get the vehicles out of here in case other drivers stop to see what's going on."

Samantha looked down the long, flat road ahead and behind. Nothing in sight, yet. They began to work their way through the dozens of deliveries stacked in the van.

"There are two cylinders here, both addressed to the site," she pulled the lid off them. J.J. squatted beside her. He looked in at the liquid contents and sniffed.

"Gasoline. Why would they need all this gas delivered to them?" he said before discovering a tag on the side of the cylinder. "Avgas."

"What's Avgas?" Samantha asked.

"Don't know, remind me to check that out."

"Here's another delivery for them." Samantha found a small sealed box. J.J. reached over and cut the tape with a Stanley knife.

"It's full of small bottles of cyanide! Why would they want a fuel substance and cyanide?" She resealed the box as best she could with its own tape.

"The lab can tell us what it means."

Samantha heard the sound of an engine and a car came into view.

"Shit, I don't like this one bit," J.J. said in a lowered voice.

"I think we're stuffed," Samantha agreed.

Samantha stood at the back of the car as J.J. closed the van doors. He did up the zip on the blue courier overalls, turned and began to wipe his hands on a towel.

"Top up the air when you get to town," he spoke in clear earshot of the driver who pulled over to check if everything was OK.

"Thank you. I'm sorry to trouble you," Samantha smiled.

"No trouble at all." J.J. looked over at the driver. "Thanks for stopping, buddy. I think we're right. The lady had a flat; she's got enough air in the spare to get her into town."

The driver waved and continued. Samantha watched him drive off and turned back to J.J. "Let's do it."

"OK, head back to the hotel. I'll make this drop now. Should take me about an hour for the round trip. I'll call you on the way back to pick me up here so we can bolt as soon as the driver begins to stir."

Samantha nodded. "What if Mitch calls back?"

"Tell him the surveillance is under control."

"Right. Good luck and be careful, J.J. Hopefully they'll have something they want you to bring back."

Samantha watched J.J. drive the truck towards Broad Arrow.

I hope Mitch is caught up in meetings and doesn't call, she thought, because he is going to freak out about this one.

J.J. eyes roamed around the site, looking for details and a glimpse of Maria. *Nothing out-of-the-ordinary.*

He pulled out three items from the back of the van; the two heavy cylinders on a trolley and a small box of cyanide bottles. He glanced towards the front of the load; the driver remained concealed.

"Just need you to sign for these, buddy," he said, handing the worksheet to the security guard. He took the clipboard back, followed the guard to reception and was asked to wait for a return package. He looked around again. *Two vehicles on site and one person.* He glimpsed through the narrow glass panel at reception.

A few maps on the wall in the back room. Otherwise, no signs of any kind of industry.

J.J. looked at his watch. *Hurry up for God's sake, I've got to get moving.*

———

Samantha's phone rang. She answered it, recognizing J.J.'s number.

"Is everything OK?"

"Fine. They've asked me to wait; they've got something to go back. I'll call you when I'm on the road."

"You can't wait too long … the driver!"

"I know," he whispered. "If they don't hurry up, I'll leave without it."

"Oh, no!"

"What?" J.J. asked.

"I've got an incoming call, hang on," Samantha read the screen and then put it back against her ear. "It's Mitch!"

"Let it go to voice mail. You can honestly say you were on the phone," J.J. advised.

"Who to? You?"

"Yeah, good point … think up something while you're waiting."

"OK. Hurry up, J.J."

She hung up.

"We should never have done this!" She said, between gritted teeth. "It's a stupid plan."

———

Mitch paced his office as he dialed Samantha's number. He calculated it was midday in Eureka. He was diverted to voice mail and left a message. He tried J.J.'s phone and got voice mail.

"I hate voice mail. Where are you two?" he said talking to himself.

He could see John waiting impatiently for him at the lift.

"Coming," he mumbled, grabbing a file and exiting his office. He joined John in the lift.

"More meetings, here goes two hours of my life that I'll never get back. Is there anyway …"

"No," John cut him off. "You got out of the last two. If I don't produce you today, they'll write you off as my imagination and you'll lose your budget."

Mitch grinned. "John and his imaginary friend. There is a movie in that – might have already been done with a rabbit though."

John laughed. "Yes, I'll start calling you Harvey," referring to one of his favorite James Stewart films.

"Least you've got a friend."

"Yeah, thanks Mitch," John shook his head.

———

Mitch stopped at the traffic lights on his way to meet Charlotte and Sally for drinks.

It's six p.m., three in Eureka, he thought.

He tried to call Samantha and J.J. again and got their voice mails. Damn, where are you guys? He felt the first stirring of panic as he calculated backwards. I last spoke to them at seven their time this morning; it's now after three. What's going on?

He placed a call to Ellen and got voice mail.

"Damned voice messaging," he said aloud. His mind ran through scenarios. I better pull out of drinks, I won't be able to concentrate … no, chill out. Sam and J.J. are professionals. I'll give them another hour, then I'll go on alert.

He pulled into the wine bar's parking lot and locked the car. Entering, he spotted Sally and made his way over to her.

"Hi Sal, looking good," he complimented her.

"Good God, Mitch, what happened to you?"

"Why? Oh, the bruising," he remembered and self-consciously

reached for his face. "Nothing, just a training exercise. Where's princess?"

"She's up at the bar getting a wine list. Mitch, that looks painful," Sally studied him.

"I'd say you should see the other guy – but that line's been overdone," he removed his black wool coat and placed it on the back of the chair, glancing around.

"Another Charlie discovery?"

"Yep. She's out to discover every new place in town. Are you off nightshift?"

"Only for tonight. Boss's orders, early to bed, etc." He sat back. "Actually, it was good to be on nightshift for a while; gave Charlie the house to herself to have Lachlan over."

"Yeah, well, that won't happen again," Sally informed him.

"Why?"

"You asked that quickly."

"Did I?"

"I'm just teasing you. Anyway, they're off again. They had another one of their infamous arguments – and that was it."

"Hmm! Heard that before." He poured a glass of water from the carafe on the table.

"No, he's taken a contract interstate. A six-month contract. I'm surprised she hasn't told you."

"Why would she?"

Sally shrugged. "Because she normally talks about everything—occupational hazard—and you are her roommate and friend. She's pretty upset about it."

"Maybe that's why she hasn't spoken about it. How upset?" Mitch asked with a glance to his phone.

"Morose, moody, unhappy, wallowing ..." Sally stopped talking. "What's wrong with you tonight? You're so jumpy."

"Don't you start, Sally. It's bad enough Charlie analyzes my every move."

Mitch's phone rang and he grabbed for it.

"Sorry, I've got to take this," he rose. "Ellie, have you heard from them?" He went outside the café.

Finishing the call, he turned and saw Charlotte and Sally watching him. He headed inside, sitting down next to Charlotte.

"You two are quiet. Run out of conversation? Who would have thought?" He took the wine Charlotte offered him.

"No, smarty," Sally grinned. "We were checking you out and we've decided you're not bad looking – when you're not black and blue."

Mitch laughed.

"Really? So did you both come to that conclusion?"

"Maybe," Charlotte piped in, "But I didn't really want to tell you because your head is big enough without us boosting your ego."

Mitch looked at Charlotte, a grin on his face.

"A big head?"

"Absolutely!" Charlotte exclaimed. "I've got to live with you, so I don't want your head getting any bigger. We both won't fit in the kitchen at the same time."

"Ah, a back-handed compliment. Be still, my beating heart. Anyway, like I'm the one with the big head!"

"Whoa, Mitch! You're on dangerous ground now," Sally warned.

The waiter dropped some menus on the table as Mitch's phone rang again.

"Thank Christ," he said, recognizing Samantha's number. "Sam!" Mitch listened to her.

"What!" he exclaimed. "You've got to be kidding me?" He rose and headed outside again.

"He was supposed to meet me over two hours ago. And I can't reach him," Samantha said.

"Two hours ago, why didn't you call me sooner?" Mitch groaned. "From the top, Sam, what happened?"

Mitch listened, breaking in occasionally.

"No way. What sort of plan is that? What were you both thinking? Why didn't you run it by me?" Mitch paced up and down outside the café. He rubbed his temple.

Stay in control, he told himself. Don't do anything you will regret. I just want to punch someone out ... namely, Jack Jameson.

Samantha finished.

"Mitch, are you there?"

"I'm here. I'm deciding what to do."

"I shouldn't have let him do it," Samantha's voice was choked with tears.

"He's an experienced operative, he should have known better."

"I had a gut feeling."

"He's senior to you. It's OK, Sam, don't beat yourself up about it, we'll work it out," Mitch cut her off. "You're going to stay put. Don't do a thing until I get there, understand?"

"Yes."

"I mean stay put, Sam. I need you there when I arrive. Clear?"

"Yes, Mitch," she said. "You're coming over?"

"Tonight, as soon as I can get a flight organized. I'll get back to you with the arrival time. Call me if you hear anything. Anything!" He hung up and raced back inside.

"Sorry ladies, got to go." He grabbed his wallet, slipped some notes under his wine glass while Charlotte and Sally protested and grabbed his coat. "Charlie, I'll be away for a few days."

"But where are you going? Don't you need to pack?" Charlotte asked.

Mitch was already halfway to the door and didn't respond. He headed straight to the office, calling John on the way.

———

"What's Broad Arrow like? Can we send in reinforcements without it being noticed?" John asked as Mitch paced his office.

"Unlikely. An extra person will register and trust me, they'll be watching now. I've got to extract J.J. without making waves if we can. I need to get over there now, tonight. I'll take Ellie. Can you replace her on surveillance at the university?"

"Of course."

"That will be three of us on the ground. It should be manageable."

John didn't move.

"What's wrong?" Mitch realized John wasn't getting the wheels in motion. He stopped pacing.

"Are you up to it?" John asked.

"Of course I'm up to it. What do you mean?"

"The lack of sleep, the fight with Nick ..."

"John, I'm up to it!"

"And, I heard you had a bit of an argument with Henri."

"Henri? It was nothing."

"Must have been something. He's worried about you." John picked up the phone and instructed a staff member to book Mitch and Ellen on the next flight to Elko. He hung up.

"I had a gut reaction about this," Mitch resumed pacing.

"About what?"

"About J.J. joining the team. I know he was keen for the change, but he was senior to all of us and I suspected he felt he should have been team leader."

"He's senior, but his skills aren't in leading a team. It's one thing to be able to start any engine and crack any lock, but you've also got to be a lateral thinker. When did you have this gut reaction?"

"Right from the start. He must have been itching for some independence."

The phone rang and John answered it, taking down some details. He hung up.

"No flights at this hour to Elko."

"Can we get a charter?"

"No, out of the question. You're on the last flight available to Las Vegas, leaving in twenty-five minutes from Dulles International."

Mitch listened in as John made a series of calls confirming the flight, taxi transfer to the airport, weaponry and an overnight bag to be produced for Mitch. Ellen was being picked up. John went to his computer and within minutes, received an email with Mitch and Ellen's details. He printed it out. He read from it, "You will land in Las

Vegas at ten-thirty tonight. There are no flights to Elko until seven the next morning. You'll get in at eight ..."

"We'll drive from Vegas."

"It's about four hundred miles!"

"I know, but every hour counts. We should be able to do it in ...," Mitch did the calculations, "less than six hours. If we land at ten-thirty, we should arrive at Broad Arrow around four in the morning. That gives us nearly two-and-a-half hours before sunrise."

"OK, I'll hire you a car. Share the driving."

Mitch headed for the door. "Can you email the audio transcripts through from the lab if you get any?"

"Will do," John agreed.

Mitch continued. "Can you put a trace on Johan? Leave Nick sitting tight until I get back. I hope Johan doesn't want to pull out earlier with Nick. I want to be back and right on him the whole way. I don't trust him yet." He shook his head and looked up at John. "If I lose Johan because of J.J ..."

"Go," John ordered. "I want to hear from you regularly."

Mitch sat in the taxi on the way to the airport and called Samantha.

"We're on our way," he confirmed. "We'll call you when we get close to Eureka. Should be around three-thirty in the morning, all going well, and we'll go onto Broad Arrow from there, arriving around four. Be ready to move out. And turn your tracker on," he referred to the tracking device in their wristwatches.

"I don't suppose ...?"

"No," Mitch finished. "J.J. hasn't turned his on. But don't panic, he might not have thought of it." Or is capable of it.

"How are we going to access the site?" Samantha asked.

"I'll work that out on the flight. John's sending me an up-to-date plan of the area. He's getting the layout from the leasing agents."

"Right."

"Are you OK?" Mitch asked.

"No. What if he's ... Mitch, he could be dead and ..."

Mitch cut her off.

"Hang in there, Sam. It'll be fine. Don't do anything rash; just wait for us, OK?"

"OK, hurry, Mitch."

"We'll see you soon." Mitch hung up.

The whole thing is slipping through my fingers. What a stuff-up! J.J.'s supposed to be one of our best senior agents, but this maverick act could compromise the whole mission. Why didn't he just stick to surveillance?

The taxi pulled over at the terminal. Mitch leapt out, ran to check in and found Ellen waiting.

"John's booked us into business class. Probably thought you needed it," she looked at Mitch's bruised face.

"There goes the budget. Hope it comes out of his and not mine." They boarded immediately and stowed their agency-issued black overnight bags in the locker above their seats.

Mitch sat down beside Ellen. He sighed. "Now for the plan."

———

"You missed him," John invited Henri Spalter to take a seat in his office.

Henri lowered himself into a chair.

"It's after eight, John. Catching up on the day?"

John opened his cabinet and poured them both a scotch.

"Just had to get Mitch and Ellie on a flight to Nevada before heading home."

"Ah, I've well and truly missed him then." Henri took the glass, clinked it against John's and sipped. "We had a bit of a fall out," Henri sighed.

John looked at the amber liquid and swirled it around the glass. "Mm, there is something going on with him at the moment; something's stirred him up. Do you know what it's about?"

"Skeletons in the closet maybe. He was asking me about his father, out of the blue. It must be twenty years since he's seen him."

John frowned. "Maybe now he feels the need for an explanation. I hope he's not feeling vengeful."

"No, it's not in his nature."

John nodded in agreement. "So, he didn't tell you why the sudden resurgence in interest?"

"No, I was allowed to answer questions, not to ask them."

"Ah," John said knowingly. "He's not sleeping; nightshift. Might be contributing to his odd behavior. It can throw you around a bit, give you a short temper."

"And he's had an encounter from the past I hear – Nicholas Everett."

"Yes, you know him?"

"I remember Nicholas well. He and Mitch were best friends; inseparable the pair of them."

"Hmm, well they've just about knocked each other's lights out this time."

"Good grief! The fight was with Nicholas?"

"Yes," John confirmed.

"Well, no wonder he's shook up. One of the people he most trusts or used to at least." Henri finished the scotch. "Well, best get home; you too, I imagine. Thanks for the drink. Tell our boy when you speak to him that I dropped by."

"Will do," John smiled. "Goodnight."

John swiveled on his chair, and began to log off his computer. As it went through the back up process, he sat back and thought about Mitchell Parker: strong minded, impressive recall of detail, a voracious need for stimulation and the ability to change the mindset of a team; there is no doubt under pressure he's the best … but he pushes himself to breaking point and never asks for help.

"Who do you talk to, Mitch?" John said to himself, rising to leave. "Got to work on that."

The computer screen went to black. John grabbed his jacket and satchel and pulled the door closed behind him.

14

Mitch declined the alcohol being offered by the flight attendant and opted for a juice.

Need to keep a clear head, he thought. God knows what's waiting for us in Nevada, or where the hell J.J. is.

After takeoff, Ellen leaned towards him.

"Mitch, I've got these profiles on Johan and Maria. Nick you already have. Do you want them now?"

"Thanks Ellie, may as well." He took Ellen's notes and scanned the page.

"Ah," he circled a company called Linenet. "I imagine that's where Johan met Maria – when he was working for this company in Venezuela in 2004."

"I'd say so," Ellen agreed. "They entered the U.S. together, so the romance has been on for a while."

Mitch flipped the page to Maria's profile and looked over the entries.

"Strong distribution networks throughout South America and Europe. That's handy."

Mitch stopped to read a line out loud.

"Her sister Ana was engaged to an American pilot. Ana was killed in a car accident late last year. What are the odds we know the pilot?"

"Nicholas Everett?" Ellen guessed.

"Precisely."

Mitch went through the files John had sent electronically. He gave the map to Ellen to find the best possible entrance and exit to the Broad Arrow mining site.

"We're lucky some of the tunnels still exist from the days when the area was a thriving gold mine," he said. "Odd. Usually after production ceases they secure them."

"Very lucky," she agreed. "See here," Ellen pointed to the map, "this is probably the best entry point. These underground tunnels will give us direct access to the main building if we can find the entrance to the tunnels and if they haven't been sealed. They should be external, against the south wing of the building."

"Plan B if they are sealed?" Mitch asked.

"There's always the ceiling."

―――

"Thank God," Ellen said, making her way off the plane.

Mitch went straight to the hire car desk and within fifteen minutes they were on the road. He concentrated on the monotonous highway ahead of him.

"Get some sleep Ellie; you're going to need it." He opened the window, using the cold air to stay alert and resigned himself to the drive. His mind wandered …

One hour …

… crap music, nothing to see …

… Ellie sleeping.

He yawned and flicked between radio stations.

Two hours …

… need to stop for gas … something to look forward to …

… Ellie's still sleeping … truly amazing how she does that with the radio and wind noise.

Three hours …

... one coffee and a Coke gone ...

... aching, need to take a piss; can wait until next gas stop ... more coffee ...

... if you're not dead J.J., I'm going to kill you.

Mitch's phone rang making him jump. Ellie woke up beside him.

"Parker," he answered.

"Mitch, where are you now?"

"John! Still driving; about an hour away from the destination. You scared the shit out of me, again," he said feeling his heart thumping.

"I was counting on that to wake you up." John hung up.

Mitch looked over at Ellen. "I swear sometimes he's in my head."

"Funny, that's what we say about you," she smiled at him.

Mitch dialed Samantha's number and followed her directions. He saw her waiting in her hire car, discretely parked on the outskirts of the town's limits. She jumped into their car.

"I have never been so pleased to see anyone in my whole life as I am to see you two," she exclaimed.

"No news from J.J.?" Mitch asked.

"Nothing."

"OK, Sam, tell the story from the top. Don't leave anything out."

As he listened, Mitch accelerated to get to the former mine site. Getting closer, he looked around for somewhere to hide the car.

"What's the landscape like during the day?" he pushed Samantha.

"Flat, lots of scrub."

He found a hilly area where the car could be hidden.

"Hope it holds up in daylight," he parked the rental car, killed the lights and jumped out. Opening the boot, the three agents geared up. He checked their weapons – a handgun, a ranger knife, stun guns, flares and a quantity of bullets and devices for immobilizing the enemy.

"Test your wires and trackers," he ordered. They each did so in turn.

Satisfied and with a quick glance to his watch, Mitch gave directions.

"It's just on four. We've got to be out by first light. We're going to jog down to the boundaries of the main building. If there is security —and according to surveillance there is only one officer on duty—he should be around the main building. We have to assume that the building is alarmed, so we need to get in underground somehow. If the map is accurate, those tunnels are near the fuel storage tanks. Once in, we'll break up. I'll indicate where you are to go. Cover the area, keep your trackers on and stay alert."

Hugging the back roads they jogged the half-mile distance to the site. Mitch strained to see the girls, camouflaged in black in the pitch-black surrounds. The only sounds he could hear were of their footsteps as their hiking boots hit the road surface. Mitch slowed his pace to ensure they didn't fall too far behind.

He arrived at the first of the buildings and waited for Ellen and Samantha to fall in behind him.

"Sam," he whispered, "head to the front of the building. Look out for the van, any signs of a struggle, any signs of J.J. Come back here when you're done. We'll let you know where the tunnel entrance is."

She nodded and peeled off.

"Fuel storage," he whispered to Ellen. They searched the area where it was suppose to be according to the map.

Nothing.

They covered the area again. It dawned on him.

The row of barrels is masking it.

Nudging behind one of the barrels, Mitch tipped it to the side.

Found it!

He gave Ellen the thumbs up. With another glance around, Mitch heaved the barrel out of the way, a foot at a time.

This is when you need J.J., he thought, grunting with the effort.

"OK, Ellie, let's go," he pulled up the iron lid, looked down into the tunnel and lowered himself down the steel ladder. He helped Ellen down and maneuvered the lid back in place. Mitch and Ellen stood still, listening for noises, waiting for their eyes to adjust. He could feel her touching his back in the dark.

She's freaked out.

Mitch pulled out his penlight and turned it on. Rats scuttled and he felt Ellen stiffen behind him. He saw tunnels in every direction – full size, wide tunnels that cleared his head by at least a foot. Ellen's breathing quickened.

"Are you OK?" he shined the penlight in her face.

She nodded.

"Go up if it freaks you out."

"I'm OK," she began to slow her breathing.

Mitch watched her for a few seconds more. "Ellie, go up if you need to ... I don't want to carry you out after we've gone half-a-mile underground."

"I'm OK," she assured him.

Mitch turned the penlight down to the map and studied it. He flashed the light at the nearest tunnel to their right. They followed it as it went downhill, then sideways, and then leveled out. They walked for about five minutes until Mitch came to a small timber-framed hatch above his head. He pried it open. A shower of dirt and dust fell onto him and he blinked to clear his eyes.

"This hasn't been opened for years."

Mitch pushed himself through the hatch, calculating there were two underground levels in the main building. On the other side of the cover was another iron ladder.

"Ellie," he whispered, "continue along the tunnel, and try any doors you find. Look out for anything suspicious."

She nodded.

Mitch took her arm. "Are you sure you're OK?"

"I'm fine," she pulled away.

OK, he coached himself, the ladder should hopefully land me somewhere near reception of the main building.

Mitch bound up the fifteen rungs and listened.

All quiet. He edged open the next door he found until it was wide enough to see through and get his bearings.

No security cameras; no lighting either.

He pushed the door open and slipped through.

The main building! He thought and exhaled with relief. Mitch went to the edge of the wall and squatted, taking in the area. Spotting the open fire-exit door, he bolted for the stairs, taking them two at a time. He came to a partially opened door and looked in.

This is wrong, he frowned. It looks like another storage area. Reception must be one more floor above. He glanced up to the next landing. The door was barred.

"Damn", he muttered, "I can't risk opening it in case it's alarmed and Sam's got the tester." Mitch went back into the storage area and glanced up.

Great, a ten foot high ceiling. He studied the area. Nope, no way around it. He stood on a table and pulled the grate aside, taking a leap towards the ceiling. He gripped the outer edges of the air conditioning shaft and pulled himself through, grunting with the pain in his body. *I'm becoming a master of crawling in ceilings.*

He scurried along until he came to a vent. Glancing through it, it seemed to come out in a hallway.

He pushed the frame until it fell out, crawled through the hole and put the vent cover back in place. Mitch stood, looked around and moved straight ahead, prying open another door.

Perfect! Just where I want to be: reception. He listened; there was no sound.

Where the hell is the security guard? No cameras, no dogs ... security seems pretty light on – odd.

Mitch used his wire.

"Ellie, are you OK?"

There was a slight delay before he heard her voice.

"Alive and kicking."

"Good, stay that way. I'm at reception. Anything your way?"

"Nothing,"

"OK, carry on." Mitch let his eyes adjust to the darker environment, then headed to the reception desk. He grabbed a delivery docket sitting on the desk from the courier company.

Two cylinders and a small box delivered here, he noted. Someone's signed for them.

A sound at the outside window instinctively made him duck for cover. He looked up to see Samantha outside.

"Shit, Sam," he said into his mic.

"Sorry! I'm just going to case the window for alarms."

Mitch watched her move the scanner over the aluminum window frame. She gave the all-clear sign and he pushed the window open, helping her in.

"No sign of the van outside," she said in a hushed voice. "There are several sets of tire tracks leading to a larger garage next to this building. I think that's where we should be looking; it's sealed. Can we enter it through this building?"

"We'll find out."

Mitch showed her the courier receipt. "It's signed at twelve-forty. Is that timing right? Would it be J.J.?"

"Yes," Samantha nodded, "that's about the time he arrived. They've nabbed him after he had made the delivery ... I wonder what alerted them."

"Hopefully J.J. can tell us. Let's get into the garage; it must be connected to the main building somehow." He scanned the map for clues. Mitch looked around.

"Come on." He headed down the hallway of the building, looking left and right as rooms peeled off on either side.

"No sign of J.J. here," Ellen came through on the wire. "I'm heading up one level."

"OK. When you finish the next level Ellie, head towards the back of the building, we're trying to get into the garage and we think that's where the access will be."

Mitch came to the end of the hallway.

"Two exits. One marked for fire and the other sealed by dead locks. Check them for alarms, Sam."

He stood back and watched her run the scanner over the fire door. The light remained green as she ran it around the door, looking for an alarm.

Mitch waited, his foot tapping.

"All clear," she whispered.

"I don't get it, where's the security?"

"Perhaps they didn't think they needed any … yet."

Mitch pushed open the fire door and found himself out in the open courtyard.

"Wrong door," he said under his breath. "Try the other one, Sam."

She tested the door for an alarm.

"Clear."

"Great, no alarm," he said angrily, "just a dead lock."

"And breaking into locks is J.J.'s specialty," Samantha sighed.

"Don't remind me."

"Mitch?" Ellen's voice cut across his thoughts.

"Go ahead."

"This level's clear too," she said with a mixture of disappointment and relief in her tone. "I'm done."

"OK make your way to the garage if you can find a way in, head towards the rear, we're on our way."

Mitch looked at the door and lock again.

"We need to ram that in," he said looking around for something to help throw weight against the door.

"Nothing," he said. "Well here goes." He ran at the door and hit it will full force. Mitch fell back and tried again. Samantha joined in. The door latch began to crumble and with one final kick from Mitch the lock swung off and the door flew open.

Racing through the stairwell they arrived at the garage.

"Hey, we're above you," Mitch whispered into his mic to Ellen as she pushed up a grate from a tunnel below. He helped move the grate and she joined them.

"It's all clear here," Samantha said casing the area. "This place is amazing. There are tunnels everywhere."

Mitch led the way out of the first large concrete garage bay, passing another two bays. And then, he saw it – the Rightway Express Courier Van.

"Split up."

Mitch went to the back of the van, Samantha cased the room and Ellen took the front. Mitch swung the back van doors open; it was empty.

"Shit", he swore under his breath. He jumped out of the back of the van and stood looking around the room, his hands on his hips.

We're running out of time. Think!

His eyes widened at the site of a huge mound of earth, freshly dug in the corner of the garage.

"Oh, no," he inhaled sharply. He saw Ellen and Samantha turn at the sound of his voice and they noticed the mound. Mitch swallowed the lump in his throat. Samantha ran towards it, but he beat her there, grabbing her around the waist and pulling her behind him.

"No, Sam, get back."

She moved around him, dropping to her hands and knees and began to dig. Mitch heard a muffled thump and froze. The sound came again. He signaled for quiet; it was coming from a storage unit. Mitch indicated for Samantha to check the unit for alarms. She ran the test; the green light for all-clear came on. He looked at the bolt securing the unit.

"Should we blow it?" Samantha asked.

"No, too noisy."

He reached for a small pair of bolt cutters from his vest. Mitch worked at the steel, feeling the sweat running down his back.

Come on!

With a snap, the bolt gave way and Mitch pulled open the door to find Jack Jameson alive, bound, blindfolded and gagged. Samantha pulled J.J.'s blindfold from his eyes. Ellen joined in, untying the bonds around his feet. J.J.'s face was bruised; the courier overalls were covered in dirt and blood.

"I thought you'd never get here," J.J. gasped.

Mitch let out a long sigh of relief. "Thank Christ, you're OK." He turned and walked away, feeling the anger build up inside him.

"Boss, I'm sorry …" J.J. started.

Mitch turned. "J.J., save it."

"I just thought if I could …"

"No, really. Not now," Mitch paced.

Stay calm, deal with it later. You're the team leader; just keep it together.

"Mitch, at least let me explain …"

Mitch glared at him through clenched teeth. "We'll talk about it later, not now. We're almost out of time and we've got to get out of here."

He saw J.J.'s eyes flare with anger.

"If you weren't so anal and gave us the chance to think for ourselves occasionally," J.J. hissed.

Mitch heard Samantha inhale sharply.

"Anal!" Mitch exploded. "Thinking for yourself has really paid off, hasn't it? You were on surveillance orders, in charge on the ground. You could have blown the mission, not to mention what a waste of time this has been traipsing across the country to save your sorry ass. I should kill you myself."

"Mitch," Samantha grabbed Mitch's arm and moved in front of him, cutting off his vision of J.J. "We both made the decision."

Mitch shrugged Samantha off.

"We've got a job to do, focus on that. Where's the security?" he asked J.J.

J.J. bent over, wincing. "There is one guy around: a soft, middle aged guy. He's armed."

"Then how did you get in this shape?"

"The driver and guard did it, after I was tied up."

"The courier van's here. Where's the driver?" Mitch pushed him.

"I don't know," J.J. said. "He might have been too groggy to drive and got a lift."

"Not groggy enough to give you a thrashing though. Let's get out of here before the security guard finds us."

15

Mitch sent Samantha and Ellen ahead. He walked behind supporting J.J.

"Give me a minute," J.J. stopped and leaned over, wiping the jacket sleeve across his face. "I feel hot and cold."

"It's going to be light soon, we've got to keep moving." He grabbed J.J.'s arm and put it across his shoulders. "Try and stay on your feet, put your weight on me." Mitch eased J.J. along. He saw the car coming with Ellen behind the wheel. Samantha jumped out to help Mitch lower J.J. into the back seat.

"Ellie, drop Sam back to her hire car, then backtrack and take J.J. onto Elko. It's about an hour away and there is a hospital there. Tell them he got into a fight."

J.J. began to protest. Mitch cut him off.

"Sam, bring your car down here and wait for me behind that hill, out of sight. If I'm not back in thirty minutes, call John; he'll get you all out of here. I've got the tracker on if anything goes wrong."

"Where are you going?" Samantha asked, "I'll come with you."

"No. I've got to check something out in case we don't get back here for a while."

"What?" J.J. asked, clenching his teeth in pain.

"Playing a hunch." He pushed J.J. back in the seat. "Go Ellie." He turned and ran back towards the buildings.

Mitch looked back satisfied from the dust storm that Ellen was driving away.

Mitch pushed his exhausted body one more time into a run. The building came into sight. He raced around to where the barrels had been. Again he found the manhole, and grunting, slid the lid off. His breathing was coming short and fast. Sliding down the stairs, Mitch ran down the tunnel, his hands grasping the walls on either side to steady himself in the dark.

Halfway down, he turned, took another tunnel and kept running. Finally, he stopped.

That entrance Ellie found to the garage ... it was somewhere around here. He took out his penlight and turned in a full circle.

The tunnel to the left ... found it.

He went down a few paces and saw the opening, pushing his way through, he stopped and gaped.

Whoah! A huge underground hangar.

He walked around. In front of him, almost dwarfed by the hangar's size, was a full-sized airplane sitting on a hydraulic ramp.

Mitch put it together. This is what the investors are paying for, he thought. He looked up and saw a massive garage door built into the earth. When that opens, the plane can be hydraulically lifted to ground level to sit on the runway. When closed, it disappears from sight underground, as if it never existed. Fantastic. He smiled.

Mitch checked his watch. *Ten more minutes ... I've got to get closer.*

"A Fairchild Metro turboprop aircraft," he mumbled aloud. "A nice one."

He walked the length of the plane, opened the door of the cockpit and hoisted himself in. He noted it was empty except for built-in vaults in the back of the plane. High security steel safes.

Mitch jumped out, looked around for a power box, and found it.

That's where the lift and garage door will operate from. He studied the wiring.

Out of time, got to go.

Mitch turned away and pushing himself through the opening, ran back up the tunnel, mounting the iron rungs two at a time. He stopped, checked no one was around and heaved himself out of the manhole. Closing the lid, he rolled the barrel back into place and ran flushed up against the wall.

He coached himself; *hold up ankle, just a bit longer while I beat my sprint record back to the car in case Sam takes off without me.*

As he came around the corner of the building, he looked straight down the barrel of a Glock 20 handgun.

Found the security guard.

———

"Don't move." The guard pointed his gun at Mitch's head.

Mitch sized him up and dropping low, slammed his fist into the security guard's stomach, pushing him against the wall and pinning the guard's arm and gun against the wall.

J.J.'s right; middle aged, overweight. Probably never seen action in his life.

He spun the guard around to face the wall. Mitch drew his own gun and pushed it against the security guard's neck.

"I don't want to use this," Mitch said.

The guard nodded.

Grabbing the handcuffs from the man's uniform, Mitch pulled the guard's arm behind his back and cuffed him.

"Move it," Mitch hissed, pushing him back towards the manhole.

"Please no," he begged, "don't put me down there, they'll never find me, I've got a wife and two kids."

Mitch rolled his eyes.

"For chrissake!"

He pulled the guard over to the outside of the garage door. Looking at the chain of keys hanging from the guard's pockets he asked. "Which key opens the door?"

"The green one."

Mitch could smell the sweat pouring off the guard. He found the key with the green rubber border, unlocked the steel doors and pried them open a few feet. Pushing the guard in front of him, he moved towards the storage unit that J.J. had been locked into.

"I'll assume they'll find you here," he said, remaining behind the guard's vision.

He grabbed some tape from his vest and tearing a strip, placed it across the guard's mouth and another strip across his eyes. He pushed him inside the unit and locked the door. Wiping his print off the key, he tossed the ring of keys on the floor and took off at break neck speed. After sprinting for a few minutes, he saw Samantha idling the car and scanning the horizon for him. He reached the car, opened the front passenger door and jumped in.

"Thank God," she said.

"Head to Elko," Mitch instructed out of breath.

"What happened?"

"My hunch, I think it's paid off," Mitch looked at his watch. It was nearing six a.m. "Give me five minutes and I'll tell you," He rang John.

"John, all clear and safe. We need out. We're heading to Elko with the two hire cars," he panted.

"Are you OK?"

"Fine."

John put him on hold. Mitch waited.

"Mitch?"

"Here." He listened to the instructions. "OK, we'll be there, thanks. The trip was worth it after all, aside from finding J.J alive. You won't believe what we found. I'll see you in your office," He hung up.

"Sam, there is an air force plane leaving Battle Mountain airport at seven-thirty. We all need to be on it." He dialed Ellen's number. "We'll pick them up at the hospital, leave one car in Elko and the other at Battle Mountain. John's taking care of it."

He sat back.

Got the team back and we'll be back on deck in D.C. by the end of the day. Not enough time for Johan or Nick to make a move without us, hopefully.

"How far is it?" she asked.

"From Elko, about 70 miles. We should be able to do it in under an hour." They both glanced at the clock on the car's dashboard. It read six-fifteen.

"It's pretty flat and straight, I'm told," he assured her.

———

Mitch woke with a start, his mind empty of the present. Looking around, he remembered where he was – lying flat on the floor of a 707 cargo plane, and he relaxed.

Ah, every bone in my body's making itself known, he thought, pulling himself into sitting position. He glanced at his watch. Still Friday and I've slept for half a day! Got to love time zones. Could use a shower.

He looked around at his team as they sprawled, surrounded by boxes and military gear. Samantha and Ellen were lying asleep, huddled on the floor, J.J. was awake.

"J.J., how are you feeling?" Mitch stood and stretched.

"Sore. Hey Mitch, listen, I stuffed up. I could give you a lot of shit about why and what I was thinking … but take it from me, it won't happen again … and sorry about the anal comment."

"Is this what you really want, J.J.?"

"What do you mean?"

"To work in this team, instead of managing your own."

J.J. shrugged. "It was a stupid call that's all. Don't read too much into it."

"Right," Mitch turned away.

———

"I'm surprised you're still standing given you've had little sleep and driven a marathon!" John greeted Mitch.

"I'm fine, but you should've seen this plane, it's unbelievable," Mitch's eyes were huge as he fell into a chair in John's office.

"So, J.J.'s alright?"

"Yeah, fine. Listen, they've got this huge Fairchild turboprop …"

"Did you two sort it out?" John cut in.

"More or less. Anyway, they've built a huge underground hangar with a hydraulic lift …"

"What does more or less mean?"

"What?" Mitch stopped. "John, you're missing the point … fine, forget about the plane. J.J.'s OK; bruised, but OK. He told me I was anal and we had a few words. I suggested he might want to manage his own team; he said no – that's that." Mitch clammed up.

John laughed. "Sorry, Mitch, I couldn't resist.

"Yeah, very funny."

"Anal, huh?"

Mitch grinned. "Imagine! Me!"

John laughed. "Tell me, what's this about a plane?"

"Yeah, the plane. They've built this garage door flat into the earth. You wouldn't even see it from above. It's designed to swallow the plane into it. Then underground, they've used the existing mine storage areas to build a huge hangar and they've got a Fairchild Metro twin engine turboprop aircraft in there. This one's got custom built wall-to-wall steel safes in the back – it's unbelievable," He stopped to draw breath.

John stared out the window in customary form while he thought. "Are you thinking what I'm thinking?"

"The gold plane," Mitch answered. "It's a substitute for the courier plane that does the gold route."

"Yes. Very, very clever," John agreed. "The Nevada police are going to want this."

"No way, there are too many loose ends. I don't believe this is a simple robbery. Johan and Maria with their international connections must have some other agenda – and these investors who are being duped, that's all a bit pie-in-the-sky at the moment," Mitch said. "I'm still not sure what Daniel Reid's role is either, but there is no doubt where the investors' funds are going; they need some serious money to get the plane and organize the underground hangar. And let's face it, since September 11, any mention of pilots hired for non-official flights should keep the alarm bells ringing."

"And the rest of it? The university lab?" John asked.

"A smokescreen – an address, somewhere to plan one of the biggest gold heists in history."

"And we have to keep up the charade," John agreed. "We don't want them to know we're on to them."

"They're going to know someone's onto them given J.J. knocked off their regular courier driver," Mitch shook his head.

"How did they know? Is it the same driver all the time?"

"Usually one of three. J.J. said the driver had called ahead about twenty minutes earlier to check someone was on site because he had two cylinders that had to be stored in a cool place. This time they did know him – he was a regular. So when J.J. showed up …"

They sat for a few seconds in silence.

"I've set up an alias for J.J. in the system," John said. "He's been given a petty criminal history. If they run his profile, they'll assume he was looking to steal any loot he could get his hands on. It's a long shot, but they won't be able to connect him to us at least."

"Great." Mitch rose to his feet to leave. "I need to speak with Nick now we're up to speed; I want his every movement choreographed."

"Why don't you go home and get some sleep first? Nick will still be here tomorrow." John walked him to the door. "And for God's sake, go and see Henri. He's been trying to track you down."

———

"The intruder's gone," Luis Gamboa, former head of security for international firm Securald and now on-site security manager at Broad Arrow, informed Johan.

"Where is he?" Johan asked.

"We don't know," Gamboa spat it out. "I found that idiot bound and gagged in the storage unit this morning. From now on, I hire the security staff. That was my arrangement when Maria hired me."

"Then do it. I want to know who that guy was connected to," Johan ordered.

"I ran the name on his driver's license. He's got a rap sheet a mile long, mainly break and enter. My hunch is that he's working solo and was casing the place. He probably heard the site was leased. I imagine he's cleaned out anything of value in the courier van as well."

"Maybe. We should have got more from him while we had the chance. I may have to move the project forward. Hire someone effective," he ordered.

"Done," Luis Gamboa assured him.

Mitch entered his office, sat back in his chair and stared at the ceiling. From the beginning, he told himself, going through the case in his head. He turned sensing someone was standing in the doorway, watching him.

"Henri," Mitch rose. "Sorry, I didn't hear you. I was thinking about the case."

"No problem. Are you OK?"

"Fine. Come in."

Henri stayed put in the doorway. "I've got the lads working on something, I need to get back downstairs. As long as you are fine." Henri gave Mitch a smile and turned to leave.

"Henri," Mitch raced out from behind his desk. "Wait up."

Henri turned and waited for him.

"I, um, I've been in Nevada. I wanted to talk with you, but ..."

"But you didn't want to as well," Henri finished his sentence and smiled at him.

Mitch felt like a fourteen-year-old kid again with Henri reading his thoughts. Mitch looked sheepish. "I'm sorry I got a bit angry the other day. I've been on nightshift and it has thrown me around."

"Listen, son," Henri interrupted him, "I'm happy if you tell me you're fine. I know you, and I know better than to enter your world uninvited."

"No, Henri, it's not like that," Mitch stammered.

"Mitch, if you want to talk, you know where to find me." Henri moved to put an arm on his shoulder. Mitch flinched.

"I wasn't going to hit you, Mitch," Henri stepped back.

"I know that!"

Henri nodded and giving Mitch one last look, left his office.

"Shit." Mitch swore, turning back to his desk.

16

Mitch woke up in a cold sweat. The clock beside his bed told him it was after seven.

Sunday. He sighed with relief. Raising himself up on his elbows, he leaned back on the headboard and thought about the project: they're going to swap planes, take the gold, stash it and get it out of the country using either their Venezuelan or South African networks – or both, he thought with sudden clarity. Nick will pilot the plane that will carry the gold out of the country; the other pilot will perform the swap.

He smiled.

A good plan. Very good, in fact.

He heard a knock on his bedroom door.

"Just me," Charlotte called out.

"Come in," he sat up.

"Hello," she smiled.

"Hi, Charlie. Sorry I didn't last until you got home from your night group," he pulled himself further up the bed and, conscious of having a bad case of bed hair, ruffled it further.

Are you alright? I heard you yell out?"

"Did I?" He ran his hand over his eyes. "I'm fine."

HELEN GOLTZ

She came in and sat on the edge of his bed.

"You know," she looked around, "there is nothing that says Mitchell Parker in this room. Just suits, running gear and shoes. No framed photos or books. It's like you could get up, move in ten minutes and be gone for good."

"Just how I like it," Mitch looked around.

"Are you sure you don't want to talk?"

"About what?"

She leaned back further on his bed.

"You're still black and blue, you haven't slept for days and you're having regular nightmares, Mitch – that's for starters."

Mitch propped his pillows up behind him. He crossed his arms.

"Dr. Curtis," he teased her, "I've been on a surveillance job that went wrong, so I lost a night's sleep. I had a training episode and got a bit bashed around," he looked away as he embellished the truth, "and my nightmares, if you want to call them that, are the result of being out of whack with work and sleep. I'm fine. Case closed?"

"If you want my professional opinion, Mitch, no – the case is not closed."

Mitch sighed. "Charlie, don't dig. There is nothing to find and I'm not into the self-help stuff. OK, my head's sore, my body aches and I've had a break on a case. All-in-all, it's a fair trade and things are good."

Charlotte frowned at him. "You're such a hard nut to crack," she sighed, leaning next to him on the pillows and putting her head on his shoulder.

Mitch looked down at her and smiled.

"You've got enough nuts, you don't need one more. Speaking of which, spoken to Lachlan?"

"Very funny. No, he's on a contract interstate. Didn't I tell you that?"

"Sally did – but they have phones there."

"Ha ha. I meant to tell you. In a way, it's almost a relief it's over, if that makes sense."

"It does," Mitch said. "Sally said you're pretty upset about it."

He watched her face flush.

Charlotte swallowed. "I'm tired of the pain of being on-and-off again. The geographic separation might make it easier."

"Maybe. I'm not going to say there are plenty of fish in the sea or any of that crap. It's hard to find the right fish."

Charlotte laughed

They sat in silence. Mitch felt her hand touching his.

"I'm going to take a shower." He pulled himself away.

"Mitch, don't go, just sit for a while. We haven't spoken for ages."

Mitch leaned back. Charlie, how am I going to survive being in the same house with you if you keep doing this.

―――

Arriving an hour before his team meeting on Monday morning at eight, Mitch went to see Henri.

"Ah, Mitch," Henri grinned, "I hope you stayed in bed all weekend."

"Morning, Henri," Mitch returned his smile and grabbing a coffee cup, sidled it next to Henri's as he poured, "that's wishful thinking. Tell me what you know about gold mining and refining."

Henri glanced up in the middle of pouring.

"Is this something to do with your Aurum project?"

"I think so. The project is about gold in the true sense, as in the stuff that is dug up from the earth."

Henri nodded. "Gold. OK. Let's see." He handed Mitch the cup and they moved into Henri's office to sit down. "South Africa is the largest gold producer, followed by the U.S.A., Australia, China, Russia, Venezuela and Canada, roughly in that order."

Mitch choked on his coffee as the South African and Venezuela connection fell into place.

"Sorry, continue," he said coughing.

"These days, geochemistry and satellite surveys are used to locate an ore deposit, then this is measured and a mine is designed on computer using the location and measurement of this deposit. Once all the approvals come through, construction of the mine begins," Henri paused to sip his coffee. "Holes are drilled for blasting and ore samples are gathered. These are tested and graded. For low-grade ore, a cyanide type solution is poured over the heap and it dissolves the gold which can then be collected."

"Cyanide? OK, that makes sense," Mitch said, thinking out loud. The courier company was delivering cyanide to the Broad Arrow mine. What would they be testing when they're stealing gold bars? Perhaps they've found gold on site.

Henri continued speaking. "It varies a bit, but the dissolved gold is ground to a powder, and if it contains carbon, it's roasted; if it doesn't contain carbon, it's oxidized. Eventually, it is leached with cyanide and the gold is collected. The pure gold is melted into what they call dore bars. These are bars that contain up to ninety per cent gold. These dore bars are sent out to refineries to be refined further."

"OK, so once they arrive at the refinery, what's the next step?"

"Usually the first thing they do is evaluate it again for gold content."

"How?"

"Same processes. Melt a bit, burn or grind dry samples. Once the refiner and the owner agree on the content, it can be released for refining further. This is when it goes through a roasting and electrolysis process to create pure gold. Mind you, it has been a while since I've done any work in the minerals area. The technology is improving all the time, but that's about the gist of it."

"And locally, where are the major gold producing mines?"

"That I don't know. I think there are about ten states with some level of production, Nevada being the biggest. My gold knowledge is more process-based, for what it's worth," Henri told him.

"Henri, you've made my day," Mitch smiled.

―――

Mitch watched J.J. wince as he lowered himself into a chair besides Samantha and Ellen.

"Still sore?"

"Getting better."

"Project Aurum," Mitch looked at his team, "has got nothing to do with science. The work in the lab is a smokescreen."

"For what?" Samantha's eyes widened.

"A gold heist."

"No way," J.J. snorted. "Seriously?"

"Yep. Ever heard of the gold plane?" Mitch asked.

All three shook their heads.

"You've seen the security vans around the city? The vans that pick up cash from banks?" Mitch asked rising to shut his office door.

"Usually attended by a number of security guards and looking like Fort Knox on wheels?" Ellen asked.

"That's them. This is the same concept, but it's airborne. The gold plane is a high-security plane which visits the isolated mine sites in Nevada to collect their gold, secure it and remove it from the mine locations – usually twice a week, depending on the site."

"They must be carrying an enormous amount of wealth from one mine alone," J.J. gave a low whistle.

"Exactly. And somehow, Johan and his team are going to hijack that load, and my guess is it'll be out of the country before anyone notices."

"Am I the only one who doesn't get the connection between the lab and the gold plane?" Samantha asked.

"I'll start at the beginning," Mitch said. "The Aurum Project on paper is supposed to be a drug research program to find a cure for Alzheimer's. Twenty investors from South Africa and Venezuela have put in close to a million dollars to make the drug a reality, knowing it could be worth billions. The investors have details of the university, the lab and the science team. All credible, but none of it true."

"Because nothing is happening as we found out when we brought back their tubes and petri dishes," J.J. interjected.

"Exactly," Mitch continued. "The shareholders will get a nice 'Dear John' letter saying 'sorry it didn't work out' – and by then,

Johan, Maria and Nick will be long gone; and much richer. End of story," Mitch concluded.

They stared at him.

"Why couldn't they scrap the university project and just do the gold heist?" Samantha asked.

Mitch shrugged. "Financial I guess. They would have to come up with the funds to lease the site, buy or lease a plane, hire another pilot, pay off other accomplices like the security team in advance, and support themselves while they planned the exercise. This way, they've got easy money that can be siphoned to pay for the plane, the hangar and the staff to make the gold heist a reality. Basically, they've earned a million dollars in investment money to reinvest in a project that will see them walk away with tens of millions. There are a few things that bug me though," Mitch continued. "What's the connection with the British guy, Daniel? Who's working on the ground for them in South Africa and Venezuela, and why book the lab in D.C.? Why not book lab space at the University of Nevada in Vegas or Reno? It's closer."

"I see what you mean," Ellen nodded, "but wouldn't it be more credible from the investors' perspective to have the project undertaken in the nation's capital?"

"Possibly," Mitch agreed. "The cyanide that Sam and J.J. found is used in the gold testing process. The other substance was Avgas – aviation gasoline. They've had a fair bit delivered in small runs. I imagine they didn't want questions asked about why they need aviation gas when they haven't got a plane, a visible plane anyway."

"We know Johan and Maria are romantically linked," Ellen added.

"And Nick's connection?" Samantha asked.

"He was engaged to Maria's sister. I don't know how or where they met," Mitch said.

"Was engaged?" J.J. asked.

"She died last year in a car accident," Mitch informed them. "We need to find out more about the company who run the gold plane – the courier company. Nick mentioned in the lab one night that he's done the route numerous times. I'm assuming he's talking about the gold courier route, so he must have worked for them at some point or still does. He'll be on their books if that's the case."

"I'll check it out," J.J. said. "So they've got the Broad Arrow site secured for six months, they've leased or bought an imitation gold plane, plus they've got the university lab booked to fool the investors. They've been busy."

"It's an impressive project," Mitch agreed.

Ellen spoke. "Can't we get more out of Nicholas Everett?"

"It's like extracting teeth, but I'm working on him," Mitch sighed. "He's trying to protect Maria – family loyalty I guess."

John rapped on the door, opened it and entered it. He sat on the end of Mitch's desk, listening in.

"What now?" Ellen asked.

"OK," Mitch began. "I'm going to chat with Nick. It's time we worked out how, where and when this is going to happen, and he has the answers. J.J., make some buddies on the ground at this courier company. Find out as much as you can about the exact times, routes and contacts for each of the gold plane stops. I'm sure Nick has these, but I don't trust him – I want our own material to corroborate his information. Get the names of any pilots who do the gold route and see if the pilot profile we got from Johan's briefcase matches any of the pilots employed at the courier company. Try and find out if Nick works for the company without giving away his name or identity. Be discreet."

"Done," J.J. said rising.

Mitch continued. "Ellie, I want to know who the real Daniel Reid is – go downstairs and chase them up on the photo I.D. See if you can find out who Maria Diaz's current trade partners are. Find out who's buying and selling gold in Venezuela and get your hands on any black market info you can get."

"OK," she confirmed.

"Samantha, check up on Johan. Find out what's he doing. See if he's booked flights yet for himself and Nick. Go through his phone records and listen in on anything you can get access to."

"Got it," Samantha agreed, rising and departing his office.

Mitch turned to John. "Anything new?"

"No," John informed him, "but before the close of business today, I need a written report on the Nevada incident."

Mitch nodded.

"And Mitch, that's close of business when normal people leave work, not midnight."

―――――

Mitch watched his team disperse. He sat thinking for a minute and decided to call Charlotte.

"Mitchell Parker!" he heard her answer. "The Ghost Who Walks – well, walks out early. What time did you start today?"

Mitch laughed. "Seven, I had some research to do. So, are you OK?"

"I'm fine thanks. How are you?"

"Good. Are you in tonight?" he asked.

"I am. Let's do Thai and a DVD? I can pick one up on the way home."

"Sounds great. Nothing too smulchy though," Mitch recalled her last DVD choice.

"Smulchy? Is that like smoochy and mulch together?"

"Something like that. See you after seven."

Mitch hung up. He looked over at the pile of paperwork he had to do, pushed it aside and strode out of the office.

―――――

Nicholas Everett and Mitchell Parker met in a small meeting room on the first floor at headquarters. Mitch sized up Nick in his sweat top and jeans, with his blonde hair cropped short and his dark-brown eyes watching Mitch with equal distrust.

Mitch sighed. "Feels weird sitting having a formal meeting with someone I've known for half of my life."

Nick looked away.

"Yeah, can see it's cutting you up to." Mitch pulled his chair closer to Nick. "So the plane doesn't go missing, the gold does?"

"Yes," Nick answered. "A perfect plane swap. One continues on and arrives at the bank empty, the vaults loaded with weights to simulate the gold; the other returns to the hangar, picks up Johan and Maria and heads to Venezuela that day, where the gold is siphoned through Maria's connections."

"Good plan."

"It's a beautiful plan," Nick agreed.

"It's a pretty expensive way to do it though. Why not hijack the plane?"

Nick hesitated. "It's not expensive; the plane is being leased for a few months and we'll dump it when we're done. The owners will collect it. Using the substitute plane buys us more time."

Mitch waited.

Nick elaborated. "When the gold is delivered, it's taken from the plane and placed in storage vaults. The vaults aren't touched until nine-thirty the next morning when the gold bars are moved and checked. Therefore, no one is the wiser for a day that the gold has been replaced. If we hijack the plane, we're defending ourselves straight up. This way, it gives us time to get out before they even realize the gold is missing."

"That's it?" Mitch asked.

He nodded. "Pretty much."

"What's M.M.?"

Mitch watched as Nick blinked quickly before freezing again.

"No idea, what is M.M.?"

"You referred to it on the tapes."

"I don't know what you're talking about," Nick said, not making eye contact.

They sat in silence.

"What's Daniel Reid's involvement?" Mitch continued.

"He's managing the financial side of the project."

"What does that mean?"

Nick continued. "He's organized funds for the lease of the plane, the leasing of the site and the basic expenses."

"So he's the one who got the investors on board to take part in the fake science project? The Alzheimer drug?"

Mitch noted the look of complete surprise that swept Nick's face. "I've got the contents of Johan's brief case."

Nick looked away, his tongue going over his lips.

Mitch rose and poured two glasses of water. Sitting back down he pushed one to Nick who drank it in a few gulps.

"Nick, stop holding out on us. Are you working with us or not?"

Nick wiped his hand across his mouth.

"The investors think we're working on a drug, hence the need for the lab. Their funds are backing the gold project. They'll get a letter telling them that the drug project's gone sour after we leave the country."

"Yep, we figured that. But aren't they expecting a tour of the lab?"

"Yeah, that's to keep it all above board. We'll be long gone before then."

"So, Daniel; what's his role again?"

"I told you! He looks after the finances. Are you getting Alzheimer's?"

Mitch stared at Nick.

"If Daniel is looking after the finances, why does Johan need Daniel's sign off? Wouldn't Daniel be paid by Johan and working for Johan? Or is it the other way around?"

"I've told you all I know," Nick said.

Mitch drew a deep breath and took a different tack.

"I know your connection to Maria, I'm sorry to hear about your fiancée."

Nick looked away.

"Nick, why are you involved in this? You never gave a toss about money."

Nick looked back at Mitch.

"I owe her; Maria, I owe her this."

"Maria! Why do you owe her anything? Would her sister want you doing this?"

"You don't know Ana, so don't second-guess what she would want for me," he snapped.

Mitch nodded. Fair reaction.

Nick hesitated. "I owe her because ... I was driving. It was me behind the wheel. I killed her sister," Nick swallowed and cleared his throat. "I owe her the chance to start over."

Nick rose and walked out of the room, Mitch stared after him.

"Ten pilots," J.J. groaned.

"How many?" Samantha asked, sitting opposite J.J. in Mitch's office.

"Ten. There is a roster of ten pilots for the gold plane. Strange, I thought with such a high security operation they would minimize the number," J.J. said. "How's this?" he continued. "The gold plane stops at five of the mines to collect gold bars. Man, can you imagine the value of that? I'm getting some information faxed through on it now."

"Need some runs on the board, huh?" Samantha teased him.

J.J. leered. "Something like that."

"I thought Mitch was very controlled. I would have kicked your butt if you called me anal. I was hoping for some action."

"Thanks! Just drop it. I wonder if he's going to be flying a gold plane in the next few weeks."

"Here he comes," Samantha sighted Mitch striding towards them.

"Hey, what did you come up with?" Mitch entered his office.

J.J. waved a fax at him.

"There are a lot of active mines spread from one end of Nevada to the next—Meilke, Twin Creeks, Phoenix, Round Mountain, Carlin East—and the list goes on," J.J. informed him. "There is a courier group that has the contract for gold collection in five counties from Elko at the top of the state to Nye at the other end. The runs vary. Some of the smaller mines only require a visit weekly, or even every second week. The bigger ones can be as often as twice a week – Wednesday and Friday. The pilots get their schedule the day before – they go to the same mines all the time; it's a case of when. It looks like Friday's the big day when most of them book the gold plane. Wednesday is by appointment. The plane then goes to Las Vegas where the gold is stored."

Mitch nodded. "Good stuff. My hunch is the Aurum project will happen within a week or two."

"That soon?" Samantha gasped.

"Yeah, Nick said they've been working on it for about eight weeks now and Johan's keen to move. What else J.J.?"

"The plane has a pilot, two security guards and a number of safes on board which are impenetrable. There are ten pilots who cover the route. Of those ten, seven of the pilots are contractors with the company and take other charter flights during weekdays. This means, that they are coming in contact with wider networks and not loyal to the security company."

"Makes sense. Three full-timers ensure you are never caught short and cover sick leave and annual leave," Mitch added, "and they need contractors to cover extra work."

"And," J.J. continued, "of those ten, one is South American, no South Africans, a couple of Brits, one Australian and the rest are locals. Nicholas Everett is one of them, he's been on their books for six months."

"Mm, so he'll be doing the gold run that day," Mitch mused.

"As for the pilot whose profile was in Johan's briefcase," J.J. added, "he doesn't work for any courier company in Nevada."

"Damn. OK, so he's a ring in … Nick must know him from somewhere and hired him to fly the second plane. Wonder what he's getting out of it."

Ellen walked into Mitch's office, looking satisfied with herself. She dropped into a chair opposite the team.

"Daniel Reid," she announced. "The photos you took in the lab identified him as the Daniel Reid that entered the country a few weeks back. He's British and works for the media company, Globalnet. He's here for a conference at the Hilton followed by a brief holiday and his return flight is booked for December 1. He's a lawyer by trade."

Mitch sat back. "Why would Johan be dealing with either Daniel as an individual or through Globalnet? They weren't on the list of investors for the project. Man, this is frustrating."

Samantha patted his arm. "Hang in there, Mitch, we'll get it yet."

"Not soon enough."

17

FAMILIES ARE COMPLEX. CHARLOTTE SIGHED AS SHE READ THROUGH HER young client's file. She moved to the computer and entered the National Security database.

"OK, Bradley, let's see if you have a history with the Department of Children and Families before you committed the assault," she mumbled as she flicked through the pages on screen, moving to the P's.

"Parnell, Parnell ... Bradley Parnell."

Charlotte froze.

Mitchell Parker.

Mitch ... Mitchell Anthony.

She followed his listing, reading Mitch's date of birth, religion and his mother's maiden name.

Mitch, that's definitely you! Why were you involved with the state?

She looked again at the information.

"You would have been ten or eleven when this entry was logged," she said talking to herself, her eyes affixed on the screen. "Your parents were alive, and they're listed, so it's not an adoption record. It must be a hospital record. And the only reason a hospital record would come through to the state is if there was suspicion of child abuse."

Her finger hovered over the key.

Damn, I don't have access to the file, but I know someone who does. No, it's a breach of the privacy act to read the file without relevant grounds, she reminded herself.

The phone intercom buzzed and Charlotte jumped.

"Brad's arrived," the receptionist's voice cut through her concentration.

"Thanks, I'll come and get him."

She quickly resumed looking for Bradley Parnell.

No entry for your name, Bradley. Mitch, if only I could access your entry ...

She logged out of the network.

Mitch drove out of work and merged with the steady flow of leftover peak-hour traffic. His cell phone rang; he turned down the radio and looked at the screen, not recognizing the caller.

"Mitchell Parker," he answered.

"Mitch my man, it's Marco from Info Technology."

"Hi, Marco, what's happening?"

"Thought you might like to know, that I just picked up a conversation from the lab, and Huey and Duey are stepping out."

Mitch laughed. "That'd be Johan and Nick?"

Marco continued. "Yeah, they're meeting a guy called Daniel at the Hotel George tonight."

"About?"

"Don't know, didn't pick up any convo on that, but they're meeting him at seven, so they'll be heading out in a few minutes."

"Marco, you're a legend. I'm on my way. Did Nicholas Everett happen to call in and advise us this was happening?"

"No. No record of any call from him. Hang on." A female voice familiar to Mitch came on the line.

"Mitch, it's Sam. Do you want me to come with you? Nick won't recognize me."

"Sam!" Mitch exclaimed, "Are you working back? Is everything alright?"

"Yeah, fine. I've been tracking Johan's phone records."

"Right. No, don't worry; I can go alone. But could you double-check with John that we weren't advised of the meeting, before I kill Nick?"

"OK. Hold on – Marco's checking with John now. I'll put him back on."

What's Sam doing in the I.T. Department? Ah ...

He heard Marco come back on the line.

"Marco, you sly dog!"

Marco laughed a deep throaty laugh.

"Samantha brought me a bite while I'm on night duty. A man's got to eat."

"How thoughtful; sorry to interrupt the date," Mitch said.

"No problem, it's all in the name of duty. And no, John hasn't heard from Nick either."

"Thanks." Mitch hung up. "Good one, Nick, still holding out on us?" he said under his breath.

Marco and Sam. Why not?

His phone rang again.

"Parker," he announced.

"Mitch, it's Nick. Johan's meeting Daniel at seven at the Hotel George."

"Hey, thanks. Do you know why?"

"No. I thought we were done with Daniel, so beats me. How do you want to play this?"

"I'll head over there and observe. I won't be able to bug the area; it would take me two days to get the paperwork through."

"I'm meeting Johan straight after his meeting with Daniel," Nick said, "I guess I'll fill you in after that."

"Thanks, Nick."

Mitch headed to the Hotel George.

Mitch sat at a table in the far corner of the bar, his eyes fixed on Johan and Daniel who were seated on stools at the counter.

Who is this Daniel Reid and what's his connection?

Mitch watched as Daniel pulled some paperwork from his briefcase. Johan made a few notes. He didn't look happy and shook his head several times.

Why isn't Nick involved in this meeting?

Mitch raised his newspaper as Daniel rose and departed. He kept his eyes fixed on Johan who sat finishing a coffee. Within minutes, Nick joined him, ordering something from a passing waiter. They talked briefly and then Johan departed. Mitch watched as Nick sat back and lit a cigarette. The waiter delivered him a coffee. He stirred it and eventually turned and looked around. Mitch waited until they had eye contact, rose and left the bar. He walked towards his car, while dialing Nick's number. Nick answered.

"How's it going?" Mitch asked.

"Good. Not going to join me?" Nick asked.

"Bit risky, don't you think?"

"Maybe."

"What's going on?" Mitch slid into his car seat.

"The project's coming forward a week. I've got to get over there for work anyway, but the event will take place a week earlier than we planned." Nick said.

"OK. When? What time?" Mitch asked.

"Whenever you book me on a flight. Tomorrow afternoon would be good." He heard Nick sip his coffee. "I assume you and your crew are coming along?"

Mitch ignored the question. "I'll book it. So what was tonight's meeting about?"

"A couple of the investors want an earlier tour of the lab than we had planned. Johan and Daniel were deciding whether to set up a fake situation or stall them."

"And?" Mitch pushed him.

"Johan is going to try and delay them to the following weekend; we'll be gone by then. If he can't, he's got to do it on Wednesday or Thursday this week. That's why he's not coming over with me."

"Right. So those scientists that we have profiles for really exist?"

Nick paused. "Geez, you've been busy haven't you? They're actors. They'll be hired for the day to play the part if needed."

"Nick, who is this Daniel guy?"

"For chrissake, Mitch! You're like a dog with a bone. He's looking after finances. What don't you believe about that? Do you want me to make something up?"

Mitch waited; he ran his hand over his jaw.

"Don't use that silent technique on me, I've got nothing else to say about him," Nick snapped.

"Get over yourself. I'm not using any technique on you. I was thinking, if that's OK with you? You're holding out on me, Nick. What's in it for Daniel?" Mitch demanded.

He heard Nick take a deep breath. "He coordinates the investors' money, makes the purchases, signs checks and gets a solid percentage of the gold. No risk other than financial."

"Where did he come from?"

"Don't know. He's connected to Johan."

"Why D.C.?" Mitch continued.

"What do you mean?"

"You're stalling. If the job is in Nevada, what are you doing in D.C.?"

"I don't know. I guess working out of the university is designed to impress the investors." Mitch heard Nick pay for his coffee and shortly after, he came into view, walking out of the bar.

"Do you need a lift?" Mitch asked.

"No, thanks. I've still got the hire car. The one like Dad's, remember?"

"Uh-huh, funny. I'll call you with the flight times. And Nick, thanks," Mitch hung up and pulled out of the car space.

Charlie, Thai takeaway, a DVD and a good bottle of wine, Mitch sighed, not a bad way to spend the night.

He maneuvered his Audi into the garage, parked it and hurried up the stairs out of the cold.

Mitch opened the front door and saw a suitcase in the hallway.

"Charlie?"

"Mitch, in the kitchen."

Mitch walked through.

"Lachlan," he said, seeing Charlotte's ex-boyfriend slouching over the kitchen bench.

"Hi Mitch, sorry to be a freeloader. I had to come up for a contract meeting, so thought I'd drop in."

"Sure, no problem," Mitch said unconvincingly.

"So, it's three for dinner and a DVD," Charlotte added.

"Ah, sorry, but its back to two. I'm flying out to Nevada tomorrow, so I've got to head into work tonight; book flights for the team, get gear, do paperwork, you know the story."

"Sure do," Lachlan agreed.

Mitch looked at him. I bet you do buddy, he thought.

"Right," Charlotte said. Mitch could feel her eyes boring into him.

"Have a beer though, before you go," Lachlan grabbed him one. "An after-work wind down."

"Thanks," Mitch took it grudgingly. "I'm just going to pack." He left the kitchen, hurriedly walking down the hallway to his own bedroom and closed the door.

That's it, forget it! He thought. I've been acting like a love-sick teenager. Thank God I'm going to Nevada – out of the house and away for a while. Why do I let her get to me? For a guy who's supposed to be interstate on business, he's in my face a hell of a lot. No more thinking about her, I've got better things to do.

He threw some clothes in an overnight bag.

Pathetic. No more accepting invitations to stay in her room and talk or having her fall asleep beside me. Enough. Forget it, move on.

He gulped a mouthful of beer.

He finished stuffing the small overnight bag with half a dozen black T-shirts and pants. He grabbed some socks, underwear and his runners and tossed them all in on top of each other. Mitch heard a knock at the door.

"Mitch, can I come in?"

He opened the door and Charlotte entered, closing it behind her.

"While Lachlan's in the shower, I wanted to have a quick chat."

"What's up?" he turned away, zipping up his duffel bag.

"Mitch, you're angry at me ..."

"Charlie ..."

"Don't deny it, I know you, and you've every right to be annoyed at me. I'm like a yo-yo. I waste your time crying on your shoulder and as soon as Lachlan appears whispering apologies, I'm back on with him like nothing happened. And I know you hate playing the role of therapist ..."

"Charlie, stop," Mitch interrupted her. He threw his bag on the ground and turned to face her. "It's your business, not mine. Do what you want. If you want to give it another try with Lachlan, you should – you guys have a history. But ...," he paused.

"But?"

He looked away, started to say something and stopped.

"Mitch?"

He rubbed his hand over his chin and put his hands in the pockets of his pants.

"Charlie," he looked at her. "It would be better, that is, I don't want to be asked ..." he stopped. "I don't want to be on-call to sleep next to you, like a stand-in warm body, every time things get bad between the two of you."

Charlotte stepped back.

"I mean, it's one thing to support you as a friend; and hey, I'll do that any time, every time – but the crashing in the same room stuff, we're roommates, and ..."

"I get what you mean," she retorted. "I'm sorry, I won't ask you to do that again. It was insensitive of me. I never thought of you as a stand-in warm body; more of a ..."

"More of a brotherly-type," he finished her sentence.

"Yes, no," she stammered. "I promise I won't call on you for that again."

Damn, I'm making a mess of this.

Charlotte headed for the door.

"Charlie, you don't understand," he reached for her arm, pulling her back, and turning her so that she faced him. He pulled her closer and heard her inhale sharply.

"It's not that I don't want to comfort you and be close to you – it's just that I don't think my heart could take any more of it." He let her go.

There! It's been said. He exhaled.

Charlotte stared at him, then reached for him.

"Mitch, I didn't realize. I'm sorry, Sally warned me." He felt her arms go around him and she pressed her forehead against his chest.

He slowly moved to hold her, listening for the shower running in the next room.

She looked up at him. "I'm such an idiot!"

Mitch smiled. "Charlie, this is not helping."

Charlotte laughed. They looked at each for a few moments.

He gently pushed her away. "Now go. I need to take a cold shower." He pushed her towards the door, opened it and closed it behind her.

Mitch sat down on the bed, feeling a dull pain in his chest.

18

Mitch scanned the faces in the boarding line at the airport looking for Nick. He spotted him.

Good, all going to plan.

He followed his team on board, lowering himself into a seat next to Ellen.

"I hate flying, especially take-offs," she said.

"Really? That's bad luck. We've got a stopover and you have to do this twice."

Ellen opened her eyes. "I know. I guess to a pilot, hating flying's pretty hard to imagine; but when you think about being so far from the ground with only a piece of metal between you and death."

J.J. looked over. "Thanks for that."

Ellen laughed.

Mitch looked across the aisle to Samantha on his right.

"Sam and Marco, huh?" he teased her. "No wonder you're always keen to drop tapes to Information Technology."

"Well, a girl would die waiting for a date with you," Samantha rolled her eyes.

"I'm available," J.J. piped in.

Samantha laughed. "It's OK, isn't it?"

"What do you mean?" Mitch asked.

"You know, work regulations and all that. It's OK that we see each other?"

"God, yes! It's hard enough meeting someone with the hours we work without limiting the pool of talent even more."

J.J. passed Mitch the gold plane schedule for next week.

"I hope it matches the version Nick's going to give you," J.J. whispered.

Mitch scanned the document. "Great job, J.J. – we'll soon know."

At Elko, Mitch adjusted his watch back three hours from D.C. time, as Ellen drove them to their hotel in Eureka. He turned, saw Nick following at a safe distance in his own hire car, and swiveled back in the seat.

"This is it," Samantha confirmed, recognizing the hotel she and J.J. had stayed in.

Ellen pulled the car into the visitors' parking lot. They waited as Samantha went to reception to check them in and returned with individual room keys.

"Pizza and beer for dinner?" J.J. asked.

"It's tradition," Samantha agreed handing out the room keys.

"Sounds good. I'll see you in my room in ninety minutes." Mitch grabbed his bag and scanning the doors for his number, headed towards his room.

Mitch entered the room, inhaled its musty smell and threw his bag on the bed. He pulled out his running gear and got changed. Taking the key, he hit the road, running through the main street doing surveillance and pushing the frustration from his body. With a glance at his watch, he turned back at the thirty-minute mark and mixed in some sprinting for the remaining distance to the hotel.

Mitch called Nick's room. "It's all clear. Are you coming in?"

"On my way," Nick said.

Soon after Mitch heard a knock at the door, opened it, letting Nick pass, and introduced him to the team.

"Take a seat next to Ellie," he suggested.

Nick dropped into the spare seat and accepted a beer from J.J.

"Is Johan arriving here tomorrow?" Mitch asked.

"Yeah, he managed to stall the investor tour," Nick confirmed.

"So, the gold heist is to happen this week?" Mitch pushed the pizza towards him.

"Friday. It's been confirmed." Nick reached for the tropical combination.

"The Mexican's better," Ellen said with a mouthful.

"Do you reckon?" Mitch said. "It's too spicy."

"You're a girl, Mitch," Nick grinned. "You never could hack the hot stuff." He reached for a slice of the Mexican.

"Hey!" Samantha frowned.

"At least I can handle my beer," Mitch shot back. "I'm not the one drinking light."

Nick looked at his beer. "Yeah, I have two words for you: Aloha Hickam!"

Mitch laughed. "Hickham!" he repeated and looked at Nick. He broke up laughing again.

Nick sat back joining in.

"In-joke," Ellen declared, "you have to explain it now."

"Sorry," Nick turned to her, "it's classified, but it's safe to say it has something to do with where we were stationed at Hickam Air Force Base."

"Hawaii?" J.J. asked.

"Ah, yeah, it'll keep," Mitch cut off the discussion.

"We'll find out yet," Samantha threatened.

"Nuh, selective amnesia, he'll never tell," Nick shook his head. He took a bite of the Mexican pizza.

"Spicy my ass," he shook his head at Mitch.

"OK," Mitch straightened up and pulled out his copy of the flight schedule for Friday. "I'm calling this meeting to order. Got your flight schedule, Nick? Talk us through it."

Nick pulled his schedule and map from his jacket.

"Friday is the biggest haul day, which explains why we're doing it. We've got a few biggies booked in – and we've got to visit some of the smaller ones who are still worth a look at if they haven't had a collection for a couple of weeks." Nick moved the map closer to the center of the table.

"There are five, all up," he continued. "We start with Twin Creeks and Lone Tree, which are in the Humboldt County. From there, we go to Eureka County where we pick up a load at Meikle and Carlin East. Then across to Phoenix in Lander County, and then we land in Vegas where it will be stored," Nick pointed out the locations on the map. "We may get a last-minute call to do Round Mountain in Nye County, but we won't know until the day."

"That's a lot of miles," Mitch said.

Nick nodded. "We depart at nine from the courier headquarters. We alert each mine as we begin our descent. When we land, one of our officers stays on the plane; the other will be on the tarmac to meet two security officers from the mining company. Still with me?"

Mitch nodded and Nick continued.

"The gold transfer will take place from their security van to the plane. Their storage containers will be locked in our vaults that are purposely built to hold them. They get them back empty next week once the transfer has taken place. Our security guy on board and one from the mining company sign that the transfer took place and we take off and repeat the same process at each of the locations, finishing up around noon."

Nick sat back, taking a mouthful of his beer.

Samantha exhaled. "It's a huge exercise."

"Mm," Nick agreed.

"What's the plan if anyone gets in the way?" Mitch asked. "Drive them into the bush and leave them for dead?"

Nick gave Mitch a wry look. "We shouldn't need to take anyone out. But, if we had to, I suspect Johan wouldn't hold back. He's taking this pretty seriously."

Mitch nodded. "How accurate are they on the timing?"

"Spot on. Each company has its own transmission number. We change channels for each site and confirm we're on schedule or advise the anticipated time of arrival."

"Is it a secure transmission site?" J.J. asked.

"They think it is," Nick said. "But is anything really secure?"

"What happens after the final pick up?" Mitch continued.

"After the last stop around midday, the plane goes straight onto Vegas. On landing, it's met by three security guards – one stays inside the plane, the other two are on the tarmac. The safes are transferred to a high-security van and taken straight to a Vegas bank storage. Given they arrive mid-afternoon, they're stored and not processed until Saturday morning, or sometimes Monday."

"How did you get all this info? Who's your insider in Vegas?" Mitch asked.

"Me," Nick answered. "For the last six months I've been working with them, building trust, setting up networks," he cut to the chase. "I've made a few drinking buddies at the Vegas end."

"So, you're scheduled on every Wednesday and Friday?"

"Not always, but as luck would have it, I am for the next month. I've done the route over a dozen times," Nick assured him.

Mitch braved the Mexican pizza.

"Want some water with that?" Nick grinned.

"Ha! So, what's going to happen after the final pick up this time?"

"After we do the final pick up, the substitute gold plane gets clearance for takeoff from Broad Arrow as a tourist flight and takes to the skies. It should be perfectly timed so as we take off from the last mine in either Lander County or Nye, the substitute plane takes off from Broad Arrow and takes over my coordinates, heading to Vegas in my place."

"Won't they be expecting you personally to land the plane in Vegas?" Mitch asked.

"The airport staff in Vegas don't expect the same pilots each time – they've got nothing to do with the courier company so they don't question who turns up. They're expecting the load and the signed releases. Our pilot will land in Vegas, meet with a security van on the tarmac, wait while the load is transferred and then leave. He'll find his payment in his account at the end of the day. He's oblivious to the whole thing; he's been hired to take the plane from point A to point B. The plane stays there on-site for the weekend. On Monday, the Vegas branch of our courier company does a number of runs for other clients, eventually bringing the plane back to home base and delivering the empty safes. In the meantime, I'll be landing the real gold plane at Broad Arrow, picking up Maria and Johan and heading off to Venezuela. We're long gone by the time they open the vaults the next day and find sand."

"And who's piloting the substitute?" Samantha asked.

"A pilot I've known ..." Nick started.

"Me," Mitch cut in. "Nick's organizing it."

"I guess I am," he agreed.

"Only, there'll be a change in plan. Nick you'll continue to the bank as usual with the gold load and I'll circle for the appropriate time and land back, empty in the hangar."

"It's going to be all out war when they see you and not Nick in the pilot's seat," J.J. said.

"That's right, but you'll be on board with me J.J., and Sam will be hiding in the hangar waiting for us. We've only got three on the ground to handle: the security guard, Johan and Maria. Is that right?" Mitch asked Nick who nodded confirmation. "Plus, I'll wear the same gear as Nick. They won't know it's not him until I open the doors of the plane. Nick, can you get me a uniform?"

"Done," Nick agreed. "You'll need that anyway if you're playing the part of an employee of our courier company."

"What about the security officers on the gold plane – Nick's plane? If they're on the Aurum project's side, won't there be a mutiny when Nick heads to Vegas as usual?" Samantha asked.

"That's where Nick and Ellie come in," Mitch told them, "they'll be securing that plane.

"So, who is this guy?" Johan Booysen asked again.

"He's a pilot friend of mine, from my air force days," Nick told him as they sat in a large office on site at Broad Arrow.

"I don't like changing at this late stage. It makes me nervous," Maria said. "It's not against the rules it is?"

Damn! Mitch will pick that up. Nick panicked and glanced at the microphone device in his watch switched to the on position.

"No, it's not, but I don't like it either," Johan scowled.

"None of us do," Nick assured them, "but the pilot I picked for the changeover had to tend to family business; he couldn't get out of it."

"What sort of family business?" Johan pushed.

"His mother died and he's gone back to Chicago for her funeral."

"Some things in life are more important," Maria nodded.

"So this new pilot, you've checked him out?" Johan tested Nick.

"I've checked him out and I know him. Besides, I've only told him what he needs to know. He thinks it's a charter flight; he's picking up a plane at Broad Arrow and delivering it at the other end to the Vegas landing strip."

"Except he'll be able to identify us," Johan reminded him.

"There is no need for him to see you. Our security guy, Gamboa, can take him to the hangar downstairs to collect the plane; then he'll fly the plane straight to Vegas. I'll be returning with the gold plane."

Nick saw Johan and Maria exchange looks.

"What's his name?" Johan asked.

Damn, a name! Nick panicked. "Maxfield, John Maxfield." *One of Dad's veteran friends, that'll do.* "He's discreet, he'll do the job and I've offered him double cash-in-hand if he says he only ever dealt with one person, no names exchanged."

Johan nodded. "OK. I want to meet him."

"No you don't. There is no need for him to see either of you. Trust me on this," Nick said.

Johan stared at him. Nick shrugged.

"Hey, if you want to meet him ... meet him."

"No, fine, just check him out thoroughly. We are so close to this and I want to win," Johan lowered his voice. "I want it so badly, I can taste it."

Nick gritted his teeth. *Not again, shut up for chrissake! Mitch'll be on my case as soon as I return.*

19

Mitch sat with his team in the hotel room. He saw Nick's car turn into the car park and jumped up to meet him at the door.

"What did 'the rules' and 'winning' mean?" He stood aside to let Nick enter the room.

"Hi, Mitch. Yeah, I'm well, thanks. And you?" Nick shot back.

Mitch inhaled. "Hello Nick, lovely to see you. What did 'winning' and 'the rules' mean?"

"Can I have a cup of coffee?" Nick asked. "It's been a long day at the office."

"I'll put the kettle on," Samantha said.

Mitch followed Samantha into the kitchenette. "Still white with one?"

"Yeah," Nick said surprised. "So you heard everything? You're in as the pilot."

"John Maxfield," Ellen piped in.

"Yep, good work, thanks. So, stop stalling and tell me what 'rules' and 'winning' refer to," Mitch said.

"How would I know? Some stupid game Johan's playing at. I'm not privy to everything."

Mitch stopped with the jar of coffee in his hand and glared at Nick.

"What does it mean, Nick?"

Nick moved to sit opposite him on a kitchen stool at the bench.

"I just told you, he doesn't tell me everything."

"Bullshit. It's about the fifth reference to either rules, game, winning or M.M. You expect me to believe he'd mention those things around you and you wouldn't ask what he's talking about? Tell me!" He raised his voice.

"I– don't– know!" Nick emphasized the words.

Mitch's eyes narrowed.

"I don't know," Nick stamped his hand, "drop it."

Mitch's fingers began to tap involuntarily on the counter.

Samantha cleared her throat. "Um, maybe we should talk through the plan, from the top."

The two men continued to stare at each other.

"Just damned well tell me, Nick, or I swear …"

"What will you do, Mitch?" Nick taunted him.

Mitch's phone rang. He turned his gaze from Nick and looked at the screen. "John," he answered it, moving away. He watched Nick take the coffee offered by Samantha.

"Maria?" Mitch asked. He saw Nick snap to look at him. "OK, thanks, John." Mitch hung up and returned to the group.

"What's happening with Maria? Can he organize her a deal? Get her off?" Nick asked.

"How would I know, Nick? I'm not privy to every little thing John does," Mitch said.

Nick flared with anger and lurched at Mitch as J.J. barged in between the two men.

"Hold up," J.J. ordered Nick. "Back up."

Nick stepped back.

"Let's go through the plan one last time, shall we?" J.J. suggested.

"Fine," Mitch said. "This is how we'll be playing it tomorrow …"

Charlotte woke and looked at the clock.

After seven already, she thought. I need to get up right now, she rolled back over. I should call Mitch. Wonder where he is and if he is the same time zone.

She reached for her phone and dialed his number. It rang three times before she heard him answer.

"Mitch!"

"Charlie, hi," she heard the slowness of his words.

"Have I woken you?" she whispered. "What time is it there?"

Mitch cleared his throat. "I'm three hours behind you, but it's OK. Why are you whispering?" He teased.

"Oh, no, so, it's four in the morning?"

She heard him yawn and turn.

"Yep," he confirmed.

"So, where are you?"

"Nevada."

"What on earth for?"

"A job. Hey, it's great to hear from you. Everything alright?"

"Everything's fine. Go back to sleep before you wake up fully, I'll call you later today."

"I am awake fully, talk to me."

Charlotte smiled. She lowered herself back in the bed.

"Lachlan there beside you?" he asked.

"What do you think?"

Mitch laughed. "Guess not."

"I've been thinking a lot about our talk."

"Really?" he closed his eyes. "I thought you might analyze it once or twice."

"I'm sure you did," Charlotte answered. "I think we should talk when you come home."

Mitch groaned.

"I heard that."

"Charlie, there is nothing to talk about. It's all squared away."

"Nothing? So when are you coming home?"

"If I had my way I'd be there now," he sighed.

"God, I love a man in uniform," Samantha said, sizing up Mitch and Nick dressed in the courier company's black pilot suits.

"You should see how good I look out of uniform," Nick said.

"She's a black belt," Mitch warned him.

"I wasn't thinking of fighting her," Nick smiled at Samantha.

"John Maxfield," Mitch said aloud, adjusting his tie.

"Yes, John Maxfield," Nick confirmed. "One of Dad's old buddies."

"Yeah?" Mitch smiled. "OK, let's cross-check the gear."

"Some of this stuff is fantastic," Nick said, looking at his new phone. "Zone maps, infrared camera, voice recognition and scrambler. Great!"

Mitch handed him back the black wristwatch Nick had worn with the microphone in it the day prior.

"Put your trackers to the 'on' position and the listening device should be 'off'. We can't risk hearing each other's dialogue." He showed Nick how to do it.

"Ah," Nick smiled. "I wondered how you got that backup team so quickly that night we went for a drive."

"Yeah, we have our ways." Mitch ran his eyes over Ellen and Nick. "OK, you two ready to head off?"

They nodded.

"Be careful and watch each other's backs." He glanced at Nick. Their eyes met.

"Relax, you can trust me," Nick read his look.

"God, I hope so … an ambush is not going to go down well," Mitch's brow creased with worry.

"You know, you always worried too much," Nick lowered his cap on his head. "Don't you think he worries too much?" he asked Ellen opening the door for her.

"Yeah, he does," Ellen patted Mitch's shoulder as she passed him, "but it's a good quality in a leader."

Mitch rolled his eyes and pushed them both out the door.

Nick walked into the courier company's makeshift office on the tarmac with forty-five minutes to spare before his shift. Waltzing in, he offered the usual greetings to the staff. He looked around and walked out through the back door onto the tarmac. He strode behind the demountable office and saw Ellen waiting, hidden behind the wall. He opened a wire gate and let her in. They walked towards the plane. Nick spotted George, one of the security guards who would be on his flight, milling around the plane.

"Damn," he swore. "What the hell is he doing here so early? I wanted to smuggle you on board before the guys arrived."

Nick smiled as he walked towards George, wrapping his arm around Ellen's shoulders.

"Hey, George, you're early. This is my gorgeous girl, Jessie," Nick planted a kiss on Ellen's lips.

"Hi," Ellen extended her hand.

"Jessie," he grinned shaking her hand. "Didn't know flyboy had a girlfriend. Never seen him with one. Thought he might be gay."

"I promise you, he's not," Ellen giggled.

"I'm going to show her the cockpit," Nick winked at George. "Then we should be off."

"OK," George continued to grin.

They entered the plane and Nick saw Ellen wipe her mouth.

"Hey, it wasn't that bad."

"It was wet and sloppy!"

"Well, excuse me." He pointed to a large timber box.

"In there?" she asked looking at it. "Can I breathe in there?"

"It's the only place – and yes, there are plenty of gaps to let oxygen in. It carries the daily parcels that get air delivered but, with the gold run, everything goes in the safe. The guys sit on top of it most of the journey." Nick opened the lid; empty mailbags filled the bottom.

"So, how do you think I'm going to arrest them when they're sitting on top of me?" she asked.

"You'll follow my lead and I'll get their butts off you."

Ellen looked at him.

"What?" he sighed, pushing the cap back off his forehead. "Did you and Mitch go to the same school of suspicious spies? Get in there, we don't have time to argue the toss. Cover up with the mail sacks to be on the safe side."

Ellen climbed in.

Nick took her arm. "Trust me, OK?"

"OK," she looked up at him.

"Want another kiss for luck?"

"No!"

"Right." He waited until she was in position and closed the lid.

Nick walked to the front of the plane and descended the steps to the tarmac. Seeing George on the other side of the plane, he wandered around to him.

"Ready to go?" Nick asked.

"Sure, where's Jessie?" George looked around.

"Sent her home," Nick told him, "to change the sheets."

George laughed.

At nine, Samantha and J.J. dropped Mitch near the Broad Arrow site. They then turned the car around and headed back about half a mile to hide it from passing traffic. Looking around, Samantha gave the all-clear to J.J.; they parked, exited and ran, hugging the edge of the road, all the way to the perimeters of the site.

Mitch, carrying his jacket and cap, walked the quarter-mile to the Broad Arrow site, entering through the main gates and making his way to reception. He knocked and saw a huge man striding towards him.

Hell, that's one huge guy, he thought. He must be six-foot-five and weigh as much as a tank. Got to be Luis Gamboa. No one else around.

"John Maxfield," Mitch announced.

Gamboa grunted. "This way."

Mitch followed the security guard back out of the building and around to the garage, feigning ignorance of his surrounds like he was seeing it for the first time.

Going down a set of stairs to the underground garage, Mitch saw the cargo plane.

Looking forward to having a fly.

"I've been told you've got your instructions," Gamboa thundered. "Wait in the plane until you receive a signal to take off."

Mitch nodded.

"The opening?" Mitch asked.

"I'll be here to do that. I'm your only point of contact. If you want anything, press this alert button here," he indicated an alarm on a timber pole. "Otherwise, do not move from the plane."

"Got it."

Mitch watched Gamboa walk off and then hoisted himself into the pilot's seat. He looked around the control panel.

OK, he thought, now how do you fly this baby?

———

Ellen could hear Nicholas Everett's voice as he gained clearance for takeoff. Control responded to his request.

CONTROL: Air Express 021, cleared for takeoff – runway ten right – wind zero-ninety, eight knots.

EVERETT: Roger, understand – clear to line up and take off.

CONTROL: Affirmative.

EVERETT: Air Express 021 is rolling.

CONTROL: AE021, roger.

Ellen braced herself. She closed her eyes and felt the plane rising.

———

Mitch checked his watch.

The plan's started. I hope you're safe on that plane, Ellie, with two men not on your side and one informer whose loyalties are dubious, Mitch thought. *Please Nick, do the right thing.*

He sat back in the pilot's seat, scanning for Samantha and J.J. He looked at his watch again.

Just under two hours until the swap.

Mitch checked his phone; there was a text message.

Ellie? No, Charlie!

It read "R U OK? Miss you."

Charlie, Charlie, what are you doing? I haven't time to think about you right now. OK, I have plenty of time, but I don't want to think about you right now.

He sighed and put the phone away. From the corner of his eye he saw a door being pushed up from the ground, Samantha's face emerged from the tunnel. Mitch looked around and gave her the all-clear. He watched her run to the back of the garage. A few moments later, he saw J.J. emerge, waiting for the signal. Mitch gave him the thumbs up. Running low, J.J. ran towards the cockpit. Mitch pulled him up and he scurried on board and hid behind in the body of the plane. Mitch sighed with relief.

All in place. Two on board the gold plane, two on the backup plane, and one on the ground.

20

Ellen heard Nick getting clearance for the first landing, then felt a bump as the plane touched down.

Smooth! Nice job, Nick. She stifled a yawn. *Don't fall asleep! No sleep last night, watching and waiting for that alarm to go off.*

Soon, Ellen felt the plane take off again. Her stomach lurched. *I'm going to kill you Mitchell Parker for assigning me this gig! You know I hate flying and here I am doing more landings and takeoffs than a flight attendant.*

She heard Nick getting clearance for his next landing. She retrieved her phone from her pocket and, in the light of the phone's green glow, started to send Mitch a text message:

"Just in case you're worried, Mitch, so far so good ..."

Mitch sat and fidgeted.

Should be on their third trip by now.

He looked around. No sign of Johan and Maria – guess they won't enter the hangar until the plane returns, supposedly captained by Nick.

He felt his phone vibrate and grabbed it.

Ellie. He read it and smiled. "So far, so good – two to go. Going to get you back for this gig." He sent a text back: "Good work, Ellie. Look forward to being got."

Mitch sighed. I know you hate flying Ellie, he thought. But I'm gambling that if Nick betrays us, he won't hurt you; he would never do that. But he might react differently if partnered with J.J. or Sam, who are more aggressive.

Ellen counted the landings and calculated they were on their last delivery. She could hear Nick talking with the two security guards—George and one other—like nothing was happening. She waited.

I hope you do the right thing, Nick. I guess the moment of truth has arrived.

She heard the last run finishing; the sounds of Nick pulling up the stairs and sealing the plane door. She shivered. Great. Alone with three men and no one around to help if they turn against me, she thought. Three men ... airborne. No, focus on the positive – Nick's going to be on my side. He's Mitch's friend, and if Mitch trusts him, so do I.

She felt the plane begin its final take-off.

The sounds of the security guards celebrating reached her. Nick was telling them to keep it down.

"Not until we're in the air," she heard him say as the plane rose.

OK, here we go, she thought. Nick is now supposed to head back to Broad Arrow instead of Vegas, where the security men will be paid and he'll depart with Johan, Maria, a load of gold and the promise of a new start. What are you going to do, Nick?

Ellen heard him on the radio to Luis Gamboa on site at Broad Arrow.

"All clear, send him up," he said. She felt the plane turn around as planned to give the impression they were heading to Broad Arrow.

―――――

Mitch spotted Luis Gamboa walking towards the door of the plane. He pocketed his phone.

"The signal's come through. I'll open the door, the hydraulics will lift you to ground level and take off when you're ready," Gamboa said.

"Right," Mitch watched him walk away.

"Geez, let's avoid taking him on," J.J. whispered behind him.

"He's a mountain," Mitch agreed.

He glanced towards where Samantha was hiding, closed the plane door and waited for the lift to raise the plane. He watched as the roof rolled back above him, light poured in and the lift kicked into gear taking the plane up towards ground level, towards the runway. Mitch began his instrument checks.

―――――

Once in the air, Mitch called J.J. out of hiding to join him up front. He flipped the dial to the radio frequency supplied by Nick. Minutes later he heard Nick's voice coming through crystal clear.

"Major, are you there?" Nick asked.

"Captain," Mitch smiled, "present and circling".

"OK," Nick continued, "I'm turning now, anticipated landing fifteen minutes."

"Copy. Good luck."

"And you."

―――――

Nick glanced behind him.

"Hey, George, Eddie," he called from the cockpit to the two security officers, "where's my champagne?" He pushed the captain's hat off and ran a hand through his blonde hair. George and fellow security officer, Eddie Ang, came into the cockpit.

Nick saw Ellen push up the lid of the box and he nodded at her.

"Friggin' too easy," George patted Nick and Eddie on the back.

"We've still got to land this thing and get the gold out of the country. Don't count your gold bars before they land!" Nick warned him.

"How long?" Eddie asked.

"Landing in ten minutes." Nick saw Ellen coming up behind.

"Well done guys," he extended an arm to George to shake his hand. As George took his hand in his grip, he pulled George's arm behind his back and pushed him against the wall. He saw
Ellen raise her gun muzzle to Eddie's neck.

"What the hell ..." Eddie sneered.

"Nick, you double-crossing asshole! What ..." George struggled as Nick secured him with plasticuffs.

Ellen pulled Eddie's arms back behind his back and pulling plasticuffs from her jacket, secured him.

"It wouldn't be a great idea to shoot that in here now would it?" Eddie sneered. "Ever heard of cabin pressure?"

"Yeah, I have," she yanked him around to face her, "but a clean gunshot hole through the plane will let air escape out of the hole. The outflow valves will close a little to compensate for the air leak."

Eddie looked at her.

"Then," she continued, "you can make an emergency landing in about five minutes, even going from about thirty thousand feet to under ten thousand. So, if I shoot you and the bullet passes straight through you and the wall, it won't affect anything unless I hit a cable – but there is probably a backup system."

Nick grinned at her.

"Did you get all that boys? There is an exam afterwards," he finished securing George.

"Anyway," Nick continued, "just so you don't get any ideas, we're using frangible bullets."

"Are we?" Ellen asked.

"We sure are," he turned to George and Eddie. "You know what that means lads? Thanks to the events of September 11, the bullets we're using are made of bits of metal or plastic, so that if one should hit you or the plane, they break up into small pieces. So, you can imagine it's going to hurt a lot more if one hits you because it'll break up and stay inside you – but if it hits the wall, it breaks up and won't penetrate. Good to know isn't it?"

"I can't believe you would double-cross us. Your girlfriend, huh? How much do you want?" George spat at him.

Nick wiped his face.

"He doesn't want the gold," Ellen said. "We're turning you in".

"That's right," Nick agreed, "I'll leave the gold and take the girl."

Ellen flashed him a smile. "Is anyone flying this plane?"

"Shit," he said turning back to the controls.

———

Mitch continued on the coordinates towards Vegas.

"Just waiting for a signal from Nick before we return to the Broad Arrow hangar," he told J.J. He heard Nick's voice break over the radio.

"Done and clear here. Perps apprehended and detained."

"Good on you, Captain," Mitch exclaimed. "Where's Ellie?"

"She's safe," Nick said. Mitch heard Nick pause. "You want to hear her voice don't you? You're still not a hundred per cent sure I'm to be trusted."

There was a silence as Mitch debated what to say.

"Nick, I trust you one hundred per cent. Great job. OK, wish me luck, I'm landing now."

"Oh, OK. Good luck." He heard the surprise in Nick's voice.

Mitch felt a sharp sting and a trickle of blood run down the back of his neck.

He turned – knowing the only person with him was J.J.

21

Mitch couldn't turn his head; the blade was pressing against his skin.

"I love this knife," he heard J.J. say. "It's a Russian ballistic knife. The whole blade leaves the handle when the trigger's depressed."

"J.J.," Mitch muttered. "Not you."

"Looks like it," J.J. answered.

Have Nick and J.J. teamed up? Mitch ran through the scenarios in his head.

"Get on the radio to Nick and tell him to keep circling; there is a change of plans," J.J. ordered.

"Forget it."

"You don't have a choice in the matter," J.J. announced.

Mitch's hand reached for his neck as he felt the blade of the knife slice into more skin and blood trickle down past his collar. He inhaled sharply from the pain.

"You're unbelievable – this whole time, you've been running a covert operation?" Mitch said his voice showing his disgust. "The night shift with me, the bashing you got at Broad Arrow – were they for effect?"

"Oh, no. I was every bit a part of the team then," J.J. assured him.

HELEN GOLTZ

"But I began to realize I wasn't getting anywhere fast – no promotions in sight, crap money. I can't even make a decision on location without some junior wanting to check it with you. And for what it's worth, I'm sick of being managed. This time, I'm managing the show."

"So, are you working with them? What's 'M.M.' stand for?"

"How the hell would I know?" J.J. hissed. "I'm not working with those idiots. You can do what you like to Johan and Maria. This is about the gold – the gold they're never going to receive. Now shut the hell up and call Nick."

"Not happening. I'll take us both down before I give you the chance to do this."

"I counted on that. Which is why the phone in Sam's vest has a nice little trigger in it now."

Mitch's eyes widened. J.J. patted his vest.

"I've got the detonator here," he pulled out his own phone to show Mitch and replaced it back in his vest. "Technology is amazing. All I have to do is send a pulse from my phone to her phone and she won't even have time to see her pretty little life flash before her eyes. But wait, there is more," J.J. grinned. "That assignment you gave me—checking out the courier company—really paid off. I made a buddy on the ground in Nevada, the one who was giving us all the info about the courier company, and lucky me, he was keen to go solo too. So he's planted the second bomb for me. It's on board with Nick and Ellen."

He's not bluffing. Mitch opened the shared radio frequency. *At least Nick's not turning traitor.*

"Nick, are you there? There is an emergency, stay airborne," he ordered.

———

Nick sat back; removing his jacket. He glanced at the two security guards bound in the corner.

"Nice work, Nick," Ellen said.

"And you too," he congratulated Ellen.

Mastermind

Mitch's voice broke through on the radio. Nick sat forward.

"I hear you loud and clear, Major, what's wrong?" he replied.

"We have a change in plans," Nick recognized J.J.'s voice.

"J.J., what's happened? Are you OK? Is Mitch?" Ellen jumped in.

"Yeah, yeah, I'm fine, he's fine," J.J. said.

Mitch's voice interrupted.

"It's OK. But our buddy here has decided to go solo. And before you ask, yes, I can drop him, me and the plane into the Pacific Ocean except for one little detail."

"Three details actually," J.J.'s voice cut in. "I've wired Sam to go off and your plane's also carrying a bit of C4 – beautiful stuff for fireworks. Plus there is a sharp knife pressed against the boss's neck, so we're playing it my way now."

Ellen glanced around. "Where could the C4 be?" she mouthed the words to Nick. He turned back to the console, taking charge.

"What do we need to do?"

Mitch stared straight ahead, blocking out all noise.

OK, focus, he told himself. I need to shut down J.J., get the detonator off him and get the phone off Sam just in case there is a secondary device, and get Ellen and Nick off that plane. Think!

He felt another stab of the knife and listened to J.J.'s accelerated breathing.

Good, he's nervous. That'll help.

"This is what we are going to do," J.J. said to his audience spread over two planes. "And we're doing it before they get suspicious below. Nick, you will continue with Johan's original plan and land that plane back in the hangar at Broad Arrow. Then you'll be taking me out of the country on the route you had planned. Get to it now," he ordered, "understand?"

J.J. waited for Nick's reply before continuing.

"When you land, Ellie, you'll tie Nick up – after I clean up the others, I'll need him to fly me and my partner out. If you don't, I'll blow you, Nick and Sam sky-high and finish off team leader here," J.J. looked at Mitch. "Wait until Johan and Maria see Nick in the pilot's seat, so they know it's gone to plan, then come out firing. Take out everyone and anyone in your path. Don't hit Sam though; I need her to ensure Mitch follows through. Besides, she'll assume you're on her side. Clear?"

"Understood," Ellen's cold tone came over the radio.

"I'll take her out myself if need be," he watched Mitch for a reaction. "Mitch's going to drop me as close as he can get to Broad Arrow," he shoved Mitch. "And if he behaves, I might even give him a Band-Aid; making a mess there, Mitch!" J.J. wiped the blood off his hands.

"Well, remove the knife," Mitch spat back.

J.J. raised his elbow and hit him hard in the side of the head.

Mitch swore in pain.

"Mitch?" Ellen sounded alarm.

"Shut up, he's alright. What is with you and Sam? Can't you function without him?" J.J. said, "I'm not going to destroy my only means of getting down, am I? He'll be better off if he learns to shut up." J.J. glared at Mitch. "As I was saying, when we land, Mitch will get this plane back on route to Las Vegas before we start panicking the courier company and their little track-and-trace program kicks in. If he does as he is told, I might spare Sam. My partner will be on the ground in Vegas to meet the plane, so don't think about aborting," he threatened Mitch. "When he rings through the all-clear, I'll disengage the detonator."

"That's big of you," Mitch retorted.

J.J. snapped Mitch's head back grabbing his throat, and cutting off his oxygen.

"Don't push me, Mitch. I'm in charge."

"If you kill me," Mitch gasped, "you'll have to land this yourself."

He released Mitch. "Not before I take the others down with me. Remember that before you get too heroic." J.J. stopped suddenly and looked at Mitch. "You're stalling for time knowing the courier company will panic if the delivery is not on schedule. Very clever. Get me to Broad Arrow now."

"You're going to meet Maria's contacts?"

"Why waste a good deal?" J.J. shrugged. "They don't care who it comes from as long as they get the goods. Now everyone shut up and get to it."

―――――

Mitch knew what he had to do. He pushed the throttle forward and headed up to ten thousand feet.

"What are you doing?" J.J. felt the plane rise.

"I've got to take it up," Mitch informed him.

"Why?"

"The flight path I was given has us at over fifteen thousand feet on the last leg."

"Why would they do that?"

Mitch shrugged. "A lot of the gold mines have private planes. Sometimes there is a stack of traffic in the under-ten-thousand-feet zone. If we're finished, they move us up and out of it until we are ready to land."

J.J. glared at him.

"Suit yourself," Mitch said. "If I'm not there, it's going to draw attention to us and the tower will be asking questions. Fine by me."

"Do it, but I'm keeping my finger on the detonator so don't try anything," J.J. ordered.

Won the first round!

―――――

Nick's eyes grew wider as he heard the conversation. He flicked off the microphone so he could continue to listen and not be heard.

"Shit, he's going to kill them both," he told Ellen.

"What?" Ellen gasped. "What's he doing?"

"He's going to take it over fifteen thousand feet and depressurize the cabin."

"I don't understand."

Nick explained. "Mitch and I have talked about this before. He's going to attempt to push J.J. out."

"Why? How?"

"The run over the goldfields doesn't require us to get much over ten thousand feet so, in theory, a smaller plane could do the trip without a pressurized cabin. Mitch is traveling at under ten thousand now; it's called the physiological zone."

"OK, and?" Ellen prodded him.

"People are fine in a zone from sea level to ten thousand feet; the oxygen level is OK, so you don't need any special breathing aids." Nick continued. "But Mitch is going to push over the ten thousand feet zone to what's called the physiologically deficient zone."

"So," Ellen finished, "he'll somehow depressurize the cabin, deprive them both of oxygen and try to outlast J.J.?"

"Precisely, but there is a catch," Nick said.

Mitch's voice interrupted. "Thirteen thousand feet."

"He's letting me know what he's doing so I can time how long he's going to be in the danger zone," Nick told her.

"What's the catch?" she pushed.

"He can't deprive them of oxygen without breaking something to depressurize the cabin."

"Can't he open the doors from the control panel?"

"No. The pressure on the doors makes them impossible to open in flight. There are two things he can do. He can break a window and hold tight, hope J.J.'s ejected and then drop altitude so he can breathe —which is risky in itself—or ..." Nick shook his head, "... he can get to a certain height, turn off the engines, open the doors and hope J.J. gets sucked out – then as quickly as possible, close the doors, pressurize the cabin or drop below ten-thousand feet again and breathe."

"Won't oxygen fall from the ceiling?"

"It's not a commercial plane," Nick told her.

"How long can he last if it doesn't work?"

"Assuming there is supplemental oxygen on board ..." Nick thought for a moment, "the worst-case scenario without oxygen, if he doesn't go beyond about eighteen thousand feet is twenty minutes – above this, about ten minutes. But given they will both be exerting themselves—you know, fighting—he's probably got ten minutes tops."

"And what will happen to him?" Ellen asked.

"It's called hypoxia. He'll get tired, dizzy, short of breath, get a headache. If he doesn't get oxygen, he'll become weak and uncoordinated and slow right down. His reaction time will be delayed and he'll fall unconscious. The danger is that most pilots don't feel it coming on; it's kind of hard to pick the signs."

Nick listened to Mitch's voice announcing he was at fifteen thousand feet and rising to twenty thousand.

"Isn't that enough? Why is he still rising?" Ellen asked.

"Because if he doesn't break something, he'll have to turn the engines off to open the door ... he'll lose about three thousand feet when he does," Nick explained. "He's going to have to act fast ... you'd think J.J. would have realized they don't need to rise anywhere near that height."

"Twenty thousand feet," Mitch's voice broke through over the radio waves.

Nick tensed. "Shit, here we go!"

"What can we do?"

"First off, we can let the gold plane courier company know everything is under control or there'll be more dramas. Then I need to get clearance from the tower for both of us to go to that height."

"What do you mean both of us?" she asked.

―――――

Mitch continued to take the plane higher.

J.J. leaned over him. "Patch me through to the other plane."

Mitch pushed a few buttons.

"Nick, report in," J.J. ordered. There was no answer.

Mitch listened. *Hope you're on another channel notifying the tower what's going on, Nick.*

"Ellen?" J.J. barked again.

Nick's voice came through. "We've got the runway in sight now and we're about ten minutes from landing."

"Good," J.J. sighed, easing the knife off Mitch's throat. "This is going to be easier than I thought. Get this plane down now."

Mitch could see from his instruments that Nick was nowhere near the runway at the Broad Arrow mine.

He was following Mitch skywards.

Got to get that detonator. Mitch looked at his watch. *I've got ten minutes tops before I have to seal the door again. I hope you're listening, Nick.*

"OK," Mitch turned to J.J. "That's probably the best place for me to land over there, it's a clear area and you can get to Broad Arrow by foot quickly. You can see it through the right window."

He waited for J.J. to look to the right.

Mitch cut the engines and hit the door release button. He braced for the rush of air at eighteen thousand feet as it pulled through the plane, dragging everything not tied down out with it.

J.J. screamed, falling backwards. Mitch saw the knife fall to the ground as J.J. stood spread-eagled across the door to the cabin, grasping anything he could to stop himself from being sucked out. Mitch looked down as his seat belt held him in place, but the chair pulled, trying to break loose.

He felt the plane glide before he restarted the engines.

Lost twelve hundred feet in those thirty seconds. That's about right, he calculated.

He checked the engines were on and the doors remained open. Mitch put the plane on autopilot. The roar of rushing air was deafening. He reached back as if in slow motion against the pull of air, fighting for oxygen in the rarefied state.

He saw J.J.'s face reflecting terror.

"Give me the detonator and I'll close the doors," Mitch yelled.

J.J. raged. "Close the goddamned doors," he screamed "or I'll press the button."

Mitch smiled at him.

"Sure," he yelled, "let go of the door and press the button."

"You bastard," J.J.'s face was red with anger.

"You know, at the height we're at," Mitch yelled, "you're going to hit the ground at just over one hundred miles an hour in under two minutes."

J.J.'s eyes darted around the cabin.

"Eight minutes," Nick's voice cut in over the radio.

"Eight minutes until what?" J.J. yelled.

"Until we lose consciousness," Mitch answered. "I'm taking the detonator."

Mitch moved forward in the chair towards J.J., the seatbelt giving him enough length to reach him.

So far, so good. Feeling fine, got to watch for the signs.

Mitch felt the blood begin to pour from his nose, flowing down over his lips. He looked over at J.J., who remained spread-eagled across the door, terrified. Mitch reached inside J.J.'s vest and found the phone. He looked at the screen. It was locked for safety. At least something's going right today.

Mitch gripped it. J.J. let go of the wall with one hand and grabbed onto Mitch's arm. With his other arm he grasped the door, using his feet to keep himself wedged into the cockpit.

"Seven minutes," Nick yelled over the radio.

Mitch heard Ellen cry, "I can't stand it, can't we do anything?"

"We are," Nick answered her. "Stay calm. Mitch knows what he is doing."

I hope you're right, Nick, Mitch thought. He could see J.J. was feeling the effects; he seemed light-headed, slow to move, but oblivious to it. Mitch tried to fight J.J.'s arm off.

"Are you trying to kill us both?" J.J. spat the words at him.

"If necessary, you bet," Mitch tried to push him off, leaning out of the chair.

Feeling the symptoms now, just behind my eyes. Time's running out. Got to get J.J. off me, got to close the door.

"I've got the detonator, get off me and I'll let you live," Mitch breathed rapidly.

"You'll let me live?" J.J. laughed. "You'll let me live? You might have the detonator but this is my show."

Mitch saw a flash of silver as J.J. flicked a knife out of his sleeve, while gripping onto the door with his other hand. J.J. slashed at him, stabbing him in the arm that was still holding the phone. Mitch felt an initial flash of pain, then nothing else.

Big sign of danger. I should be feeling that pain, he thought.

"Five minutes," Nick's voice cut through. "Close it up, Mitch, you can't go the whole way."

Mitch grasped the phone despite the throbbing in his arm. With his free hand he wrestled for the knife. He struggled, feeling lightheaded.

Hell, how can J.J. still be physically strong?

Dropping back in the chair and raising his foot to J.J.'s chest, Mitch groaned with exertion as he gave J.J. a huge shove, knocking the wind out of both of them. Mitch watched as J.J. went sprawling through the cabin door, screaming as he hurtled at a phenomenal speed towards the open rear door.

He could hear Nick yelling over the radio to him.

"Three minutes, close up, Mitch, NOW!"

Mitch breathed in air in huge gulps. He looked at his hands.

Blue. Nails look blue. Not a good sign.

He closed and locked the cabin door, shutting out his view of J.J. clinging on at the back of the cabin. Turning in slow motion, he squinted at the panel.

Don't pass out! Get the bomb off .... He started to give way to the blackness engulfing him. He wanted to sleep. *Stay awake!*

He moved in slow motion and turned the engines off. He closed the plane door. Fumbling, he turned the engines on again, pressurizing the compartment. He heard J.J. thump to the ground behind the door.

I'll deal with you when we land, J.J.

Mitch sucked in the air in gasps.

"Mitch," Nick yelled, "what's happening?"

Mitch looked around; everything was blurred. He couldn't find an additional oxygen supply.

About two minutes left, enough time for the depressurization to kick in, maybe.

"Mitch, report in now," Mitch heard Nick yell.

Mitch could hear J.J. gasping from behind the cockpit door. He drew in deep breaths himself.

Safe here, he thought. Got the phone with the detonator, so the team's safe. Whether J.J. survives or not, I'll leave to the gods.

Mitch heard Nick's voice clear and loud now that the rush of air had subsided.

"Mitchell, come in!" he commanded, his voice sounding strained with tension.

Mitch's voice was groggy. "Nick ..."

"I'm here, Major, and I've got you in sight. What's going on in there?"

Mitch wiped the blood from his nose on the back of his sleeve. He saw the stab wound in his arm wasn't too deep.

Can't feel it at all. Must be the hypoxia. Almost blissful.

"I've got the detonator; it was in his phone. So he can't call his partner to blow you guys up or trigger the bomb on Sam," Mitch spluttered. "Get the phone off Sam as soon as you land, just to be safe."

"We're not going to land yet."

Mitch took a minute.

"Where are you?"

"Right behind you," Nick answered.

22

Mitch knew he shouldn't close his eyes. But he did, just for a minute, to get rid of the headache ... clear his vision ... *everything's blurry.*

He tried to run through his actions: *did I put the plane on autopilot? Can't remember. What did I do before opening the doors? Nuh, gone.*

He opened his eyes and forced himself to sit up straight.

If I could just see clearly.

"Mitch," Nick's voice jarred him, "do you think you can land?"

"I don't know," Mitch said, "it's dim in here, I can't see a thing."

Nick exhaled. "Mitch, you're speaking very slowly and it's not dim in there, it's your vision ... this is not good."

Behind Nick, bound and listening, George and Eddie exchanged glances.

"Nick, it's not too late. Forget about him," George said. "We can still land like planned and pull it off. He's out of your hair now."

Nick turned to face George and Eddie. For a moment he hesitated, running his tongue over his lip.

Ellen reached for her gun. She looked from Nick to the two men and back.

"Who are you going to shoot first love?" George taunted her.

Eddie spoke up. "Nick, we can still do it. We'll just move faster to get the gold out of the country or hide it and come back for it."

"Don't do this Nick," Ellen said in a controlled voice.

Nick looked at the control panel and back at the two men.

"Mitch is your childhood friend, Nick," Ellen broke into his thoughts. "Can you leave him to die?"

"It's the chance of a lifetime, Nick," Eddie said. "You've done all the hard work for God's sake. Bring it home."

"What's this chick mean to you?" George asked. "We don't have to hurt her, just lose her later."

Ellen's hand shook as she held the gun. Nick glanced at her and dropped his eyes. He turned back to the panel.

"Mitch? Focus and stay with me here, how many feet are you at now?" Nick asked.

Ellen breathed a sigh of relief. She slowly put her gun down.

Mitch blinked trying to clear his vision.

Nick continued to push Mitch. "What are you feeling?"

"Nothing. A bit tingly, that's all."

"Shit," Mitch heard Nick swear under his breath. "OK, how many feet are you at now?"

Mitch could see the altimeter, but the numbers were blurred. He moved closer to the panel, straining to read them.

"Mitchell?" Nick barked at him over the radio.

"Yeah, give me a minute," he slurred.

"OK, sorry, just take it slowly. Focus and stay with me here, how many feet are you at now?"

"Fourteen, no twelve thousand ... I think."

"Can you see the numbers?"

"No," Mitch answered.

Mitch heard Nick mutter, "This is not good."

———

Samantha saw Johan and Maria enter the hangar. She crouched out of sight, fidgeting, glancing again at her watch.

Fifteen minutes behind schedule. What the hell's going on?

From her hiding position, she could see Maria and Johan looking anxious as they discussed something intently and looked skyward.

Samantha reached for her phone. No text messages. Should I send one to Ellie? No, best to sit tight. If only we had a microphone on and I could hear what's going on.

She returned the phone to her vest. Peering through the open hangar doors, her eyes moved from Maria to Johan, then to the sky.

Samantha froze.

There is the plane and it's high, way too high and nowhere near ready to land.

Then she saw the other plane right behind it.

———

"What settings are in the autopilot?" Nick continued to push Mitch.

"Um … I can't remember," Mitch answered.

"Mitch, think!"

"I can't remember!" he snapped.

There was a silence over the radio.

"Mitch, what's your middle name?"

There was a silence again. Mitch rubbed his forehead.

"Great," he heard Nick mutter.

"Can you see the numbers below the autopilot light?" Nick continued.

Mitch leaned closer to the panel.

"Mitch, what can you see?"

Mitch exhaled. "A lot of lights, but I can't distinguish which one's the autopilot light," Mitch swore, leaning back in the seat exhausted. He felt himself drifting off.

"OK, Major, let's do it by touch. Put your hand out directly in front of you." Nick's voice continued over the radio. "Done that? Mitch? Don't black out on me now!" Nick yelled.

Mitch could hear him remotely.

"Try to see the numbers. We need to get below ten thousand feet."

Mitch pulled himself forward again. "I can't see them, OK? I can't see them!" he shouted the words haltingly.

"It's OK, Mitch, we're here," Ellen intercepted.

"We'll work it out, stay calm. We'll get out of this," Nick assured him. "I guess changing coordinates is out of the question?"

"Oh, God!" Mitch muttered.

"What?" Nick asked, his voice full of alarm.

Mitch leaned over and vomited.

"I guess that's 'no' to the coordinates. Mitch, listen to me, can you hear me?"

Mitch wiped his mouth on his sleeve.

"Can you hear me?" Nick barked.

"Yes, I need to lie down."

"You can't lie down. Now listen …"

"Nick …"

"What?"

"I'm OK. Just give me a few minutes, my vision's improving," he sat back, drained.

"Mitch, this is what we're going to do," Nick ignored him. "Ellen's going to join you and help you land the plane."

"What!" Mitch heard Ellen exclaim. "No way. There is no way I can go out there."

"It's OK," Mitch cut her off.

"No. Sit tight for instructions. Ellie's on her way," Nick ordered.

———

Mitch turned around in his seat. He looked at the closed cabin door.

"J.J.?" he called. He leaned over and vomited again and spat, clearing his mouth.

"J.J.," he yelled, thumping the door with his foot. "If you're alive answer me. Otherwise we're going to crash. I need help to land."

He heard a noise on the other side of the door and J.J. answered.

"You think I'm going to help you?"

"No," Mitch sighed. "I think you're going to help yourself."

"What's in it for me?"

"You'll live."

There was dead silence.

"What do you want?" Mitch groaned.

"A chance to run," J.J. called out.

Mitch thought about it. It's not promising anything but a chance.

"Deal," he agreed. "I'm going to open the cabin door. For your info, I've disarmed the detonator, and if you're planning on killing me, wait until we land since you don't know how to fly." Mitch leaned forward and unlocked the cabin door. He watched as J.J. tried to raise himself from the floor. Mitch couldn't help. J.J. crawled in and pulled himself into the co-pilot's chair next to Mitch.

"What do I do?"

"Depends. Can you see clearly?" Mitch asked.

"Almost."

"Clear enough to punch in some numbers."

J.J. hesitated. "I think so."

"I need you to put in the coordinates," he stopped for breath. "I'll do the rest."

"OK," J.J. agreed. "You know these planes are designed for two pilots?"

"Yeah, next time I get hijacked, I'll bring a backup," Mitch said. "Listen," he stopped for breath again, "shut up ... we're wasting energy on small talk."

———

"Are you insane?" Ellen turned to Nick.

"I can't do it, can I? Besides we can't keep flying in circles until we both run out of fuel. Unless you want to land this one by yourself and I'll go sit beside Mitch, you're doing it."

Ellen glanced at George and Eddie tied up in the corner.

"We can't trust them," Nick followed her gaze. "Come on, we haven't got time to waste. It's been done before. I'll strap a parachute onto you, so if anything should happen, like we overshoot the mark, just pull the cord and jump."

"I know how to parachute," she mumbled.

"Good. I'm going to position us over the top of Mitch's plane. We'll be separated vertically."

Nick glanced towards the front and saw Mitch's plane in slow descent in front of him.

"Hell, no!" he ran back to the controls.

———

Samantha watched as Maria and Johan became increasingly agitated. She could hear them arguing about whether to abort the project now and run. Glancing upwards, she could see the two planes clearly now, one was breaking away and heading down towards them.

The show's about to start, Samantha thought, reaching back to feel for her gun.

———

"Mitch! Come in, what's going on?" Nick yelled into the radio controls.

"Sorry," Mitch answered.

Nick heard the surprise in Mitch's voice.

"I thought ...," he took a breath, "thought you'd be listening in."

"How could I be listening in when I'm down the back of the plane preparing to save your butt? I thought you'd passed out. You gave me a heart attack."

"Sorry, I'm OK."

Nick noted Mitch's speech was still slow.

"I've enlisted J.J. to…"

"J.J., shit, you have lost it!"

"No, he knows if we don't land, we both die."

"OK, OK … I'll talk him down," Nick said taking control.

"No, I can do it. I'm feeling better."

There was a silence for a moment.

"Can you see straight?" Nick asked.

"Pretty much, between the two of us we can."

"Alright, leave the channel open. We're going to follow you down."

"We need to let the courier company know …" Mitch started.

"Done," Nick informed him.

"And the tower …" Mitch continued in a slow drawl.

"Done, it's all done, focus on landing safely," Nick ordered him. "And Major, I'm in charge, until you're on the ground, got that?"

"Sir!" Mitch snapped at him.

A smile flickered across Nick's face.

———

The smell of vomit made Mitch feel nauseous again. He looked over at J.J. They were both covered in blood and J.J. looked pale.

Mitch forced himself to sit up straight. He fell slightly forward and J.J. pushed him back in the seat.

"Thanks," he muttered. He issued orders to J.J. and in slow motion, moved his hand over the controls. He heard Nick cross-checking his orders and adjusting his own controls.

"Talk it out, Mitch," Nick's voice came over the radio, "So I can hear what you're doing."

"OK," Mitch began speaking the words for Nick's benefit. "Adjusting speed from 320 to 240 knots. Reducing altitude from twelve thousand to seven thousand. Extend flaps. Ten thousand five hundred feet," Mitch continued, panting. "Engaging auto approach." Mitch directed J.J., "hit that switch that reads APR."

J.J. scanned the controls in front of him, finding the APR switch. He flicked the switch and Mitch saw the shaking in J.J.'s hands was more severe than his own.

"Seven thousand feet, reducing speed to two hundred knots," Mitch continued, blinking.

"Check," J.J. confirmed the numbers.

"Good job," Nick's voice cut in. "How are you feeling?"

"Better, my vision's clearing."

"Right. I'll leave you to land it on the runway. I'm taking the hangar."

"OK," Mitch agreed. "Hey, Nick – thanks, and listen," he stopped for breath again, "when we land, be prepared."

―――――

Nick felt Ellen looking at him and turned to face her.

"Yes ma'am?"

"You're a bit of a hero aren't you?" she teased him.

"Well, you know, I do my best."

"I mean, except for wanting to push me out of the plane, you're a really nice guy."

"Don't let that get out," Nick smiled at her, "you'll ruin my bad-boy image."

"What's going to happen when we land with two planes?" she asked.

"By now the courier company will have staff on the way. They've got to protect the load in the back – it's an automatic response if the flight is late," he said with a shrug towards the gold in storage. "They can take George and Eddie with them too," he glanced at them.

"How are you going to explain to Johan and Maria why we're late and why the second plane's landing nearby?" Ellen asked.

"I'm not, it's business as usual, like nothing ever happened."

―――――

Samantha watched the gold plane land on the runway. Several minutes later it taxied onto the hydraulic lift. Inside the plane, she could clearly see Nick at the controls, and she could swear she saw another plane landing further afield.

So, you betrayed us after all, Nick! Mitch was wrong to trust you, Samantha shook her head. *But why is the other plane here?*

She watched Johan and Maria.

They haven't seen the other plane. Where's Mitch? He must be in the second plane. Something has gone wrong, she thought.

Samantha pulled her gun, taking off the safety catch and keeping her eyes on Johan, Maria and the security guard.

———

Mitch and J.J. landed the second empty gold plane successfully in the next field. Both of them sighed with relief. As they taxied to a stop, Mitch looked over at him.

"A chance, remember?" J.J. said.

"I don't have time to pursue you J.J. I've got to get a bomb off Samantha, and back up Ellen and Nick. You can get lost and I'll worry about you later."

Mitch saw J.J. had retrieved his knife and was gripping it tightly. He moved to the door. Mitch hit the door release.

"Hey, I'm sorry about the bomb," J.J. said.

"Sure you are," Mitch watched as J.J. leapt from the plane and ran, stumbling. Mitch stood and did the same, running in the other direction. He felt shaky on his legs, but didn't stop. He saw Nick's plane taxing towards the hangar.

———

Nick pulled the plane to a stop; he looked back at George and Eddie.

"Wish we could use you boys," he said. He turned his eyes to Ellen squatted further back out of sight, gun drawn.

"Ready?" he asked.

She nodded.

Johan and Maria ran towards the plane, the large security guard flanking them, weapon drawn.

Nick opened the door. "Break out the champagne," he smiled.

"What happened?" Johan growled.

"Air traffic control kept us circling, too much traffic in the air above the gold fields and we lost time at one of the mines – they had a bigger haul than usual."

Johan's eyes narrowed. He pushed past Nick going on board, and saw the two bound guards. He turned.

"You've already secured them! Excellent! I had no intention of paying them either or letting them go. You surprise me, Nicholas," Johan said. "Stick them down in the mine and use the cyanide I had delivered. It'll look like they were accidentally trapped in the tunnels and the residue cyanide poisoned them. Scientifically possible. Remember to take the cuffs off though."

"Johan!" Maria exclaimed from the steps of the plane.

"Come on, Maria, it's just tying up loose ends."

Nick saw the look of terror on the guards' faces. He alighted from the plane, taking Maria's arm and whispered, "run, get out of here now." She looked up at him bewildered. "Trust me Maria, get out of here now."

In the distance he saw Samantha looking confused and with his eyes, he motioned to the security guard on her right. She nodded slowly.

Great, she thinks I'm a traitor, he realized.

As Nick pushed Maria in the direction of the hangar exit, he saw Samantha running full speed across the hangar and raising her gun. She yelled at the guard to drop to his knees. Luis Gamboa grabbed his gun as Samantha leapt up, kicked him in the stomach and under the chin. He groaned with pain. Samantha slammed into him, knocking him to the floor. Nick reached him, knocking the guard out with a solid hit.

"Who is that?" Johan yelled at Nick, "What's going on?"

Nick saw Maria slowly backing out of the hangar.

He nodded to her.

As she rounded the corner, she ran straight into Mitch. Nick cursed under his breath.

"Mitch!" Samantha exclaimed.

Nick watched as Mitch grabbed Maria, wheeled her around and secured her hands with plasticuffs. He pushed her into a seated position inside the hangar.

Nick turned to see Gamboa regain consciousness.

"Sam!" he yelled. Gamboa swiped Samantha with a huge blow across the face, knocking her backwards. Nick moved in, hitting Gamboa under the jaw while Samantha struggled up beside him, pulling her gun and holding it to the guard's temple. Gamboa sank back to the ground.

Nick heard the click of a gun and felt the metal at his temple.

23

"What the hell is going on?" Johan hissed, barely inches away from Nick.

Nick froze.

"Why did you secure the two in the plane?" Johan asked.

"Double-crossers," Nick spat. "Tried to take us hostage on the flight and hijack the gold."

"Then, who are these two?" he nodded towards Mitch and Samantha, keeping the gun pressed against Nick's temple.

Nick hesitated.

"As I thought," Johan said.

"No Johan, Nick's on our side," Maria yelled, defending him as she squatted on the hangar floor. Nick felt a stab of pain. He looked away from her.

"Shut up, Maria," Johan ordered. "He might have started off that way, but it hasn't ended like that."

Nick raised his eyes to meet hers. They stared at each other.

"Start talking," Johan shoved Nick, "or I'll take them out. Starting with the two on board."

"You can kill the two on board for all I care," Nick shrugged looking back to Johan.

HELEN GOLTZ

"OK, let's see how much your friends care for you," Johan turned to Mitch. "You've got one minute to tell me what's going on or your friend here's history," he pushed the gun harder into Nick's skull.

Nick exchanged looks with Mitch.

Read my mind, Mitch. Make a deal, do something.

"Maybe we can do a deal?" Mitch suggested.

"A deal?" Johan laughed. "I'm always up for a negotiation. What did you have in mind?"

Nick took his cue. "Hold on."

"What? You want to counter offer, Nicholas? And I haven't even heard the first deal yet!" Johan looked at Nick, amused.

The few seconds were enough. Nick saw Mitch reach into Samantha's vest and withdraw her phone with the bomb in place.

"What ... Mitch?" she looked at Mitch.

Johan caught the movement and cocked the gun at Nick's head. Nick flinched, his eyes appealing to Mitch.

"Let's talk a deal," Mitch moved towards Maria. "In this phone is enough C4 to blow your lady friend sky-high. Release Nick and I'll disarm it."

"Why should I believe that?" Johan scoffed.

"Are you prepared to risk her life not believing it?" Mitch asked.

Johan glanced towards the plane. "If I agree and release Nick?"

"May the best man, woman, win," Mitch said.

Johan kept the gun barrel firmly pressed against Nick's temple.

Nick could feel the sweat running down his neck. He swallowed.

"It's not great odds for me. It will be three of you against an unarmed female," Johan nodded towards Maria, "and me."

"At least she'll be alive," Mitch said.

Johan continued to think. Nick watched Maria, her face registering shock.

"No deal," Johan announced.

Nick's eyes widened.

"I need a pilot. My chances of getting out of here are better taking Nicholas hostage. So, do what you've got to do."

"Johan!" Maria screamed.

"It's business, dear," he said. "Business always comes first."

Mitch never took his eyes off Johan – never even gave a flicker of a glance as Ellen stole up behind him from inside the plane.

He held his breath as Ellen pressed her gun to the back of Johan's neck. "OK," she said, "what's your life worth?"

Johan froze, Nick reacted, grabbing Johan's wrist and removing the gun from him. Mitch turned as Luis Gamboa got to his feet. He rolled his eyes.

This guy does not give up. Mitch landed him a solid punch knocking him out again.

"Shit," he shook out his hand, "this guy's got a solid rock head."

Nick grinned at him. "You big girl, Mitch."

Mitch shook his head. "Is it too late to renegotiate?" he said looking Johan's way.

"Very funny," Nick said. He looked up at Ellen who was standing on the steps of the small plane.

"You're not just a pretty face are you?"

"God, no," she grinned. "And I'll be sure to keep reminding you that I saved your butt today."

"Love your work, Ellie," Mitch touched her shoulder.

"Mitch!" Samantha yelled.

Mitch turned to face her. "What?"

"Hello! Am I missing something here? Are you telling me I've been carrying a bomb?" She looked stunned. "You took so long. Where's J.J., why do you have blood on you? You look like shit," Samantha's words stumbled over themselves as she tried to make sense of everything.

"It's a long story," Mitch replied. "We'll tell you on the way back – but trust me, we had no intention of letting you blow up."

Mitch gave her the detonator. He walked over and grabbed Maria's arm, pulling her towards Johan. He heard the sound of squad cars and within minutes the police arrived followed by the courier's security firm.

"We'll want to talk to him later," Mitch told the head agent on the ground, indicating Johan.

Mitch watched as Nick spoke with Maria and walked beside her as the police put her in the back of the squad car.

Mitch followed and leaned in to speak with Johan, just before the officer closed the car door.

"M.M?" Mitch asked. "Tell me what it means?"

Johan turned and looked away.

"For chrissake, won't anyone tell me what M.M. stands for?" Mitch muttered walking away.

Mitch had a hell of a hypoxia hangover – his head was pounding. He slid down in the back seat of the second police car, hitching a ride back to Eureka. He looked over at Nick, who stared out the window.

"Nick ..."

Nick turned to look at him.

"You OK?"

"Sure," Nick shrugged and turned back to the window.

"I'll arrange for you to see her tomorrow ... if you want. John's flying in tonight to interview them and get the paperwork started; he can get you access."

Nick nodded without looking back.

Mitch closed his eyes until the car pulled up. He entered his hotel room and went straight to the shower, standing underneath the steamy hot water, washing vomit, blood, sweat and dirt from his body. Eventually he turned off the taps, wrapped a towel around himself and crashed on the bed.

He woke with a start.

Geez, how long was I out for?

He heard a loud knock at the hotel room door and Nick's voice yelling: "Are you alive in there?"

Mitch got up and opened the door.

"Just."

"We've been knocking for five minutes," Samantha said. "We're going out to find a bar. Are you coming?"

"Not dressed like that he isn't," Nick answered.

"I'll meet you there," Mitch agreed.

"Call us when you're ready and we'll give you directions," Samantha said, taking off with Nick and Ellen.

Mitch sat back down on the bed.

What a day, he thought. At least Nick's out with the girls, that'll be a good distraction for him. And at least he didn't turn on us – wouldn't have put money on J.J. doing that. Mitch exhaled, staring at the ceiling. After all that's happened today, all I want to do now is ... speak with Charlie.

———

Johan reached for the phone to make his permitted call. He rang a number and Daniel Reid answered. Johan said one word, "Failed." He hung up and sat back in the chair.

———

"Isn't that the end of it?" Samantha asked as they sat in the bar at Salt Lake City airport the following afternoon waiting for their flight back to D.C. "John's done the interviews, charges are pending, the gold is safe and everyone's happy?"

John and Ellen returned with a round of drinks.

"No," Mitch looked at Nick.

They picked up their glasses and John made a toast. "Welcome on board, Nicholas."

"Thanks. It's all who you know," Nick shrugged.

"And there was a vacancy," Samantha added.

"Don't undersell your credentials, Nick," Mitch added. "You're handy to have around ... sometimes."

Nick smiled. "You think?"

"You're going to move from Nevada to D.C.? Big move," Ellen said.

Nick shrugged. "I was only there for the work. I've been on the road for a while before that."

"So, what becomes of J.J. now?" Ellen changed the subject.

"We've got an alert out for him," John said, "I don't suspect he'll get far. He'd be clever to lay low for a while."

Mitch looked at his watch; it was after two. He glanced around.

"What is it?" John asked.

Mitch moved to the edge of his seat.

"Nick, tell us what 'M.M.' is and honestly, who is Daniel Reid?"

Nick groaned. "What is it with you and Daniel?"

"It doesn't fit and you know it," Mitch pushed. "Why would a Globalnet employee be meeting with Johan? What's the connection? Globalnet was not on the investors list. Plus, I don't get the reasoning behind the D.C. location."

He watched and waited as Nick sipped his drink.

"It's like I told you," Nick eventually answered.

Mitch glared at him, shook his head and looked away.

Forget it, let it go. He told himself. Pisses me off, though. He knows something and he's holding out.

"Mitch ..." John began.

"Nick, just spill it!" Mitch interrupted returning his glare to Nick.

Nick ran a hand through his hair.

"Ah-ha! There is something. You always do that when you're holding out," Mitch exclaimed.

"Bullshit!" Nick shook his head, hiding a smile. "Since when?"

"Always! Just tell me for God's sake."

"Great, now you're Columbo – you just need the trench coat," Nick turned to the team. "Is he always like a dog with a bone?"

"Yeah, most of the time," Samantha said, "but we like him."

Mitch smiled.

Nick sighed. "It's a long story and bigger than you can imagine."

"We've got an hour here," Mitch urged him on.

Nick frowned, then shrugged. "Telling you this could be dangerous for you."

"Nick!"

"You asked for it," Nick sighed. "M.M. stands for Mastermind."

"Mastermind," Mitch repeated after him.

"Yes, Mastermind. And you've only closed down one crime. Mastermind is international."

24

Lawrence Hackett leaned on the windowsill.

"You're telling me two of the six have failed – two foolproof Mastermind projects have bitten the dust? It's bitterly disappointing. This is going to be the worst result in the competition's history." He looked down at the streets below and the colorful parade of umbrellas as they crossed the street at every light change.

"Sloppy, disappointing, unprofessional, uncreative!" He turned back to the boardroom table taking in the directors sitting around it.

"Richard, what happened in Tokyo?"

Richard Sinclair opened his file.

"Truly, you wouldn't read about it," he started. "The project team entered the I.T. area according to plan, disarmed and created a duplicate main server in a matter of seconds, downloaded all the bank's major clients' information, swapped back to the original server before anyone realized what was happening, got as far as the exit hallway with the information and the earthquake struck."

Lawrence noticed his Chief of Staff, Andrew Kenny, suppress a laugh.

"It measured eight on the Richter scale," Richard continued. "Everything shut down, they couldn't get in or out and, of course, by the time it was declared safe and the place was re-opened, they were recognized as intruders."

"Any link to us?" Lawrence asked.

"No. It hit the press, but is old news now. Charges were laid on Seika Tajimo and two accomplices."

Lawrence swore. "That was a brilliant plan."

"Act of God ... timing's everything," Andrew shook his head.

"Phillip, what happened in Munich?" Lawrence continued.

Phillip Saunders put his reading glasses on and read from a report.

"The international press has been all over mine. Initially, everyone believed another set of manuscripts and diaries from a Gestapo leader had been uncovered. At one stage, the competitors even had a bidding war going for them. It was up to the equivalent of $2.4 million U.S., but then they were ousted as fakes – the rest is history."

"They should have cut a deal and disappeared much earlier," Lawrence shook his head.

"Egos got in the way," Phillip continued. "They were riding high on the fame – in demand for media interviews, talk-back radio, you name it. I think they enjoyed the celebrity status."

"Yeah, well they can keep a diary in prison and see where that gets them," Lawrence retorted.

"They'll write a book and sell the rights; they'll be fine," Phillip shrugged.

"Are we safe?" Lawrence asked.

"Absolutely. Who'd believe anything they have to say after that?"

Lawrence turned to his Chief of Staff.

"What's the latest, Andrew?"

Andrew sighed. "More bad news. The Nevada Mastermind failed."

"Not the gold plane?" Lawrence exclaimed. "Bloody hell, how did that go wrong?"

"Daniel Reid tells me one of the team, the security guard or the pilot, decided to hijack the project for a bigger cut."

"Bloody hell!" Lawrence shook his head and returned to looking out at the streets of London's Docklands.

With a glance around to make sure it was safe to talk, Nick began. "I'm not supposed to know about Mastermind," he said.

"Why not?" Samantha asked.

"Because they only deal with one person; if the job fails and they fall out of the competition, there is less risk of it being traced back to them," Nick explained.

Mitch interrupted. "Can you start at the beginning? What are you talking about and what is the competition?"

Nick sighed, leaned into the group and lowered his voice.

"'M.M. or Mastermind is a competition that happens once every five years. This is the third season."

"Who runs it?" Samantha asked. Mitch glanced at her impatiently.

"That I don't know."

"Keep going," Mitch urged.

Nick continued. "I found this website called Mastermind – it was an Internet game site where you had to mastermind the perfect crime," he shrugged. "It was a bit of fun. You had to think through all the elements – how you would do it, all that. Anyway, if you submitted an entry, once a month this panel, calling themselves The Directors, would select the best one for the month and the winner would get a prize of five hundred British pounds – it was obviously a British-based site," he drew breath. "I thought it could be connected to a movie studio looking for ideas and the directors were possibly real directors. Some of the stuff was genius level. So, one night when the four of us were out to dinner …"

Mitch cut in. "Four of whom?"

Nick hesitated.

"Me, my partner, Maria and Johan," he bit his lip. "We were out and Johan started talking about some bank robbery in Sweden and how it was the perfect crime. So, I mentioned this website. Anyway, I was flying the gold plane route around this time and he was fascinated with it. So next thing I know, he's put in a Mastermind entry to the site with the theft of the gold plane – and he won the prize for that month."

"Go on," Mitch encouraged him.

"It was about four months later when Johan got a call from Daniel Reid. They met and he told him that the directors not only awarded a monthly winner, but once every five years, by invitation, selected six of the best entries to play for real. They had checked out Johan and invited him to play. They provided a small fund and strict terms and conditions – the prize money was unbelievable. Johan wanted to do it."

"Was Daniel acting on behalf of Globalnet?" Mitch asked.

"Yes, but at the time we didn't know anything about Globalnet," Nick explained. "We knew Daniel as one of the website directors, a stand-alone guy, and we had no contact details for him. It was pretty scary not knowing if it was a set-up or genuine. That was the risk both parties took, I guess – we could squeal on them and vice versa. We talked it through and decided to play. We named our entry the Aurum project."

"How much was the prize money?" Samantha asked.

"Five million ... pounds sterling."

"Holy shit!" Samantha said. "That's nearly ten million U.S. dollars."

Mitch frowned. That kind of money could only come from a huge global company – Globalnet. At least, that would make the Daniel Reid connection fall into place. This is enormous, if it's for real, Mitch thought. He exchanged looks with John. Nuh, too implausible.

He looked back and saw Nick watching him. They held each other's stare. Mitch realized his team was watching him and Nick as they sized each other up.

Nick broke the silence. "Do you seriously think I would make this up?"

"How do I know, Nick?" Mitch shrugged.

"Do you have any idea of the danger I have put Maria in, and myself for that matter, by talking about this? Contestants have been killed for less. When do you begin to trust me? What does it take?"

"Nick, I'm sure Mitch …" John started.

"Come on," Mitch cut off John. "You're one of my long-term friends and this time last week you had a gun pressed to my head out in the middle of nowhere. How's that for trust? You think now that you've helped me land a plane that I have no doubts about your allegiance?"

"My allegiance!" Nick spat at him. "I handed over my fiancée's sister, double-crossed her for your stupid mission, the only person left connected to Ana." Nick looked away. "Anyway, since when did you become the guru of trust? Does East Timor ring any bells?"

"You know that was a trap. I can't believe you'd bring that up," Mitch straightened, glaring at Nick. He ran his hand over his mouth.

"Do I know that?" Nick snapped.

John intercepted.

"Mitch, Nick, not here," he said sternly.

Mitch came to his senses and looked around, his eyes scanning the area.

"Right," he said, "sorry. I forgot where we were."

He retreated, getting a measure on his anger. John turned back to Nick, dropping his voice.

"So, Nick, given the prize pool, can we assume Globalnet is involved?"

"Assume what you like," Nick reached for his coffee. Mitch bore John's frustrated glance.

Nick took a deep breath. "John, I don't know for sure and to be honest, at the time we didn't care. Daniel Reid was our point of contact, which was all we really needed. Johan was privy to more than Maria and I – that was part of the conditions of entry so it was less risk to the organizers."

"Why would you and Maria agree to do this?" Mitch asked.

Nick shrugged. "I didn't give a toss. She had lost her sister and I think she needed to feel something – fear, hope, I don't know. Maybe to keep Johan happy."

Maybe that's why you did it too, Nick. To feel something. Mitch watched him. He listened to an announcement advising they would be boarding in twenty minutes.

"So, Daniel Reid looked after your project?" Mitch continued.

"Yes," Nick met Mitch's eyes. "Johan was told there were six entries selected. Each entry was assigned a director who stayed in the capital city of the country staging the Mastermind job."

"Daniel in D.C.," Mitch nodded.

"Yes, that's why he was located in D.C. Happy now? It's also easier to justify that they are here on business if they stay in the capital. Less likely to draw attention than having a British businessman located at Broad Arrow."

"Makes sense, he was supposedly here for a conference." Mitch recalled. "So, with the competition, can there be more than one winner?"

"Yep. There can be as many as six winners sharing the prize pool, or just one. And as there is only one point of contact on each team—in our case it was Johan—if we failed, he was forbidden to link it to Mastermind – or they'd send in the cleaners."

"Shut up or you're dead," John said.

"Yes, and they've kept their word in the past, from what I understand. That's why I had to try and keep you unaware of that side of it."

"This is enormous; international crime on a major scale," Mitch drummed his fingers on the table. "And the gold plane failed, so that's one of the six out of the running. Are there any Masterminds still to take place?"

"I don't know," Nick answered.

Ellen reached for her drink. "If Johan won't talk, what evidence is there linking the Aurum project to Mastermind?"

"Nick!" Samantha suggested.

"Nah," Nick shook his head. "I'm working on both teams, almost related to one of the crims; I'm not the credible witness you need."

"We need to find Daniel Reid and confirm he's acting as an agent for Globalnet on this project. Nick where would he be now?" Mitch asked.

"Probably packed and on his way to the airport as we speak. The representatives leave as soon as the plan is completed or fails."

"Then we'll be following him, I guess," Mitch thought out loud. John pulled out his phone, made a call and gave a directive.

"The office will get back to us in a minute and tell us what flight Daniel is booked on," John said, hanging up. In less than a minute, his phone rang. Mitch watched him as he took down the details.

"Looks like he couldn't get a flight until three tomorrow afternoon," John informed them.

"Good, we can sort out how to handle him in the morning," Mitch said hearing the boarding call for their flight. The team rose. Mitch lagged behind with Nick as Samantha and Ellen headed for the boarding gate. John lingered.

"I can't believe you'd bring up East Timor," Mitch said.

"Forget it," Nick told him. "I was riling you. It's not important."

"Bullshit, Nick, it obviously is."

John coughed and Mitch looked over at him. John came closer and stood next to the pair. "Can you two work together?"

Mitch looked at Nick.

"Of course we can," he answered.

"Then sort this out later somewhere in private, not here," John ordered them, "and sooner rather than later."

Mitch nodded. Grabbing his duffel bag, he strode past Nick and John, following Ellen and Samantha on board.

It was close to ten p.m. when Mitch turned the key in the front door of his house and entered the warmth of the living room. He looked around for signs of Charlotte's on-again, off-again boyfriend, Lachlan. She appeared in the doorway.

His eyes washed over her; this girl who did his head in, the girl that he wanted to hold, kiss and own, who belonged to someone else.

"Hey Mitch, welcome home."

"Hi, it's good to be home."

"Are you alright?"

"Sure, why?"

"You're bruised again and you look ... thinner," she walked toward him. "Don't they feed you when you're away?"

"I'm fine." He threw his bag from the doorway into his room and stood looking at her.

"Uh, want tea or coffee?" she asked, turning towards the kitchen.

"Yeah, coffee would be great," Mitch removed his coat and followed her. "God I feel like I've been away for a lifetime," he dropped onto a stool in the kitchen.

"I know, feels like that for me too," she said, then looked up. Mitch saw her flush. "So, did your trip go according to plan?"

"More or less. How's did your first group therapy session go?"

"It went well. It's a bit easier than one-on-one."

There was a brief silence and their eyes met. They both spoke at once and then stopped.

"So, will you do more of them?" Mitch filled the silence. "Group sessions? Or are you a one-on-one girl?"

"No, I enjoyed it, I'm up for more." She poured boiling water into two cups.

Again they were silent. He watched Charlotte add milk to their coffees. She pushed a coffee cup towards him and sat on one of the kitchen stools near him.

"Mitch," she met his eyes, "I'm going to cut to the chase – um, do you think we should talk about what you said at ..."

"No" he cut her off.

The last thing I need is an analysis of my comments. I'll look like an even bigger idiot, he thought.

"But ..."

"Forget what I said, Charlie. I said too much. Everything's fine." He looked down at his coffee. You're an idiot, why did you say anything?

"Is it?" he felt her watching him.

Mitch leaned back against the wall.

Great, I've just walked in the door and straight onto the psychiatrist's couch!

"Really, Mitch? Is everything fine? So when you tell a girl that you … that you can't be anything but friends because your heart … because you like them more than … you know what you said," Charlotte stumbled with frustration. "So you didn't mean it or did you have time to think about it and change your mind while you were away?"

He turned to face her.

"Look Charlie, I love living with you, that's all there is to say. I don't want to change that situation because you think I can't handle it. I know you think of me as the brother-type and you're still working things out with Lachlan … I spoke out of school. End of story. End of talk. OK?" He sipped his coffee.

Charlotte looked at him.

"No."

Mitch glanced up at the clock. "Listen, I've got an early meeting tomorrow; I need to read some reports before bed."

"Mitch, you've just got home! You can't be all work."

Mitch sighed.

"You have to have this discussion with me sometime and I don't want to be dodging each other for the next month."

"Exactly Charlie," he leaned across the counter. "I don't want to be avoiding each other either, that's why we are going to forget it and not have this conversation."

Charlotte persisted. "Mitch, I don't work for you."

"What does that mean?" he bristled.

"It means you don't get to make all the decisions and close down every conversation when you've had enough," she said.

"Charlie, it's not about me being in charge, it's about you and me wanting to discuss … how we feel. And it's my right not to discuss my own feelings. You don't force your counseling clients to talk do you?"

Charlotte considered this. "Nice deflection, Mitch. Won't work with me though."

"Charlie," he pleaded.

"Mitch, I didn't know you felt that way. Why didn't you say something much earlier?"

Mitch ran a hand through his hair. "We're having this discussion aren't we?"

Charlotte smiled.

"Why didn't you tell me?" she said.

He exhaled and rose, moving to the window. He could see their reflections in the glass.

"Mitch?" she pushed.

"When?" he turned to face her. "When would I tell you? In the whole time we've lived together you've been on-and-off with Lachlan. The timing wasn't right. I didn't want to make a move when you were still rebounding from Lachlan."

"Why now? Why this time?"

He shrugged. "I don't know. You got too close," he returned to the stool. "Nothing would have changed if you hadn't come to me and ... I mean, when you're lying that close." He felt the color rise in his face.

"You could have said something; it would have been OK."

"If I felt less for you ... if it was going to be just a fling, I might have," he said. "I couldn't say anything without betraying how I felt, and I didn't think the risk was worth it—worth our friendship, our roommate situation, the whole package—particularly when you made it clear that you didn't feel the same way about me that day we had drinks with Sally. In fact, I wish I had never said anything at all, I didn't want to get into all this." Mitch looked away, he felt exhaustion starting to override him. "So can we forget it and carry on as usual?"

"I've been thinking about that day," Charlotte ignored his request, "I was embarrassed when Sally said we should date, that's why I said we were like brother and sister; it was an instant reaction. It doesn't mean I wanted you to agree."

She reached out for his arm and he stiffened.

"Listen, Charlie, I'm really tired ..."

"We need to finish this discussion, Mitch."

Bet this is the subject of a future Charlotte and Sally discussion!

Mitch sighed. "I can't second-guess you or how you feel – you're not that easy to read. I'm OK with us being friends. So, can we drop it, counselor?"

He felt her withdrawing her hand, then touching the bandage under his shirt.

"What happened to your arm?"

"A few stitches. It's nothing," he recalled the stabbing.

"Mitch, what about me?"

Mitch groaned. "OK. What about you?"

"What if I felt the same as you?"

Mitch started to speak then stopped.

Is she testing me, playing me or sincere? Surely she wouldn't be playing. Would she? God, my heart's beating a thousand times a minute. Can she hear that?

"What are you saying?" He cleared his throat.

"I'm asking if I felt the same way as you do, what becomes of us then?"

"Well, hypothetically, if you did … if you did …" His eyes met hers, "I would ask you out."

She nodded. "So, ask me out." She smiled.

Mitch stared at her, a slow smile forming. "OK, Charlie, I will."

"Good!"

And leaning across the counter, he pushed their coffee cups to the side and pulled her closer, within inches of him.

He stopped to look at her again. "Are you sure?"

"Shut up."

"Right." He heard her hold her breath as he closed the gap between them, and kissed her.

25

"What are you looking so happy about?" Samantha prodded Mitch as she walked into his office bearing the team's coffee order.

"Nothing. Can't a man be happy?" he asked.

"Did you get laid?" Nick cut to the chase.

"Geez, give me that coffee," Mitch took his flat white from Samantha's tray.

"I bet it's the painkillers," Ellen told them. "They can bring on euphoria."

"I'm not euphoric, I'm not on pain killers and I'm not saying whether I got laid," he shot Nick a glance.

"I did," Samantha gloated.

"More information than we really need," Mitch grimaced at her.

"Marco, of course," Samantha added.

"Of course," Ellen agreed.

John entered the room. "Where are we up to?" He seated himself around Mitch's meeting table and reached for a coffee.

"We're taking score on who got laid last night and who didn't," Nick said.

Mitch choked on a mouthful of coffee, as Samantha and Ellen exchanged looks and smiled.

"Nice one, Nick. So much for protocol." Mitch nodded towards John. "Have you met the Executive Director for the Trans-national Crime Unit?"

Nick grinned and shrugged.

John smiled at Nick and turned to Mitch. "So?"

Mitch looked at him. "So what?"

"Did you?" John asked.

Nick laughed out loud.

Mitch rolled his eyes.

"You do look pretty relaxed this morning," John continued.

"I'm happy to be home, OK?" he said, trying not to smile.

"No, there is more to it than that." Nick grinned at him. "I've seen that look before."

"OK, it's the drugs, can we move on now?" Mitch smiled, not making eye contact with them. He pulled out a file on major international crimes in the last two weeks.

"I'm not playing anymore," he said ignoring their banter. "Let's get to it."

―――――

Waiting in the boarding lounge at the Washington-Dulles Airport, Daniel Reid returned his phone to his coat jacket.

Great, I've pissed off the boss, Daniel mused on his situation. Failure spells trouble and the gold plane was supposed to be a sure thing. How did they stuff it up?

OK, need to run over the submission again, he thought over the plan. Did I miss the weak links? Did I run tight enough checks on Johan's team? The woman was fine. The day and night security guards were hired muscle. There was that change of pilot at the last minute; Johan assured me he came recommended. Who was he?

Daniel opened his briefcase and went through the files.

I need that pilot's name. Nicholas Everett … no, that was the first pilot and I got his profile from Johan. He was connected to the woman and checked out alright. It was the second one, the one that came in when the other guy had to return to Chicago.

Daniel went through all his paperwork.

There is no record of him, no name, no photo. Was this guy a loose cannon? This could be risky. Does he know anything about Mastermind? Where the hell is the second pilot now? Bloody hell.

If I ring Lawrence back and say there might be a possible threat to Mastermind, my balls are on the line. If I don't and all hell breaks loose, I'm a dead man. Great choices.

He called Lawrence Hackett.

John listened as Mitch discussed the team's next move. He watched the interaction between Mitch and Nick.

They seemed to have sorted out their dramas, John thought. It's going to be good for Mitch to have an ally; someone who won't put up with much stick, will add value and push him. Just what he needs to keep him interested.

He looked up as Marco hurried into the room and handed Mitch and him a piece of paper each. John saw Marco give Samantha a smile and wink.

"You might want to move sooner rather than later on that one," Marco said departing with a wave.

"Damn, why couldn't he do a bit of sightseeing?" Mitch said rising from his chair.

John pushed the paper into the middle of the table.

"Daniel has got himself on an earlier flight for London, it leaves in forty-five minutes," he told the team. "How do you want to play it, Mitch?"

"We should head to the airport, make sure it's him taking off," Mitch started. "Nick can identify him. I'm pretty sure I'd know him, even though I only saw him from the ceiling." Mitch grabbed a file, pulled out an angled shot he took of Daniel and passed it around.

"At least ensure he gets on the flight; no point following him once he's taken off," Nick added. "He'll be going back to his U.K. office."

Mitch agreed. "We need to get him tracked on the ground when he does land. Be even better if his luggage went missing. I want to see what's in that briefcase," Mitch paced.

"If we could get his phone to lift the address book, it might prove useful too," Nick added.

"Exactly," Mitch nodded. He began to issue orders.

"Sam, get airport security to remove his luggage. I want the hand luggage too. Do whatever it takes, even if you have to get everyone off the plane on a drill. Ellie, you take the hand luggage, photocopy it and get it back on the plane ASAP. John, can we get one of our agents in the London office to track him when he lands?"

"Done," John agreed.

"Nick, get some photos of him at the terminal, don't let him see you. Would he recognize you?"

"He never met me, but he's got my profile."

"OK, you confirm I've got the right guy and I'll get photos," Mitch reached for the digital camera in the desk draw. "He won't know me unless ...?" Mitch looked to Nick.

"No, your profile never went to Johan," Nick confirmed.

"Let's go," Mitch raced out the door. John smiled as he watched the team jump to catch up.

———

"You did the right thing calling me," Lawrence Hackett assured Daniel Reid. "Was there anyone else?"

"No," Daniel said, "he was the only change to the plan."

"Can you identify him?"

"No. Johan said he was a contact of the other pilot, Nicholas Everett. Johan trusted Nick; said he was family."

"Have you got access to Johan?"

"He's in custody. I could go in as his legal rep."

"What about Nick?" Lawrence continued questioning Daniel.

"Skipped."

"What do you mean he's skipped?"

Daniel swallowed. "Only the woman and Johan were arrested."

Lawrence said nothing. Daniel waited.

"That's a problem. It doesn't sound right that the pilot got away," Lawrence said eventually.

Daniel heard pages rustling.

"I'm going to send two assistants to Nevada immediately. They'll be there in the next twenty-four hours. Meet them at the airport, Daniel. They can handle whatever work you need done, get it cleaned up, no loose ends. Find Nick and get out of him the whereabouts of the other pilot."

"What if we find everything's OK and both of the pilots know nothing – they're laying low?"

"I don't buy it. If Nick was family, Johan would have spilled something about Mastermind to him; my gut instincts tell me it's too risky. Find both the pilots and fix it. Let me think what to do about Johan and the female – we may have to clean that up as well. When does the lease end at the mine site?"

Daniel fished through the paper work. "Uh, three more weeks."

"Right, head back to Broad Arrow. Ask questions; see if anyone can identify the second pilot in case Nicholas Everett tries to pull something over on us. Is there a surveillance tape at the Broad Arrow office?"

"I don't know, I doubt it."

"OK, check that out and get your hands on any surveillance tapes that could have captured their image. Like the nearby hotel might have one."

"Lawrence I haven't been there, but I hear it's the back of nowhere, the odds aren't good on the tapes."

"Probably not, but it might work in your favor getting him identified – small town, not too many people pass through. We'll run Nick again and his background." Lawrence paused. "Daniel, do whatever you have to do, but clean it up before you return home. I'm counting on you." The phone line disconnected.

Daniel stood temporarily frozen; then he grabbed his briefcase and jacket and headed to the counter.

I've got to get off this flight and get on a flight to Nevada.

———

Mitch couldn't find Daniel Reid at the boarding gate for the London flight. He checked the flight again.

Right flight, but no Daniel.

Samantha joined him. "His luggage has been taken off the flight."

"Any reason why?" Mitch asked.

"He told them that he had pressing business elsewhere."

"Damn it. He may still be in the terminal. Sam, take Nick with you, he'll recognize him and head that way," he indicated straight ahead. "I'll take the other half of the airport. And call Ellie – tell her to forget the briefcase and to check out the taxi ranks. If anyone matches his description, tell her to call Nick to positively I.D. him."

"Done," he watched her hurry off, signaling for Nick to join her.

Mitch called John. "He's done a runner. Can you put him through the system and see if he has transferred to any other flight?" He hung up, stopped, exhaled and gathered himself.

If Daniel is staying, it means he has found out there is a risk to the game's security. It'll be a much bigger fight than we planned, and we'll have lost our element of surprise.

His phone rang. It was John.

"His name's come up on a flight to Elko," John told him.

"Elko? Why is he going to … uh," Mitch put it together. "I think Daniel has found out that only two of the three have been arrested. He's looking for loose ends and he thinks they're still at Broad Arrow."

"I'm guessing given what's at stake, he isn't going there alone," John added.

"No, but depending on where his allies are coming from time might be on our side," Mitch said. "We know the insides of that place now, Daniel doesn't."

"How many flights do you want?"

"Uh, I don't know what we're up against, book four. Can we be on his flight going out?"

"You might be cutting that fine. Leave it with me."

"Listen, if you don't want to go, three on the ground's probably enough," Mitch said walking alongside Samantha as they made their way through the airport.

"Why wouldn't I want to go?" she looked at him surprised.

Mitch shrugged. "Well, you know, you've started seeing Marco – you might want to actually see him."

"You mean because I'm a female, I need to nest?"

Mitch stopped dead.

"No, I didn't mean that at all." Risky territory. Back off!

He started walking again. "I just meant, we haven't been home much and ... forget it."

"Hey, I'm sorry."

"No, it was stupid of me," Mitch said. "Forget it."

"No it wasn't, it was considerate of you. But I love my work; I don't want to stay at home and play families. I want both."

"I hear you."

They caught up with Ellen and Nick in front.

"What are we doing for clothes?" Ellen asked.

"We'll get issued some in Elko. John's organizing it, along with the hire car."

"Something black in military one size fits all?" Samantha asked.

"Yep, three sets of it each," Mitch recalled the issued packs.

Mitch turned to Nick. "Try and stay incognito. I don't want him recognizing you."

"I'll keep the baseball hat on and try not to draw attention to myself. As hard as that will be."

Mitch smirked at him. "True, with that big head you do stand out in a crowd."

Mitch spotted Daniel sitting, waiting to board. He was dressed in a blue pinstriped suit with a white T-shirt underneath, his brief case across his lap.

Nick followed Mitch's gaze.

"That's him," Nick confirmed. "Looks like he just stepped out of a Calvin Klein catalogue. So, what's the plan?"

"It's a work in progress," Mitch said, sitting on the opposite side of the departure lounge watching Daniel's reflection in the window.

"No idea, huh?" Nick sat next to him.

"That's it," Mitch agreed. "But I'll know before we land."

26

"Should we panic?" Andrew Kenny, Chief of Staff, asked Lawrence Hackett.

"No need to yet, Andrew," Lawrence answered, "I have the best security money can buy."

"And money buys loyalty," Andrew agreed. "So, what about Daniel?"

"I'm sending Daniel two of our best: Colby and Westwood. There's a lot at stake and I'm not spending time in any prison, anywhere."

"We've still got fall guys set up to do that," Andrew assured him. "There is always someone prepared to go to jail for enough money to ensure their family's long-term financial security. We can buy our way out of almost any charges, as long as the evidence isn't watertight."

"And if there is no one around to give evidence …" Lawrence smiled.

―――

Daniel kept his eyes closed and stewed over the Aurum project.

Why didn't I get one of the European postings? He thought sulkily. I'm supposed to be the golden boy, so why the hell was I sent to Nevada?

Unless ...

Andrew Kenny! That's why! Andrew wants to get me as far away as possible. Andrew's threatened by me, the little pisshead. He's been Lawrence's right-hand man for years and he can't take the competition. Well, I'll be back, Andrew, Daniel gloated – and I'll wrap this up so tight, that I'll be back with a promotion.

He opened his eyes and everything looked better.

Charlotte sat at her desk.

Focus, she told herself. Stop thinking about Mitch and concentrate on the next client. Her phone rang and Mitch's number flashed up.

"Hi," she answered.

"Hi there, Charlie. Listen, I can't talk," Mitch said, "I'm going to be away for a few days."

"How many?"

"Maybe four or five. I'll call you when I get a clearer picture."

"OK. When do you leave?"

"Now."

Charlotte could hear the sounds of a boarding call in the background.

"Sorry, Charlie. I'll see you by the end of the week. I promise to spend my time planning that date."

"Sure. Take care." She hung up.

Here's the first downside of a relationship with Mitch, she thought. Plus the fact that he might be an impenetrable closed book.

Mitch put his phone away and returned to the group.

"Pretty hard to hold down a relationship in this job," Nick said watching him.

"What makes you think …"

Nick interrupted him. "You're allowed to have a life you know."

"Anything happen?" Mitch sat down next to him, keeping Daniel in sight.

"Nothing."

Mitch sat bolt upright. He stood and walked away. He paced up and down the far end of the terminal a few times.

"What's he doing?" Nick asked watching him.

"Thinking," Samantha said, "he always does that."

"I hope he doesn't explode," Nick remarked.

Ellen laughed beside him. "Give him a break."

"Why?" he turned to look at her.

"He's got a lot on. There is a fair bit of pressure in his job you know," she said.

"That's why I'm good for him. Lighten him up a bit," Nick said.

"You're pretty direct with him," Ellen commented.

"You don't need to protect Mitch from me," Nick scoffed. "We go way back – we're past that stage of watching our p's and q's around each other. I was hanging out with him in high school. I was there when he got his driver's license and when he first got laid. Geez, he's even had Christmas lunch at my parent's house a half-a-dozen times."

"OK, point taken," Ellen said.

Nick continued. "I bet you and Sam wouldn't even recognize him after he's had a few drinks, loosened up a bit. He's so uptight now, I barely recognize him."

"I don't get you guys. One week you're beating the crap out of each other, the next you're having a beer together. Why did you fall out? Was it because of the East Timor incident you mentioned?"

Nick watched Mitch coming towards them. The question hung in the air unanswered.

"What's up?" Nick asked him.

"We're going about this all wrong," Mitch said. "We're bringing the fight to Daniel Reid – a small fight. He's out of our hair if he's heading back to Nevada. We need to take the fight ..."

"Straight to the source," Nick finished Mitch's sentence.

"Exactly. Two of us can go deal with Daniel in Nevada; the other two need to track down the source in the U.K. As much as I'd rather you were on deck in the U.K., Nick," Mitch started, "Daniel is going to be looking for you in Nevada and he needs to see you. I'm not sure what resources he'll bring with him. Best you handle it and we'll split Sam and Ellie. I can pick up one of our agents in the U.K. when we get there – someone who knows the lay of the land."

Nick rose and moved closer to Mitch, ensuring he couldn't be overheard. "No problem. Ellie and I will stay here and board the plane with Daniel – you and Sam go find the source."

Nick saw Mitch studying him.

"Why Ellie?" Mitch asked.

Nick shrugged. "I heard she's a great shot and accurate. The best in the unit, didn't you tell me that?"

"Uh-huh, probably," Mitch said with a slow smile forming.

"Piss off," Nick grinned.

27

"Can I say 'I told you so'," Sally asked, looking at Charlotte over lunch.

"No."

"Oh, come on, you've got your man, let me gloat."

Charlotte sighed. "Fine, you were right, I was wrong; you told me so – there it is, happy now?"

"Very. But not as happy as you, by the looks of it."

"Hmm. It will depend if we're ever in the same place at the same time. He's away now for the rest of the week on business. And don't say absence makes the heart grow fonder and all that; I've never bought that crap."

Sally laughed. "It will be good to take it slow; after all, he's not going anywhere – you live together! Did he kiss you?"

"Good grief, how old are we?"

"So, was it good?"

"Great."

Sally sighed. "At last. I'm almost jealous."

Charlotte lowered her voice. "Hey, I wanted to ask your thoughts on something confidential."

"OK."

"I think Mitch was abused as a kid. I think he had a violent parent; I'm assuming it was his father."

"Did he tell you that?" Sally frowned.

"No. But I found out that he has a file with the Department of Children and Families. You don't get those unless there has been a reported incident. I have seen the signs a thousand times with patients. You know, limited family contact, doesn't give out his home number, never talks about his past and has few intimate personal relationships. Plus, he has scars that he goes out of his way to avoid discussing; avoiding stimuli associated with the trauma is quite common. And since he's been on night shift and is a bit out of whack, he's been having these amazing nightmares. He wakes himself up yelling in his sleep."

"About what?"

"I only heard a few times. He called out for his father once, then someone called Henry. The other times it was quite violent; he's woken up shaking and sweating."

"Could be work stress or ..."

"No. I've seen it before," Charlotte lowered her voice. "It's a post-traumatic stress disorder; a traumatic event is experienced, like a violent assault, and the affected person will disassociate themselves from it until a trigger brings it back to the surface."

"So, you think Mitch's nightmares are because the recent bashing he got triggered the emotions of being hit as a child? Seems a bit simplistic, and it's not the first time he's been in a fight."

"No, there is probably more to it ... other triggers."

"Did you read the file?" Sally asked.

"No. I can't access it," Charlotte took a sip of water. "But I spoke to him about his dreams and he shut down. Told me to stop digging. I'm worried that it will affect him at the wrong time or he'll react unexpectedly to something and place himself in danger."

"Does that happen?" Sally asked surprised.

"All the time. You hear about people who flip out and do something out of character over little things that send them off. Everyone comes out of the woodwork to say they're so surprised – so-and-so always seemed so mild-mannered. It's delayed onset."

"Hmm. Look Charlie, I'm with Mitch on this. I know it's an occupational hazard for you and you think that talking about it can cure everything, but I don't. I like the philosophy of get over it and move on. If it happened and if he wants to tell you he will. Let him do that when he's ready."

"Stop trying to save him?" Charlotte asked.

"Precisely."

Ellen pulled the hire car into the car park of the Eureka Best Western Hotel. She shook Nick's shoulder to wake him up.

"We're here."

Nick stirred and began to sit up.

"John called while you were out to it; you can sleep through anything," Ellen said. "He said Daniel used his credit card to book three rooms at this hotel and he's hired a sports utility in Vegas. He's also changed his flight from Elko to Vegas."

"No doubt to meet his backup team," Nick stretched. "Sounds like they're coming in too late to get connecting flights to Elko. They'll have to do the five-and-a-half hour drive from Vegas to Eureka."

"Gives us time to be seen, so that when Daniel asks around about you, he'll know you're in town," Ellen said.

"Yeah, let's go be seen," Nick got out of the car and waited for Ellen. They walked into reception.

"Daniel Reid, Cambridge Law School, graduate attorney-at-law, 29, employed by Globalnet. A media company run by …"

"Lawrence Hackett," Mitch filled in the rest as he sat in John's office.

"Yes," John continued. "Billionaire and successful media man."

"And," Mitch sat down opposite him, "in his late forties, been at the helm for over twenty years."

The two men looked at each other.

"It's a big call associating the masterminding of a perfect crime with someone like Lawrence Hackett," Mitch shook his head, "it's so extreme. Why would he do it? Risk it?"

John reached for his coffee. "Bored. Looking for a thrill. Thinks he's above the law."

"Maybe," Mitch agreed.

Samantha knocked on the door. "Got it." She grinned. John moved to give her access to his computer.

"This is the Mastermind site," she called it up on the screen. "It's set up as Nick said it would be."

Samantha clicked into a number of different areas. "When you go through to the engine room ... for want of a better term," she said, leaving the front page, "you'll find the site is coming from a company called Globalnet." Samantha showed them the connection between the company and the game site.

Mitch and John exchanged looks.

"Guess it's not that extreme, after all," Mitch rose. "This is huge."

"Bigger than we thought, that's for sure," John looked at the Aurum file on his desk. "How much back up do you want?"

"Can you get me one of our U.K. guys for starters?" Mitch asked.

"Done. Your flight leaves for London in less than two hours," John reminded them. "I'll get the U.K. agent to liaise with you at your hotel."

28

Federal Agent Adam Forster scanned the wall of pigeonholes at the London headquarters of the National Crime Squad, found his name and pulled out his mail. Adam shuffled the envelopes, tearing open the one containing his orders for the rest of the week. He read the slip of paper.

Meet Agents Mitchell Parker and Samantha Moore from the U.S.A Washington D.C. Trans-national Crime Unit at 0800 hours at room 244, the Four Season Hotel, Westferry Circus, Canary Wharf.

Adam stuffed the paper and the rest of his mail into his suit pocket. He took the black band from around his wrist and tied his shoulder-length brown hair back. Raising the collar on his black overcoat, he pushed out into the street into the rain and headed towards the underground entrance.

So, what are these two Yanks doing in town? He wondered. Hope it'll get the juices running, I could do with a challenge. Should just pack the medals away, buy a fruit and vegetable store and settle down with a nice girl, have a few kids, the usual thing. Nuh. Wouldn't work. I'd have to have the best fruit and vegetable store, then a network of stores – soon I'd want a monopoly on the market. Who knows? I'd probably create a new line of vegetable, he thought.

And then, I'd be bored with it. There has to be more to life, but what?

Yep, he sighed, mid-life crisis. He cheered up again. Who knows what these two are doing in London, Canary Wharf of all places. Might be interesting.

Samantha watched Mitch as he slept beside her, leaning against the window – his long legs stretched across the exit row space in front of them, his arms folded across his chest. Mitch frowned and his dark eyelashes fluttered as she covered him with one of the airline-issued blankets.

What I'd give to be able to sleep on a plane, she thought enviously. Now cargo planes, where you can lay full length on the floor if room permits, that's the only way to fly!

Mitch woke with a start. Samantha grabbed his hand.

"It's OK, we're still in flight," she whispered.

He looked around; she watched his eyes come into focus on her. Samantha removed her hand.

"Right," he rubbed his hand across his eyes. "Are we there yet?"

"No. Bad dream?"

"Sort of," he sat up. "I dreamed I was on a plane going to London to break up a criminal game."

"Ah, that's actually not a dream," Samantha teased him.

"Damn!" Mitch pushed off the blanket, reached for his water bottle and seeing the file on Adam Forster, grabbed it.

"Twistie?" Samantha offered him the packet, "they're chicken, my favorite. Although, I don't mind the cheese-flavored."

"God, no. How can you eat that stuff at this time of the day?"

"What time of the day?" Samantha shrugged, putting one in her mouth. "We're about to eat dinner but it's really midnight isn't it?"

"Fair point," Mitch handed the file to Samantha. "He's a bit of a hot shot our London assignee. American born, though looks like he's lived in the U.K. most of his life. Check it out."

Samantha opened the file and glanced over Adam's record. She gave out a low whistle.

"Impressive," she looked down the list of his credentials. "MI5 and MI6, served in Northern Ireland, commanded an armored squadron in Germany, completed a tour in Bosnia, deployed to Macedonia in 1999, a stint in Kosovo, counter espionage work for the British foreign intelligence service and further postings in Russia and China," she flipped the page and continued. "Fluent in four languages, that's handy, and originally a member of the British Royal Air Force. He's a fly-boy like you," she noted. "He's jumped around a bit. Why do you think he joined the TCU after a career like that?"

"I'd say he's keen on a few trips to the States each year, or ..."

"Or?" Samantha looked up from the paperwork.

"He's hankering for a life change. The TCU would have snapped him up; no relocation fees, he knows the ropes and has the contacts – that's probably the biggest challenge for our agents based in the U.K."

"Would you do a London posting?"

Mitch shrugged. "Maybe. Anyway, let's hope he's a team player and not a renegade."

Mitch looked at his reflection in the mirror of the male restroom at Heathrow Airport. *Need a shave, need to brush my teeth, need to sleep.* He splashed water on his face, ran his hands through his hair and went back to meet Samantha at the luggage carousel.

"You look like death warmed up," Samantha nudged him.

"After an eleven hour flight, bet I smell like it too."

Samantha inhaled. "You're not bad on the nose. I've smelled worse."

"Thanks, I think."

Mitch smiled as she rested her head on his shoulder and closed her eyes, as they waited for the luggage to appear on the carousel belt. Mitch turned his phone on.

"I'll check on the other two and see how they're going. Geez, got to get the brain working … let's see – the time difference, if London's five hours ahead of D.C. and eight hours ahead of Nevada, that would make it around eleven p.m. in Eureka." Mitch dialed Nick.

———

"Daniel Reid has booked into two hotels; one in Vegas, and the one we're staying at here in Eureka. John confirmed it earlier," Nick informed Mitch over the phone. "My guess is he's waiting for a flight to come in or he'd be here now."

"I agree," Mitch said. "He's probably booked the Vegas room to hang out in during the day. When's the next flight due from the U.K.?"

"There is one at five-thirty in the morning."

"Any idea of how many people Daniel is waiting on?"

"He's booked three rooms here, so I'd say he's got two joining him. John's working on identifying them from the U.K. flight manifest. There are forty passengers getting off in Vegas, and John can't account for twelve of those yet."

"OK," Mitch said. "Got a plan?"

"Yep. First thing in the morning we'll head to the Broad Arrow site."

"Then?"

"We'll case the joint, make sure we're alone. Then we're going to look at how we can close off the underground tunnels somehow to create an ambush situation. We're going to be outnumbered by one, but Daniel will be pretty ineffectual. We need to control the situation."

Mitch tensed.

"Nick, don't underestimate Daniel. He's not going to be making small talk. I think we should get you more back up."

"Hold off until we work through it in the morning."

"Alright, but get back to me ASAP. I think playing in the tunnels is dangerous, you could end up ambushing yourself."

"Boss, it'll be alright," Nick assured him. "We'll come up with something and let you know if we need more back up."

"Make sure you do."

"I will."

"I mean it."

"I hear you."

There was a silence on the line.

"Can you put Ellie on?"

"Sure."

Mitch waited hearing Ellen move to the phone.

"Hi Mitch, what's the protocol once we have them?" Ellen asked.

"John will interview them. We can only hold them for a short time unless we get something concrete. So we need them to reveal their hand to make it stick. Now listen Ellie," he warned her, "keep your head, OK?"

"OK," she replied. "What makes you think I wouldn't?"

"Nothing, but don't go ..." he hesitated, "don't go soft on me."

"I'm not following."

Mitch ground his teeth. "Don't let Nick distract you."

"Oh. It's not an issue," she snapped.

"Ellie, don't get pissed. You know it can happen, so stay focused."

"Yes, Mitch."

Mitch hung up. *Not winning any popularity contests this week.*

Mitch threw his gear on the floor of his hotel room and with a glance to his watch, headed to the bathroom; thirty minutes until Adam Forster was due to arrive.

He had a quick shower and reached for his razor when he heard a knock at the door. He opened the door, wet and with a white bath towel around his waist.

"Uh, Mitchell Parker? I think you're expecting me?"

Mitch smiled. "Adam Forster," he sized up the tall, built man who looked impressive in a well-cut black-grey suit. Mitch offered his hand.

"Sorry, we just got here ten minutes ago."

"That's fine. No need to dress for the occasion – after all, it's just me," Adam said in his British accent. Mitch laughed standing aside to let him in.

"Bet you feel like shit," Adam said.

"Feel and probably look like shit," Mitch agreed. "Come in. I'll ..."

"Sure, get changed. Tea or coffee?" Adam took charge.

"Coffee, white, thanks."

———

Adam walked in and headed straight to the counter, grabbing the kettle to fill it. He turned to watch Mitch go.

Wow, more battle scars than me. The ones on his back are impressive.

Adam opened and closed a few cupboards looking for mugs. He looked up hearing a knock on the shared internal door and stopped as a tall brunette walked straight in. She froze.

"Samantha?" he asked.

"Adam Forster!" she exclaimed. "Sorry, I thought I had the wrong room. What did you do with Mitch?"

"I've finished him off. It was easy! Elite agent? Ha!"

Samantha laughed. They shook hands.

"Please, call me Sam."

"Sam it is. Tea or coffee?"

———

Mitch emerged dressed, his dark hair wet, his blue eyes observing Adam. He took the offered coffee.

"What are we in for?" Adam asked removing his jacket.

Mitch ran through the brief, rising and looking out at the silver Credit Suisse building where Lawrence Hackett worked. When he finished, he turned to face Adam and Samantha.

"That's great," Adam said sitting back and extending his arms over the back of the sofa.

Mitch smiled.

"I mean, that's really brilliant," Adam said. "It's amazing he's already had two seasons of the competition."

Mitch nodded in agreement. He ran his hand over his eyes. Glancing at Samantha, he could see she was struggling to stay alert.

"This is what we need to do," Mitch started. "Lawrence's got six directors and a number of board executives. I'm assuming those six directors are the Mastermind board. We need to find out how many are here in London now. The ones that aren't here, we can assume are in a designated country, playing the game. We need to find out which country, track them, track the crime they are waiting on and see if we can assist the local authorities to thwart it before it happens. We need one or all of them to testify."

Adam let out a low whistle. "Tough one," he sighed. "At least you know the U.S. is out of the running."

"Assuming there was only one Mastermind entry there," Mitch agreed. "We need to bug Lawrence's offices, I want to record every gathering. I want to know what's going on and I want proof."

"That's easier," Adam took a notepad from his jacket pocket and scribbled some notes.

"I want access to the files, to the hard drives, to his bank details. In fact, I'd love to get an insider into his world," Mitch frowned, rising again and pacing around the room, "time's going to be against us there."

Mitch looked at Samantha, then back to Adam.

"Has Lawrence got a girlfriend?"

"Many," Adam confirmed. "Wealth and power – an age-old aphrodisiac."

"I'm sure he could use one more," Mitch said.

"Ah, I've been set up," Samantha clicked to his plan.

"Perfect match," Mitch smiled. "So, how's this work, Adam ... with you on board I mean?"

"You get full access to me as your TCU rep, and through the TCU's partnership with the U.K. National Crime Squad, I can get you access to any intelligence we need and shortcut the system, which most outside agencies can't do. I've got to keep the NCS hierarchy in the loop as we go along, otherwise, everything's sweet."

Mitch nodded. "Great, because I need you to pull strings."

29

"There is something I should mention," Ellen whispered, making her way through the empty Broad Arrow mine site at one a.m. in the morning. She moved aside, avoiding some stacked boxes and followed Nick as he led the way to the hangar. She noticed his eyes lit up at the sight of it.

"You boys are all the same," she shook her head. "Mitch was beside himself when he found your hangar and the hidden plane."

"I bet he was. Boring without it here." He squatted to lift up the door on the floor of the hangar and peered down into the mineshaft.

"Been down here?" he asked.

"Yep, they're all still functional; plenty of tunnels and rabbit warrens. I thought you knew this place?"

"I cased it for our needs, but didn't venture down into the tunnels. No point really. Come on." He lowered himself down the stairs, drawing a torch from his black vest. Ellen followed behind him, bumping into him when he stopped.

"Sorry," he whispered. "Just listening for any movement."

They continued along the shaft by torchlight. Ellen shone her torch up side tunnels, opening and closing the occasional entrance and inspecting them as they came along.

HELEN GOLTZ

Breathe slowly in, wait, breathe out, she coached herself as the tunnels went deeper.

"Hey, what did you want to tell me?" Nick remembered.

He looked back at Ellen, shining the torch towards her.

"I'm a little claustrophobic," she said.

Nick rolled his eyes.

"Fine time to tell me. You're scared of flying and claustrophobic! Anything else?"

"I don't like rats," Ellen said as a huge one ran past her feet.

"Yeah, me either," Nick moved aside as it scurried past. "Are you going to be able to do this? I can't carry you out while holding back the others on my own."

"Of course I can do it," she took a deep breath, "or I wouldn't be here. I thought I'd mention it, so if you saw me hyperventilating you didn't panic."

"OK, now I'm panicking," he grimaced.

———

Mitch, Samantha and Adam sat in the hotel suite surrounded by the floor plans for Lawrence's building.

"Thanks for getting these, Adam," Mitch poured over them.

"Easy one," Adam said.

Mitch's phone rang. He looked at the screen.

"What's up, Nick?" he answered.

"Did you know she's claustrophobic?" Nick whispered. "We're down in the mine shafts with my brilliant combat strategy and I've got Ellen hyperventilating on me!"

"Yeah, I knew she was a little cagey in tight spaces. She's great in water, a divemaster actually."

"That's going to be real useful here," Nick cut in.

"She managed before; keep her distracted. Besides, she's great with a gun, remember?" he ragged him.

"Yeah, yeah," Nick took the badgering. "Got to go."

"Wait, what do you mean you're down in the mines?" Mitch

looked at his watch. "It's got to be midnight there. What are you doing?"

"Couldn't sleep, doing a pre-rendezvous. Speak to you later." Nick said hanging up.

Mitch stared at the phone.

"Dramas?" Samantha asked.

"Potentially." Mitch returned to the maps, his brow creased with concern.

Daniel waited at the airport for Colby and Westwood to arrive. He looked at their schedule; they weren't coming from the U.K., but from a job in Shanghai, arriving at nine p.m.

He read the dossier Lawrence sent him on the two security men: Wayne J. Colby served in Beirut, Afghanistan and Iraq. He took a payout after a potential court-martial came to light over inappropriate behavior with women prisoners.

That'd be right, Daniel thought. He'd be pretty happy to take up Lawrence's offer to come on board.

He scanned the profile for Aaron P. Westwood: Raised in Brooklyn, fought wherever a war was raging. Retired but missed the life. On-call for special emergencies. I guess this is one of those situations. Daniel sighed. He turned the page and looked at their photos. *Scary guys! Not two people you'd want to take on.*

Nick had been in bed for an hour when he heard the sound of a car's engine idling outside his room.

"Keep the noise down," he grumbled with a glance to his watch. Three-fifteen. He rolled over. The noise of car doors slamming and people talking drifted into his room.

Wake up the neighborhood for God's sake!

He got out of bed, pulled his jeans on, grabbed his sweater, and went outside. He cupped his hands around a cigarette and lit it.

That'll be around eleven a.m. in London. Wonder what the boss is up to, Nick thought. He looked around. Lights were on in three rooms from the newly arrived guests. Then, he saw the sports utility.

Shit! Three rooms, a sports utility hire car! It's got to be Daniel. We need to move now and get to Broad Arrow so we're on site at first light! Otherwise we're sitting ducks, especially if he shows my photo to the manager.

Nick put out his cigarette and turned to go. A door on the upstairs veranda opened and Nick looked up. Daniel stepped out onto the landing. Their eyes locked. Nick broke off and bolted to his room.

"Look, I know this techno stuff excites you," Mitch yawned as he sat next to Samantha waiting for her verdict on the security installed in Lawrence's building, "but can you give it to me in ten words or less?"

He heard Adam laugh as he placed a call to room service for sandwiches and Cokes.

"No, Mitch," Samantha turned to him. "It's complex. On the first floor, Lawrence's building has a security officer at the front door; all other commercial occupants of the building organized their own security initiatives."

"Lawrence will know better than to rely on human security," Adam said, rejoining them around the table.

Samantha agreed, "He's installed a sophisticated motion sensor system. He's got a different system for each of his nine floors."

"That's a chronic pain in the ass," Mitch frowned.

"I need to find the main server," Samantha continued, picking up one floor plan after another. "Logically, it should be on their Information Technology floor, but hey, who's logical these days."

Mitch closed his eyes as Samantha rifled through the diagrams.

"Here it is!" she announced, making Mitch jump. "On the eighth floor. The I.T. room has a motion sensor beam about one foot up from the floor, running in a perfect square around the room," she grabbed another plan from the table, "There is a different security system on floor nine. I haven't seen this type before."

"Can you shut it down?" Mitch asked.

"It should be manageable. However," she bit her lip, "he's got a variety of sensors in place. The top floors are more complex; they house I.T. and the mainframe area. My guess is that floor nine is his office," she looked at the grid. "We want the eighth floor in order to access the computers and mainframe."

Mitch pulled the plans closer and studied them. "Won't the different security systems on each floor be linked through the mainframe, so if one floor is cut, all other floors are on alert? I'm assuming that's what those markings mean?" Mitch pointed to a number of figures and lines.

"Damn, I didn't see those," Samantha took the plans off him.

The room buzzer sounded and Mitch glanced at Adam with a relieved look. He noticed Samantha remained oblivious, burying her head in security plans for the lower floors.

Nick ran into the room, grabbed his bag and vest and headed straight out again, pulling the door closed behind him. He ran to Ellen's room, swearing under his breath.

"Ellen, quick," he knocked, speaking in a hushed tone.

He heard her stir and within seconds she was at the door. Nick rushed past her into the room.

"Get dressed, hurry!"

"What's happened?"

"I'll tell you on the way, leave everything, let's go."

Ellen grabbed her bag and phone. They raced out of the door.

"Hurry," Nick led the way to the car park, leaping over the iron banister. He rounded the corner and stopped suddenly. A Smith and Wesson was pointed at his head.

"Nicholas Everett," Daniel appeared behind the man holding the gun. "What a surprise. Going somewhere?"

Ellen stopped dead beside Nick. He glanced over at her, scanning the area for an escape route.

―――

Ellen and Nick sat, hands tied behind them, in the back seat of Daniel's hire car, surrounded by Lawrence's men. Daniel drove.

"I never thought it would be that easy," Daniel grinned at Nick in the rear view mirror.

"Listen you're only after me so let the girl go," Nick said.

Nick felt a strong blow to his eye socket. His head jolted backwards with the impact. He heard Ellen scream and everything went momentarily black.

"Bloody hell, Colby, don't kill him yet," Daniel barked.

Nick pulled himself forward in the seat. He looked at Colby.

"Was that really necessary?" he squinted with the pain.

Colby sniggered.

Nick turned his attention back to Daniel.

"What do you want?" he persisted, the pain rushing from his eye to a dull ache at the back of his head.

"To finish off a mistake," Daniel said.

"What mistake? So we didn't pull it off, so what? It's not like I'm on the run with the gold. None of us got anything."

"No, but you're on the run from me. Why is that?"

Nick felt like he had hit the ground with a thud.

Shit. I'm an idiot! I wasn't supposed to recognize Daniel given I'm not supposed to know anything about Mastermind – Johan was the point of contact. Shit ... shit!

"I assume Maria Diaz knows as well?" Daniel asked.

"No," Nick looked at Daniel in the rear view mirror. "I know it's somehow connected to the Mastermind Internet game; Johan let it slip. She doesn't know anything."

"I find that hard to swallow, since they were bed friends. But she's safe while she's in prison. For now anyway."

Nick stared out the window. *When will it stop? First Ana, now I've signed Maria's death warrant,* he thought.

He glanced at Ellen, bile rising in his throat. *And Ellen's going to pay the price as well.*

30

Mitch removed a ceiling panel and looked down at the eighth floor of Lawrence's building. He felt his phone to vibrate on silent in his pocket.

"Damn."

"What is it?" Adam asked.

"Phone."

He reached for it, taking it out of his pocket slowly.

"Whatever you do, don't drop it," Adam said. "It just has to pass through that sensor below and the place will be all bells and whistles."

"Yeah, thanks for that," Mitch gave Adam a sideways glance. His eyes strayed back to the phone screen.

"John," he answered, "everything alright?"

"Fine my end, how about your way?" John asked.

"All OK. Got to go though, we're inside."

"Call me when you're done."

Mitch hung up.

"That it?" Adam asked.

"No, I thought I'd call my mother," Mitch grimaced. "I've got other operatives on the job, I need to take their calls in case there's a problem."

Mitch returned the phone to his vest pocket and secured it.

"Ready, Sam," he said into his microphone.

"OK," she started. "On each floor is a blue light motion sensor."

"We've got that in sight," Mitch confirmed.

"Good. What we need to do now is find the security box on the floors that we want to enter, isolate the wiring and use the laser beam to fuse through it to disconnect that sensor. Cool?"

"Right," Mitch said.

Samantha continued. "When we find the security box, we need to pinpoint the laser beam onto the correct circuit and burn that area with the laser; it will shut it down and kill the alarm."

"Easy," Adam said frowning at Mitch.

Mitch scanned the room looking for the box.

"The only problem ... " Samantha's voice broke his concentration.

"Yes?" Mitch responded.

"Is that there are two security boxes that appear to be linked on floor eight and two on floor nine – double the security, I guess."

"Good," Mitch said without enthusiasm.

"And on your floor, it looks like one's a wall unit and the other is ... in the telephone."

Mitch and Adam looked down and around.

"We've got them. I'll take the phone," Mitch told Adam, "you take the wall box."

"Now, Mitch, Adam ..." Samantha continued, "we need to count it down and you need to be synchronized in the timing or one of them will read the other is not functioning and start the alarms. Once you give me the all-clear, we've got a window of a few seconds for me to isolate the eighth floor from the other areas so that the sensors don't pick up that there has been a shut down."

"What happens if they do?" Mitch asked.

"They could set off the alarms or override the system and turn it back on."

Mitch frowned. "It can do that?"

"It can," Samantha confirmed.

"OK, let's get to it," he said facing Adam. They crawled along the ceiling frames, removing two panels closest to the security boxes. Wedging a boot on each side of the frames, they lowered themselves upside down from the ceiling.

"Sam, I've got three telephone lines here, any idea which is the main one?" Mitch asked into his headset.

"No. My guess would be the one in closest proximity to the security box," she answered.

"Guess?"

"An educated guess," Samantha assured him.

Mitch selected the nearest telephone line. He reached for his laser pen. With a quick glance to check on Adam who was propping himself up on the security box, Mitch prompted Samantha. "We're ready."

"OK, let's do this," she issued instructions. "Adam, in the main box, find an input line with a yellow circle around it."

"Hang on," Adam surveyed the box, "there are a thousand buttons, lights and gadgets. Got it."

"That's the one you need to disable. Now, Mitch, you're looking for where the yellow wire joins the blue wire, use the laser to burn through them. Try and slice the yellow cleanly off and avoid the blue. Basically, your laser light has to penetrate an area no wider than a pinhead."

"Right," Mitch said. "OK, go on three."

Mitch and Adam, hanging next to each other, aimed their narrow pen laser beams at their targets.

Stay steady, Mitch concentrated. Breathe out, relax.

Mitch counted it down.

"One, two, three."

Mitch tensed his body. Aiming for accuracy, he used one hand to steady the other, listening to the soft buzz of the lasers in the silence of the room.

Hold on, Mitch felt the ache in his arms. Just a bit longer. He tried to control the shaking and groaned with the effort of keeping steady.

"Done," Mitch breathed out.

"Me too," Adam announced.

"Clear and hold," Samantha called, "both lights have gone to black ... isolating now ..."

Mitch waited for Samantha to do her part. He looked to Adam; they both hung in limbo.

"Done," she confirmed.

Mitch and Adam swung back up and grabbed the ceiling beams, the blood rushing down their bodies. Mitch looked down, the blue beam had disappeared. He lowered his feet to the ground and landing with a soft thud, froze and waited.

"OK, Adam, I think we've done it."

Adam dropped down beside him.

Mitch and Adam headed to the two nearest computers. Mitch looked up as Samantha lowered herself through the ceiling minutes later.

"You alright?" Mitch asked not taking his eyes from the computer.

"Fine," she headed towards another computer terminal. "I'll try and get you your external access so you can log into this system from outside the building."

"Great. Thanks, Sam."

Adam and Mitch waited while the computer went through its processes. They were prompted for a password.

"Password?" Adam asked.

Mitch fished a list out of his vest. He read the first one on the list.

"Try Mastermind."

The computer rejected the entry.

"No go," Adam reported.

"Try MM3," Mitch suggested reading from the list.

They both tapped it in and gained instant entry. Adam dropped back in his seat.

"That was too easy. Who's that stupid?"

Mitch shrugged. "Reverse psychology, maybe. I'll get the Mastermind files. Can you get anything financial?"

"Done," Adam agreed.

Mitch put a memory stick in the USB port and downloaded the files listed in the Mastermind folders.

They worked silently. Mitch glanced up occasionally, keeping his ear tuned for any noise.

"Almost done. Where are you at, Adam?" Mitch asked.

"Right behind you."

"Sam?" Mitch enquired.

"I think I've done it," she said.

They heard the lift doors open.

"Shit," Mitch whispered. "Adam, Sam, log out, get up there now!" He indicated the ceiling.

Adam pulled his memory stick from the computer and turned it off. Samantha logged out.

"They're going to notice the blue screens ... they should be black in standby mode," she panicked.

"Doesn't matter, keep going." Mitch rose and closed the system.

"Quick," Adam called to Samantha.

She stuck the memory stick in her vest and running towards him, leapt straight into his cupped hands and he pushed her up into the ceiling frame.

"No time, Adam," Mitch hissed. "Drop!"

Mitch could hear numbers being keyed on the pad outside the door as Adam dropped to the floor beside him.

That keypad sequence was supposed to cut the security. Please don't let it somehow turn the blue sensor back on again, Mitch prayed.

"Sam, cover!"

He saw her slide the ceiling tile back in place.

Mitch glanced up at the door from where he and Adam hid below desk level. He saw the door open and the legs of someone enter the room. The lights came on.

―――

Mitch moved to get a better view.

It's a kid ... can't be more than eighteen. He watched the kid with a spiky hairdo, oversized jeans and a sweatshirt with hood, pull out an iPod, ram the earplugs into his ears and drop into a chair at one of the computers closest to the door. The kid started the computer up, pulling a memory stick from his pocket and putting it in. He sang along to the iPod.

Mitch and Adam exchanged looks. Mitch shook his head and looked at his wristwatch.

Nine p.m. Thank God we're ahead of schedule, he thought and started to calculate backwards – according to Sam, the system goes into backup mode from midnight. Cleaners in from ten p.m. Ideally, I'd like to be gone by ten p.m. if possible – or worst-case scenario, dodge the cleaners and be out by midnight. If we stick with the first scenario, we have one hour to get out of here.

Mitch heard a machine whir nearby.

The printer!

Rising, the kid started around the desks towards them. The two men scuttled along the floor on all fours, Mitch followed Adam.

Go back the same way kid. We're toast if this kid does a 360.

The kid grabbed the printout from the computer and returned to the desk the same way. Mitch gave a silent prayer of thanks; he didn't want any casualties.

The kid sat back down again. Mitch and Adam made themselves comfortable.

Anthony Jenkins tapped on the keyboard in beat to the music from his iPod.

"That's it," he said out loud. "Log off and Anthony has left the building," he announced in a low, monotone voice followed by an impersonation of a crowd roar. He grabbed the mouse – then froze.

Hey! This system was last accessed at eight tonight. That's only twenty minutes ago. He looked around. *Who was here at eight?* He keyed in a number sequence. *MM3. What's that? I can't access it without a password. Hang on, it's linked to another site.* He hit the link.

Anthony's eyes lit up. *Mastermind. Haven't played this one before.* He hit on a few links, reading information on the site. *Cool! Should I report someone was in here or let it go? Probably all cool, they must have had an access card to get in here ... but I could really use the attention for that senior programmer's job coming up. If I had a bit of profile ... you never know,* he thought.

He pulled his memory stick free, logged out and stood up.

I'll mention it to security; get some good kudos happening.

He headed to the door, glanced around the room and killed the lights, closing the door behind him. Mitch heard him enter numbers into the security pad on the outside of the door.

———

"Adam!" Mitch whispered. "The numbers he's keying in might allow the mainframe to turn the motion sensor back on."

Adam tensed. "Shit!"

"Get up on the counter!"

The two men jumped onto the counter.

As the kid finished entering the numbers on the outdoor pad, blue beams flicked around the perimeters of the room. Mitch and Adam sat perched three feet above the sensor.

"Close call!" Adam exclaimed.

———

Anthony Jenkins caught the lift to the first floor and found the security guard.

Solid white dude! Anthony thought as he approached, taking in the bulging arms and square body. Anthony mentioned MM3 and the security guard suggested he waited while he made a call.

That's when Anthony should have run.

"Bloody hell," Adam swore. "Stupid kid."

Mitch was thinking. "OK, we'll have to take a running jump for the ceiling. Sam, are you up there?"

Samantha pulled open the ceiling tile. She saw the blue light around the perimeter of the room.

"Shit!" she exclaimed.

"Doesn't matter," Mitch said, "we've got what we need from this room."

"It does matter!" Samantha said alarmed. "If this room is back on, then it needs to be turned back on simultaneously at the main box. Or else, in five minutes it's going to register as a malfunction and sound the alarm."

"Move!" Mitch ordered her.

He watched her scurry out of sight on the steel beams in the ceiling over to the fire stairs to get one floor up.

"How much time did we lose?" Mitch turned to Adam.

"At least a minute and a half."

"Sam," Mitch spoke into his headset. "You've got about three minutes thirty seconds left. What can we do?"

"Nothing. Get out of there just in case."

Mitch looked at the ground and up at the open part of the ceiling.

"Twelve feet roughly in length from the counter and over seven feet up," he said thinking aloud. "We'll have to run off the end of the counter and hope for the best."

"We could try leaping from here to the next desk," Adam suggested.

"It's not much closer."

"True."

Mitch looked at his watch. "Sam, two minutes thirty seconds. Where are you?" He could hear her puffing through his head set.

"I'm on the ninth now. It's going to be close."

Mitch paced along the counter bench. He turned to Adam. "We've got about fourteen feet of counter as runway. Let's get to it."

Adam pushed everything to the side. Mitch, standing at the edge of the counter with the roof opening in view, inhaled.

"Here goes."

He took four huge strides along the counter and leapt from the edge, projecting himself upwards and forward. He was inches from the opening. Stretching full length, he gripped the metal edge with one hand, raising the other to secure himself. He hung there for a second, relieved.

"One minute fifty," he called for Samantha's benefit, pulling himself up into the ceiling. "Adam, go for it."

Adam went to the end of the counter.

"Sprinting was never my thing, I'm more of a cross-country guy," he said taking off from the end of the counter. Copying Mitch he took a huge leap. Mitch moved out of the entrance to allow him to grip. But he didn't. He came short by a few inches.

With lightning-fast reflexes, Mitch reached down and grabbed Adam's arm. Adam jolted to a stop, pulling his feet up, short of the blue light. Mitch groaned as the impact put his shoulder out. Adam reached past him, grabbed the edge and pulled himself up.

Adam thumped Mitch's shoulder. "That help?"

No, thanks," Mitch gritted his teeth.

"One minute ten, Sam. How you going?" Mitch's voice broke into her concentration.

"I'm nearly there … getting into place," she lowered herself next to the system. "Looks like everything's still in order, but the eighth floor is blinking, registering as on."

"One minute," Mitch's countdown continued.

"I'm there now … just finding the right wires."

"Fifty seconds."

"Got them … damn," she fumbled. "Mitch, get out of there, we're not going to make it."

"It's OK, Sam," Mitch spoke calmly through her headset. "Slow down ... breathe ... do a step on each of my counts."

"But ..."

"Sam," he snapped, "on my count."

She slowed her breathing to correspond with his words.

"OK," she concentrated, "ready."

Mitch counted her back.

"Twenty-five ... twenty-four ..."

Separating the two wires that she previously disconnected, Samantha prepared them, lining them up to reconnect at exactly the same time.

"Fifteen ... fourteen ..."

Samantha took a step on each count; touching the wires, connecting the wires, applying equal pressure at the same time.

"Five ..."

"All clear," she sighed.

"Well done," Mitch commended her.

Samantha closed her eyes and took a deep breath. She jumped to full alert as alarms began to wail throughout the building.

"What the ...?" she exclaimed.

———

Hours had passed—five, six, maybe more—Nick had lost count on how long they had been at Broad Arrow. He looked out into the hallway, seeing Ellen bound to a chair in the front office. Colby moved in again, blocking his view, standing in front of him.

He felt another hit and saw the ground rising to meet him.

"I think he needs some more persuasion," Colby said to Westwood, flexing his fist.

"You could be right," Westwood nodded.

"Just don't kill him," Nick heard Daniel say. "Have your fun, but keep him conscious."

Nick could see the blackness; he began to drift towards it. He heard Westwood speaking again.

"I think he needs higher stakes. Let's work the girl over."

Nick struggled to sit up. He blinked trying to focus on the men.

"Thought that might work. Welcome back, sunshine," Westwood grinned.

I have to tell them something, Nick panicked. And get help. He remembered the tracker and struggled with the ropes binding his hands. Getting enough movement in his wrist, he pushed in the small button on the side of his watch.

Has Ellen already sent a signal?

Please Mitch, get that message and send help.

31

The alarms rang all around them. Mitch dropped the ceiling tile back in place.

"Sam, what's going on?"

"I don't know," her voice answered over his intercom.

"Which level has triggered the alarm?" Mitch asked.

"It's the fourth floor."

"OK, sit tight."

"What are we going to do?" she asked.

"Nothing, yet," Mitch turned to Adam. "Any experience in shut-down mode? What happens next?"

"In these buildings, all emergency doors are locked, all exits and windows sealed."

"For how long?"

"Until the code is put in and the room is secured again," he answered.

"Sure?"

"Positive. They've had a few security scares in recent times here and other buildings in the area."

Mitch sighed. "We might be here for the long haul."

A light flashed on his watch. Mitch looked directly at it.

Nick's tracker.

"Oh, God no," he said alarmed.

"Trouble?" Adam asked.

"More of the same," Mitch answered. "Alarms ringing on two fronts now." He grabbed for his phone and called John.

It's one p.m. in Eureka, that'll make it four p.m. in D.C.

John answered on the first ring. "I've got it," he said straight off.

"We need to get someone in there fast, John. Can you get a chopper?"

"Done. There is a chopper leaving from Elko now; it's less than eighty miles to Broad Arrow. It'll be there in no time. We'll get some guys around the perimeter and check out the situation."

"They're not going to question Nick … it's going to happen fast. Are they above ground?"

"Can't tell from the signal. What the hell is going on there, I can hardly hear you?"

"We're in the ceiling of Lawrence's building waiting for the alarms to …"

Silence. The alarms stopped and Mitch dropped his voice.

"… go off."

"What happened?"

"We're waiting to find out."

"Are you going to be able to get out of there?"

"Yeah, no drama. Can you call me back ASAP? John, don't let them …"

"As soon as I know something," John hung up.

Mitch ran his hand over his face.

A great night's work. Two agents in trouble thousands of miles away, and three trapped in the ceiling.

He refocused. "Sam, is it all clear on the system panel?"

"Green like a Christmas tree; all's back to normal," she reported.

"Then what's happening on the fourth floor?" Adam said.

"Let's check it out." Mitch led the way.

———

Samantha stayed on the ninth floor, putting bugs in place around the ceiling of Lawrence's office and boardroom. Reaching in near the ceiling lights, she attached a small audio device, not noticeable from below. Her hands shook as she attached one at a time.

Don't drop it ... steady ... that's all we need is for one of these to drop into the blue light and set off the alarm again.

She bit her tongue with concentration.

His office is bigger than my whole apartment, she thought. *Bet he's seen some action in here.*

She looked around.

That's enough bugs.

She headed to the eighth floor.

Mitch and Adam made their way down to the fourth floor via the internal fire staircase. Mitch found the manhole and gave Adam a leg up into the ceiling. Adam reached down, pulling Mitch up behind him. They stood motionless, listening. Adam pulled out his phone and hit sensor. He waited for the reading.

"No movement in the room below, but there is heat in one corner. Something, someone's sitting there," Adam whispered. "It's not moving, but it's set off the alarms somehow."

"What's located on the fourth floor?" Mitch asked.

Adam pulled out a layout of Lawrence's building from his vest.

"Fourth floor is admin and staff facilities, gym, sauna – nice."

"Nothing better than sweating with your colleagues," Mitch said.

"Photocopy room, binding room, lunchroom, that's about it," Adam concluded.

Mitch thought for a moment. Then glanced at his watch. "We've got thirty minutes left."

"It's probably that same kid photocopying something," Adam shrugged.

"Yeah, we've got what we came for, let's leave it. Agree?"

"Agree."

Mitch whispered into his headset. "Sam, where are you?"

"On the eighth floor. I had one left so thought I'd bug the computer systems room for good measure."

"Good thinking. How much longer do you need?"

"Hang on ... I'm putting it in place now."

Mitch waited.

"There!" Her voice came back on line. "I've done two in Lawrence's office, two in the boardroom and one on the eighth floor. That should do us. They're all recording to my laptop, as we speak."

"Great work, Sam. Move out. We'll meet you where we came in. Wait for us."

"Check that."

Adam opened the manhole and began to lower himself back down into the stairwell.

"Just give me a minute," Mitch said. He went through a mental checklist in his mind. A minute later he joined Adam. "OK, we're done. Let's get out of here."

———

Daniel heard it in the distance; the sound of a chopper. He saw Nick glance towards the hangar doors.

"What the hell is going on?" he roared shaking Nick.

Nick spat out a mouthful of blood and saliva. "How do I know?" he slurred.

"We've got to hide them," Daniel turned to Colby and Westwood.

The two men moved in, dragging Nick to his feet. Daniel followed as they pushed Nick forward down the hallway. Westwood and Colby shoved him down onto a seat next to Ellen.

"Oh, my God! What have you done to him?" She gasped.

"Shut up or you'll go the same way," Westwood sneered.

"Let's finish them off and dump them," Colby addressed Daniel.

"We can't. I need to talk to Lawrence first."

"What for? He said to clean it up," Colby snarled.

"Listen Einstein, there were two pilots. We've got one. I may need to keep these two for bartering. I've got my orders, you've got yours, so play the game." Daniel looked up as the sound of the chopper drew closer. "Here's the plan. Westwood, you and I will take care of these two, hide them somewhere in the mines – there is no shortage of tunnels below. Colby, you guard the perimeter, shoot whatever you like. Warn them if they come in, the girl dies first, followed by him," he nodded towards Nick.

"Then?" Colby asked. "We can't risk any connection to Lawrence."

Daniel shook his head. "Don't panic, I'll speak with him. Let's deal with it one step at a time."

Westwood hauled Nick and Ellen to their feet and marched them towards the door leading to the tunnels.

Daniel followed behind.

Another bloody mess to explain, he ground his teeth.

———

Colby ran towards the front entrance of the Broad Arrow site, two automatic rifles at the ready. He closed the iron gates in front of him and set himself up beside a barrier near the gate. He watched as the chopper landed and four combat-dressed figures scuttled to the perimeters.

———

"Hurry up," Westwood grunted as he pushed Nick down the stairs that lead to the mine.

Nick struggled to get his footing, bumping into Ellen in front of him. He could hear her breathing faster as they went underground.

This is not good. Who's in the chopper and what the hell are they doing? He caught Ellen's eye and held her gaze.

"It's OK, Ellie," he whispered.

"Keep moving." Daniel ordered turning the torch onto the two captives.

Nick counted the number of steps they walked until they came to an underground concrete room with benches, a former underground lunchroom for the miners. Westwood pushed Nick down on a bench, Ellen dropped down beside him. The room was lit only by the glow from the torch.

"This'll do," Westwood said, checking the ties around their hands. He grabbed a torch from his belt.

"I'm going up to help Colby."

Daniel nodded and shone his torch in Nick's eyes.

"Might be a good time to talk, Nicholas," he said. "Who was this other pilot friend of yours and where is he now?"

Nick glared at Daniel. *Arrogant little prick.*

"Nothing to say?"

"I thought you knew everything," Nick watched him.

Daniel looked over at Ellen. Nick followed his gaze; she was white as a sheet and breathing fast.

"What if I take your girlfriend here for a walk further down into the tunnels. Think she'd like to sit somewhere in the dark in a closed in part of the mine all by herself?"

"Nick!" Ellen gasped.

"Ellie, it's OK, close your eyes and breathe deeply," he coached.

"Yeah, it's OK, Ellie," Daniel mimicked "Look at your boyfriend here, covered in blood, had the crap beaten out of him – but don't worry, we're really nice guys."

Nick glared at Daniel. He bit his tongue for Ellen's sake.

You couldn't beat the shit out of anyone. Wouldn't want to damage that expensive designer suit. Forget it ... don't get him angry, he'll take it out on Ellie. Stay calm.

"Well?" Daniel said above Ellen's breathing.

"I'll tell you if you get her out of here."

"You'll tell me and I'll leave her with you. That's as good as it gets."

Nick turned back to Ellen who was breathing in shallow gasps.

"OK," he said. "Ellie, look at me, these tunnels go for miles and miles. There is so much space and air in here that we won't run out."

He saw Ellen's eyes were huge as she stared at him.

"Breathe with me," he instructed her.

"You can play doctors and nurses later. Who's the other pilot and where is he?" Daniel demanded.

"He's a friend of mine, totally trustworthy. Been flying for years and doesn't know a thing about your stupid game," Nick said through gritted teeth.

"Name?" Daniel kept the torch shining in Nick's eyes.

He squinted. *Hell, what was his name? The alias Mitch used?*

"Name?" Daniel pushed.

Remembering in a rush he spat out the name.

"John Maxfield." Dad's friend.

"And where is Maxfield now?" Daniel asked.

"He's in D.C. on a job," Nick felt Ellen looking at him. Can't give away the London connection.

"On a job or cleared out to save his ass?"

"From what?" Nick asked. "I've told you we didn't come away with anything. He was a hired hand paid to do the run and he got paid for delivering his end of the deal."

"How did he get paid? Wasn't Johan arrested before the job was done?" Daniel smirked.

Shit! Forgot about that, slipped again. Think!

"I paid him his usual hourly fee in advance," Nick announced.

"Well, he's got twenty-four hours to get himself back here. We'll do a bit of trading," he said looking at Ellen. "Him for her. And if that doesn't work, there is always your life." Daniel pulled out his phone. "Good, still got some reception in this hell hole."

"He's not going to drop a job to come back to Nevada."

"He had better if he's any sort of friend. Phone number?" Daniel demanded.

Shit, Nick thought. I don't know Mitch's number.

"It's ... uh, it's programmed into my phone, I don't know it off the top of my head."

Daniel eyes narrowed, then putting his own phone away, he patted Nick down, finding his phone. Daniel began to scroll through the address book looking for the name John Maxfield. Nick looked at Ellen; the only John in his phone book was John Windsor.

Thank God I put it in there with no surname. Nick swallowed.

"John! I assume that's your John Maxfield?" Daniel flashed the screen at Nick for confirmation.

"That's it."

Daniel rang the number, pressing the phone to Nick's ear.

"Don't try anything stupid Nicholas; after all, it won't be your life at stake."

John answered. "Nick, we got your tracker call and sent reinforcements in. Have they arrived?"

"John, uh, it's Nicholas Everett here," he began.

"OK, Nick, tell me what you can."

"I know you've taken a job there, but I need you back here. The person who hired us wants the two original pilots back for another job urgently and, trust me, it will be worth your while – much more lucrative than your current job."

"Are either of you hurt?" John asked.

"No. I wouldn't ask it of you, but he really wants the two original pilots and you would be doing me a huge favor."

"How much time do we have?" John asked.

"In the next 24 hours. Can you pull out of that job? You're costs will be covered and more," he stressed again.

Daniel interrupted. "Tell your friend, we have someone who can identify him, so it must be him."

Nick glared at him.

Who? Is he bluffing? He ran through potential witnesses in his head.

"I heard," John said. "Does he?"

"Ah, it must be you," Nick assured John. "Sorry, matter of life and death – he won't accept anyone else. You know, top security stuff ..."

"Where's Ellen?"

"I'll be here. I'm staying with a friend, she'll head off when you arrive and we'll get to work," he said.

"Stall them, Nick, I'll have to get Mitch back," John said. "Hang in there, I'm onto it."

"Thanks, John; I owe you."

Daniel removed the phone from Nick's ear and hung up.

"Well done, Nicholas, very well done." Daniel turned and walked out, taking the torch with him. At the door he looked back. "Make yourselves comfortable, you'll be staying overnight."

Nick and Ellen sat in total darkness. Total pitch-black darkness. Nick was thinking.

Who could identify us? Ah, I know! The security guard, Luis Gamboa. He led Mitch to the plane. Could they find Gamboa?

"I hope John doesn't risk sending someone in Mitch's place," Ellen said between breaths. "Poor Mitch, flying all the way back again."

"He'll be pissed."

They sat in silence. Nick could smell the dirt around them. He heard Ellen draw in an enormous breath. He moved closer to her.

"I feel blind. It's so dark my eyes can't adjust to it," she said.

"Ellie, listen to me. Are you listening?"

"Yes," she said with labored breath.

"Think this through ... the chopper's here because I hit the tracker. Mitch and John know we're in trouble. There are reinforcements outside."

"I know, but they won't move in unless ordered to. Who's giving that order? And Daniel wants Mitch, and he's on the other side of the world. It's going to take longer than we've got."

"John's getting him back; it's going to be OK. Daniel will wait ... he's got no choice."

"Uh-huh," she breathed. "But he doesn't have to keep us both alive."

Nick swallowed.

"Nick, I'm sorry ..."

"It's my fault, not yours. I'm an idiot, I wasn't supposed to recognize him."

"It wouldn't have made any difference," Ellen gasped. "Even if you had ignored him, he wouldn't have waited until morning."

"Maybe. If I'd given up smoking I wouldn't have been out there," he joked. Ellen drew another round of short, sharp breaths.

Just what I need; she's going to pass out on me here, Nick thought feeling her head on his shoulder. He moved down, leaning back further against the wall to support her weight.

It's going to be a long, indistinguishable day and night. Hurry up, Mitch.

32

Andrew Kenny, Chief of Staff for Lawrence Hackett's Globalnet company, looked at his pager.

"Code One," he muttered. He rang Lawrence and arranged to meet him at the office. Twenty minutes later Andrew walked in. He saw the security guard waiting.

"What's the Code One?"

"Intruder into our security systems," the guard answered.

"The game?"

"Yes. Detained a kid; he's one of our programmers, not the intruder. It gets worse ... he discovered an intrusion, went in to check it out and then reported it."

Andrew nodded. "Call the head of I.T. in now. Get him working on finding out who's entered the system."

The guard nodded. "The kid, Anthony Jenkins is his name, doesn't know what he's done wrong except set off the fourth floor alarm. I've detained him in the staff room. He's crying for his mummy."

Andrew smirked. He spotted Lawrence coming out of the first floor lift and joined him, filling him in as they followed the guard into the lift. They entered the fourth floor staff room. Anthony sat with his hands bound in front of him, his mouth taped, his eyes huge from shock and red from crying.

Andrew looked down at the security report he had been handed. "Anthony," he said. "Let's chat."

The guard walked behind Anthony's chair and pulled the tape from his mouth. Anthony's eyes darted around the room.

"You found something of interest?" Andrew asked.

"Yes ... no ... I don't know, sir. I thought you should know about it," he said.

"Let's take a stroll to the eighth floor shall we?" Lawrence suggested.

The security guard nodded and grabbed Anthony's arm, pulling him out of the chair and walking him in front. Lawrence and Andrew entered the lifts without speaking. Anthony could barely walk.

"Mr. Andrew, I didn't ..."

"Shut up," the guard ordered.

They exited on the eighth floor. The guard put a code into the pad near the door to the I.T. room and the blue motion sensor went off. He pushed Anthony in. Andrew and Lawrence followed.

"Which computer?" Andrew asked Anthony.

"This one, sir," Anthony indicated with a nod.

The guard sat Anthony down in front of the screen, keeping his hand on Anthony's shoulder.

Andrew could see Anthony shaking. "So what were you doing here?" he continued questioning while Lawrence observed.

"I came in to make a copy of a web page I'd been designing for one of our clients; I wanted to do some work on it at home because I got this new software package that has ..."

Andrew cut him off. "I get the point. So, when did you see the file marked MM3?"

"I logged out and as I did, I noticed the computer had been logged into about thirty minutes before me and whoever was on it, had accessed that file, the MM3 one with a link to a game. I didn't open the file, but the game was a site called Mastermind. I figured, you know with hackers and everything today, I thought I should mention it."

Lawrence spoke at last. "Impressive, Anthony. Your loyalty is appreciated." Anthony's head spun to look at him.

"Do you know what MM3 is?" Lawrence asked.

"No, sir. I haven't heard of it."

Andrew looked towards Lawrence who nodded once, turned and walked out of the room. Andrew said a few words to the guard.

"Mr. Lawrence!" Anthony yelled after him.

The guard stuck the tape back over Anthony's mouth.

"You did the right thing, Anthony," Andrew said, "unfortunately, you know about it now."

He watched as Anthony shook his head and tried to yell through the gag, losing control of his bladder as a stream of yellow urine ran down the leg of his jeans. Andrew stood by as the guard went to the cupboard and removed two large black plastic bags. The guard grabbed Anthony's arm, lifting him out of the chair. He pulled Anthony to the front of the room and pushed him down on top of one of the bags.

Andrew watched, fascinated, as Anthony's eyes looked for some way out, his body whimpering and shaking. As the guard drew his knife, Andrew kept watching as Anthony's eyes became lifeless. The guard closed the bag around him and tied it up with rope at the neck and feet. He pulled a second back over the top and secured it. He hurled it over his shoulder in one easy movement.

"Been a while since I've had to call on my military skills, but they came back like riding a bike," the guard chortled.

Outside the room, Andrew entered the security code. The blue motion sensor came back on.

"I want a full report from I.T., ASAP," he ordered.

"I'll let them know, sir," the guard answered.

Andrew watched as the guard took the body bag away to dispose of it. He removed his phone from his coat pocket and rang his wife.

"Emergency over love, on my way home."

Samantha's microphone in the ceiling recorded it all.

"A good night's work," Adam said arriving back at Mitch and Samantha's hotel room just after ten p.m. "Bugs in, files downloaded."

"I'm exhausted," Samantha said. "Not only did we have an eleven-hour flight, but a week of on-and-off night shifts and an all-nighter in Nevada. I feel like I'm in slow motion."

Mitch glanced at his watch and began to pace. "Test the equipment, Sam, will you? See if the bugs work."

He saw her give him an exasperated look.

"What?" he asked.

"You haven't heard a word I said."

"Sorry, I was thinking. What did you say?"

"Doesn't matter. I'll test the bugs," she dropped down on the sofa and opened her laptop.

Mitch continued to pace. *Why hasn't John called back? Why has Nick got the tracker on?* He sat down and watched over Adam's shoulder as he loaded the laptop with the files copied from Lawrence's office.

Adam turned sideways. "You're making me nervous," he joked.

"Good." Mitch grinned.

"Transfers have worked," Adam announced. "Now, we need to go through all the Mastermind material and find out where the missing directors are, and get some evidence to prove Mastermind really exists."

"I hope the data's not too cryptic," Mitch mumbled distracted.

Adam opened the financials. "All here," he reported.

"I can't test the bugs, until the cleaning staff start or some early-birds arrive to get some noise feedback from the receivers in the room," Samantha said taking off the earphones.

Mitch looked over at Samantha, noting she looked drawn; her

eyes were dark from lack of sleep. He sat back exhausted, hitting a low after a tense job.

"Listen," he started, "as much as I'd love to do this right now ..."

"You need to sleep," Adam finished his sentence looking from one agent to the other. "You two hit the sack. I'm going to work here for a bit longer on these files. I'll let myself out and see you in the morning."

"OK," Mitch said. "Sam, go to bed. I've got to try John again." He stood, pacing the room while trying the number.

"I'll wait. I want to hear what John says," Samantha stayed seated.

"Who's this John guy?" Adam asked.

"John Windsor, our Director," Mitch answered. "We've got two other agents working on this same case in Nevada and they've run into a bit of trouble. John's trying to help them."

Mitch frowned as the phone continued to ring out.

Where the hell is he? Why hasn't he called me about Nick and Ellen?

Finally, John answered.

"What's going on?" Mitch said straight up.

"I was about to call you," John said. "We've got a standoff happening. Ellie and Nick are being held hostage somewhere in the mine. Two of Lawrence's heavies are guarding the perimeters and Daniel is inside the joint."

"Great!" Mitch groaned.

"It gets worse," John warned him. "They want to talk trade. They want the second pilot."

"What for? What's the trade?" he asked, knowing the answer.

"The second pilot in return for Ellie."

"For chrissake," Mitch said exhausted. "How did all this happen?"

"I don't know. I haven't been able to speak with Nick in detail. I've had a stinted conversation with him talking trade."

"Gut instinct. I knew it," Mitch mumbled.

"What?" John asked.

"Nothing. Was Daniel there?"

"Yes, he was directing the conversation," John confirmed.

"Right," Mitch pictured the scene. "I should have given them a concrete plan. After the J.J. incident, I was trying not to be so anal and let them be more independent."

"Mitch, anal is good. Stick with your instincts. If they don't like your management style, they can transfer out of your team."

"Hmm. Can you get someone to act as the pilot, John Maxfield?"

"No. Daniel can I.D. you."

"How?"

"I don't know, but Nick sounded sure of it. Who saw you?"

Mitch thought about it.

"Bet it's the guard that worked at the Broad Arrow site. Big Brazilian guy who showed me to the plane. Wasn't he charged?"

"No, he was found to be just an employee at the site. But if he was on the payroll for the job, Daniel had the master file. One call, a promise to make it worth his while ..."

"Yeah, he took me to the hangar, had a good look at me."

"I hate to do this ..."

"It's got to be done," Mitch cut in. "What time?"

"I've got you on a military flight at one in the morning your time from Northolt; it's about six miles north of Heathrow. You'll change planes in Miami."

"Northolt?" Mitch said out loud. Adam nodded.

"I'll be there. Thanks, John." Mitch hung up the phone. He looked at his watch – nearly ten p.m.

"Are they alright?" Samantha asked, alarmed.

"No. They've been taken hostage. I've got to go make a deal."

"Can't someone else negotiate, or are you it for the whole coastline?" Adam asked.

"Someone else did negotiate and I'm offered in exchange for Ellie."

Samantha's eyes widened.

"So, can you both keep going on this until I get back?" Mitch dropped to the sofa.

"Of course," Adam said. "Put your head down for a few hours, and I'll wake you before midnight. I'll drop you at Northolt on my way home."

"That'd be great. Thanks, Adam."

Mitch saw Samantha flash Adam a look.

This'll be interesting, Mitch thought. Sam will want to make it known that she intends to run this show. So will Adam. Should I declare a leader? Nah, stuff it ... too tired. They'll either kill each other or ... we'll see.

33

At eleven p.m., Lawrence Hackett paced in front of the window observing the stillness of the square below.

Why is this year's event going so badly?

He had called an emergency meeting and turned to face his three executives: Alan Peasely, Andrew Kenny and Rishi Patel and the directors whose projects had failed – Phillip Saunders and Richard Sinclair. He counted them off; Daniel Reid and Ian Gare were still in the U.S., Michael Germaine and Brian Davies were out of the country overseeing their Mastermind projects. Lawrence turned to Andrew Kenny.

"Go ahead."

Andrew began. "At eight tonight, someone logged into the mainframe. They logged out at eight fifteen. The area they accessed was MM3."

Several of the directors drew in sharp breaths.

"After eight, one of our employees came in to collect some work and found the computer had been logged into and saw the file MM3 and the game link. He went through to the game link but didn't open the file, or so he said."

"Where is he now?" Rishi Patel asked.

"Disposed of," Lawrence said.

Andrew continued. "According to our systems, no one has physically broken in or entered the premises. No one has set off the alarm with the exception of the fourth floor which we are aware of and it is accounted for."

Phillip Saunders spoke.

"So someone has seen the file – we don't know who, we don't know how. I think we should abort the project now."

Lawrence looked around the room at his directors.

"Opinions?" he asked.

"If we sit tight," the American, Alan Peasely, cut in, "what are the consequences?"

Lawrence nodded at Andrew.

"It could fall into the wrong hands and we'd have to defend ourselves in a court of law," Andrew said. "Or if it's a maverick, we might be blackmailed."

Alan looked at Lawrence. "It's all part of the game; I say we keep the project alive."

Andrew disagreed. "I'm for abort."

Lawrence paced again in front of the window.

"There are two weeks left. How watertight are our accounts?" he asked Andrew.

"Unbreakable. All funds are non-traceable."

Lawrence sat on the edge of the window frame, facing the directors.

"Might be fun to see what they'll do with the information. Better still …" Lawrence rose. "Let's raise the stakes. Let's invite them to play."

"What?" Andrew choked.

"My gut instinct tells me it's an inside job," Lawrence looked around at the directors. "Someone has got in without setting off any alarms and knew what to look for. Let's sit tight until we hear from them. They know how to navigate our system, so I imagine it's only a matter of time. Then, we'll invite them to participate; give us back the information and we'll pay them what they want. What they don't know is they'll need to survive the handover." He smiled.

"Lawrence," Andrew started, "let's think this through ... none of us are skilled at combat or stealth."

"Or surviving jail for that matter," Alan cut in.

"Andrew, Alan, you worry too much. That's why you're good at what you do. We're talking about meeting them for a handover, nothing more. Who's in?" Lawrence looked around the room, his eyes alive with excitement. "I'll make it worth your while. If we pull it off, I'll double your bonuses; if we don't, my lawyers will talk us out of trouble. Come on, it's a win-win situation."

"Lawrence, you need to think about the consequences of this," Andrew started.

Rishi Patel cut in. "I'm in."

Lawrence walked around and put his hand on Rishi's shoulder.

"Excellent. Who else?" he asked with a grin looking around the table.

———

"A 3.4 litre?" Mitch asked, yawning and sliding down in the leather front seat of Adam's Porsche Boxster S.

"Yep, 3.4 litre. Zero to sixty miles an hour in just over five seconds; sport suspension," Adam said with pride.

"Beautiful."

"Yeah. Did you get any sleep?"

"About two hours before you woke me. I feel worse for it."

Adam accelerated, driving the Porsche out of the hotel onto the traffic-free road.

"So," Mitch began, "why the Trans-national Crime Unit, if it's not too personal?"

"Why not?"

"I've seen your record."

"Ah," Adam smiled. "So, you think I'm either on reprimand or having a career crisis."

He glanced at Mitch waiting for a reaction.

"Something like that," Mitch watched London go by from the window.

"It's a bit of both – self-inflicted reprimand and career crisis," Adam sighed. "I was on a mission in Bosnia, my third one and I saw something I shouldn't have seen. So, instead of following orders, I intervened." He looked over at Mitch. "It was one of those moral dilemma situations – you help or you turn a blind eye. I got hauled over the coals for helping. After that, I decided I needed a change to shake things up a bit and given I was born in the States, I decided to apply for the TCU. Now I do intelligence gathering with the occasional deployment instead of the other way around."

Mitch nodded his understanding. "How did that go down with the British office?"

"With my record, they're not real happy that I've changed to the TCU, but they're giving me time out to think about everything. I gather they think I'm on the edge of a breakdown." He smiled at the thought.

"How long have you been in time-out mode?"

"Six months."

"Frustrating," Mitch said. "I can't imagine being desk-bound doing research, with only the occasional deployment throw in."

"It hasn't been easy. They're waiting to see if I'll crack and throw in the TCU, beg for another field assignment."

"Are you planning to crack?" Mitch asked.

He shrugged. "Your mission has given me a bit of excitement … change in routine."

"Our gain," Mitch said.

"Thanks," Adam said.

―――――

Mitch boarded the military plane bound for Miami. He scanned his fellow passengers, some in uniform, some in civvies. One of the airmen approached him.

"Sir, Mr. Windsor wanted me to give you this." He handed over an envelope.

Mitch thanked him, settling into a seat, he opened the envelope to find instructions for the next leg of the flight once he landed in Miami and two Temazepam tablets. Mitch recognized the heavy-duty sleeping pills.

Bless you, John, Mitch smiled.

34

Samantha pulled off her sweatshirt and tied it around her waist. Keeping up a steady jogging pace along Fisherman's Walk at six that morning, she scanned other joggers looking out for a face: Lawrence Hackett.

Come on, Lawrence. I know you jog here, show yourself. Samantha thought as she looked out over the water. Glassy. Nice when it's like this. Soon it'll be choppy when the city wakes and the water traffic begins. She inhaled the cold morning air. *I love these tree-lined promenades; just beautiful.* Stopping to stretch and rub her knee, which played up in the colder weather, Samantha heard a voice behind.

"Are you alright?"

She turned to find Lawrence Hackett jogging on the spot in front of her.

Too easy, job half done!

———

Adam Forster used Mitch's key to enter the hotel room. He found Samantha doing sit ups. She filled him in on her encounter.

"Can't believe it was that easy," Samantha exclaimed.

"I can," Adam shook his head. "As soon as he saw your tan and heard the accent, he knew you needed a tour guide. Men, they're all the same."

Samantha laughed.

"Can you borrow a dress for me from your wife, girlfriend or mistress?" she asked, stretching her leg along the counter as she warmed down.

"I'm short on all three," he said, his eyes taking in the long legs. "You're going to have to go shopping."

"Really?" Samantha smiled. "The things I do in the name of duty."

Mitch adjusted his watch as he crossed another time zone. He could still feel the remnants of the sleeping tablets and the effects of sleeping on-and-off during the flight to Miami.

I am now so out of whack that it'll take me a month to sleep normally again, he thought.

He followed the crew and a handful of passengers out of the plane at the Homestead Air Reserve Base in Miami, bracing as the cold air hit him. He looked at the note from John with his instructions, and looked around for a second military plane. He saw it in the distance and increased his pace, grabbing his phone to make a quick call while walking. John answered on the first ring despite the hour.

"Mitch!"

"Sorry, John, I know it's early, but I guessed you'd be up."

"I am. Where are you?"

"Just landed in Miami, about to board the next leg. Any news?" Mitch asked.

"I've spoken with Nick, Daniel controlled the call. I confirmed what time I was arriving, pretending to be you of course."

"OK, thanks."

"Call me when you get to Vegas."

Mitch hung up and boarded the plane.

Only five hours now to Vegas. Hang in there, Ellie and Nick.

At Broad Arrow, Nick and Ellen waited. They were given some water and left again in the pitch black.

"Is it day or night?" Ellen asked.

"Impossible to say," Nick answered.

"Where are you, Mitch?"

"Hang in there, Ellie, he'll come."

Five hours later, adjusting his watch again, this time to eight a.m. local time, Mitch stumbled from the plane at Nellis Air Force Base in Las Vegas. Thanking the crew for the lift and pulling his jacket around him, Mitch pulled out his phone to call John for the arrangements to Broad Arrow.

"John, me again," he announced.

"You've landed?"

"Yep."

"How are you feeling?"

"OK."

"You sound terrible. Are you up for this?"

Mitch heard the concern in John's voice.

"I'm fine," he cleared his throat and started walking faster, waking his body up. "So, how do I get to Broad Arrow?"

"OK, there is a chopper waiting for you somewhere there," John informed him.

Mitch looked around. "Got it, thanks, John."

"We've got five men on the perimeter. They're waiting for your orders. Good luck and call me as soon as you can."

Mitch checked his watch; it was just after four in the afternoon in London. He dialed Samantha.

Nick felt Ellen waking.

"It's OK, Ellie," he said before she had a chance to panic. "I'm here."

"Oh, my God," she took shallow breaths. "Are we going to get out of here? It's so dark I feel like I've been buried alive."

"Of course we're going to get out of here. Our guys are outside now," Nick said.

"Nick, I can't stand it …" he heard her breathing quicken.

"I think we should start moving," Nick suggested.

"What? You're kidding?" Her words came in bursts. "It's pitch black … we could fall down a mine shaft … or anything."

"It's just tunnels. If we head up …"

"How do we know if we are heading up?"

"Because you're going to reach into my vest and get the penlight."

Ellen stopped. "Yes, good idea. Can't we find something to cut the ties with?"

"That'll take too long. Let's move first, hide, and cut later. Stay where you are, I'll come closer to you," Nick said. He stood in the dark, swaying. "It's hard to stay balanced in blackness. OK, I'm going to drop to my knees and try and align my chest with your hands." He started to move to his knees. "Now, my vest should be at the same level as your hands; if you turn slightly, you should be able to feel it."

He felt her tracing the inside of his vest and pulling out a thin object.

"Got it." Nothing happened.

"Shit! I think that's a pen."

"OK," Nick coached her. "Try again."

He felt her work her way along the vest with her fingers. She pulled out another pen-like shape and the light came on.

They both gave a small cry. Ellen smiled at him with relief.

"Nice to see you, Ellie. How you doing?"

"OK," she smiled. "Glad we're at least here together."

"You should be," he teased. "It's not every girl I take on dates down dark mines, you know."

Ellen laughed. "Next time, can we just go out to dinner?"

"Nah, everyone does that."

"I think we should get the other penlight," Ellen suggested. "We won't turn it on until we need it, but let's be prepared."

"OK," Nick said, "but that means I'm delving into your vest; if I touch anything I shouldn't ..."

"I'll kill you later."

"Fair deal. At least we can see this time." He found the penlight easily and pushed it into the back pocket of his jeans.

"There is one more thing," Nick said. "Can you reach into my top pocket and grab my cigarettes?"

"You're not going to smoke in here?"

"No," he rolled his eyes, "I'm going to leave a trail, like breadcrumbs. Grab the box from my shirt pocket and hang on to them. I'll turn around and grab them from you."

"Won't Daniel notice?"

"I'm not going to leave them every few feet. He won't notice, but Mitch will," Nick assured her.

She found the cigarettes. Nick turned and she pushed them into his back pocket, near his tied hands. Leaning over, he took the penlight from Ellen's hands in between his teeth.

"Let's go," he mumbled, leading the way. "Stay close."

"Don't lose me."

"I won't."

Nick could just reach the cigarettes and breaking one in thirds, he dropped pieces along the way.

———

As he spoke to Samantha on the phone, Mitch walked across the tarmac to the waiting chopper.

"Three hundred pounds!" Mitch exclaimed. "Sam, that's over five hundred dollars."

"Do you want me to look the part or not?" she whined. "It's not like there's a lot of choice, and the shops here are expensive. Anyway, that includes shoes."

"Oh, good. That makes me feel much better. Couldn't Adam get you a dress from his harem?"

"Apparently not. Men! I swear you wouldn't care if I showed up in a paper bag."

"I think you would look great in a paper bag and it would be a lot cheaper, not to mention recyclable. That's a whack of my budget just gone out the window."

"I can take it back."

"Forget it; give me the bill when I get back."

"Thanks, Dad," she teased.

"Don't push it. Now, tonight, make sure Adam's watching your back the whole time while you're with Lawrence."

"Already organized."

"And let Lawrence pay, for chrissake! Don't be a feminist for once – remember I'm on a budget and he's loaded," Mitch ordered.

"Yes, sir!"

"What are you doing now?"

"We're working through the material. We think there are still agents in four countries. And we're going to listen to all the tapes we've recorded from the rooms."

"OK. Now listen, Sam, I don't know when I'm going to get out of this one, so if you need more help, John can take care of it. Are we on speaker phone?"

"No."

"Good, be careful with Adam. He's obviously skilled but he's a bit edgy."

"Did he tell you something?"

"Nothing much, he's fine. Just don't test him."

Mitch arrived at the chopper.

"I've got to go. Are you going to be alright?"

"Mitch, don't worry. Everything that could go wrong, probably already has. We'll be fine."

"How reassuring, thanks. Good job getting the date," Mitch gave the pilot a nod as he climbed on board.

"And Mitch ..." he heard Samantha's serious tone.

"Yeah?"

"Please, please be careful," she begged, "and call me as soon as all three of you are clear."

"Sure. Speak to you soon."

Mitch hung up and muttered, "Five hundred dollars on a dress."

He felt the pilot looking at him.

"Girl trouble, buddy?"

"She just spent five hundred dollars on a dress and pair of shoes!"

"That's nothing. My girl can spend that on the shoes alone."

Mitch took a deep breath. *Right, focus,* he told himself. *I've got twenty minutes to get fired up and be ready to take on Daniel and his on-the-ground team. Got to think this through.*

"Man, what does it take to get some action around here?" Colby muttered, as he lay flat on his stomach, gun loaded and ready. *Twenty-four hours stuffing around ... these clowns in camouflage camping outside the gate must be waiting on instructions. No one's moved for hours.* He turned at the sound of a chopper coming and watched it land some distance from the site.

Some fresh blood. Must be a change of shift, he thought. He counted four men in the chopper. Four in, four out? Here's my chance, if I can get a clean shot of them as they swap shifts, I'll be a happy man.

Rising, he aimed at one of the camouflaged men alighting from the chopper. He pulled the trigger and waited as the soldier fell to the ground at the sound of gunfire. The others followed, snaking along on their bellies.

Well trained, he thought, watching them split apart and cover the perimeters. The chopper rose leaving all eight on site.

Colby saw movement in his peripheral vision. He fired another round – then came the intense pain.

God! I've been hit. He pulled his shirt up, off the burning skin on his chest. Collapsing, gasping on the ground, he choked as the blood pooled in his throat.

―――

Daniel watched from inside the office. He saw Colby fall into the grass, a spurt of blood rising on impact of the bullet. He watched as Westwood came out fighting from near the tunnel and surrendered, raising his arms in the air, when he saw eight men around the perimeters.

"These are supposed to be Lawrence's best men? Bloody hopeless!" he muttered.

Daniel moved out of sight, inside the building. He spotted an armed solider near the gate, edging his way closer toward the administration building.

"Don't come any closer," Daniel yelled, bluffing. "The mine's wired, I have the detonator here. You've got no chance of finding anyone alive if you try anything, I'll blow it up. So back off! I'm not negotiating until you produce the pilot."

Daniel waited. It was quiet inside and out. Nobody moved.

35

If I was getting frequent flyer points, I could send a small nation on holiday by now, Mitch thought. He felt his blood pressure rise at the same time as the chopper began to ascend. He knew there was no reason for Daniel to keep Nick and Ellie alive once he was identified.

So, how am I going to do this? There are three of them and our guys are all on the perimeter. He stared out the window, not seeing anything.

Mitch's phone vibrated. Charlotte's name came on the screen.

"Hi, are you OK?" he answered.

"Fine, why wouldn't I be?"

"I don't know. Sorry, nearly everyone I know is in some kind of shit at the moment!"

He heard Charlotte laugh, thinking he was joking.

"No, all's well. I've taken the day off to catch up on a few things and thought I would try my luck and call you. It's quiet around here without you."

Mitch felt his stomach lurch.

"I miss you," he said. *Shit! Is it too soon to say that? I'm so tired, it just came out! Shit, shit, shit! I'm an idiot.*

"Really?" she sounded pleased. "Good. What's that noise?"

"I'm in a chopper."

"Where are you?"

"In the air," he teased. "Where are you?"

"In bed with my paperwork," she answered.

"At eleven in the morning?"

"See, you go away and the rot sets in. Hey, you knew it was eleven in the morning ... that means you're on the same time zone or you calculate quickly."

Mitch laughed. "Ah, you should have been a detective instead of a psychiatrist."

"Hmm, OK don't tell me then. Hang on, Mitch, there is someone at the door, I won't be a sec."

Mitch's phone beeped. He scrambled around in his utility vest for the spare battery.

"Hey, Charlie ..."

She wasn't listening.

Where the hell is it? He pushed gear in his bag aside.

He heard her greet someone in the background. A male voice.

"Mitch, sorry ... everything always happens at once. Listen I've got to go," she continued, "When are you coming home?"

Mitch's phone gave him a series of warning beeps.

"I don't know. Listen, Charlie, my phone's about to die ..."

Mitch heard the sound of silence.

Damn!

He dug around, finding the battery and swapped them over.

She was home with someone. I hope it's not Lachlan. If he's there ... then ...

I wish she hadn't called now; I've got enough crap on my plate without running through the scenario of who's in her room.

He felt the chopper making its descent.

I'll call her later. If Lachlan's there ... no, it's probably someone else, someone from her work, he thought it through. Who? I'm away too much, that's the problem, and she'll go back to him because he's around.

Focus!

The chopper touched down with a light bump and with a wave of thanks, Mitch grabbed his bag from behind the seat, jumped out and cleared the area. A cloud of dust and leaves engulfed him as the chopper moved away. A glance at his watch told him it was eight-fifteen. He ducked down low and scanned the area to see what movement he could make out at the site entrance.

Great! I can't concentrate now. He reached for his phone again. *I'll call her back, check out who's there and then I can focus on the job ahead.* He dialed Charlotte's number and got the voice mail.

Could anything else go wrong?

The phone vibrated. Not reading the screen, he answered it, expecting Charlotte's voice.

"Where are you?" John asked.

"I'm near the front gates of Broad Arrow," Mitch snapped.

"You sound angry. What's wrong?"

"Every goddamned thing at the moment!"

"Mitch, calm down."

"Telling me to calm down, John, just makes me angrier!" Mitch clenched his jaw.

He heard the silence on the line.

"I've gotta go. I'll call you later."

"Mitch, wait."

"What?" he barked.

"Listen to me. Get your head in order; you're tired and acting on a short fuse. I don't want you going in there until you've calmed down. Sit tight for five minutes."

"John, I don't have five minutes. I've got all this shit going down, I've got to go!"

"Mitchell, wait! Talk to me here … what's going on?"

"Nothing's going on. Don't worry. I'll call you later."

Mitch hung up. *Yeah, yeah, therapy 101.*

Staying low, he took in the area and saw two of the squad near the gate. He stopped and exhaled.

I'm doing exactly what I warned Ellen about; losing my head over the opposite sex.

Great, really great, dickhead. Calm down. He drew a deep breath and talked himself through it. "OK, think ... Charlie wouldn't be seeing Lachlan; not now after we've just said all that stuff to each other. Surely. Focus on Nick and Ellie ... I need to establish they're alive and then find out where Daniel' men are located. If they're on the boundaries, I can isolate them ... if all three are indoors, it's going to be harder ... a whole lot harder."

And I've got to call John back. Five more minutes won't be a matter of life and death. I hope.

He redialed John's number.

"John, it's me."

Mitch rested his head in his hands and closed his eyes, listening to John's dressing down.

―――――

Nick and Ellen continued to wind their way up the tunnels.

"Some of the tunnels go back through the offices," Ellen said in short, sharp gasps.

Nick moved the penlight to the side of his mouth, between his teeth.

"That'd be perfect," he muttered, "would you recognize which ones?"

"No ... maybe. I was too distracted on the way down to see how far we were going."

"Don't worry, we're still too far down at the moment to be anywhere near the offices," he swallowed. "I've got a rough idea of how far it is to the top, I counted our paces on the way down. Can we go a little faster?"

"Yes, I'm fine. Let's go."

Nick started to walk faster, feeling Ellen following close behind near his bound hands.

―――――

Mitch sidled up to one of the armed officers at the front gate and identified himself.

"What's the go?" Mitch asked.

"He's got the male and female down in the mine and he's armed. Says they won't be found if we try anything. Claims he's wired the area."

"That old chestnut," Mitch sighed.

The officer continued, "There is one other male with him, a big guy in a security outfit. We don't know if he's carrying. We've taken out his two other security people."

"Excellent," Mitch exclaimed. "That's the best news I've had all day."

"It's only eight in the morning."

"Ah, yeah, long night. OK, this is my plan ..." he explained in detail. Finishing, he watched the officer crawl back into position and waited for the signal that the details had been passed along. He saw the agreed sign, and coming out into the open, Mitch walked into the site.

Feel like a walking target! Breathe. Take it slowly.

I'm not supposed to know Daniel's name, what he looks like, or what he wants, so I shouldn't look like I'm worried about anything! He coached himself.

"Stop right there," Mitch heard a voice yell from inside the building. "Identify yourself."

"John Maxfield, pilot," he recalled his identity. "Nicholas Everett said to meet him here. We did a job ..."

"Yeah, you've got the right place," Daniel cut him off as Mitch rambled on intentionally.

Mitch squinted as two spotlights came on in the front yard. Even in daylight, the lights blinded him. He turned away.

"Look to the light," Daniel ordered him.

Mitch did as he was told.

Yeah, get a good look at me, I'll be busting your ass in a minute.

The lights went off. Mitch blinked, trying to rid his eyes of the white spots.

"Been talking much about your recent gold flight, Maxfield?" Daniel called.

Mitch hesitated. "I didn't know it was a gold flight. I just got paid to deliver the plane from here to Vegas."

Daniel called out.

"I'm taking him into the mine. I'll be back to release the girl to you. If you follow me, I'll kill him and blow up the other two. Maxfield, get over here!"

Daniel waved a gun.

"What's going on? Where's Nicholas Everett?" Mitch tried to sound panicked to buy time.

"Shut up and get in here now," Daniel snapped.

Mitch walked the length of the yard to the building entrance. He checked out where the officers were positioned as he moved towards Daniel.

I could take Daniel now, he thought, *but what if Ellie and Nick are impossible to find? What if he has wired the place? He's had plenty of time to do it. No, I need him alive ... the original plan's good ... stick to it ... otherwise, as soon as I put my foot in there, I'm a goner and he'll go back for the other two.*

Mitch cleared his mind and returned his thoughts to the plan.

So, the window of opportunity will be for around ten seconds when Daniel opens the door, and while the officers are there to back me up. The only loose end is Gamboa. Is he armed? Will he defend Daniel?

Mitch arrived at the door.

Daniel opened the door wide enough to let him pass through.

You're out of your league, Daniel. Your eyes give you away; they're reading pure fear. If it weren't for the gun ...

Mitch stepped in, running his eye over the Brazilian, Luis Gamboa. He saw a sidearm.

In one swift movement, Mitch slammed the door against Daniel knocking him back against the wall. He grabbed Daniel around the neck, turned him and used him as a shield against Gamboa. Mitch's grip on Daniel' wrist sent the gun falling to the floor.

He heard Daniel yell, "Get him, you idiot!"

Mitch drew his gun and pointed it straight at Gamboa.

"Turn, hands against the wall," he yelled. Gamboa did as he was told.

Daniel struggled.

"Don't push me," Mitch wrenched Daniel arm higher. He called out for backup and four officers barged in.

"Feel him down for the detonator. I think he's bluffing," he put his gun down as Daniel was manhandled from him.

Mitch watched two of the officers secure the area while the remaining officers fleeced Daniel and Gamboa, collecting the gun from the floor. They cuffed both men.

"Clear, no detonator," one of them announced.

Mitch breathed a sigh of relief.

"You can kiss-off seeing your pilot friend and the girl again," Daniel threatened.

Mitch whipped his gun back to Daniel's temple. Daniel froze.

"You can kiss-off seeing your next birthday unless you lead me to them," Mitch snapped.

"You won't kill me, you need me. You think I'm going to be your prize informer."

Mitch moved closer to Daniel; inches from his face.

"Let me tell you something, Daniel," he hissed. "I've got more info on Lawrence Hackett than I know what to do with, plus two other directors who are prepared to squeal and I've had a shit day. Trust me, you're dispensable. Start walking," Mitch pushed Daniel ahead of him towards the hangar and tunnels, "and they had better be OK."

"The financials are crap," Adam rubbed his eyes. He sat on the large cream leather sofa in their hotel room, surrounded by paper print outs and a laptop screen displaying numerous columns of figures.

He continued. "I've spent all day wading through nothing usable.

If there has been any entry fees paid, he's got it so tightly wound up you'd never find them." He ran his hands over his face.

Samantha dropped down near him, a ream of paper in her hand.

"Same here. I've got a few leads, but it's so ambiguous. Everything is called the project or the fund. We'll have a hard time proving this is anything but project work."

"It's very clever," Adam agreed.

"Listen to this," Samantha read from her paperwork. "Six projects are listed as requiring director assistance between October and now. I went into their system yesterday and three of the six are now marked project completed. Three remain open. My guess is that these are the Mastermind entries and there are only three left to run."

"Can they tell you're going into their systems?"

"Not if I've done it properly."

"Are directors' names with the projects?"

"Yes, location and title."

Adam sat back. "OK, this is going to be like working out a cryptic crossword ... start the clock now?"

"Speaking of the clock," she leaned over to read the time from her wristwatch resting on the coffee table; it was just on five p.m.

Adam caught a flash of a black lace bra as her T-shirt gaped at the front. His eyes ran over her.

Great body. That's one workout I'd enjoy, he thought.

"I need to listen to those tapes before it gets too late, see if we picked up anything from the microphones," she was talking and Adam realized he wasn't listening, just staring.

"Why hasn't Mitch called?" she said, frustrated.

"Perhaps he hasn't got anything to tell us yet," Adam pulled his mind back on the job. "It's about nine in the morning over there; he's probably just arrived."

"Perhaps it's bad news," Samantha worried.

"Let's take a coffee break," Adam said rising. "When we come back, I'll split the tapes with you before you get ready for the date. I'll work on the three puzzles tonight while you're sucking up to Lawrence."

"I'm so tired – I hope it's a quick date. I'd rather stay in and get a pizza," Samantha yawned.

"Well, drag it out for as long as possible. Don't forget, if you come back here, I'll be in the next room if you get in trouble," Adam assured her.

"I'm not bringing him home to bed," she snapped.

Adam shrugged, rising. He grabbed his jacket. "That's not very dedicated."

He waited until she looked up, eyes flaring and gave her a wink.

"Shut up," she picked up her jacket and followed him to the door. "Just for that, you can buy the coffee – and I want a large one."

———

They had been stumbling uphill for fifteen minutes. Nick listened, stopping at every sound in case Daniel or his henchmen re-entered the tunnels. He could hear Ellen's breath was short and labored; his own was not much better.

"Door number six," he grunted, kicking it in and losing his balance. "Nothing." The sweat was pouring off him and the penlight began to dim.

If that light goes out before I can change pens, Ellie's going to freak out. I've got to find a door ASAP; a door leading into the office building would be perfect.

———

Mitch continued to push Daniel in front of him, slowing down for the officer following behind to catch up.

I'm beginning to understand what Ellie was feeling. He shuddered. *These tunnels are like tombs; pitch black and damned cold.* He kept the torch trained in front of Daniel, straining for any sight of Nick and Ellen.

Daniel rounded a corner and stopped dead, his eyes grew huge.

"They've gone, they were here," he exclaimed.

Mitch pushed him aside and walked into the cement room. There was no sign they had been there. He grabbed Daniel and pushed him against the wall, his hand around Daniel's throat. The officer ignored them, continuing to look around.

"I swear, I left them here," Daniel wailed.

"How do you know it was this room? There could be a hundred like it?"

"It was number fourteen; the marking on the wall says fourteen."

Mitch glanced at the number.

"Take him up and charge him with whatever you can come up with ... kidnapping, threatening an officer, attempted murder, you name it," Mitch handed Daniel over.

"Yes, sir. Do you want me to send someone back down?"

Something caught Mitch's attention. Bending down, he picked up the butt of a Dunhill cigarette. Nick's brand, not smoked. He stood and walked out of the room, glancing up the tunnel to the left and right, shining his torch along the edges. He spotted the tip of another cigarette.

Nice one, Nick. That's got to hurt, he thought with a faint smile.

Mitch looked up at the officer who was waiting for an answer.

"Uh, no, thanks." He ran down the hall, shining his torch on the floor. He found half a cigarette, sometimes a third.

Hope you've got a full pack, Nick.

―――――

Nick pulled Ellen into a side tunnel. "Someone's coming and coming fast." He whispered, pushing her behind him.

"Don't turn off the light," she pleaded.

"I have to. Ellie, close your eyes."

"What? Why?"

"Just do as I say, no arguments. Lean on me and close your eyes. Breathe as quietly as you can and listen for my breathing."

He waited until Ellen closed her eyes, and turned off the penlight. He heard the footsteps getting closer and saw the faint beam of torch.

It's got to be one of Daniel' apes, he thought, and they'll be pissed that we've escaped. He could hear his heart thumping, the adrenalin coursing through him. I could do without another beating ... don't think I'm up to it. And Ellie ... I don't want to think about what might happen to her.

"Ellie, you're breathing too loudly, try and control it," he whispered.

They'll hear her for sure. I've got to do something.

He heard the footsteps slow down.

Sound like just one, but I'd say he's heard us. Need the element of surprise.

Nick ran out from the side tunnel and rammed the figure against the dirt wall. He heard Ellen scream as he moved away. Moving in again, Nick slammed his boot in to the man, pushing him on his back. He kicked again aiming for the rib cage, kicking hard and fast. Light bounced around the walls as the torch rolled forward. He saw Mitch's face.

"Mitch! Crap, sorry," Nick stepped back, dropping to his knees beside Mitch, his hands still tied behind his back.

"Mitch!" Ellen exclaimed.

Mitch coughed, gasping.

"Ellie, Nick, thank God you're OK," he winced with pain. "Geez that hurt," he gasped pulling himself up on all fours.

"Buddy, sorry, I only had one chance, so I had to make it count."

"Yeah, well done."

Mitch rose, pulling Nick to his feet.

"Geez, Nick, nice shiner."

"Courtesy of the Neanderthals. We should get moving," Nick looked around.

"No," Mitch grabbed the torch, "it's over. Daniel and the other two are out of action."

Mitch reached into his vest for a box-cutter. Nick turned and felt the rope fall away from his wrists. Mitch put a hand on Ellen's shoulder as he cut the ties.

Ellen turned and threw her arms around Mitch's neck and

hugged him. Surprised, Mitch stood there not moving. Nick frowned at him, motioning to hold her.

"You OK?" Mitch asked looking down at Ellen.

"No," her voice caught. "I thought we were going to die this time. I'm sorry,"

Ellen continued to grasp Mitch.

"There is nothing to be sorry for." Mitch stroked Ellen's hair. Nick watched them, rubbing his rope-burned wrists

"Do you hug all your team members?" he asked.

Ellen pulled away laughing and wiped the tears from her face.

"Usually. Come here big guy." Mitch grinned.

Nick laughed.

"I'll pass on the hug, but I've got to say, I've never been so pleased to see anyone ever," he slapped Mitch on the back. "Now, can we get out of here?"

36

MITCH HUNG UP FROM TALKING TO JOHN AND READ THE SIGN requesting all phones to be turned off before entering the hospital. He frowned, hit the silence button and ignored it. Mitch followed Nick and Ellen through the doors of the outpatients' wing.

"Doing a roaring trade here for ten in the morning," Nick commented as they struggled to find three seats together in the waiting room. Mitch saw a nurse glance at Nick, who was covered in dried blood, and she quickly motioned them into a small room.

"Ah, this is more like it," Nick smiled.

"Be even better if they had a coffee machine in here," Mitch added. "So, while we wait, can you tell me what happened?"

Nick sighed and sat back against the wall, resting on a stretcher. "It was my fault."

Mitch listened, looking from Nick to Ellen as they told the story together. He stiffened, motioning for silence as a doctor entered the room.

"Good grief, bit early for a fight isn't it?" The doctor exclaimed looking at the two men. "You know I may have to report this ..."

"Not necessary," Mitch flashed his I.D. and gave a brief overview of injuries.

"Ah, all in a day's work then," he looked them up and down. Mitch watched as the doctor placed an I.V. into Ellen and Nick's arms for re-hydration, then divided the room with a curtain. He left Ellen with a magazine and the fluid dripping into her on one side of the curtain, and reappeared to dress Nick's wounds.

"Nothing broken. Just some bruising and you'll need an assortment of stitches," the doctor announced pulling out a needle.

Mitch caught Nick's eye. "Nick, I'm sorry I got you into this."

"I'm not," Nick cut in. "Don't look so worried, boss; it's not as bad as it looks."

Mitch frowned.

"I'd still sign up even if you told me this might happen," Nick winced as the doctor applied some antiseptic to an open cut. The doctor moved from Nick to Mitch, who brushed him off, and then cleared both men to leave while he checked Ellen.

Outside, Nick pulled Mitch aside.

"Listen, Mitch, I need to help Maria."

"Nick, you've got to be kidding …"

"Daniel knows that she knew about Mastermind. He'll try and win brownie points by making that known," Nick cut him off.

"She's locked away," Mitch reminded him.

"They won't risk leaving her alive. They'll kill her, Mitch."

Mitch exhaled. "OK, OK."

"I've got to go to her."

"No way," Mitch shut him down. "I'll talk to John. We'll get her in maximum security. Can you live with that?"

"Does that ever work?"

"It'll work."

Nick nodded. "When can you do it? It has to be now or …"

"I'll call as soon as we leave here."

Mitch saw Ellen walking towards them.

"Cheer up you two," she smiled at them.

"All OK?" Mitch asked.

"I'll live to see the next round of action."

"Speaking of which, I'm surprised the doc didn't tape your ribs.

Are you going to be OK for the next round?" Nick jabbed at Mitch's ribs.

Mitch inhaled at the sharp pain. "Yes, thanks. Now, beat it!" he said as he moved away.

"They don't do that anymore," Ellen said. "Tape or strap the ribs. You're supposed to breathe deeply and cough to prevent lung collapse and pneumonia. Try it, Mitch."

Mitch breathed deeply which brought on a bout of coughing, his face winced with pain. "Nuh, I'll stick to the breathing," he gasped. "If Nick could stop giving me thrashings it would help."

"You deserved it the first time," Nick said.

"You're kidding?" Mitch glared at him.

Ellen interrupted. "So what happens to Daniel now?"

"I'm leaving him to John. He's arriving late tonight and he'll interview Daniel tomorrow," Mitch told her. "We'll have a conference call later and then fly out of here as soon as we can."

"Do you think Daniel will testify against Lawrence?" she continued.

"No," Mitch answered.

Nick agreed. "Not unless he's got a death wish."

"We've got enough to put Daniel away at least," Mitch assured her.

Ellen nodded.

"I'm starving," she changed the subject. "It's just after eleven, near enough to lunchtime – let's eat."

"I'd kill for a steak," Mitch agreed.

"With a huge potato and sour cream," Ellen continued.

"I'd kill for a cigarette," Nick sighed.

"You should give those up, they'll kill you," Ellen told him.

"They saved our butts today." Nick turned to Mitch. "She's bossy for someone who barely reaches your waist."

"Aren't you bruised enough?" Mitch grinned watching Ellen punch Nick's arm.

Samantha paraded in front of Adam in a black, shimmering dress and strappy black sandals. Her hair was down, full and shiny, and diamonds glittered in her ears.

"How do I look?"

"Absolutely lovely," Adam told her. "If he stands you up, come back and I'll take you out."

Samantha laughed. "OK, so you'll be around?"

"I won't let you out of my sight. Where's the microphone?" Adam asked.

Samantha turned over the edge of her dress to reveal it clipped to her bra.

"Good," Adam said, "don't get drunk and forget you're wearing the wire. You need to remove it if you decide to get amorous."

"Hmm, let's not go there again."

He saw her glance at the transcript work on the sofa.

"Don't panic. We've only got the eighth floor tapes to do. I'll start them when we get back tonight."

"Alright," Samantha agreed. "Best go. I'll try and keep the conversation lively so I don't bore you while you listen in."

"Bore away. I'll just sit there, dateless, eating my salad, and eavesdropping."

He opened the door and followed Samantha out, a bundle of paperwork tucked under his arm. "I'm going to attempt to crack the remaining Masterminds over dinner."

"Good luck," Samantha said.

"Hopefully, we both won't need it."

———

Adam saw Lawrence waiting as he followed Samantha across the square to the nearby restaurant. He watched Lawrence's eyes move up and down Samantha admiringly. Adam waited for them to enter and followed, requesting a table in the far corner. He observed the staff fawning over Lawrence. Adam pulled out the first printout from his folder and started to cross-check Lawrence's missing directors with the three projects still unaccounted for.

A waiter passed, he ordered a mineral water and accepted the menu. He heard Samantha order the calamari salad as a starter and grilled perch with steamed vegetables for the main course. *Nice choice, I'll have the same.*

He closed the menu and sat back, looking at the passing pedestrians. The corner paper seller caught his eye. He glanced at the headlines. Jumping up, he ran out and bought a copy, returning to his table and spreading it out before him. A young man's picture covered the front page.

I know that kid!

He scanned the article. 'Anthony Jenkins, a programmer for multimedia giant Globalnet was missing, feared dead ... last seen by his mother before leaving to collect a file at his office ... expected home at eleven that evening but did not arrive ... there is no record of him having entered the Globalnet premises that night ... Globalnet President, Lawrence Hackett, said Jenkins was an ambitious young man with a bright career ahead of him. Lawrence has posted a sizeable reward for any information that could assist police with their investigation ... and provided for Jenkins's mother.'

Adam stopped reading, feeling a wave of nausea. He looked at the front-page photo of the kid from the computer room.

Samantha had just finished her entrée when Lawrence's phone rang. He apologized and reached for it. She studied him; Lawrence's face was unreadable.

"Excellent, I'll be there." Lawrence hung up and returned the phone to his pocket.

Leaning across the table, he took Samantha's hand.

"Samantha, I've got to be unthinkably rude and leave you."

"Emergency?"

"I'm afraid there is a small problem at the office, something I need to attend to."

"Another time," Samantha smiled.

"I told you I wouldn't get laid," Samantha said as Adam walked into their hotel room.

"Bad luck! Is the audio on?"

"Yep, he hasn't entered his office yet, but we'll hear it if he does. I'm guessing that's where he's heading."

"Look at this," Adam slid the newspaper across the table towards her. "We need to listen to those tapes tonight. I bet it's all on there."

He watched Samantha's reaction; a look of confusion crossed her face.

"It's the kid from the computer room ... when Mitch and I were in there."

Samantha gasped. "Are you sure?" She read the headline and stared at the photo of Anthony Jenkins.

"Positive. He was in the building."

"We could have saved his neck." Samantha looked up at him.

"It's worse than that. I suspect we're the cause of his death."

They weren't waiting long before voices were heard in Lawrence's office.

"Sounds like a conference call," Samantha said. "That's Lawrence's voice. Who's the other?"

"Don't know. He's bound to call them by their name soon enough," Adam added.

They listened as Lawrence appeared to be enjoying a description of a successful crime from a voice over a phone line.

"He cut our date short for that? He could have got that news later."

Adam shrugged. "You've got to put it in perspective. He has a bevy of beautiful women like you at his fingertips—not saying you're not one of a kind—but Mastermind is played only once every five years. It's hot on his list. And I'm guessing they've just pulled one off."

Samantha sniffed with disgust. "Sounds like something in Monaco's succeeded."

"Ah-ha, there you go!" Adam picked up a name. "He said 'good work Brian'. We need to check our paperwork, find a director by the name of Brian and see where he's located at the moment."

They heard Lawrence terminate the conversation and the sound of a door closing.

"That sounds like the end of it," Samantha said. "I'm exhausted. I'm going to call Mitch and fill him in. Then I'll take some paperwork to bed and see if I can find this Brian guy."

"Work out the time difference before you call."

Samantha had the phone pressed to her ear. "Too late ... anyway, it's gone to voice mail. How weird, Mitch's always reachable."

"Try again in a few minutes; he might be out of range." Adam loaded the audio recordings for floor eight. "I'm going to go through the tapes, see if I can find anything about the kid on them."

"I'm going to get changed."

Adam put the headphones on and watched Samantha walk out of the room. Nice butt, he thought.

He glanced again at the front of the newspaper.

It's one thing to kill the baddies, Adam thought with a sigh, I can do that with the best of them – but if we're responsible for this kid's death, that would be hard to stomach.

He fast-forwarded through the tape for a few minutes, stopping and starting. He caught the sound of a young voice and rewound the tape. He heard the kid pleading for his life with three males.

Lawrence and ... Andrew. Must be Andrew Kenny, Lawrence's right-hand man, and I'm guessing the third is the security guard.

The incident finished. Taking off the headphones, Adam ran his hands over his face. He heard Samantha call out to him and he went in, taking the files she wanted with him.

"I found our Brian guy," she said propped up in bed in a gold-colored slip. "It's Brian Davies and he's in Monaco," Samantha waved a piece of paper at him. "So it looks like a Mastermind entry has succeeded in Monaco tonight."

Adam sat on the edge of her bed.

"What's wrong?" Samantha scanned his face.

He told her what he had heard. "That poor kid probably hadn't even started shaving yet," Adam sighed.

———

Samantha woke with a start. The red digital numbers of the clock read 12:10 a.m.

Mitch! I forgot to call him back.

Dialing, his number, she got the voice mail again.

Odd.

She put in a quick call to John and got diverted to his voice mail. Are they on the phone to each other? She lay back on the pillow.

Why hasn't anyone called with an update? What's happening at Broad Arrow? Maybe it's worst than I imagined, she thought.

Samantha got up and went for a glass of water.

It's got to be about five in the afternoon in Nevada. Where are you, Mitch?

She tried again.

———

Mitch was sound asleep when his phone rang. He woke on full alert, reaching for it.

He heard a rush of words; "Mitch, it's Sam. Is everyone OK? You didn't call to let us know. What's happening?"

"Who?" he stumbled, he looked around at the unfamiliar room trying to get his bearings.

Where the hell am I? Nevada ... yeah, that's right.

"Sam ... Agent Samantha Moore!"

"Sam." Mitch sunk back down onto the pillow.

"Are you there?" Samantha's voice snapped at him.

"Yeah, I'm here. How are you?" he asked rubbing his hand over his eyes.

"I'm good. Did you hear what I asked?"

Mitch thought for a minute.

"Sorry, ask me again."

Samantha sighed. "Where are you? You sound half asleep. Isn't it five in the afternoon there?"

"I was asleep ... I'm wiped out."

"Is everyone OK? Nick and Ellie? I've been worried."

"Everyone's fine. Sorry, Sam, I meant to catch you up. We've arrested um ..." Mitch couldn't think of his name. Geez, I'm losing it.

"Daniel Reid," Samantha filled in.

"That's it."

"Thank God. Now listen, Mitch, I know you're exhausted, but you need to know there is some serious shit hitting the fan here. There has been a successful entry in Monaco; they were talking about it in a roundabout way earlier tonight, and Lawrence knows someone's broken into the system." Samantha kept talking and Mitch struggled to keep up with her. "There is some bad news. They killed the kid, the computer kid with the spiky hair."

Mitch sat bolt upright in bed. He noticed he was still fully dressed, his combat boots and jeans still on, his T-shirt twisted around him. He pulled it straight and swung his legs over the side of the bed.

"What do you mean?"

"The kid you and Adam saw," Samantha said. "We've got it on tape."

"No, seriously? Are you sure?"

"Yes."

Mitch groaned. He rested his head on his hands.

"That's my fault. He'd never have been killed if he hadn't seen our logout on the Mastermind file."

"The poor kid thought he was doing the right thing reporting it."

Mitch felt a wave of guilt wash over him.

"Shit. What did they use?"

"I don't know. Adam said I didn't need to hear it, so I didn't push it."

"I agree. Where is he now?"

"Here. We worked until late, so he crashed here for the night."

"Can you put him on?"

"Sure."

Mitch heard Samantha whisper, "Adam, Mitch wants a word."

Mitch listened to the sounds of Adam stirring on the bed.

"Mitchell?" His English accent came down the line.

"Are you in bed together?" Mitch exclaimed.

"Ah, let me check ..."

"Forget it. What happened?"

"It's definitely the kid," he said. "No gun noise – must have used a silencer or a knife."

"Shit!"

"Listen," Adam changed the subject, "we've emailed you the transcripts. They know someone's on to them and they don't know whether it's MI6 or whether to expect a blackmail note."

Mitch thought for a moment. "Blackmail ... that could work."

"There is more. They're going to invite the blackmailer to meet them in person. Lawrence wants to play. And he's doubling his board members' bonuses if they take part and manage to eliminate the blackmailers."

"He's out of control. Adam, leave it with me to process when I wake up. It would be great to catch him in the act, this might make it possible."

"OK. Now in respect to the next two Masterminds," Adam continued, "I think I've cracked them. It's a hunch ..."

"Two?"

"Yeah, it was three earlier today, but Sam went into their system tonight and another one of them has been marked project complete. We're assuming that's the Monaco one."

"Right, I think she just told me that. Anything we can use on the tape to hang it on them?" Mitch asked.

"It's pretty ambiguous unless we've got a witness," Adam said.

"So, somewhere tonight your time, they've pulled one off?" Mitch reiterated.

"So it seems." Adam stopped. "Are you alright?"

"Yeah, sorry, I just woke up. I'm catching up."

"I'll speak slower."

Mitch laughed. "Thanks."

"Anyway, I need a few more hours on the other two, it's cryptic. I'll fill you in tomorrow, or today in your case."

"Yeah, thanks. I'll need that to finalise our next move."

"OK. Do you need to speak with Sam again?"

"No." Mitch sighed. "I'm blown away by the kid though; it pisses me off. You know that was probably him on the fourth floor, that reading we got ..."

"I know; it crossed my mind too. You don't want to hear the tape."

"They didn't torture him, did they?"

"No. But he was terrified."

Neither of them spoke for a few seconds.

"Hang on, Sam wants to say something."

Samantha came back on.

"Mitch ..."

"Yep?"

"About the bed thing ..."

He cut her off. "Sam, who you share a bed with is none of my business. I'll talk to you later today." Mitch hung up.

Poor kid ... and poor Marco, he thought wondering if Samantha would come clean with her Caribbean Casanova. I hope Charlie's not in bed with anyone.

Samantha hung up the phone and turned to Adam. She looked at him lying on the pillow, a smile on his face.

He's gorgeous, she thought. Gorgeous face and eyes, the body ... beautiful.

"That was subtle," he reached for her.

"I could have handled it better," she agreed, running her fingers down his chest. "You know, for the record, I don't make a habit of bed-hopping. I am a good Catholic girl."

"Ms. Moore, I beg to differ. I think you're a very bad girl indeed." With one quick move, he pulled her on top of him. "Your penance is ..." he kissed her, "two good deeds – and make love to me."

Mitch got up and headed for the shower. Shivering in the chilly room, he stripped off his gear, struggling with his boots. Turning on the cold water first, he braced himself for the impact and stepped in. It hit him like needles and he gasped. He turned up the heat, adjusting it to a comfortable temperature.

Was it really necessary to get rid of that kid? He thought of the young man in the computer room.

If they had thanked him for reporting it, would the kid have given a second thought to what MM3 was?

Mitch closed his eyes and let the water run over him.

Kid was probably so excited to be working for Globalnet. Lawrence's going to pay for this, Mitch decided. Whoever orchestrated it, is going to pay for it.

He could hear John's voice telling him to keep his head.

Sometimes, it's worth losing it.

Bet I haven't heard the last about hanging up on him either. Better lay low for a while; first the fight with Henri, now losing my cool with John. Not playing it smart ... then again, running on no sleep, crap food and a different time zone every day, they've got to expect a fall out.

His thoughts drifted to Charlotte. I'm not even getting any action and Sam's getting enough for all of us.

He took a mouthful of water, swilled it round and spat it out. He drank the next few mouthfuls.

At this rate, the chance of getting to first base—or is it second—with Charlie anytime real soon is up there with walking on the moon. Shit! I meant to call her back. When this one is over, I'm going to take a week off, maybe two. No, one week will do.

Mitch wrote a note to Nick and Ellen, telling them to go to dinner without him and come to his room around nine p.m. for a conference call.

That'll give me enough time.

Walking down the carpeted hallway, Mitch slid the note under each of their doors and headed down the stairs of the three-level motel. He stopped on the street and looked left and right, feeling the cool air hit him. Mitch walked towards the main street, searching for somewhere that served coffee. He spotted a McDonald's.

No matter where you are in the world, there is bound to be a McDonald's, he thought.

He went into the warm surrounds of the familiar store, ordered a coffee and found a booth in the corner.

Parked looked around; people were having real lives. He watched the kids with their parents, trading their toys and food; the mother with her kids who were more excited about the playground than eating; the young couple that must have lived with their parents and had nowhere to go to be alone.

He remembered coming to McDonald's as a kid.

We loved it; maybe it was the food or it was kid-friendly, or bright and happy. Everything home wasn't. Or maybe we always went when Dad was away on his road trips. They were the best times when he was away; Mum was happy, the house was peaceful, and I could look after them both – Mum and Dylan.

Mitch swallowed and looked away from the kids playing.

OK, he refocused. Six p.m. in Elko, and after nine in D.C. Will Charlie be home? Home alone?

He dialed her number.

———

"Of course I'm here, you know I hate going out Sunday nights with work on Monday. What are you doing?"

"I'm having a coffee with Ronald."

"With whom?"

"Ronald McDonald."

Charlotte laughed.

"Sorry about my phone battery, running out," Mitch continued.

"It's fine. I tried to call you back, but no luck."

"Me too, I got the machine. Who was at the door?" *Oh no, did I just ask that?*

"What door?"

He hesitated.

May as well keep going now.

"When I rang, you had to answer the door."

"Oh God, yes, that seems like a lifetime ago now. That was Dad. I promised Mom a book I'd been reading, and he dropped in to get it on his way home from his shift."

"Ah." *I am an idiot. To think I let it affect my work. And let John see that.*

"When are you coming home?" she asked.

Mitch sighed. "I don't know. Soon, I hope; I'm a bit plane weary."

They caught up for a while until the conversation waned, and Mitch heard Charlotte's landline going in the background.

"Hey, I'll let you go," he said. "I'll call you soon."

"OK. Take care."

"You too."

Mitch waited for her to hang up, but she remained on the line.

"Very high school." He smiled.

Charlotte laughed.

"See ya," she disconnected.

Mitch realized he was sitting there smiling.

I am such an idiot, he told himself again. OK, everything's in order on the home front.

He felt invigorated. Even the coffee tasted better. He opened the folder, thinking about the team's next move.

Got to get to work or the plan won't be finished before John arrives.

37

Mitch grabbed his phone and downloaded the update and two final projects that Samantha and Adam guessed to be Mastermind entries. They were encoded names.

I'll give these a go, he challenged himself. See if I can give Adam a run for his money. Let's see; Michael Germaine, Paris, Czars' project, 2711; and Ian Gare, Washington DC, Bedouin project, 2711.

Mitch sat up straight. He looked at the two entries.

D.C.! Another U.S. one?

Mitch mulled over the first one. The Czar's project … Russia, aristocracy, history? He threw the words around in his head. 2711 must be 27th of November. That part's easy. He went online and entered the words, 'Czar Project'.

Great! Everything from the last Czar to Rasputin to current projects with the acronym C.Z.A.R.

He narrowed it down, putting in the current date, the word Czar and Paris – the possible location of the crime, and waded through several pages of search engine topics.

Romanov history, relics, jewelry … all money spinners.

He dropped Paris and substituted it with France, aware, thanks to Nick, that Paris was just the head office for the directors.

No luck. Frustrated, Mitch sat back, took a large sip of coffee and stared up at the ceiling, thinking it over.

The Czars Project, The Czars Project ...

A Google link for the Russian eggs caught his attention.

The Fabergé collection of royal eggs that are doing a world tour. When will they be in Paris? He entered 'Fabergé tour Paris' into the search engine. His eyes lit up.

Bingo! The royal eggs! This has to be the Czar Project. The Russian Fabergé Eggs International Exhibition on tour at the Musée du Louvre, Paris, for one week from November 23 to 30.

Mitch absorbed the press article as the McDonald's waitress refilled his bottomless cup of coffee. He looked up, thanked her and scored a winning smile before returning to his reading.

The first Fabergé egg was made in 1884 as an Easter-egg gift for the Russian Czar, Alexander III. From then on, Fabergé made an Easter egg each year for another eleven years until Alexander III died. Nicholas II, Alexander's son, continued the tradition. It was agreed that the Easter gift would always be egg shaped, would hold a surprise and be inspired by historical events or art in Russia, such as the coronation of Czar Nicholas II or the completion of the Trans-Siberian Railway. They were made of various metals combined to produce different colors. Fabergé added precious stones including diamonds, sapphires, rubies and emeralds. A total of fifty-six Imperial eggs were made, twenty of which will be on display in the Louvre's Richelieu Wing from November 23 to 30. The display will be opened daily except Tuesdays.

That's got to be it!

He reached for his phone to ring Adam, just as it began to ring.

"Mitch," he answered not looking at the screen.

"Mitch, it's John. I've just arrived. Where are you?"

"Come to my office at McDonald's," Mitch suggested providing the addresses. He hung up.

Twenty minutes until John gets here. He looked at his watch. Six-fifteen local time, that's after two in the morning in the U.K. I hate to wake you Adam, but I've got no option.

"Exactly!" Adam exclaimed. "That was my conclusion too, once I ruled out the science path. Those Fabergé Eggs are worth a fortune and they'd fetch a good price through private collectors."

"I'm surprised they didn't schedule the crime for the Tuesday when the Louvre's closed," Mitch said.

"Yes, but they might be going to use the public to create a distraction. I don't know; I'm working on it."

"Good, keep on it for now. I've got John arriving in about ten minutes and I haven't started the second one yet. I need to assign it. How did you go?"

"I could use a bit more time, but I think I've got it – and guess what?" Without waiting for an answer Adam continued, "it's back on your home turf, the Washington D.C. Bedouin project – it's the Dead Sea Scrolls in the Library of Congress."

"Fantastic!" Mitch said excited.

Adam continued. "The Library of Congress is hosting the exhibition for a month. The last day is November 30. The exhibition's called 'Scrolls from the Dead Sea' and it includes twelve of the scrolls written two thousand years ago."

"Man, these Mastermind teams aren't thinking small."

"Well, they're by invitation after all," Adam reminded him. "It's like a criminal talent quest … Criminal Idol!"

Mitch laughed. "The project's called Bedouin; what's the connection with the name?"

Adam continued. "The scrolls were discovered in 1947 by a young group of shepherds from Bedouin. They were searching for a stray goat and went into this long cave and found these jars filled with ancient scrolls. At first they found seven scrolls, but after the experts moved in and the search spread to eleven caves, they found thousands of scroll fragments dating back to before Jesus lived."

"It's got to be that, what else could Washington D.C. Bedouin mean?"

"I agree."

"Great work, Adam."

"Thanks, I enjoyed it."

"So, does that means we've got another director – in D.C.?"

"I guess so," Adam agreed.

"I want you with me in London, so I'm going to hand the Fabergé Eggs project over to Ellie. I'll fill you in at the nine o'clock meeting."

"Five in the morning," Adam reminded him of the time difference.

"Yeah, sorry about that. Get some sleep, I'll wake you in a few hours," Mitch hung up.

John looked out of place at McDonald's in his suit and tie. He studied Mitch's face expecting to see dark eyes and signs of strain.

"I'm pleased you're looking so well; except for wincing every time you move," he said.

"I'm fine," Mitch agreed.

"Coffee?"

"Ah, you better get me a juice, thanks. I've had a jug of coffee."

John returned with their drinks and dropped into the booth. He listened to Mitch's sitrep and plan, and the thoughts on the remaining Masterminds.

"Good," he announced at the end. "Consider it approved."

"Thanks, John."

"We've got a few hours until the conference call. I wouldn't mind checking in, then we should talk," John suggested.

"About what?"

He noticed Mitch stiffening.

"About what your team might need for the next stage ... how you're feeling."

"Right," Mitch answered.

While he waited for John to check in, Mitch grabbed a handful of clothes from his hotel room floor and stuffed them in his duffel bag. He looked up at the sound of a knock on the door and opened it to find John.

"Mitch, walk with me. Let's talk."

"Can we walk to a laundromat?" Mitch grabbed his bag and stuffing the remaining items in, followed John out the door.

Thought I got out of it lightly. Here's the lecture for my Broad Arrow performance.

He followed John out of the hotel, onto the street. They passed John's hire car and walked towards the main street.

"How did you go with Daniel?" Mitch asked hitching the bag over his shoulder.

"Won't talk. We'll get him on deprivation of liberty and attempted murder, but he won't say a word against Lawrence, yet." John shrugged, "It's still early days; they usually buckle after their lawyers haven't got them out by the week's end."

"I need him to talk to confirm we're on the right track with the Czar and Bedouin Masterminds. I can't afford to be off on the wrong tangent. Whatever it takes …"

"Leave it with me," John assured him.

"And Maria Diaz, can we help her?"

"She's in maximum security as you requested. I've made it clear to Daniel if anything happens to her it will go on his rap sheet. I think he's got the picture."

"I'll let Nick know."

"You don't entirely trust him yet, do you?" John asked.

"Who, Nick?"

"Yes."

Mitch thought before answering. "I trust him to do the right thing by us, but I think he's still going to try and do the right thing by Maria too. So I'm watching him in case he does something stupid."

They walked in silence for a while.

"So …" John said.

Here it comes, Mitch thought. Psych 101 and 102! Bet this was the only reason John came to Elko. He could have extradited Daniel to D.C. for questioning – but no, he had to check on me in person to make sure I haven't grown two heads.

"I want to know why you lost it, Mitch?"

Mitch looked up surprised at John's directness. He spotted a laundromat and nodded towards it.

I hate this self-analysis shit. I get enough of this at home living with a psychologist, now work has got all touchy-feely with this workplace health and safety crap. It was better in the old days. You lost it, you moved on. You got shot, you healed. Now, you have compulsory counseling every time you need a band-aid.

Mitch sighed. "It's not complex," he kept his voice neutral. They crossed the street to the laundromat. He avoided looking at John.

"I'd crossed a thousand time zones in the last week, I was out of whack, it was the second rescue attempt with my team who should know better ... I got a bit impatient, that's all."

"Mitch, as you know, we have few units like yours for political and cost reasons. In fact, at last count, there was only fifty Trans-national Crime Units across twenty-six countries. The leaders of these units are picked because they don't lose it; they have proven themselves to have uncanny strengths mentally and physically. I want to know if there is some other agenda here," John asked. "I've watched you in action for over three years now. You've been sleep deprived before, you've been stressed before and you've never cared about picking up after your team. Your actions of late, even in the office, have been a bit ... unlike you. Yet, if something's wrong, you haven't asked for help. I want you to step me through what brought you to the point of snapping."

Mitch bit his tongue, holding back his frustration.

"If you're referring to Henri and me, that's not work related. That's history between us. It goes way back, we're OK."

"Maybe, but he's worried about you."

"Did he say something?"

"Not really."

Mitch frowned at John. Great, now they're talking about me like I'm a case file.

"Start with the incident when you arrived at Broad Arrow," John prompted.

What do I say? OK, think ... tiredness and time zones are not going to work.

They walked into the laundromat and John took a seat on a blue timber bench along the glass wall. They were alone except for one load spinning in the dryer, the owner nowhere to be seen. Mitch looked at his load. It was almost all black and anything that wasn't was about to be. He emptied it into a washing machine and searched his pockets for change for washing powder, buying time.

"Mitch," John called his name.

"Yeah?" he looked up.

"Relax, it's not the Spanish Inquisition. Stop thinking and tell it to me as it is."

Mitch nodded, running his tongue over his lower lip, he looked back to his laundry.

What do I say? He thought. That the girl I can't stop thinking about isn't going to wait forever while I traipse around saving the world; that she's got an ex hovering around like a vulture; that Sam is compromising her ability bed-hopping and I'm not home long enough to get past the first kiss; that Nick, who tried to kill me is now my best agent on the ground; J.J. who betrayed us is still out there; that Ellie folded under pressure and can't function underground; Adam's a time bomb waiting to go off; that I want one night in my own bed and to know where I am when I wake up; that I can't bear the sight of another plane or the thought of one more flight; my bones ache and breathing has taken on its own level of pain; that three of my team have all been threatened in the space of two weeks – but otherwise, all is well.

Mitch started the machine, his time had run out. He turned and sat on the bench at the opposite end to John.

The kid. I'll tell him about Anthony Jenkins.

He started, "the kid got to me."

Not exactly true. In fact, I didn't know about the kid's death at the time of our argument; but John won't know that.

"The kid?" John asked.

Mitch recounted the death of Anthony Jenkins. When he finished, John looked at him and nodded. Mitch could read the sympathy and understanding in his face.

I hate that. He's probably thinking I need to see a shrink now.

Rising, he turned his back to John, on the pretence of checking on his washing.

"You know what I think?" John asked.

Mitch turned back to face him.

"Sit down, Mitch."

Mitch swallowed, sitting back down.

"I think that over the last few weeks, you haven't had one uninterrupted night's sleep and when you have managed to sleep, you've had nightmares. I think Nick's appearance has triggered some of those. You've had several severe bashings; you've traveled across multiple time zones and are out of whack. You've witnessed a fairly traumatic incident with three of your team having their lives placed at risk and you've felt responsible for rescuing them. You've had a gun held to your own head and you're feeling guilty about this young boy. Plus, something's going on at home that you won't discuss. It all falls into the critical incident stress category."

Mitch knew what was coming. He shuffled uncomfortably.

"John ..."

"Mitch, let me finish. Whether you like it or not, you know I should send you and your team to Critical Incident Stress Debriefing and refer you onto the staff psychologist for a set number of sessions. I'm required to do that. Give me one reason why I shouldn't?"

Mitch looked down. He felt John watching him.

John cleared his throat. "But, I'll buy your story this time."

Mitch looked up and smiled.

"But this time only," John smiled back.

Lawrence Hackett sorted his mail. He threw the envelopes back in his in-tray.

Nothing, I want a blackmail note! It'll be like being invited to participate in my own Mastermind. But they had better know what they're doing, because we will.

He smiled and looked down over the Docklands.

This will be a great swansong.

———

At nine p.m.—five a.m. in the U.K.—Mitch sat in a small hotel room in Elko, Nevada, with his team: Ellen, Nick and his boss, John Windsor. Adam and Samantha joined them via a conference call. Mitch laid it on the line.

"We need to regroup and think before we act ... me included," Mitch added. "We've been lucky so far to have escaped injury at the hands of J.J. and Daniel, but let's not assume we're invincible. We've had one casualty," he referred to Anthony Jenkins, "I don't want anymore."

John agreed. "Especially now that you're coming up against a more aggressive competitor with endless resources."

Mitch confirmed their mission. "Our aim is to capture Lawrence Hackett committing an illegal activity and pick up his directors as cohorts – we already have Daniel. We need to shutdown any remaining Mastermind projects, namely Washington and Paris. Finding Anthony's body would be a bonus." He repeated the mission. "Everyone clear?"

He heard murmurs of consent.

"I don't care if you think I'm anal but, until this project is over, don't breathe without running it by me. No more experiments, no more try-it-and-tell-me later, no more 'it'll be right on the night, boss'. It's not on. And if anyone has a problem with that, now's the time to get out. Clear?"

They agreed in unison.

"OK. Nick and I will be working with Adam in London, preparing for Lawrence's next move."

That gives me a strong local presence with Adam, and I can rely on Nick. At least he's not likely to sleep with Adam.

Mitch continued. "We'll be doing surveillance and setting up a trap to snare Lawrence in the act. From our base in the U.K., we will also oversee the remaining two Masterminds in D.C. and Paris. Adam, tomorrow, could you find a serviced apartment for our use on a week-to-week basis and check us out of the hotel? Get it in the same area with a view of the square and Lawrence's building if you can. You might want to stay there too rather than go home at all hours ... up to you though."

"Will do," Adam's voice came through.

"As for the remaining Mastermind projects, the contestants have until November 30 to complete their projects or be disqualified. That gives us a window of seven days. Sam, you'll head back to D.C. tomorrow to shut down the Mastermind project at the Library of Congress. I'll email you a full brief after this meeting. I'll copy everyone, and I suggest you all read it to be across what's happening. It's scheduled for November 27, so it's going to be tight. John will get you some backup."

John interjected. "Sam, I'm partnering you with a member of the Criminal Investigative Division, the CID, and you can run the show with their backup."

Mitch continued. "After that, you'll be on standby to return to London if needed."

"Right," Samantha confirmed.

"Ellie," Mitch turned to her, "you'll take Adam's research on the Fabergé Eggs exhibition at the Louvre and head to Paris tomorrow. It's scheduled for November 27 as well, so you've only got a few days to work out this Mastermind."

"Got it," she said.

"After that, wait for orders. Now Ellie, Sam, forget about the directors on the ground in Washington and Paris; we'll pick them up as part of Lawrence's sweep in the U.K. Just make sure the Mastermind projects don't happen. I want you to remain fully accessible twenty-four seven. Any questions?"

"No," Ellen answered.

"Maybe after I read the email," Samantha said.

"Fine, just call me back then. I'll hand you over to John who'll fill you in on the protocols for working with local operatives from the TCU or CID."

Mitch tuned out as John began to speak. He grabbed his phone and sent off the email brief to Samantha and copied the team as promised.

Mitch ground his teeth subconsciously as it left his out-box. *The Library of Congress is like Fort Knox. Can the Mastermind entry really pull this off?*

38

Monday 0900 Paris
(London 0800, Washington D.C. 0300)

"Ellen Beetson, American citizen," the French immigration officer read the name on her passport out loud.

"How long are you staying?"

"Between three to five days."

"Business or holiday?"

"Business," Ellen answered.

He looked at her again and stamped her passport.

"Enjoy your stay."

"Merci," Ellen walked past him into the frenzy of France's Charles de Gaulle airport and checked the boards for her luggage carousel number.

It's good to be alone, she thought. I know Sam wants to be in London, working with Mitch and the boys, but I'm happy for some time out and to manage my own project for a while. Glancing at her watch, Ellen quickened her step. Midday meeting!

Three hours later, Ellen walked through the Louvre with the Head of Security, Gilles Revault, and the English-French speaking agent from the Trans-national Crime Unit based in Paris, Gerard Astier. Ellen got straight down to business leaving Astier and Revault no choice but to take the potential threat as genuine.

As they entered the Louvre, Ellen felt a rush of excitement.

"Can we see the area where the Fabergé Eggs are housed?" she spoke in French as the head of security did not speak English.

"Yes, of course. That's in the Richelieu Wing," Revault led the way. Ellen's eyes ran over each work as she followed.

"Magnificent," she murmured.

"Yes, indeed," Astier agreed, walking beside her.

Revault stopped in front of the exhibition. "This is it."

"Truly incredible," she said. "I've seen photographs of the Eggs, but never seen them in person," she leaned closer.

Breathtaking; so many shades on such a small surface area.

Ellen read the sign; 'The Fabergé Imperial Easter-Egg collection commissioned by the last of the Russian Czars'.

"Of all the Fabergé Eggs in the collection, those commissioned by the last Czar were considered the most outstanding," Revault said.

"They are stunning." She went to the edge of the room, taking note of everything around the Fabergé display from floor to ceiling.

OK, we've got two days to work out how the eggs are going to be stolen. Clock's on!

Monday London 0900
(Paris 1000, Washington D.C. 0400)

"Shit landing," Nick groaned as they touched down at Heathrow airport in the U.K., fifteen hours after leaving Nevada. "Wonder where he learned to fly."

"Did they need to announce we've landed? Was anyone unaware of it?" Mitch agreed.

"Landing was never your forte as I remember it," Nick said.

"You're kidding aren't you?" Mitch said. "I'm great at landing. Remember that landing you did in Singapore? Now that was shit."

Nick scowled. "Nice to reacquaint myself with my injuries. Hello sore body."

"I can't get back into a plane for at least a week," Mitch steadied himself as he rose to stand beside Nick.

"I can imagine," Nick sympathized as he pulled two duffel bags from the overhead locker and tossed one at Mitch.

They followed the other passengers out, avoiding the luggage carousel.

"Are you going to call Adam?"

"Yep, right now," Mitch turned his phone on.

"I hope the apartment's got two showers – otherwise, you'll be waiting," Nick yawned.

"Dream on. In your condition, do you seriously think you're going to beat me in there?"

———

"How did you go for accommodation?" Mitch asked.

"Good," Adam Forster gave him the address. "It's the biggest self-contained apartment I could find with three-bedrooms close to the tube and Lawrence's building. If Ellen or Sam join us, we'll have to take the sofa."

Mitch and Nick lowered themselves into a taxi and Mitch advised the driver of the address.

"OK, on our way," Mitch told Adam.

"Sorry I couldn't pick you up … the Porsche has only got two-seats," Adam said.

"Yeah, yeah, show off," Mitch retorted. "See you soon."

———

"Here's home, lads!" Adam greeted them at the front door.

"No place like it," Mitch agreed and threw his duffel bag into the room Adam indicated. He introduced the two men.

"Do you guys want to get some shut-eye first?" Adam asked.

"Nah. I'll hang out for tonight or I'll be out of whack," Nick said.

"Me too," Mitch agreed, "I'm beyond tired now."

After settling in, Adam played the tape where Lawrence decided to wait for a call from the group that hacked into his system the night Anthony Jenkins was killed. Mitch could hear the concern in Lawrence's Chief of Staff's voice. They listened as several of the directors challenged Lawrence's decision.

Andrew spoke. "OK. So, say they make contact with us; you transfer them the blackmail fee and they give you back the file, where's the thrill in that?"

"I'm not going to transfer it to them electronically, Andrew. We're going to pay it to them in person. Then we test them – how do they know we won't follow the collector home? Or bring in our own security? Or injure the public during the handover?"

"What if they don't agree to do it in person? What if they say they want to send you back the files in the mail and want the money paid electronically?" Another male voice asked, clearing his throat with a cough.

"Then, our I.T. people better be good because I want to know who we're transferring funds to and how we find them. Look, Alan," the three men listened as Lawrence addressed the male speaker, "they're likely to want cash. They won't risk an electronic transfer in case it's traceable. And if they want cash, they're going to pick somewhere safe, somewhere public, so they can walk out of there unnoticed. And I want the file in my hand before I hand over any cash."

"And who is going to do the drop?" Andrew's familiar voice asked.

"Me, of course."

"But ..." Andrew began to protest. Lawrence cut him off.

"I'll wear glasses and a baseball cap; the cameras won't be able to pick up any features. Stop worrying Andrew, it's supposed to be fun."

"Fun, of course," Andrew said.

"Thank you, gentlemen," Lawrence said. The listeners heard chairs being pushed back and the door opening.

Adam turned the tape off and turned the volume down on the live feed. He looked at Mitch and Nick. "He's out of control."

"He's going for broke," Nick said, "and taking the directors with him! Can't we get him now with what we have on tape?"

"No," Mitch said. "He could say it's a game or he had to protect his business or it's not really him speaking; any number of things. We've got to catch him in the act. This has got to stick."

Lawrence Hackett called his Monday-morning meeting to order, the empty chairs of Ian Gare and Michael Germaine indicated there were still two Mastermind projects outstanding. Daniel Reid's chair remained empty. Lawrence circled the table and refreshed their memories about Thursday night's discussion.

"So, the idea is we wait for the intruders to contact us and foil them at the point of paying the bribe. Let's have a show of hands from those wanting to play."

After the meeting, Andrew Kenny and Alan Peasely, took the lift down the nine flights to the streets below. Once they were clear of the building, Andrew turned to Alan.

"He's gone too far this time; he's going to blow it for everyone."

Alan looked around. "We can't win," he agreed. "If we pull out, he'll have us cleaned up; if we stay in, we could spend the rest of our lives in prison. These people with the file, they're not going to hand it over cleanly ... this is turning ugly."

"I know. I don't know what to do. Do we run for cover, or keep hanging in there and hope we'll survive?"

"We could do a Rudolph Hess and deliver some information to the authorities," Alan suggested.

Andrew shook his head. They entered a sandwich bar. "I can't be an informer. I've done everything he's done – I'm as accountable. This is sheer stupidity." He wiped a film of sweat from his upper lip.

"Not to mention that some of the directors are young idiots. They're bound to stuff up on the job," Alan grabbed a pre-made sandwich and a Coke and paid for it. "Can you get us out of the country on project work?"

Andrew hesitated. "It'll be transparent, but it's one option. Can't see him going for it. Lawrence is up to something; it's like he's got a whole other agenda. I want to know what's going on in his head."

———

"Contain it," Mitch said pacing in front of the windows in the apartment. "We need to contain it, yet have it in a public area."

"I agree," Adam leaned over the kitchen bench. "If we meet Lawrence somewhere isolated, we're leaving ourselves wide open. If we can pick an area that we can control like …"

"Like the Underground," Mitch continued, "where we can account for everyone in the station."

"And we can keep it in this neighborhood," Nick added.

Adam reached into a folder and withdrew a map. He unfolded it, spreading out a detailed plan of the London Underground on the center table.

"Canary Wharf is on the Jubilee line; the train runs every five to ten minutes."

Mitch stopped in front of the windows and squinted as the midday sun hit the side of the building. His brow was creased in thought.

"What are you thinking?" Adam asked.

"Huh?" he turned. "Nothing …"

"Really?" Adam pushed him.

Mitch rejoined them. "I was thinking about that kid – there was less than ten feet between us while he was still breathing, if we had known … I wonder where his body is."

"My guess would be weighed down in the Thames," Nick said casually.

Mitch shot him a look. He turned to the map.

"OK, we want Lawrence down in the station where we can control the environment and we want him to think that we've planned it so we arrive on the tube, do the file and cash swap, then leave on the same train. There will be no time for hostilities and we'll be surrounded by the general public, so he won't want to try anything, agreed?" Mitch asked.

"Agreed." Nick continued. "We'll need to follow him all that day. He might walk into the Canary Wharf tube stop from the street, or he may get smart and take a train from further out to give himself some observation time."

"Good point," Adam said.

"Are the trains regular?" Mitch asked.

"Pretty much," Adam explained, "they call it a metro service, which means trains show up every few minutes. There are no daily timetables, except for the first and last train, you just go and get on."

"That's going to make it a bit hard to get the timing right," Nick mused.

"Where's the last stop on that line?"

"Uh, that's the Jubilee line ... it's four stops later at Stratford, Mitch."

"To play it safe, we could make Canary Wharf the last stop for that particular service, but there will still be some commuters coming in and out of the platform area," Nick said.

"Unless ..." Mitch squinted at the two men as he thought. "What's the chances of us keeping that train at the platform and closing down the line, so that it can't get out and no other trains can get in?"

"If we own the driver we can keep the train at the station. As for preventing other's coming in, we can get the police to do that," Adam continued the train of thought. He broke into a P.A. announcer's voice. "Due to person under train, your service has been delayed."

Mitch smiled at him. "Exactly," he recognized the kind of public announcement that most Londoners had experienced the misfortune of hearing. "We get the police to block off the area, but to make it seem authentic to Lawrence, we could make the 'person under train' announcement ... play it right after the handover when the train stops at Canary Wharf," Mitch paced. "So, we get the timing as close to the mark as possible – the train stops at Canary Wharf, the driver calls through a jumper, all other trains are halted coming through on that line and we can't move out either. The platform is ours. Any passengers left on board are only going as far as the last stop, in this case Canary Wharf, so we get them out. Outside, we can position police at each of the entrances to the tube to tell commuters the station's temporarily closed. That gets rid of our general public coming in." Mitch looked to the two men for comment.

"That will work," Adam said. "But we can't position those cops until Lawrence has entered the station. They'll be on standby. Our guys will be in the last carriages and around the station looking like commuters."

"Lawrence'll have the same, it's a matter of identifying them," Nick said.

"On hearing the announcement, Lawrence will panic – his guys will either act or wait, but we'll have him by then," Mitch concluded.

All three men stood in silence thinking about it. Mitch stared at the Underground map, his dark head bent over it.

"What time of the day are we thinking for the handover?" Adam moved to his laptop.

"The quietest part of the day. Any idea of what time that will be?" Mitch asked.

Adam opened the Underground website. "This site is unbelievable. They've got everything except our plan up here. Check this out," Adam clicked through several pages. "It's an annual entry and exit frequency chart."

"A what?" Nick asked.

"A list per station of the average number of commuters coming and going at different times," Adam clicked through to the Jubilee line and then to Canary Wharf.

"Impressive," Mitch agreed sitting next to Adam. "Odd all that info is available, from a security point of view."

"OK, the quietest time of the day for commuter activity is at first train. Nearly seven hundred people in the station."

"I'd rather operate under the cloak of darkness outside and with a little more traffic around; we'll be less noticeable," Mitch said.

"And it can't be the last train for the day, because in theory we want to make a getaway with the cash," Nick reminded them.

"What time is that last train?" Mitch asked.

"One a.m.," Adam read from the site.

"How about eleven p.m.?" Mitch suggested.

"Anywhere between eight at night and one in the morning, we're looking at around eight thousand people entering Canary Wharf and around three thousand exiting," Adam read from the site.

"Geez, seems a hell of a lot," Mitch exclaimed.

"That's not on one train though, that's on numerous services in non-peak time, which spans five hours – so, you might average one hundred on the train," Adam calculated.

"Right, that sounds more manageable." Mitch yawned.

Exhaustion and jet lag were creeping up on him now. Nick, too, looked like he was in slow motion.

"Let's wrap this up and get out of here, I need a coffee," Mitch said, his eyes glazing over. "So, the blackmail note goes out at close of business Wednesday. That night, we do surveillance on who goes in and out of Lawrence's offices and the car park, to check which directors are on board and how many security guards are coming and going."

"Bet it'll be all hands on deck in Lawrence's office that night," Nick shook his head.

"We give him a day to organize his team and the cash. So, I'm proposing we do the handover the next night, Thursday, at around eleven p.m. What do you think?" Mitch asked looking from Nick to Adam and back.

"Sings!" Nick rubbed his eyes.

Adam agreed. "So, who's good at writing blackmail notes?"

39

Monday 2100 Washington
(Tuesday 0200 London, Tuesday 0300 Paris)

Samantha read between the lines.

It would be easier to send me to break up the Paris Mastermind given it's only an hour by plane from London, she thought. But no, Mitch is bringing me home, getting me away from Adam. She threw her luggage on the floor of her apartment and headed for the kitchen, flicking on the kettle. Then, after a thirteen-hour flight, I get stuck with the Center Intelligence Division guy who's the biggest skeptic on the planet! Three hours to convince him that Mastermind's for real. For chrissake! Just wait until I tell Mitch about that guy.

Samantha exhaled, and stretched, moving her head from side to side. She felt a tinge of pain. Here I am, doing my first job by myself and I never wanted to work by myself. Plus, I have to deal with a dick-head at CID. Samantha looked at the time. Mitch is probably asleep ... I'll try anyway. She dialed his number.

Mitch groaned, turned on his side and opened his eyes to read two a.m. on the clock. He closed his eyes again. *If I could just get to sleep, I'm over tired.* His phone rang and he jumped to get it, feeling for it in the dark. Samantha was talking before he had a chance to say hello.

"If that CID agent calls me ma'am one more time, I'm going to kill him," Samantha told him.

"Keep those lethal weapon hands to yourself, ma'am," Mitch whispered trying not to wake Nick and Adam in the next rooms. He raised himself on his elbows and glanced at the time again.

"We've got to get these time zones right," he stifled a yawn. "You're five hours behind us. So it's two in the morning here."

"Sorry."

"No you're not," Mitch said, "you're getting back at me. Lucky for me I was half awake."

He heard her suck in a breath.

"Why would I be getting back at you?"

"Because you think I'm punishing you for sleeping with Adam. So, instead of sending you to Paris, which was closer to you, I've sent you back to D.C.," he finished with a sigh dropping back on the bed. Again, he waited for her reply.

"Well, maybe."

"Hmm." Mitch closed his eyes. "Tell me what happened with our guy on the ground?"

"When he finally decided I wasn't making the story up or a nut case, he got excited," Samantha said. "His name's Sebastian Roe. He's about forty-five, and seems to be well respected. Do you know him?"

"Not in the flesh. John'll know him."

"He found the whole Mastermind thing surreal at first ..."

"Yeah, well, you can't blame him for that," Mitch interrupted.

"Sure, but he can't afford not to take it seriously. He wanted to call you or John to verify it."

"He did call, I spoke with him earlier."

"You're kidding me!"

"Sam, you've got to expect that," Mitch explained. "People at a certain level, like to talk with others at the same level. It's not a male versus female thing. I've had people who want to talk with John before they'll deal with me. Pisses you off, but deal with it!"

"How many times has that happened to you?"

He heard the skepticism in her voice. "Sam, stop testing me."

"I'm sorry, Mitch, I'm just frustrated. Anyway, he's on board, so we're meeting at eight in the morning. He's bringing some of his best people, as he calls them, to work out a plan."

"Good," Mitch sighed. "John's working on Daniel. He's not giving anything up, he'll keep us posted."

"I'm meeting with John tomorrow after I meet with Roe. It would be good though if Daniel spilled something—what time they're planning the heist, where they intend to enter, how they're going to do it—I'll take anything."

"Fingers crossed. Call me tomorrow after your meeting with Agent Roe," Mitch instructed her.

"Sure, sorry to wake you, Mitch."

"Yeah, really?" Mitch noted the insincerity in her voice. "Listen, Sam, for the record, I sent Ellie to Paris because …"

Samantha cut in.

"You don't have to tell me, I'm not questioning your orders."

"Yes you are. You're just not questioning them out loud," he yawned again. "I sent Ellie to Paris because she speaks French." Mitch hung up.

Tuesday 0700 London
(0800 Paris, 0200 Washington)

Early Tuesday morning, Adam and Mitch arrived at the headquarters of the London Metropolitan Police in New Scotland Yard, Westminster. Adam led Mitch through the building on a quick tour, sensing Mitch was keen to get to the armory.

"OK, niceties over. This way." He led Mitch downstairs into a high-security area. "This is the home of a specialist operation branch, SO19. These guys will be with us on site. They're the best, the equivalent I guess to your SWAT teams; they know what they're doing. They've also agreed to issue us with some weapons, which I had to offer my first born to get, but it was worth it."

He noticed Mitch looked surprised.

"Our guys don't carry guns," Adam explained, "they're issued batons and incapacitant spray. So getting weapons comes with a truckload of paperwork."

Gaining clearance through several more areas, Adam led Mitch into an enormous armory stacked with everything from combat gear to missiles. He pulled out a list.

"I've organized for six men to be assigned to us: one in sniper position, two outside at the entrances, one on the platform, two on board, plus our team of four – or five, if Sam makes it back on time."

Mitch pulled out his detailed map of the Canary Wharf line.

"So, covering both sides of the platform of the Canary Wharf tube, we'd locate them like this," Mitch placed crosses where the manpower would be.

"Yep. That enough manpower?" Adam asked.

"I think so. When can I get them?"

"From four that morning for the run through, and from five-thirty on the evening of the handover."

"Perfect."

Adam continued. "I've ordered these," he pushed the list to Mitch, then turned and pulled guns out for Mitch to inspect.

"I've got one, or in some cases two firearms per person," Adam elaborated. "There are two of these .224Boz modified 10mm Glocks. They were part of the .224BOZ ammunition project. Heard of it?"

"Yeah." Mitch held the small handgun. "Enhanced ammunition."

"Right. Basically the barrel of the original weapons is exchanged for a more powerful, ballistically-matched barrel. It makes it pretty potent for a small gun with the added benefit that it can penetrate body armor."

"Almost unfair, isn't it?" Mitch said.

"I know what you mean," Adam smiled. "They'll go to the two officers, Skinner and Watson, who'll be on board the carriage with you. I've booked two of these Super Magnums for our sniper team in the ceiling. They'll be good for long range platform use and will achieve a first-round hit at six hundred. They're superbly accurate."

"Nice," Mitch checked them out.

"Got five of these L85s. These produce an amazing volume of fire, about seven hundred rounds per minute. They're good at long range."

Mitch felt their weight. "Around ten pounds. Not bad at all."

"We don't need this, but check out this Under-slung Grenade Launcher," Adam pulled them out, watching Mitch's face light up.

"Excellent!"

"They're great," Adam agreed. "They're designed for mounting beneath the barrel of each individual weapon. They can fire explosives and smoke if you need to destroy or obscure anything." Adam put the weapon back. "I've got several SIGARMS P226 semi-automatics for your team to conceal somewhere on their bodies. They're accurate and reliable."

Mitch nodded.

"Or you could stick with the Glocks you guys brought over with you," Adam continued.

"We won't be able to move for weapons," Mitch handed back the Super Magnum. "Has everyone on the team used these weapons?"

"Them or some version of them," Adam assured him. "And then there is the gear." Adam pulled out the combat clothing. "Interceptor body armor ... we've got the tactical vest with a Kevlar weave that will stop 9mm ammo. You can stick extra protective inserts in if you want to – I suggest we go for throat and chest inserts." Adam tapped on one. "It's pretty hard material and can stop or catch any fragments up to a 7.62 mm round with a muzzle velocity of nearly three thousand feet per second."

Mitch repressed a smile.

Adam gave him a sheepish look. "I've had a lot of time on my hands to study this stuff. It's the usual – flame resistant, infrared reflection, thermal signature. They'll be worn under civvies for those of us meant to look like passengers. I've also ordered four transmitter-receivers. It'll only be a few of us that can wear them to communicate without risking breaking cover."

"Great job Adam, thanks," Mitch said, fitting a slung grenade.

"Hey, check this out, Mitch …" Adam continued.

"Get the guns?" Nick asked.

"Yeah, Adam's got it under control; I left him there to finish the paperwork. What did you find out?" Mitch asked.

"Well, according to the receptionist, all of Lawrence's directors featured in the current annual report are still on the payroll and while she wouldn't tell me exactly which ones would be at the meeting, she did say several of them were away on 'special project work'," Nick said, cupping his hands around a cigarette and lighting it. He pushed several torn out pages from an annual report to Mitch. "There's a photo of them in there."

Mitch stirred his coffee as they sat on a bench in Canada Square Park, several blocks from Lawrence's building and their apartment block. He looked at the photos.

"So, that's the Andrew Kenny who ordered Anthony Jenkins to be bumped off. Weak bastard. Not one of these guys will stand up to Lawrence when it comes to right or wrong."

"They either genuinely agree with him or are shit scared."

"Or just spineless." Mitch's eyes moved to Daniel's photo. "Well, Daniel's career is over at least. How did you get the receptionist to talk to you about the directors?"

"I played the part of a cranky shareholder who was coming to town for the Company's General Meeting and I wanted to know who would be there."

"Works for me," Mitch nodded.

"We used to get them calling all the time when I was working for FedEx. It's usually retired folk with plenty of time on their hands who attend – I guess it's an outing."

"Geez, that'll be us one day ... cranky shareholders going to meetings to keep the directors honest."

"And to have our free sandwich and cup of tea," Nick laughed.

"Yeah? There's something to look forward to," Mitch joked. "Hey, if you were off flying FedEx's planes, how did you know shareholders were calling?"

Nick shrugged, "I was sleeping with the receptionist for a while."

"Figures." Mitch pointed to the photo of Brian Davies, "this guy is the one they had the conference call with after the Monaco Mastermind project."

"He's due back in the next few days, according to the receptionist."

"Did you get time to check out the entrance?"

"Uh-huh," Nick exhaled smoke. "One camera above reception, two security guards at a desk to the left. Courier deliveries go directly to the security counter. Three companies have come in so far; Rightway Express, Fast-track and City Bike Couriers. I'm thinking I'll slip on a reasonable imitation outfit to the City Bike Courier driver and do the delivery so I can get in closer."

"I was thinking the same thing," Mitch looked around to make sure he couldn't be heard. "I'm a little wary after the way they handled the kid. For chrissake, be careful."

"I'll be in and out before you know it. Besides, how else could we do it? Letters and email are too risky. I'll keep my head low and wear a baseball cap so I don't get caught on the camera. It's the best way." Nick stubbed out his cigarette.

"Probably."

They finished their coffees in silence, watching a variety of people passing through the park grounds. Mitch checked his watch. "Let's pick up Adam, and go play on the trains."

40

Mitch, Nick and Adam stood with William Irwin, the head of the SO19 unit and David Byrnes, the head of security for the London Underground. They waited while Byrnes spoke to a staff member. Mitch looked around; the office had no natural light, was tucked into a forgotten corner at Charing Cross station and had a distinct damp odor. Taking up most of the back wall was a map of the Underground that had begun to peel away from the wall at each corner.

Mitch referred to his notes and Byrnes's title. He whispered to Nick: "Byrnes looks like his room: out-of-date, faded. He's been in the job too long."

"Was thinking the same thing," Nick agreed. I'm guessing the biggest security scare he's had is probably a parcel left on board a carriage."

"Even then, he would have called in the cops."

Byrnes turned to his waiting audience. "Sorry, gentlemen. Welcome to the Underground. You know, people used to take refuge in the Underground during the war; it was used as a bomb shelter."

Mitch showed polite interest then cut to the chase. "Mr. Byrnes, we have a situation and we need your help."

"What do you need?" Byrnes puffed with importance.

"This Thursday I need full access to the Jubilee line from ten to midnight," Mitch continued, laying their requirements on the line. When he finished, he noted Byrnes looked pale and turned to the chief of police.

"Wouldn't it be easier to go into his offices with a warrant, search the place and arrest him?"

"If this was The Bill or Law and Order, maybe," Mitch said. "But Mr. Byrnes, you will have to trust us on this one – we need to let the subject bring evidence to us."

Mitch turned to the head of the SO19 unit, William Irwin, for back up.

"Special Agent Parker is right, David, it has to be done this way," Irwin concurred.

"Then, I'll do anything I can to help," Byrnes agreed.

Mitch and Adam exchanged quick looks.

As they took the stairs back up to street level, Mitch turned to Adam. "Keep him out of our way; he's more of a liability than an asset."

"I'll assign him an important task," Adam agreed, "maybe clock watching."

———

TUESDAY 0800 WASHINGTON DC
(1300 LONDON, 1400 PARIS)

Samantha met CID agent Sebastian Roe in his boardroom at eight sharp Tuesday morning, the day before the crime was due to take place in Washington's Library of Congress. She noticed the room was surprisingly modern despite the old façade.

He offered her tea and coffee and pushed a plate of shortbread cookies towards her.

Breakfast, she thought, rather have scrambled eggs.

Sitting back with her tea and cookies, Samantha watched as people began to arrive; eight senior police staff – six men, two women. Once they were seated, Roe called for attention. Samantha had nothing new to report – she had heard that morning from John that Daniel was still holding out, which no one had expected. Roe brought the team up to speed. There was a high level of disbelief in the room.

Typical. They'll believe it when it damned well happens, she thought. At least, I hope it happens.

She yawned through the presentation on the current security procedures undertaken at the museum delivered by the Director of Security at the Library of Congress and tried to stay alert while his voice droned on.

"All members of the public on entering the Library go through a metal detector, and everyone exiting passes through an electronic theft-detection system," he explained. "We also check all bags and folders. Anyone booking a reading room or a conference facility has to register with photo identification and a complete security check is run on them. Any material that needs to be brought in for conferences is subject to restrictions. There is video surveillance on all levels and security staff at each stairway, entry and exit."

He resumed his seat and Samantha noticed all eyes turned to Roe.

"Agent Samantha Moore will now explain what information she has to date," Roe announced.

Samantha stood and explained, without any reference to Lawrence, the international Mastermind game up until now and how the Library of Congress fitted into the plan.

———

TUESDAY 2230 LONDON
(2330 PARIS, 1730 WASHINGTON)

Mitch, Nick and Adam rode the Jubilee line several times between ten-thirty and eleven-fifteen that evening. Pacing around the station, Mitch determined where their marksmen would go and where he would stand when he met Lawrence.

Right in the line of fire, but with plenty of back up.

He saw Nick checking out the security cameras.

"Could Lawrence access the live feed from these cameras in the twenty-four hours before the handover? We don't want to risk him seeing us doing our run-through," Nick asked.

Mitch turned to Adam. "It's a good thought. He could buy or hack his way into anything."

I'll get them disconnected on this line from midnight Wednesday," Adam said.

"What's to stop Lawrence coming in here in the twenty-four hours between the delivery of the blackmail note and the handover, and setting up bombs and who knows what?" Nick asked.

"We'll have plain clothes security in this station from the moment we deliver the letter to the handover," Mitch informed him.

"What about when the stations close after one a.m. and before five?" Nick continued.

"Security will stay on."

They threw back and forward scenarios for the next twenty minutes. Eventually, they ran out.

"You've earned a drink," Mitch slapped Nick on the back.

"A warm beer?" he said with a look to Adam.

"I'm sure we can find you a cold one somewhere in London, Nick, even at this hour!" Adam promised him.

―――

On their return, Mitch sat at his laptop finishing the blackmail letter, which was to be delivered tomorrow afternoon. Nick and Adam sat with earphones on, listening to the transcripts from Samantha's planted microphones. They divided up the tapes.

Mitch finished his first draft, stood and walked to the window. He swallowed back the tension rising inside him; even his bones were feeling stiff. Below, the Docklands area was a blaze of lights and several floors were still lit up in Lawrence's building. Mitch slid the glass door open and went out on to the apartment balcony.

He thought about what was to come: tomorrow's going to be one of hell of a day; everything's happening at once. Should think this through again ... at four in the morning we'll have a practice run in the Underground with the SO19 team and the designated train driver. That should take about an hour, before the line opens to the public at five in the morning. Then, Ellie will be on full alert at the Louvre and Sam on alert at the Library of Congress – and I'm not with either of them to provide back up.

Maybe I should take the one-hour flight across to Paris. No, Ellie should be able to manage it with backup from the local agent and his on-the-ground resources. Trust her, he told himself. Hopefully, it would be contained to the area where the Fabergé Eggs are being displayed. Sam on the other hand, worries me. The Library of Congress Mastermind is too ambiguous for my liking. I hope Sebastian Roe's good. I need to speak to John about more backup for Sam.

And by tomorrow, close of business, we deliver the blackmail note and kick in with surveillance of Lawrence and his men.

Then, Thursday night will be deliverance time.

Mitch leaned on the railing, stretching his back, trying to relieve the knots of tension.

I've got to trust the team and try not to control everything – even though I'd feel better about it if I could.

As Nick listened to the tapes, he watched Mitch leaning against the balcony rails.

I know how you feel, Mitch, I'm a bit uptight myself.

He glanced at Adam, sitting opposite with his headphones on.

Adam's the only one who looks like he can't wait for the fun to start. No vested interest, I guess.

The tape finished and Nick turned it off. Adam finished a minute later.

"Shit, that's boring," Nick groaned removing the headset. "Nothing usable there."

"Nothing here either," Adam agreed. "I'm going to bed. I'll see you at three."

"Look forward to it."

———

"Anything?" Mitch asked as Nick joined him on the balcony.

"Nuh. Nothing major on either tape." Nick pulled a cigarette out of the packet in his pocket and lowered himself into one of the white steel chairs, shivering in the cold air.

Mitch glanced through the glass door. "Has Adam turned in?"

"Yeah."

"Should be pretty interesting tomorrow night in that boardroom." He sat down next to Nick. They watched the night traffic, the lights, and the occasional person coming and going.

Nick lit up. "How's your mom these days?"

Mitch looked over at him. "She's good. Keeping busy with her committees and clubs. How are your folks?"

"Good. Dad retired last year. He and Mom are planning an overseas holiday." Nick chuckled. "Can't see it happening though, Dad won't put up with the language barriers and changing money."

"Seems like a lifetime ago we spent summers in your pool." Mitch smiled at the memory.

"Yeah, they were good times. Dad used to give me such a hard time after you'd gone home – nagging me to get a scholarship like you to save him a fortune in school fees. I can hear him now ... why don't you apply yourself like Mitch does ... blah, blah, blah," Nick rolled his eyes.

Mitch grinned.

"Do you ever hear from your dad?" Nick asked.

Mitch stiffened and shook his head. "That summer when he

decided to clear out, that was the last time I saw him," he looked the other way.

Moments later, Mitch turned to face Nick and began to speak, then hesitated. "Did you see him at our air force graduation?"

"No! Was he there?"

Mitch shrugged. "Henri saw him there."

"Did you want to see him?"

"God, no. His clearing out was the best thing that ever happened."

Nick cleared his throat.

"I've got a bit of a confession to make about that."

Mitch froze.

Nick continued. "Remember that long weekend before your dad went away ... the one that was like a heat wave?"

"Yeah ..."

"And we were hanging around the pool but you wouldn't get in, so my Dad threw you in fully dressed?" Nick smiled.

"Yeah," Mitch grinned. "He had a habit of doing that." His smile faded as he remembered it clearly. *I was twelve then, old enough to know not to take on Dad when he came home from the bar. Geez, he was strong when he was drunk.* He locked his jaw, tensing at the memory of his father's fist and leather belt.

He realized Nick was watching him. "What's your confession?"

"When you got out of the pool your T-shirt stuck to your back. You didn't know it, but there were huge blood marks on your T-shirt where the welt marks were."

Mitch shuffled uncomfortably at the memory. Both of them looked out over the balcony.

Nick continued. "Dad was so angry; man, I've never seen him so mad. He was pacing around the kitchen, swearing and carrying on how he couldn't believe any adult could do that to a kid. That night he confronted your father. I was there, waiting for him in the car. Do you remember your dad coming home with the shit beaten out of him about the week before he cleared out?"

"Yeah," Mitch said in a quiet voice. "For a whole week he didn't touch any of us. I thought maybe it was because he realized how much it hurt." Mitch shook his head at the memory. "It was like living with a time bomb waiting for him to start up again. The week after that he was gone and we never saw him again. Best time of my life after that. I'd love to thank whoever beat him senseless."

"Dad did it," Nick cleared his throat. "He told your old man that if he ever laid a hand on you again, he would dish out the same treatment every time. And to prove it, he gave him a walloping. After, Dad got back in the car, told me to keep it to myself and we went home."

Mitch's throat tightened. The memory of his fear and pain as clear to him as if it were yesterday. He struggled with Nick's father's actions.

Mitch inhaled. "Wow."

"Hell, Mitch, it's no big deal; we were like brothers," Nick tapped him on the back.

"Are you kidding? It's a huge deal to me, Nick." The words caught in his throat. "No one stood up for us—no teachers, coaches, friends of Mom's—no one interfered while Mom, my brother and I were copping it regularly. By the time Henri had come on the scene, Dad was gone." Mitch swallowed a lump in his throat.

Nick's father … I was so jealous of Nick having a dad like that, and he's the one who stuck up for us.

"You OK?" Nick asked looking at Mitch.

Mitch nodded, turning away. "I could use a coffee," he said in a low and controlled voice.

He heard Nick stub out his cigarette and rise to go make coffee.

Grateful to have Nick away from him, he gathered himself, breathing deeply and wiping his eyes and face with his hands.

Pull yourself together, he told himself. *Unbelievable. All this time … it was Nick's father that looked out for us.*

Several minutes later he heard Nick return. He handed Mitch one of the cups of instant coffee. "Are you alright?"

"Fine," Mitch's voice broke. He coughed, clearing his throat.

Nick nodded and sipped his coffee.

Mitch ran his hand over his eyes. He rose. "I've got to turn in; early start." He hurried past Nick.

"Mitch ..." Nick stood up behind him.

Mitch didn't risk speaking; he slid the glass door closed behind him, leaving Nick with his coffee on the balcony.

On Wednesday morning at three o'clock, the three men moved around each other, dressing and preparing for the rehearsal. No one spoke. Mitch, who was ready first, waited at the door. Nick and Adam filed out and Mitch locked it behind them. They entered the Underground stop at Canary Wharf where a security officer had been briefed and was expecting them. He opened the caged wire door to let them through. Within thirty minutes, the full team was present – six officers, plus David Byrnes from the Underground, William Irwin head of SO19 and a train driver assigned to the police service.

Mitch directed teams to go with Adam and Nick. He moved between both, listening in as Adam took aside the two officers assigned to the entrances and the three men who would be on the platform; two as passengers, one in a concealed sniper position with Ellen when she returned from Paris. Mitch distributed photos of Lawrence and the directors, leaving Adam to run through the scenarios, contacts and the plan for that evening with his team.

Mitch moved over to Nick's group and watched as Nick directed the men he would be managing, allocating them carriage positions and advising them they would get on at Waterloo station. William Irwin followed Mitch and moved between both teams.

After thirty minutes, Mitch called them together and, with Adam, talked through the weaponry, which was stored underground at Canary Wharf. Mitch called for questions and between the three men, they fielded a few. Close to five a.m., Mitch wrapped it up, confident with the group. The three men spent another hour with David Byrnes and William Irwin before leaving.

As they walked along the main street, looking for somewhere to eat breakfast at six in the morning, Mitch did the time calculations.

Six a.m. here; Paris is an hour ahead – Ellie should be up.

"This do?" Adam pointed to a modern café with its lights on.

"Perfect," Mitch nodded entering the warmth of the café. The owner welcomed them to sit and they slid into a booth as the waiter dropped over the menus. Mitch dialed Ellen's number. He glanced around, but there was no one in listening range.

She instinctively answered the phone in French. "Bonjour."

Mitch smiled. "Very sexy!"

"Mitch!" she laughed. "Sorry I wasn't thinking ... totally in the zone. Thanks for saying I sound sexy though, I must use my French more."

"Did I wake you?" he asked.

"No way, I went for a jog about five this morning and now I'm on my way to meet Gerard Astier at the Louvre."

"What's the plan?" Mitch asked Ellen as Nick took the menu from him and ordered on his behalf.

"That's the frustrating part," Ellen continued, "I wish we knew their plan. The best we can do is monitor the area all day. I'm going to be the curator so I'll be standing next to the Fabergé Eggs to answer questions about the collection. I've had a crash course."

"Will you be armed?"

"Yes. Plus Gerard will have agents in the roles of tour guides, so any tour group in the Richelieu Wing will have an agent leading it."

"Excellent. It's great he's taking this so seriously."

"Yes, well pardon the pun, but there would be serious egg on his face if these objects d'art that have traveled the world were stolen at the Parisian exhibition."

"True."

"We've left the existing security in place. The head of the Louvre's security, Gilles Revault, swears by his staff. Gerard and I agreed to this so we didn't raise suspicion and also, if it is one of them, we don't want to forewarn them."

"So, they don't know what's happening?"

"No, they've been told that some new tour guides are in training and they are to do their usual duties. We also have an additional five security contractors brought in who'll be playing the part of tourists, visiting curators – an assortment of roles, all armed and alert. Basically, we don't know what we're in for, but we're ready."

"Ellie, great job. I'll be sweating it out until I hear from you, so keep me updated when you can."

"I will."

Mitch lowered his voice. "Ellie, faites attention s'il vous plait; au revoir."

He waited as she translated the words in her head – Ellie, please be careful. Bye for now.

"Well done on the French," she teased.

"Yeah, I might have cheated on that last one. I looked it up earlier."

Ellen laughed. "Talk later."

Mitch hung up, turning back to the two men just as an English hot breakfast arrived for all three.

"I'd love to hear her speak in French," Nick passed Mitch the salt before he asked for it. "In fact, you sounded so good, if I was gay, I'd be doing you now."

"Thank God for small mercies," Mitch said taking the salt.

"Good breakfast," Nick concluded.

"Now, that's a decent English breakfast. Bet you can't get that at home," Adam sat back.

"You're right. At home it's called an American breakfast!" Nick grinned.

Adam laughed. "You'll keep."

Mitch sat back with a mug of tea and pushed a piece of paper towards them both.

"What do you think? It's the blackmail letter."

The two agents read it: Bring one million pounds this Thursday

November 28 to the Canary Wharf tube stop. Meet the last carriage of the northbound train at eleven p.m. Give the male who steps from the carriage carrying a black folder, the one million pounds in exchange for the folder. You will turn and leave via the stairs to your left. The folder will contain the MM-3 file disc. One other electronic copy exists. If the collector returns safely and if you come alone, the existing copy will be deleted. If not, the information will be sent electronically to MI5 and the newspapers.

"Clear enough? Too wordy? Did I miss anything?" Mitch asked.

The two men read it several times.

"Too educated," Nick said.

"What do you mean?" Mitch looked at him.

"It sounds too educated. You want these guys to think you're not the sharpest knife in the draw; you don't want them to be too prepared"

"OK," Mitch agreed. "Edit it."

Nick grabbed a pen from his jacket and went to work. Adam and Mitch watched him, while they finished off a pot of tea.

"Here," Nick passed the edited version back.

Bring one million unmarked pounds to the Canary Wharf tube stop this Thursday November 28. Look for the last carriage of the northbound train at eleven p.m. A man carrying a black folder will step out. Exchange the money with him for the folder containing your files. Leave taking the steps to your left. One copy exists. If we get the money safely, it will be destroyed. If not, we'll send it to the press and cops.

"Better," Mitch agreed, "much better. Thanks."

"Let the games begin," Adam said with a smile.

41

WEDNESDAY 1300 PARIS
(1200 LONDON, 0700 WASHINGTON)

ELLEN SAW GERARD ASTIER, THE U.S. FRENCH-BASED AGENT, IN HER peripheral vision. She could see he too was on high alert, watching every movement. Ellen counted twelve tour groups that had come and gone. Acting as one of the curators, she answered a thousand questions shamelessly making up what she didn't know. She kept moving to take in all aspects of the room.

Ellen watched the security guards swap over for their lunch break at one p.m. The head of security, Revault, came to check on progress. Abrupt and distracted, he suggested Ellen take a break.

"Thanks, Gilles, but this is one day where I intend to stay put, even if it means concentrating for nine hours straight." She sighed with frustration. "We've been here half the day and nothing yet. The tension is killing me."

"I understand. It is difficult to maintain security in a building that was not designed to be a museum," Revault shook his head as he took in the surrounds of the eight hundred-year-old palace.

"I can't begin to imagine," Ellen agreed answering him in French.

"We house over thirty-two thousand works of art here," he continued, "in over sixty thousand square meters of space – and you know, more than five million people come through here in one year. We're still recovering from the criticism we received when Carot's painting was stolen nearly eight years ago – and that was exhibited in a room with protective glass and video cameras!"

"How did they do it?"

"They cut the painting out of the frame with a razor blade."

"It must be twice as hard for these temporary exhibitions," Ellen said nodding towards the Fabergé collection.

"Exactly," he said. "I would prefer not to have them, but we can't profess to be a contemporary, international museum if we cannot display significant pieces. A few years ago we appointed a security company to revise all of our security at great expense. Now, we've got eight hundred video surveillance cameras and over fifteen hundred intrusion alarm points. Still, it is not enough and the staff complain that they are stretched trying to secure too large an area each. Excuse me," he said distracted by a tourist with a flash camera.

Ellen found no comfort in the Head of Security's words; her senses were sharpened to overload. Even the flash of a camera, which was banned, triggered an alert state in her. She turned to see what the fuss was about as security made it known that flash cameras were not to be used. Ellen felt a rush of panic and excitement. I have to get this right, she thought. I need a win on the board. After the breakdown in the mines, I've got to prove to Mitch that I can be counted on.

Ellen gasped. She saw it! She almost couldn't believe it.

As a large tour group moved away, another camera flash went off. The second security guard on the floor called out that flashes were banned and all eyes turned towards the elderly couple in question. That's when Ellen turned back from the scene of the flash to look at the Fabergé Eggs. Out of the corner of her eye she saw the security guard, who had stepped in during the lunch break, swipe his access pass across the alarmed glass box, shutting down the alarm. In a matter of seconds, he opened the glass door, removed a Fabergé Egg from the shelf in front of him and replaced it with a perfect replica, pocketing the original, fragile miniature egg into his jacket pocket. He closed the glass, swiped the card and reactivated the alarm. He looked around, thinking he had got away with it and nodded to the other guard who was continuing to distract crowds by arguing with the elderly couple with the flash camera. Ellen noticed all eyes were turned to the elderly couple who were complaining that they were told they could take photos.

Ellen was stunned – it was perfect in its simplicity. Frighteningly easy for the security guard. She glanced towards the security cameras; they were pivoting, yet to make their return cycle to the glass cases that housed the eggs.

Given that two camera flashes had gone off now, one earlier, has the security guard substituted two eggs? He still has over thirty minutes before the original guard returns from lunch, is he going to do more?

Ellen debated what to do. *Do I let them finish the swap ... I don't want to risk letting it get out of hand.* She looked around. *The other security guard is obviously in on it to create the diversion. Are the people with the cameras as well? Revault will be disappointed it's an inside job.* Ellen waited thinking through the process, not letting the substitute guard out of her sight. She needed to catch him with the eggs in his jacket.

This is unbelievable!

She caught Gerard Astier's eye and nodded, giving him the sign that the action had taken place. His eyes grew huge for a moment then he went poker faced. The accomplice guard was pacing, his back to Ellen. She indicated him with her eyes and the other guard behind her with the Fabergé Egg in his jacket. She patted her jacket pocket once as a sign. Astier nodded. He raised his eyebrows as if to ask should he intercept now. Ellen nodded, she wanted to contain this while she felt confident that she had the upper hand and she wanted to avoid drawing weapons and damaging the gallery in any way. She waited while Astier went about his business.

Outside, Astier halted a tour group from going into the room. He placed an officer at the entrance to hold back the public and dispersed four of his own team to wait outside the room's two entrances for his signal. He sent another two plain-clothed officers into the room to take up the boundaries. He looked around, satisfied everyone was in place and bracing himself, Astier re-entered the room.

———

Ellen saw Astier enter and walk towards her. He waved to the two suspect guards as though nothing out of the usual was happening. With a brief nod to the officer in the wings behind the security guard, the room erupted with noise.

Ellen felt her heart pounding.

She saw the flash of guns. Heard the shouting as manpower invaded the room.

Behind Astier, two more officers pounded in from the entrances and sealed the room. People strained to see what was going on. The two security guards were forced to their knees, weapons removed. There was no return fire, no struggle. Astier came close to Ellen.

"I don't know if it's just the two of them," Ellen said. "They created a diversion and swapped the eggs. There were several people with cameras who used flashes; they might be involved."

Astier called over two of his officers and ordered them to lock down the Richelieu wing. No one was to go in or out. He radioed Revault, to seal the entrances. The officers opened the doors and burst out into the waiting crowds, securing the area. Ellen could hear loud voices telling the public to remain calm. Astier and Ellen walked towards the guard. Revault was let in through one of the entrances.

"The honor is yours," Astier said to Ellen.

With a smile, she reached into the security guard's jacket and carefully removed two eggs, one at a time from each side of his large jacket. Revault could not accept it.

"Francois!" he exclaimed looking at his staff member amazed.

Francois scowled.

"Oh, my God," Revault continued in French, taking the two eggs. He glanced at the first one, no more than five inches high and covered in a multitude of pearls. "The Lilies of the Valley Egg. This was presented to Czar Nicholas II in 1898," he muttered in shock, "and the Coronation Egg," Revault moaned, gazing at the translucent yellow egg. He looked inside and breathed a sigh of relief on seeing the miniature coronation coach intact. "It was presented in 1897 by Czar Nicholas II to his wife Alexandra Feodorovna," he told Ellen, turning both eggs around looking for damage.

"It was an uncomplicated plot by trusted people," Ellen consoled Revault in French.

"But not quite good enough," Astier smiled. "Is that it?"

Ellen gently patted down the guard's jacket, it was empty.

"Hang on," Astier said. He frisked the other guard. A smile swept over his face as he removed another two from him.

"Four in total," she said. "I suspect those two are fakes that had not yet been swapped."

Two of the officers who were searching the room for bombs, joined Astier.

"All clear, sir," one of them pronounced.

"Good; help Chassat and Briard outside. We need to speak to anyone who used a flash in here in the last hour," Astier ordered.

The two men hurried from the room. Ellen could see the officer speaking with an agitated elderly couple.

"We'll never be trusted again," Revault continued talking to himself and holding the two eggs.

"I suggest, given the workmanship on the replicas, that you get all the collection authenticated again," Ellen said to Revault as she studied the four eggs.

He nodded, still in shock.

Officer Chassat entered the room.

"Sir," he said in French, "the older couple with the camera said they were told they could use a flash in the Richelieu wing by the security guard outside the door."

"Thank you Officer, detain them for a minute. We may need them to identify the guard who gave them permission."

"It was a female guard sir."

"The only female guard in this area is Ami Porte," Revault stepped in. He hurried to the door. There was no guard there now. Using his intercom he called down to the entrances to detain Ami Porte if she is seen. Within fifteen minutes, Revault's security team radioed they had found her at the main entrance to the Louvre, trying to leave via the courtyard of the Pyramid, Cour Napoleon. Astier sent an officer down to interrogate her. Thirty minutes later it was confirmed that there were three Louvre guards involved. Astier departed to oversee the removal of the arrested guards.

Ellen waited with Revault as he called the exhibition curator to remove the eggs for authenticity testing. He ordered a sign to be placed in front of the area apologizing for the temporary removal of the exhibition.

"There is one thing I don't understand," Ellen address Revault in French. "Why didn't they attempt this at night when no one was around? Surely it would be easier."

"No, at night the collection is put in a vault which they can't access. The guards only get access to certain areas within their patrol zones. It's another one of our safety initiatives. These men have been working on exhibitions for years, that's why their cards could disarm the alarms in that area," he said in a flat voice.

Ellen nodded her understanding. Revault turned away.

Twenty minutes later, Astier returned. "They removed the tape from the security cameras before doing the job. They thought of everything."

"They had access to everything in this area," Ellen looked around.

"I believe I owe you a drink Mademoiselle Ellen. Champagne?"

"Champagne would be wonderful," Ellen exclaimed.

"I'll just see my officers out," he said.

Ellen nodded. Walking out of the Pyramid entrance to the Louvre, she felt the relief coursing through her. She rang Mitch.

———

Mitch's phone rang. Recognizing Ellen's number, he nearly dropped it in his haste to answer.

"Ellie?"

"Mitch, we've done it!"

Mitch exhaled with relief. He realized he had stopped breathing when the phone rang. He turned to give Nick the thumbs up sign. Ellen told him everything.

"Beautiful," Mitch exclaimed. "I can't believe it was that easy and they almost got away with it."

"I know; security here is a bit of a sore point," Ellen told him. "And as they were staff and had been for some time, they weren't subject to the same security checks that the public were. They could swan in and out of here and no one was any the wiser. We came so close to not seeing it happen, it was so subtle."

"How many did they swap?" Mitch asked

"They were going for four, I only saw two swapped. They're testing them all now. Those four alone are priceless," Ellen said. "I wish we were able to get Lawrence's director as well."

"We'll get him soon enough. He'll be flying back before you, I imagine. Ellie, you've done a great job."

"Can I get John to book me on a flight to London tonight?"

"I thought you were keen to have a break from us?"

"I never said that."

"I know. I kind of sensed you needed some breathing space. Glad you want to come back. Call John, a flight tonight or tomorrow morning is fine ... we're not operating until eleven tomorrow evening. Go out and do some sightseeing."

"I'm being taken out for champagne, real French champagne, by Gerard."

"Is that so," Mitch teased, "I'd better not tell Nick that; he'd be over there like a shot to escort you back."

"Really?" she laughed pleased.

"Ellie, well done, I'll let John know you have wrapped it up. Go have some fun." Mitch hung up. He looked over at Nick who was looking worried.

"She's not going out with a Frog, is she?" he asked.

"No, having champagne to celebrate with the American agent on the ground, although ... with a name like Astier ..."

"Hmm. What happened?"

Mitch glanced at his watch. "It was the security guards. I'll fill you in ... just give me a sec, I've just got to call Sam. Let's see ... should be nearly nine in the morning in D.C." Biting his bottom lip, he dialed her number. "Well that's one down – two to go."

"Worried?" Nick asked.

"Yeah," Mitch frowned. "I feel like the D.C. Mastermind is slipping through my fingers."

42

WEDNESDAY 0845 WASHINGTON DC
(1345 LONDON, 1445 PARIS)

"THE LIBRARY'S DUE TO OPEN IN FIFTEEN MINUTES," SAMANTHA TOLD Mitch. "The exhibition's on the second floor of the Thomas Jefferson Building, so that's where we'll be concentrating, as well as the entrances on the first floor."

Samantha kept talking as she walked, flashing her badge to the library's security officers and Roe's people to get clearance through the main entrance. "Roe's got more cops here then you've had hot breakfasts – well, English hot breakfasts. We've got six acting as tourists milling around on different levels, a further four in plain clothes on each of the entrances, two in the reading rooms and four security guards around the display on the first floor. He's also organized extra security checks at the entrances; it's going to be a long day."

"What are you doing?" Mitch asked.

"I'm playing the tourist." Samantha looked the part in jeans, a jacket and loose sweater, a camera around her neck, and a small Glock handgun hidden from view and clipped to the inside waist band of her jeans.

"What's the general hunch?"

Samantha groaned, mounting the stairs two at a time to the first floor. "Given the layout of the room, it's anyone's guess. The exhibition is in front of the Great Hall, near the Congressional Members Rooms. Access to the stairs and First Street, which is down one level, is close to the display, so getting in and out quickly is not impossible."

"How big is the exhibition?"

"Not that big. The display area itself is no more than twenty by six feet, and the display consists of twelve Dead Sea Scroll fragments and some artefacts."

Mitch let out a low whistle. "There would be religious factions who would pay big money for one scroll, let alone twelve. Who's organizing the exhibition?" He continued to drill Samantha.

Samantha shuffled through her notes. "The Israel Antiquities Authority. We've checked them out."

She heard silence on the line.

"What are you thinking, Mitch?"

"I don't know; to be honest, I'm struggling with this one. Been processing it in my head all night."

"Me too," Samantha stopped to watch Roe directing his men. She looked dwarfed amongst the high arches and deeply decorated ceilings of the building's interior.

There was another long silence.

"Sam, we're talking about someone trying to steal probably the oldest copy in existence of the Hebrew bible and parts of the Ten Commandments. It's making me nervous – it could be more dangerous then we assumed."

"If I wasn't worried enough before, I am now," she told him.

"I don't want to panic you. I'm just making sure you are aware of the ramifications. This might not be a nice little snatch and grab. Who's coming in on the tours today?"

"Tours, hold on," Samantha shuffled more papers. She sat down on a bench, her sneakers squeaking on the marble floor. "There are public tours running every hour from ten until three o'clock and eight group tours booked in starting at nine-thirty, the last one's at one-thirty. They're limited to fifty people per tour."

"That's two per hour, fairly heavy traffic. How long is each tour?"

"One hour including the security checks. And, there is one constituent tour today at eleven."

"What's that?"

"It's a tour arranged through the Congressional offices. Basically, constituents can arrange special tours through their representatives," she told Mitch.

"Did Roe not think to cancel any of them to reduce the amount of traffic going through?"

"No," she answered. "Sorry, I should have thought of it."

Samantha stood as she heard the crowds gathering outside. "The library's about to open; there are tour groups here already."

"OK," Mitch sighed.

Again she heard silence on the line.

"Mitch?"

"Thinking."

She waited.

"Give me the travel agents names and any names you have for the eight group tours," Mitch ordered.

Samantha read them out, waiting as Mitch wrote down each one.

"Nick, take these," she heard Mitch say. "Sam, I'll call you back, and lay low. Don't be a hero."

"OK." She hung up and raced down the stairs as the doors to the building opened for the day.

WEDNESDAY 0900 WASHINGTON DC
(1400 LONDON, 1500 PARIS)

"Adam, I need your networks," Nick yelled to him from the laptop in the lounge room.

Adam appeared wet from the shower, a towel wrapped around him.

"I need to do international security checks ..."

"Shove over," Adam sat next to Nick opening an Internet page and logging in. After a few minutes he was through. "That should give you a person's record if they've got one."

"Perfect, thanks," Nick said his eyes not leaving the screen. Adam returned to the bathroom to dress.

Within seconds Nick was on the phone to a travel agent, faking he was with the Library of Congress Security team. He requested a full list of names for the touring party. The first group took five minutes to come via email. He ran the names through the international database. "These all check out – a group of senior citizens from Scotland on a Trafalgar Tour. No one on board had anything more than a speeding ticket on their file."

Mitch leaned over Nick's shoulder and tore the list he wrote in half. He started by calling the travel agent and requesting the information while Nick ran names through the database.

"The second group are primary school students," Mitch announced. "Nick, run checks on the teachers listed as attending."

Nick typed in the names.

"All clear," he announced after a few minutes.

"Can't get the individual names for this group," Mitch said hanging up the phone. "Not as obliging as Trafalgar Tours."

Adam came up behind him.

"American Express travel ... I know a lady in the New York office. Let me try."

Mitch passed him the details.

"Next group's clear," Nick said. "Sports group package with a few cultural things thrown in. No one on board is interested in anything but sport, they'll be in and out before you can say 'offside'." He took a few mouthfuls of water from a bottle beside him.

"No records?" Mitch asked, surprised.

"Other than a few drink driving charges and a case of minor assault—alcohol related—we're clear."

Nick moved onto the last name on his list. He entered the data and his eyes lit up. "Hold on. We're onto something here. Who are these guys?"

Mitch joined him.

"They're booked under the name United Theological University; eight theology students due to go through the library at twelve-thirty. Check this out ... if I run the contact's name, he comes up with a criminal record and a connection to a group called Atheos."

Mitch felt his heart rate quickening. "Atheos – that's Greek, it means 'godless'."

Adam overheard. "I know them. They've got networks in the U.S., here in the U.K. and throughout Europe. They're about two thousand strong. We came across them six months ago – they call themselves purists."

"Explain what you mean by purists?" Mitch asked Adam.

"They're atheists; they believe in pure science. They don't believe in any form of religion and consider organized religion to be corrupt. They aim to put an end to faith through scientific proof, and they're growing in number."

Mitch let out a low whistle. "Can you imagine?"

"People wouldn't know what to do," Nick added. "Right and wrong, heaven and hell – it's all part of our psyche. Even our calendar is set up around holy days – Christmas, Easter, etc."

"Exactly. It would be incomprehensible, if it could be achieved," Adam agreed.

"Well, we're getting too smart for our own good," Mitch added. "Weren't they doing carbon-date testing on the Shroud of Turin a few years ago?"

"Yes, and that's my point," Adam said. "Even when they concluded it could be the real thing, there were as many reports that came out faulting the testing process and its authenticity. While the print on the material matched that of wounds received by a crucified man, there was no evidence that it was wrapped around a man named Jesus. Let's face it, even if they had proven it wasn't as old as it should be, would everyone accept that as gospel, so to speak?"

Nick shrugged. "The world doesn't need to lose any more faith in my opinion."

Mitch looked up surprised. "I thought you had lost all faith."

Nick smirked at him, and continued. "All of them go to university—not the same university—but they are all third-year theology students. That would make them around twenty years of age, I'm guessing."

Adam nodded. "These guys spend every cent they raise trying to disprove religion. When we were investigating them, their U.K. branch was fundraising for a mission to find the remains of Jesus Christ."

"Won't finding that prove that there is a God?" Nick asked.

"No, the opposite. Most of western faith is based on the principle that Jesus was resurrected after being crucified. This gives people hope that there is life after death. If they find the bones ..."

"I hear you!" Nick said, "I bet a five million pound Mastermind prize pool would make that trip a reality."

"Exactly. Plus, I imagine some of these Dead Sea Scrolls may interest them greatly." Adam reached for some papers he had printed out earlier. He read, "The Dead Sea Scrolls predate Jesus by approximately eight years and, as a consequence, there are no direct references to his life and teachings. The manuscript copies are at least a thousand years older than previously known biblical manuscripts and highlight the fact that several versions of the same biblical texts were in circulation at that time – and views differed about which versions were more authoritative," he looked up. "No doubt Atheos want to study them to see how else they might discredit religious faith."

"They may just want them to sell to the highest private bidder, take the money and put it towards their work," Nick suggested.

"True," Mitch agreed. "OK, Nick, check that this Atheos group are still on schedule for the tour – and see if you can get any photo I.D.s of them."

"Will do," Nick returned to the laptop.

"Adam, can you start running the names of the Atheos tour group members through the system and see who else has got a criminal record, beside the head contact?"

"Done," Adam agreed.

Mitch went out on the balcony for fresh air and to think. He could hear his heart beating it was so loud. He paced the balcony waiting for Adam's list of names.

Maybe this job's too big for Sam ... I should have sent Nick with her. Then again, it is in a closed environment and she has a full squad with her. I hate leading by remote control. He went back inside. Adam was hanging up.

"A couple of trespassing, and break and enter charges between them – all with a religious motivation," Adam informed him.

"Here's their pics coming through," Nick opened the photo files one after the other, printing them out.

"I'd say we've got our Mastermind team, due at the library at twelve-thirty," Adam confirmed looking at the profiles as they came off the printer. "Hold on, this guy looks familiar – he's a local."

"Five from the U.S., one from the U.K.?" Mitch asked.

Adam checked the photos and I.D.s.

"Yep, looks like it. Wonder why the U.K. lad got a look in," Adam thought out loud.

"Must be some reason for the collaboration," Mitch answered.

"So they're playing United Nations, but how are they going to do it? If we could get that we'd have the element of surprise," Nick said.

Mitch paced the room. Nick kept searching on the net. He printed out several more pages.

"I should have gone to D.C.," Mitch ran his hand over his jaw.

"Mitch, you can't be in every fight," Nick came over to join him. "OK, let's think it through; we might come up with something between the three of us." He placed the map of the ground and first floors of the Thomas Jefferson building of the Library of Congress in front of them.

Mitch pounced on it with renewed focus. "Here's the Great Hall on the first floor. The exhibition will be at the end of the Great Hall right next to the Congressional Members' Room. In front is the staircase which goes down two flights and exits out onto First Street," he pointed to the ground floor map.

"What's going on in the Congressional Members' Room today?" Adam asked.

Mitch dialed Samantha. She took a few minutes to find the information. Hanging up, he relayed it to Nick and Adam.

"Nothing, it's not booked," Mitch reported back. "Let's get back to basics. The group is on an hour-long tour starting at twelve-thirty. They're going to be with a staff member tour guide and they're doing the whole museum – so, in theory, they should be getting to the Scrolls exhibition at around one-fifteen. Why would they book a tour when they could wander in and look at the scrolls anytime?"

"So, what's the benefit of being in a tour group?" Adam asked.

Mitch dialed Samantha again instructing her to find out what this group would be getting as part of their tour.

"How well do we know this tour guide?" Adam asked when Mitch hung up.

"All the tour guides checked out … but as the Paris Mastermind taught us, that doesn't guarantee anything. But we can't risk replacing the guides in case any of them are working with Atheos – it'd blow it wide open." Mitch closed his eyes picturing the scene. "They're going to be there in less than two hours. We've got to get this; we can't risk those scrolls being taken."

"What if they destroy them then and there?" Nick asked.

Mitch opened his eyes. "It's possible, but not logical that they would destroy them. Firstly, the scrolls support their case in as much as they create questions about the bible – and second, they could sell them off to fund-raise."

"Fair enough." Nick glanced at the clock. "Mitch, you'll have to take five minutes off that case and focus on the other one. Print me out your bribery note and I'll push off."

Mitch rose. *If I could just slow things down,* he thought, *it's all happening too fast.*

Nick watched Mitch print out the blackmail note, being careful not to leave any prints on it. He stuffed it in an envelope, addressed it and gave it to Nick who took hold of it with a gloved hand.

"I'd better go," Nick said looking at his watch. Heading for the door he grabbed his baseball cap and folder.

"Thanks," Mitch called after him. "Yell if there are any dramas."

"It'll be fine. Keep your shirt on," he said seeing Mitch look at his watch for the fourth time in the last minute.

Closing the door behind him, Nick increased his pace to Cabot Square to make the delivery by four-thirty.

Need to be there when the last courier run for the day happens, otherwise it might arouse suspicion or attention. I want Lawrence to get our letter by close of business so he can have tonight to plan.

Entering Cabot Square, Nick dodged the swell of traffic as shift workers hurried to get home. The skies opened and he ran under cover in the courtyard of a building opposite Lawrence's offices, out of the rain. For the first fifteen minutes there was not one courier driver in site.

"Shit, shit, shit!" he swore to himself, hoping to blend in with another delivery.

Nick was thinking up Plan B, when two bike couriers pulled up. One ran into Lawrence's building, the Credit Suisse, with a parcel. Nick took the opportunity to make his delivery while the other courier was at reception. Keeping his head down, he bolted across the courtyard, entered Lawrence's building and waited his turn. Nick handed over the envelope to the security guard, collected a signature on his fake delivery sheet and followed behind the other courier as he headed out of the doors.

He sighed with relief, returning to his former position to see who would come down to collect it. Five minutes later, he saw a young woman, possibly Lawrence's personal assistant, arrive to retrieve it.

That whole exercise took less than fifteen minutes and the letter is on its way. *Clean!* He hurried back to the apartment.

WEDNESDAY 1615 LONDON
(1115 WASHINGTON DC)

Mitch heard Nick return and turned to get feedback. Nick gave him the thumbs up as he collapsed onto the sofa and put in one earphone to listen in on any conversation in Lawrence's office, keeping the other ear free to talk to Mitch.

"All OK?" Mitch asked.

"Done and all-clear. It was even collected as I watched from across the road," Nick said.

"Thanks, Nick."

"This should be fun," Nick said.

"For some," Mitch frowned. "We've already caused the death of a kid. I'm more worried about who might be next."

"Oh lighten up. Could you be any more uptight? You'll keel over with a heart attack at this rate," Nick said.

"That's fine for you to say Nick, you only have to watch your own back. I'm responsible for that kid's death."

"How are you responsible? Lawrence is responsible. And if you are saying I wouldn't stand by the team ..." Nick glared at him.

"Well you haven't been tested yet. It's been pretty much about self-preservation so far, oh, and protecting Maria."

"You're completely off the mark," Nick's eyes narrowed with anger. "I've had Ellie's back in the plane, not to mention yours and ..."

Adam whistled and both men turned to look at him.

"Time out. Can you two work together?" he asked.

Mitch and Nick answered in unison.

"Of course we can," Mitch said.

"Yeah, we did it for years in the Air Force," Nick agreed.

Adam shook his head. "I've got something if I can interrupt?"

Mitch turned his concentration to Adam who was frowning at the photos of the six students.

"What's up?" Mitch asked.

"There is something wrong here." Adam jumped to his feet.

"What?"

"I've just thought of something," reaching for his phone, Adam made a quick call. He wrote down two names. After hanging up, he rejoined them. "Paul and Ronin Asher! You know how I said we came across members of the group here last year?"

Mitch nodded.

"At that time, six months ago, they were under scrutiny for making a scene during the playing of the national anthem at Wimbledon – it has the reference to God Save the Queen."

Mitch pushed him along. "Yep, and now one of those UK members is in the Library of Congress group taking a tour?"

"Yes, Ronin is, the other one isn't." Adam waited for Mitch to catch up.

"But as you said, there are hundreds of members ..."

"But I remember this lad ... he has a twin, an identical twin."

Mitch and Nick stared at him for a minute.

"Ronin Asher, the boy on the tour doesn't have his twin with him. Where is he?" Adam concluded.

Mitch's eyes flared with excitement. "Adam, call the Library of Congress. Get them to search through their tour group lists, their research library booking lists, staff lists, any list they can find for the names, Paul and Ronin ...?"

"Asher!" Adam said, picking up the phone.

"Nick, we need to send their photos to Samantha's phone; Paul might wander through the Library on his own."

"Done," Nick confirmed.

Mitch paced. "I can see why Lawrence gets off on this Mastermind stuff. It's riveting."

"I know; I'm almost disappointed when they don't work," Nick agreed.

"Anything happening in Lawrence's office?"

"Not yet," Nick answered, listening in through his earpiece.

After a few minutes, Adam turned to Mitch. "How about that?" he said hanging up the phone. "Paul Asher was awarded a Library of Congress Junior Fellows Internship for the summer. He's working in the artefacts preservation project area. What are the odds that area works with the scrolls?"

Mitch made a call. Hanging up, he stood by the fax, grabbing at the printout when it came through moments later.

"Ronin's on a holiday visa in the States; Paul is on a short-term work visa." Mitch looked up at the two men and smiled. "That's fantastic," he exhaled, "absolutely fantastic." He dropped onto the sofa, sitting back and allowing himself a few moments to enjoy it, but couldn't keep still. "So how are they going to do it?" he stood up. "They've got six members from their group taking a tour, Paul's working inside and Ronin is on the tour. What are they going to do with him? How could they use a double in a crime?"

Adam and Nick looked frustrated.

"There has got to be some way they're planning to fool security by using the twins masquerading as one person," Nick said.

Adam turned around from the computer.

"Here's some info on the Junior Fellows Programs." He read it out loud. "The Library of Congress Junior Fellows Program offers a small number of fellowships each year for students enrolled in or completing undergraduate or graduate academic programs. Applicants from outside the United States are welcome, however it is entirely the responsibility of the successful applicant to obtain a U.S. work visa and to meet all personal expenses necessary to work at the

Library of Congress." Adam continued. "The Junior Fellow will carry out a variety of tasks dealing with topics in artefacts preservation, religion, philosophy, psychology, manuscripts and/or law. A Fellow may be involved in cataloguing, analyzing or classifying material. This provides students with an excellent opportunity to experience what takes place behind the scenes at the Library of Congress."

"These kids are good," a smile swept across Mitch's face.

43

WEDNESDAY 1145 WASHINGTON DC
(1645 LONDON)

"FOR THE LAST TIME, I HAVE NOTHING TO SAY!" DANIEL REID GLARED AT John Windsor who sat opposite him in an interrogation room in the D.C. Central Cellblock.

John nodded at the guard. "The charges, please."

The guard began to read; "shooting at a police officer, attempted murder, and deprivation of liberty."

"Do you understand those charges?" John asked Daniel.

"Do you understand I have nothing to say?" Daniel continued in his British accent. "I've heard the charges before."

"Play the tough guy all you like, Mr. Reid, it's your neck on the line."

"My neck? You fly me back here from Nevada to read the same charges to me, lock me up in the same size cell and refuse to release me. What's the point?"

"Convenience. I didn't want to travel to Nevada every time I thought of a question."

"Screw you."

John watched him. "You're not as impressive in your orange jumpsuit, Mr. Reid. But we've put aside your slick suit and polished shoes for when you get out in the distant future." John rose to go. He put his suit jacket back on and picked up several files, noting a slight panic in Daniel's face. John turned to the officer at the door.

"We're done here, thank you."

The officer nodded.

"What do you mean you're done here? You pull me out of my cell and drag me here to read me my charges?" Daniel blurted.

John turned. "I thought you would like an outing. Don't worry, we'll take you back to your cell now. You've probably got about twenty years in there, what's the rush to get back?"

"Come on, you've come down here to offer me a deal?" he smirked. "No reduced sentence for some information? Why the hell are you here?"

John stopped.

"Not to see you. I've other business in this building. One of the prisoners has been found beaten to a pulp, you just happen to be on the way. Killing two birds with one stone you might say."

"So you're not even going to try and cut a deal?"

"No, no deal. I have all I need now. Oh, I did want to mention that Lawrence has left you high and dry. Claims he's never heard of you. But I've got all I need from Lawrence's director on the Fabergé job at the Louvre. He's cut himself a pretty good deal," John bluffed. He saw his words had the effect he wanted; Daniel's eyes enlarged and darted from the security officer to John.

"He'll be out in a few days, new identity, new life. You, on the other hand, are a loyal employee. I'm sure Lawrence prizes that above all else."

Daniel ran his tongue over his lips. "Wait."

"Mr. Reid, there is nothing you could say that would be of value to us now."

"I know about the Washington job."

"So do we." He glanced at his watch. "In fact, as we speak, I think we're finishing that one up."

"If I speak against Lawrence ..." Daniel licked his lips again.

"There is no need to. I've got him."

Daniel fidgeted in his chair. "What about the Monaco job, I can tell you about the Monaco job!" John stopped and returned.

"I'm not familiar with it," he said knowing it was already over.

"If it succeeded, you wouldn't know about it."

John closed the door and sat back down.

"I'm all ears."

"Not until we make a deal," Daniel said.

"Alright, we can do a deal; but first, I want to hear about the Washington job ... I hate waiting for the reports to come in," John tried not to betray the urgency in his voice.

He saw the realization dawning on Daniel.

Yes, you've been had! John gloated.

———

WEDNESDAY 1150 WASHINGTON DC
(1650 LONDON)

Mitch's phone rang; Samantha's name came up.

"Sam?"

"Mitch, I've got more information on that university tour group. They're doing a specialist tour. That's where they go behind the scenes to the storage area and see any extra pieces that get rotated with the pieces on display or considered too fragile to display. I don't know if it is of any significance, but the twelve-thirty and the two o'clock groups are both booked on these. It's high-security stuff, all lock and key."

"The twelve-thirty group? Is that our lads?" Mitch asked.

"Yep."

"Find out what's behind the scenes for the scrolls collection. I want to know what is not out front on display. I'll hold."

Mitch listened as Samantha took the stairs effortlessly. He overheard the conversation. It was as he thought; more scrolls were in the storage area.

"Did you hear that?" Samantha asked, returning to the phone.

"Yes, thanks. I think we're onto it; that tour group at twelve-thirty is the Mastermind entry," Mitch gave her an update on their findings. "Now, I need you to find out exactly where Paul Asher will be working. He's in the Junior Fellows Program assigned to the artefacts preservation area," he looked up at Adam for confirmation. "But," Mitch continued, "don't—I repeat don't—raise any suspicion about him; we don't want to blow it at this stage. If he has access to that storage area, call me back."

Mitch hung up and joined Adam and Nick.

"Our Atheos team has booked a special behind-the-scenes tour. It gives them entry to a high-security storage area where an extra ten scrolls are stored that get rotated as part of the display. I imagine it's to preserve them; I know the Israel Museum rotates the scrolls every three months to give them a rest from exposure."

"Ten-to-one, that's when it will happen," Adam's eyes lit up.

Mitch's phone rang again.

"Yep?" he answered.

"There are three Junior Fellows assigned to the artefacts preservation project area," Samantha told him. "Edward Sparkes, Allison Coetzee and Paul Asher."

A smile swept across Mitch's face. "Got him!"

"And," Samantha continued, "They've access to the storage area; in fact, most of their work is conducted in there. The three are assigned to projects, including documenting the archival collection. Most of the material is still under lock and key inside the storage area, but they do have access to some of it, or at least can see it without being constantly monitored."

"Beautiful," he answered. "Give me a few minutes and I'll call you back with the plan. Brief Roe on what we've discussed." He hung up.

"What's the story?" Nick asked.

"I'm guessing somehow the lads are going to get all of their team in that high security area and ... and ... what?" Mitch exhaled with frustration, his hands on his hips. It came to him! "One of the twins has to remain in that high-security area while the other masquerades as him and is somewhere else at the same time. What would be happening at the same time that would require them to be in two places at once?"

"Beats me," Nick concluded. "But, Paul Asher has to lift the scrolls. He may share the same DNA sequence as his twin, but Ronin's fingerprints will be different. It's logical that Paul's prints would be in the work area." Nick concluded.

Adam agreed. "It's a great plan if they can pull it off. Questions still remain: how are they going to pull it off and what are their buddies in the tour group doing? Will they hide scrolls somewhere where the Junior Fellow twin can get them later, or will the twin masquerading as the Junior Fellow walk out of there with them, not drawing attention to himself?" Adam rubbed his forehead.

"We've got less than thirty minutes to work it out," Mitch said, feeling the walls of the room closing in on him.

WEDNESDAY 1215 WASHINGTON DC
(1715 LONDON)

Mitch's phone rang making them all jump. They exchanged sheepish looks.

"John!" Mitch said surprised. "What's new?" He listened for a few minutes.

"Great. We got the twin connection—the Asher boys—Adam identified them, but then we got stuck. We've gone through it a thousand times and come up with a thousand scenarios." Again he listened. "That's under twenty minutes from now! We're onto it!"

Mitch hung up.

"Good news?" Adam asked.

"Yes and no," Mitch said, hitting Samantha's number on his automatic dial. "John's had a session with Daniel. He's up for a deal and spilled it on D.C., it's about to go down – there is going to be a bomb scare. The twins duplicated the Junior Fellows access passes. One will stay in the storage area, load himself up with the scrolls – the other will head to the gathering point for staff which is in the staff parking lot at the back of the building and be marked on the roll."

He waited but Samantha did not answer.

Mitch continued. "The one remaining with the scrolls is going to wear an iPod. When the bomb squad finds him, he'll play dumb and pretend he didn't hear anything and be personally escorted out the front of the building for his own safety. Personally escorted out – with the scrolls!" Mitch redialed as his call went to voice mail.

"Where the hell is she?" he muttered. He continued to fill in Nick and Adam. "His colleagues will never know he was missing since, physically, his twin was at roll call."

"What happens if they escort him out the back where his twin will be?" Nick asked.

"I don't know if the back exit can be seen from where the staff gather in the parking lot. Check on your diagram where the exit and car park are located," Mitch nodded towards the table where the maps sat. "With a bomb scare, I'm sure they'll be moving people well away from the building where he'll be able to slip out unnoticed. According to Daniel, one of the Atheos team will call in the bomb scare and have a car waiting once they're evacuated. Paul Asher will be out of the building with the scrolls before the bomb scare is over."

Fifteen minutes remained.

Mitch exhaled. The tension in the room was electric.

Wednesday 1215 Washington
(1715 London)

Samantha was milling around the sales shop on the ground floor of the Library of Congress when she saw them: six young males walking towards the entrance. They looked between eighteen and twenty-five, she estimated. The two in front were obviously in charge; one of them was Ronin Asher. The other boys followed their lead.

Samantha noticed the CID agent, Roe, had them in full view.

You'd never guess those innocent faces were about to commit a crime – at least, I hope they attempt to or I'll look like a total idiot, she thought.

Samantha sized the boys up. They were dressed casually, nothing unusual about them. *How are they going to do it?*

She noticed a couple of the plain-clothes male and female officers in the area. Samantha inconspicuously snapped a few digital photos. *To show Mitch.*

One of the boys glanced at her, checking her out. She looked away. She could feel his eyes on her again; she pretended to be absorbed in a calendar featuring the Gettysburg Address. In her peripheral vision, she saw them stop at the group-tour counter. A middle-aged woman came out to greet them, introducing herself as their tour guide. She was a motherly type and the boys seemed to play up to her, being overtly polite.

Samantha watched them with fascination. She felt her phone vibrate and, looking at the screen, saw it was Mitch calling. At the same time, the boys headed to an administration area with their tour guide.

She ignored the phone and hurried upstairs to get ahead of them.

I don't have time to update you now, Mitch. They're here.

She shook her head. *He's always such a control freak.*

Wednesday 1220 Washington
(1720 London)

Ten minutes.

Mitch redialed Samantha's number for the third time.

"Answer the phone, Sam, or I swear ..." he paced. It rang out. He dialed again and she cut it off.

"You've got to be kidding, she's cut the call off!" he said looking at Adam and Nick.

"I'll text her, you keep ringing," Adam used his own phone. He sent her a text message that read: "Call URGENT have info" ... and waited.

Fifteen seconds passed ... no call.

Thirty seconds.

Forty-five seconds.

Mitch redialed again shaking his head in disbelief. Again it went to message bank.

"What the hell is she doing?"

"What's the CID agent's name?" Nick asked.

"Sebastian Roe."

"Spell it."

"Romeo, Oscar, Echo," he answered, hearing Nick in the background dialing the Counter Intelligence Division in Washington.

Mitch tried again.

"Hello," Samantha answered.

"Sam, listen!"

"Mitch, I can't talk now, the boys are here, I'll call you back."

"Sam, wait!" The phone went dead.

HELEN GOLTZ

He redialed and the number went to message bank. Mitch hurled the phone clear across the room.

"Got him," Nick announced.

Mitch took the phone and briefed Roe on what the boys were planning to do, when and how they were going to do it. When Mitch finished, he hung up and handed the phone back to Nick.

"Thanks."

"No problem. You're not riding solo here, you know," Nick reminded him.

Mitch shook his head in disbelief. "She could have blown it. It will be pretty hard to pick how the twins are going to strike."

Mitch walked out on the balcony, his anger simmering near the surface and sweat running off him. He closed his eyes, annoyed at himself for losing it in front of Adam and Nick, and angry at Samantha for bringing that out in him. He heard footsteps behind him.

"Alright?" Adam asked.

Mitch turned to him. "I'm going to kill her." His voice was tight with control. Inside, his phone rang.

Adam leaned in, collected it off the floor and answered it. It was Samantha.

"Be afraid, be very afraid," he said to her with a laugh in his voice as he returned to the balcony and handed the phone over to Mitch.

"Sam, Sebastian Roe will give you an update," Mitch said with exasperation lacing his voice.

"He has. I'm sorry."

Mitch cut her off. "Be careful, call me when it's done," he hung up and looked down on the street.

"It's a normal day down there, like nothing's happening," Adam commented.

Mitch exhaled. "You know, I've been lost at sea, shot at, even imprisoned for weeks on end and coped, but she's doing my head in. If she's not questioning orders, she's running her own show or ..." he hesitated, "sleeping with team members!"

Mastermind

Adam looked sheepish. "Samantha doesn't play the game. You, me, Nick, we're from military backgrounds, trained to follow commands; trained how to think, not what to think. We go into a situation knowing the standard operating procedures. Sam gets under pressure and she reacts to the play. Anyway you handled her well. Very controlled."

"Only because I want to kill her in person," Mitch headed back inside.

WEDNESDAY 1230 WASHINGTON, 1730 LONDON

Samantha feigned interest in a sculpture so she could get a better view of the six young men in the administration area below. She counted heads: there were five now. She re-counted. Ronin Asher was gone. Alarmed, her eyes scanned the area for him. Pulling out her phone, she refreshed her memory with his emailed photo. Then, it occurred to her he was most likely waiting outside, somewhere near the emergency rally point for staff so he could mix in when they were being exited.

She glanced at the boys again; they were filling in paper work. Samantha caught Roe's eye and indicated she was heading out. She made her way to the back of the building and wandered past the cloakroom, past the local history and genealogy room and to the stairs that headed out to Second Street. Outside, she sat on the stairs, reaching for her water bottle. It took a few minutes to spot Ronin Asher sitting with a number of other people, listening to his headset and watching the building. Samantha felt a rush of excitement as the plan unveiled. She glanced around and saw one of Roe's agents lounging on a bench watching Ronin. Their eyes met and she turned, put the lid on her water bottle and headed back inside.

She saw the boys had their visitor tour passes around their necks and were walking towards the first exhibit with four plain-clothed officers following behind. Samantha followed from a distance, passing Roe.

As the tour group gazed at an exhibition, Samantha left them and joined the two plain-clothed officers allocated to the library's storage area. They met the tour guide who agreed to escort the three through the locked storage area to look bona fide. Samantha entered the area and put her phone on silent and vibrate. She did not want to attract attention.

Good grief, it's enormous, she thought.

In one area was a young girl with her dark hair tied back, concentrating over an opened manila folder. That must be Allison, one of the three Junior Fellows, she concluded. Looking around, Samantha spotted the twin, Paul Asher, working at the far side of the room. He was identical to the boy she saw seated outside and dressed the same. She tried not to stare but was mesmerized by the likeness. The third Junior Fellow was nowhere to be seen. She watched Paul as he removed items from the glass cabinet, checked them off on his list and returned them. Occasionally, she turned back to the tour guide, feigning interest in the exhibitions. The storage area door clicked open and Samantha saw the boys' guide enter with the boys in tow. She felt her heart beat increase as the younger boys gave the game away; their eyes glanced towards Paul, who gave them a subtle nod.

Samantha waited.

One minute.

Two minutes.

Three minutes.

Then one of the boys a tall, redheaded boy interrupted the tour guide to ask for directions to the bathroom. Their guide stopped and pointed him to the security door, telling him to press the exit button, and turn left outside the door. She advised him that he wouldn't be able to re-enter without her, so wait outside until the group rejoined him in ten minutes.

Samantha watched fascinated, as the redheaded boy headed to

the exit. At the same time, a stocky blonde boy wearing a black Kurt Cobain T-shirt, drew the guide's attention to a display. She turned to look. The redheaded boy glanced back towards Paul again before pushing the exit security button. Their eyes made contact and he exited. Samantha moved with her own small tour group, absorbed in the movements of the Atheos group.

Outside Sebastian Roe was in position. He watched the redheaded boy head for the payphone in the hallway. Roe whispered into his microphone.

"OK, he's at the payphone – everyone on standby."

The redheaded boy dialed three numbers, said a few words and hung up. He looked around, then headed towards the bathroom. Roe's phone rang, he answered, listened and hung up. He announced through his headset: "We have confirmation – a bomb threat has been made from a phone inside the Library of Congress."

Roe braced for the alarms. Suddenly, the library went on full alert. The evacuation alarm rang and people poured out. One of Roe's men, the guide and four boys raced out of the high security storage room. Roe watched as the guide fidgeted while she waited for her fifth charge, the redheaded boy, to exit the bathroom. As soon as he did, she hurried her group downstairs; Roe's staff followed close by. He heard the wail of police vehicles and glanced out the window to see the area being cordoned off. Security officers ran past him, scanning the area, checking the staff had evacuated.

"The boys are on their way," he announced through his headset.

"We've got the motive and method: but what's bugging me is how, with all that security, are they going to get the scrolls out the door?" Mitch paced.

Adam shrugged. "Given Paul Asher is staff and there is a bomb scare, he'll probably walk straight out the building under escort – and no one will be the wiser."

"And," Nick continued, "they're only paper. If they're not encased, they're not going to set off alarms when he walks through the exit."

Mitch nodded in agreement. "He wouldn't be able to take a folder or bag out with him during a bomb scare, so he must be going to hide it on himself, somewhere."

———

Inside the storage area, Samantha stayed out of sight. She could see one of Roe's men doing the same as they were left alone with Paul Asher. She felt her phone vibrating.

I can't answer it ... she read the screen ... shit ... It's Mitch. If I don't take the call, he'll kill me. She answered it without speaking. *He'll understand that.*

"Sam, I assume you can't talk, so listen up," she heard Mitch say. "We've been thinking – Paul must be going to hide the scrolls somewhere on himself to avoid detection. We can't think of any other way. Anyway, watch him like a hawk in case he slips a scroll somewhere."

Samantha breathed close to the voice box on her phone.

"Gotcha," Mitch hung up.

She slid the phone back into her pocket and concentrated on Paul Asher, who remained hidden, waiting for security to make a check of the room. He was oblivious to the fact he wasn't alone. Moments later, Samantha heard the security fire wardens enter; the two men glanced around the room and, satisfied no one was left behind, exited and closed the door behind them.

At the sound of the door clicking shut, Samantha saw Paul rise from his hiding place and move towards the scrolls. Behind him Samantha moved slightly, allowing her to monitor him in progress. He squatted in front of the scrolls, reached into his pocket and pulled out a pair of thin plastic surgical gloves, putting them on. He used a knife to pry open the cabinet door, struggling with it until he heard the snap of the cabinet lock.

Must be an area they don't have complete access to, Samantha thought, with some satisfaction.

With quick motions, the twin pulled a scroll out of the storage unit. He lifted his T-shirt and Samantha saw, attached to his chest, two flat, white elastic bands holding a leather pouch. He pulled off the leather pouch and opened it. Laying the scroll flat and taking great pains to preserve it, he surrounded it with parchment and waterproof sheets. Reaching for another, he did the same.

After collecting four, he closed the leather pouch and placed it back under the elastic bands around his chest, closing his shirt and leather jacket. Paul Asher ran his hand down the front of his jacket. No obvious bumps.

Nice work, Samantha thought. It concealed the scrolls perfectly. Impossible to tell he was carrying anything. This kid is good. Let's see him get them out of here.

Samantha looked over at Roe's man squatting nearby. He gave it the thumbs up.

The boys split up as they were herded outside of the Library of Congress building. Roe had an officer assigned to follow each of the boys. He listened as officers called in their movements. Three headed for the subway, while Ronin Asher loitered with the staff to be seen and accounted for; two of the boys collected a navy sedan from a parking station in a nearby street.

"Update on Ronin Asher," Roe ordered.

"Sir, we've got Ronin Asher in sight. He's just shown the I.D. tag around his neck and had his name checked off the staff list. Looks like he's on the move. Hang on."

Roe waited.

"Yes, sir. He's told some of the staff he's going to get a coffee."

"Follow him," Roe ordered.

Inside the storage area, Paul Asher looked towards the door.

Samantha smiled. *It's a waiting game for you now, Paul. Let's hope you get found and escorted out according to plan.*

Paul pulled a phone from his pocket and made a call. Samantha listened as he said one word, "Ready".

44

With the D.C. Mastermind now out of their hands, Mitch and Adam joined Nick to listen to the conversations from Lawrence's office. Nick removed his headphones and connected the microphones to broadcast the dialogue.

"Nothing yet," Nick updated them.

Mitch nodded, sitting down opposite him. Moments later he stood up again and walked towards the balcony to look outside.

"What's wrong?" Nick asked him.

"I'm still in D.C."

"It's out of our hands now," Adam told him. "We've given Sam enough to nail the boys, it should just play out."

"I know," Mitch agreed looking over at them. "You're right."

"Close call though," Adam said.

"Mitch, sit down; you'll hear soon enough," Nick assured him. "You picked Sam for the job; you must have thought she could do it."

Mitch looked away.

"... or maybe not."

"It's not a matter of trust," Mitch started. "It's about limited resources ..."

"But she's got backup with the local CIDs," Nick reminded him.

"Yeah," Mitch swayed on his heels. He saw Nick and Adam exchange looks.

"OK," he pulled himself together, "let's focus on the blackmail."

———

Samantha saw Paul Asher glance at his watch. Waiting for the bomb squad, are we Paul? Should be coming any minute, she thought. Paul put his earphones in and continued to work, constantly glancing towards the door.

Samantha waited. Finally, she saw the door open and two officers in black came in. Not Roe's men – must be the bomb squad. Their expressions said it all when they saw Paul Asher working away oblivious to what was happening. As they grabbed his arm, he feigned surprise.

One of the bomb squad snapped at him: "If you weren't wearing that headset you would hear the evacuation alarm." He looked at his partner. "This place is unbelievable," he complained, "so much for fire drills; they don't even know one of their own is missing."

Samantha remained hidden, watching it all unfold.

A museum security officer entered the room.

"Ah!" he exclaimed, "we were looking for him. I'll see him out," he told them, grabbing Paul Asher's arm and moving him towards the storage door exit. The look on Paul's face was one of pure smugness. Samantha waited, slipping out behind the pole and startling the two bomb-squad members.

"Shit!"

She indicated for them to be silent, flashed her I.D. and followed Paul out. She heard them complain as Roe's man came out of hiding.

"Paul Asher's left the storage area," she whispered into her throat microphone for Roe's benefit. "He's being escorted out and he has four scrolls on him."

"Copy that," Roe came back at her. "We'll pick him up after he's shown out. All officers on exits to be on alert."

Samantha followed at a safe distance as Paul was shown out of the building; he walked down the stairs and, spotting his two companions in the car, headed towards them.

"He's on the move," Samantha heard an officer in her earpiece. She kept her eyes on Paul as he stepped off the sidewalk towards the approaching car. Tour groups were being loaded back onto buses, unsure as to how long the library would be closed during the bomb alert.

"He's in the public domain and he has the scrolls next to his chest," Samantha added in a whisper through her microphone. "Move in."

WEDNESDAY 1745 LONDON
(WEDNESDAY 1245 WASHINGTON D.C.)

Mitch, Nick and Adam waited, listening to the audio feed from Lawrence's office. Mitch's foot tapped impatiently, his eyes constantly returning to his phone, waiting for a call from Samantha.

He looked up at the sound of a door opening through the audio feed and a female voice announced she had a delivery. Lawrence could be heard thanking her and rustling the envelope. Within minutes, he was on the phone, urgency in his voice.

"Andrew, get in here now," Lawrence's voice commanded. Mitch heard the door to Lawrence's office open and a discussion began about raising one million pounds sterling.

Mitch looked to Adam and Nick. They grinned like schoolboys.

Lawrence ordered Andrew to call the directors together immediately.

Samantha saw it happen in slow motion. Plain clothed officers swarmed in, surrounding the car and Paul Asher. The look of shock on the boys' faces relayed just how close they were to the perfect crime. The officers moved in and, hauling the two accomplices from the car, frisked and handcuffed them. Roe gave the order and the remaining boys were apprehended in the subway, including the twin, Ronin Asher. The public watched in disbelief.

Samantha ran down the front stairs to meet Roe who was standing with Paul Asher and the arresting officer. She had to see the scrolls for herself. She stopped in front of Paul. He was her height, young and angry, swearing and resisting arrest; his staff pass still dangled from his neck. She raised his shirt. He tried to step back but found himself wedged against a huge police officer.

Samantha gasped.

There was nothing there.

———

Samantha looked around confused.

"What the hell do you think you're doing?" Paul Asher hissed at her, through clenched teeth. He struggled to free himself from the police officer detaining him. Roe frisked him up and down.

"Damn," Roe hissed through his locked jaw, "this is one serious screw up!" He glared at Samantha.

"Where are they, Paul?" Samantha snapped.

"Where's what?" he asked.

"Don't play cute with me. I've been watching you, your twin and your band of merry men. I was with you in the storage area when you filled the leather pouch with the scrolls."

"Yeah? Sounds like fiction to me." He gave her a smug smile.

She had a brainwave. "Whether you produce the goods or not, I've got it all on camera," she bluffed, showing him her miniature video camera.

The smile faded from his face.

"So, where are they?"

She felt Roe watching her.

"Never mind," she smiled at Paul. "I'm sure one of your team will tell me when we offer a plea bargain to save their own butts."

Paul Asher glanced over at the two boys sitting in the back of the police car.

Samantha felt sick; a mixture of dread, fear and anger surging through her. In her mind, she ran over the scenario, trying to keep a hold on her rising sense of panic as she thought it through.

It was Paul Asher in front of me. I never let him out of my sight but somehow, between leaving the storage unit—escorted by the museum security officer—and arriving outside, he has off loaded the scrolls. Where? How?

"Holy crap!" she said, glancing around. Leaving Paul with one of Roe's officers, she grabbed Roe.

"The museum security officer that escorted Paul out of the building! He's not on staff; he's one of them. Paul called him to say he was ready. Where is he? He's got the scrolls."

Roe issued orders through his microphone, putting everyone on alert. Somewhere, within a mile radius, one of Paul's team was parading as a security officer carrying some of the world's most valuable artefacts.

―――

I have to find those scrolls, she panicked. *God, I'll never live down the embarrassment with the CID and TCU. Imagine the scorn of all these officers on site ... and I'd have to tell Mitch!*

She waited, sick to the stomach. She felt like everyone was waiting and watching her. She prayed Mitch would not call at this precise moment. Finally, it came, the radio call she wanted to hear.

"We've got him," a male voice came through her head set. "Picked him up two blocks away, still in uniform. Can confirm that he has a leather pouch with the documents in it."

"Bring him in," Roe said.

Samantha closed her eyes. She felt the weight falling off her shoulders. Roe patted her on the back.

"Close one," he said.

She opened her eyes and smiled.

I want to throw up! She watched Paul Asher being led away.

"It was a beautiful plan," she called to him, "one of the best if not almost the perfect Mastermind." She saw the look that flickered on his face at the mention of the word Mastermind.

"But game over."

45

Lawrence Hackett passed each of his directors a copy of the blackmail letter, watching them as they read it.

"Andrew," Lawrence turned to his Chief of Staff, "organize the money."

"Done," Andrew replied.

"Gentlemen, we need a plan. I'm happy to lose a million pounds, but frankly, where's the fun in just handing it over?"

"Do we trust they will destroy the file copy?" Alan said.

"Unlikely. I wouldn't, would you?" Lawrence asked.

"So, you're thinking of giving them a bit of scare?" Richard asked.

Lawrence strolled around the oval table.

"The problem is," he began, "that we don't know what we're up against. Is it a couple of crooks with a gun in their pocket, or a network that will have the train surrounded? Or is it just a pimply-faced kid fresh out of college who's hacked into something he shouldn't have? I'm open to suggestions on a course of action."

"I say we go in ready for action," Brian Davies said.

"Ah, all fired up after your success in Monaco, hey Brian?" Lawrence smiled.

Brian returned his grin. "Maybe. I think we should reverse the situation – bring him or them here for a little blackmail of our own."

"I like that thinking."

"Except," Richard Sinclair stepped in, "if they are sitting online ready to send the file off to the police or MI6, as they've threatened to do if the collector doesn't return, we're screwed."

Lawrence nodded his head in agreement.

"Let's track them," Rishi Patel suggested. "Put a few of our people on board and follow the collector home. Then we can be sure we get the cash back, get the file back and get rid of the collector."

There was a general murmur of consent around the table. Lawrence took his chair at the head of the table.

"I think Rishi's plan is the soundest. However, I'm keen for a little action. I say we play ball and have a little fun. Let me think on it and we'll meet again in the morning."

He turned to Andrew.

"Andrew, before you go, get me the phone number for our security company."

———

In the apartment, the three men listened as the meeting dispersed. Mitch fidgeted, his foot tapping.

"Mitch, chill," Nick told him. "You've given it to Sam on a platter, it should be easy now."

"I hope so. Thanks for your help, Nick, Adam. Couldn't have cracked it without you both, especially the twin link."

Adam shrugged modestly. "Let's hope that's it."

Nick rose. "I'd say that's it until tomorrow in Lawrence's office anyway."

"The problem with this guy is that he's bored stupid, literally," Adam shook his head. "Why would you risk everything you've got on this?"

"Maybe everything he's got doesn't interest him anymore. Haven't we got enough from that recording to put him away?" Nick turned to Mitch.

"No," Mitch said. "Lawrence's got a huge bank account ... he'll pay for a defense. I want him for this year's Mastermind and the previous ones over the past years – and I want to get him for Anthony Jenkins' death. I want him to make the payout to get the information back; I want the recordings, Daniel's testimony and anything we can get from the directors. I don't want to fall short with this, there's too much at stake."

"It would be nice to know what we're going to be up against when we hand over that file though," Nick said.

"Hmm," Adam agreed, "or what his definition of fun is."

Mitch's phone rang. He grabbed it. "Sam?"

Mitch hung up after Samantha's brief and sank back on the sofa. He closed his eyes. Nick grasped his shoulder.

"One more down, Mitch, one to go."

Mitch opened his eyes and smiled.

"It's six-thirty, let's go eat," Adam suggested.

There was a knock at the apartment door and all three men looked up, surprised.

Nick motioned for the other two to get out of sight. He opened the door; Ellen stood there with her duffel bag over her shoulder.

"Hey Ellie!" he grinned and pulled her into the room. He gave her a quick hug and grabbed her bag from her.

Mitch appeared back in the room to greet her. "Ellie, you're a sight for sore eyes," he said, placing a hand on her shoulder.

Adam introduced himself. They shook hands.

"This is cosy," she smiled. Mitch followed her gaze, traveling over the running shoes, socks, newspapers and pizza boxes.

"Ah, yeah, tried to get the boys to clean up but they're just slobs," Mitch sighed.

Nick punched his arm.

"You look strained, Mitch," she said, studying his face. "So, how is everything?"

"Well, we're all sick of each other," Nick teased. "Mitch is driving us nuts ... can't sit still, can't sleep, doesn't feed us."

"All true," Adam agreed.

Mitch rolled his eyes.

"Poor Mitch. I'll give you a massage later," Ellen offered.

Mitch grinned at Nick. "That backfired didn't it?"

Ellen looked over at Adam.

"And poor Adam," she took in the newcomer, "stuck with you two for the week."

"Oh, that's nice, isn't it?" Nick turned to Mitch.

"Ellen's right though," Adam got into the swing of it, "but that's why I'm paid the big bucks."

A sound came over the speakers and they all froze. Ellen looked around to see where the audio was coming from. Lawrence had re-entered his office. They listened to him dialing.

"Chris, it's Lawrence Hackett here," he said, followed by a few seconds silence. "Ah, good, I was hoping Andrew called you; we've got a high-security priority. Good. Well, we'll see you first thing tomorrow. Goodnight."

They heard the click of the phone followed by Lawrence's footsteps and the sound of the door closing.

"That's his security guy and that's a wrap," Nick said.

"Did you eat on the plane?" Mitch asked Ellen.

"No, just drank."

"A girl after my own heart," Adam said. Mitch gave him a quick look, their eyes connected.

Don't even think about bedding another one of my agents, Adam!

"Let's get out of here and grab a bite," Adam looked away.

Mitch reached for his coat and followed his team to the lift.

"If only my mother could see me now," Ellen teased as they let her enter the lift first. "I must be out with three of the best looking guys in the U.K."

"Come on, I've seen better heads on beers than on these two,"

Mitch nodded at Nick and Adam.

Mitch's phone rang.

"Saved by the phone," Nick told him.

———

"Hi, Sam, how is it going?" Mitch asked while the other three continued to talk. His watch read nearly seven – he calculated it was two in the afternoon in D.C.

"All done, cleared and squared away," she answered. "Thanks Mitch for the input, and thank the guys for me; it went like clockwork. Listen, I can get a flight that leaves at seven tonight and gets into London tomorrow morning at nine. Is that OK?"

Mitch hesitated.

"Mitch, don't make me stay at home ... please."

Mitch remained silent, thinking.

"I want to be there and you need all the resources you can get," she pleaded.

Mitch exited the lift and fell behind his team.

"Sam, I don't have a good feeling about this."

She's way out of sync, he thought. The incident with J.J. in Broad Arrow, sleeping with Adam, the drama today at the Library of Congress. She'll get herself killed trying to prove herself to me or matching Adam move for move. I don't want that on my conscience when I could have prevented it.

"Mitch?"

"I need to think this through. I'll call you back." Mitch hung up. Picking up the pace, he fell back into stride with his team. He inhaled; the air was fresh after the rain.

Mitch wasn't listening to the conversation around him. What do I do about Sam? If anything happens to her on this next job, and it was my doing putting her in there ... yet, it's important to her; this is what she lives for, he thought.

Dropping behind, he called her back.

"Sam, book the flight. Call John and get him to authorize it."

"Thank you, Mitch, I promise to ..."

"Listen, Sam," he interrupted her and dropped his voice. "I'm not going to beat around the bush – you're way out of step at the moment."

She waited to see if he would elaborate, he didn't.

"I'm sorry about today."

"No, it's not just today, think about it. We'll talk tomorrow when you get here. I need the old Samantha back before we go in tomorrow night. OK?"

"OK," Samantha agreed.

"I'll see you in the morning," he said.

Mitch caught up with his team.

———

The apartment only had three rooms; Mitch surrendered his bedroom to Ellen and took the large, cushioned sofa since—as he admitted—he wasn't sleeping much anyway.

That night was no exception; he drifted in and out of sleep, the job going through his head.

How hard can it be to capture a white-collar guy?

How much backup will he bring? What's the calibre of the backup? Are we talking directors or ex-soldiers?

How many passengers in that carriage will actually be Lawrence's people?

Where do I put Sam so that she doesn't get herself killed?

At two in the morning he gave up. Rising, he threw on his black track pants, grabbed his jacket and a bottle of water from the refrigerator, and went out onto the balcony. He shivered in the cold, lowering himself into one of the steel chairs. Mitch checked out the entrance to the Canary Wharf Underground station. He saw the silhouette of a man.

Good, our security guy's standing on the other side of that grill.

Out of the corner of his eye, he could see a guy sprinting at full pace towards the square.

Another person who can't sleep; fit guy, good stride, Mitch thought as he watched the runner cross the street and slow down as though he had crossed an imaginary finishing line. The runner stopped, doubled over and drew in air in gulps.

I need a run like that, he rubbed his ribs. *Nothing better than a good work out, sweat pouring off you, head and body tuned when you're finished.*

The sprinter stood up and raised his T-shirt up to wipe the sweat of his face. Mitch leaned forward to look again. *Nick! When did he go out? I must have drifted off to sleep at some time.*

Mitch sat back watching him, thinking about what might be going on in Nick's headspace ... is he nervous about tomorrow? I guess he could be; Nick's foremost a pilot; he hasn't been exposed to unpredictable hand-to-hand combat.

He watched Nick drop onto a bench and put his head in his hands. Mitch looked away, feeling like he was intruding, then looked back; he couldn't take his eyes off him.

Maybe he's thinking about more than work ... maybe he's thinking about his fiancée, or her sister, Maria.

Nick sat back and extended his legs in front of him. A light rain began to fall and he turned his face skywards. Mitch saw him pull out a phone, dial a number and begin to speak. Nick hung up and dialed another number. The conversation was much quicker this time.

Who are you calling at this hour of the morning and on which side of the world, Nick?

This is not good.

———

Nick felt better now, after the run. He looked around and sighed.

I hate the early hours of the morning, he thought. *What am I doing?* The haunting track in his mind began to start again ... the regular thought process.

So, I've got a new job ... does it make it all worthwhile?

When you're the one who is supposed to die; when you're driving and you're responsible for the accident ... when you're left behind ...

how do you make a good enough go of the rest of your life to justify that you're the one alive?

Is it all worthwhile if you save a team mate or wear the good-guy cape?

Is it about finding someone else and being more attentive to them, giving everything like there is no tomorrow?

Can there be someone else?

Tears stung his eyelids and he opened his eyes to let them wash down his face with the rain.

Didn't think I had any left to cry.

Ana, Ana, Ana. Six months since …

There are so many losers in prison, so many people who make nothing of their life; people shooting up with some habit or another – and they get to live on, while Ana …

A movement caught his eye.

———

Mitch stood up against the rails moving out of the rain and catching Nick's attention. He raised a hand in salute. Nick returned the salute. Even from a distance, Mitch could make out the hesitation in his movements, as though he was wondering how much Mitch had seen. He decided to say nothing. Mitch looked up as the sliding glass door behind him opened and Adam came out onto the balcony.

"Is anyone except Ellen asleep tonight?" Adam asked.

"Apparently not," Mitch indicated Nick.

"Let's run, you can pace yourself if your body is giving you grief," Adam said. "You need to unwind a bit."

———

0830, Thursday, The Apartment, London

"We're on," Ellen called out to Mitch who was making coffee in the kitchenette. He raced over to join her on the sofa, giving his full attention to the broadcast from Lawrence's office. They could hear the directors taking their seats and the shuffle for chairs by the extra security team.

Lawrence addressed the room. "Gentlemen, tonight ..."

And then, the audio became static.

"What's happening?" Mitch turned to Ellen.

The static was so loud that nothing could be heard above it. Ellen jumped up to check the equipment.

"They're using a scrambler."

Mitch got to his feet. "The security team must have brought in something to scramble anyone who is bugging or ..." he looked to the computer, "or hacking them?"

Ellen raced to the computer to check if they still had access to Lawrence's files – it was blocked as well. Mitch stood hands on his hips, looking out at Lawrence's building.

"This is not good. We've no idea what he's planning to do tonight ... damn, damn, damn!" He rubbed his fingers over his temple.

1045, THURSDAY, THE APARTMENT, LONDON

Mitch couldn't breathe. Too many people; not enough air.

He opened the glass sliding door letting in a rush of cold air. He looked around at his team gathered in the apartment; Nick had returned from surveillance at Lawrence's building, Adam was checking weapons, Ellen was listening to the audio and Samantha arrived, Mitch noted, with a tentative glance his way.

"Take my room," Nick offered, grabbing her bag, "I'll camp out here with the boss."

"Just share my bed," Adam said.

Everyone turned to look at him.

"Come on, who are we kidding? We're all adults. Besides, it's only for a few nights and we need the space," he shrugged. Nick handed Samantha's bag to Adam. Mitch could feel everyone watching for his reaction.

"Whatever," he mumbled. "Nick, who came in and out of Lawrence's building this morning?"

Nick gave his report. Mitch walked back and forth as he listened.

"If we can't hear what's going on in Lawrence's area, can we get access to Lawrence's security company's systems to see what they're planning for tonight?" he asked turning to Samantha.

"I can give it a go," Samantha rose and headed to the computer.

"We could track their security guy who came to the meeting this morning, do surveillance on him for the day."

"Would you recognize him?" Mitch asked.

"Sure. Adam, let's go. Can we take your car?" Nick said, already halfway to the door.

Adam reached for his keys. "Right behind you."

The two men walked out. Mitch opened his mouth to say something, but Nick beat him to it.

"They're called SafeGuard Security – and yeah, we'll stay in touch," he said with a wave at the door.

Mitch nodded. "Ellie …" he noticed her shiver and turning, closed the sliding door behind him. "Call our security guards at the train station. See if anything suspicious has been happening and tell them to check in with you every hour from now on."

"Onto it," Ellen said.

"Sam, let's talk," Mitch grabbed his coat and held the door open.

Samantha rose, grabbed her coat and passed by him.

"Want me to bring you back a coffee?" he asked Ellen.

"Yes, please. A caramel mocha with cream."

Mitch shook his head. "You should be twice the size."

———

Adam drove his silver Porsche Boxster through London Docklands, stopping several car spaces from the main entrance of SafeGuard Security. It was a white, concrete, inconspicuous office, in-between a dry-cleaning store and Chinese takeaway in Millwall.

"Handy for those late shifts," Adam said, noticing the restaurant.

"That's him!" Nick exclaimed. "The guy in the white shirt was the one at Lawrence's meeting this morning. Unbelievable, thought we'd be waiting here for hours."

"Bugger, me too. We just got a good park." Adam started the car, waiting for the two security men to get into the white van so they could follow.

Mitch carried the coffees to an outside table at the sidewalk café on ground level of their building.

"Remind me to get Ellie's coffee before we head back," he pushed the sugar towards Samantha.

"OK."

He heard the nervousness in Samantha's voice.

"Listen Sam, this is not my forte, but it is part of the job description ..."

Samantha nodded.

"Putting it bluntly, you're out of control; you're unpredictable and you're pissing me off. I can't count on you. I'm scared to put you in there tonight and I don't want to spend the next ten years kicking myself for not listening to my instincts."

He looked away. *Keep a cool head.*

They sat in silence. Mitch continued. "You need to think before acting. Think about the consequences ... you knew what J.J. was doing wasn't the right way to go, regardless of what you thought my reaction would be. You know the dangers of bedding a team-mate on a job – after is fine, but on the job! You knew we were working on the Library of Congress case with you and talking with John trying to get anything we could from Daniel right up to the last minute. You couldn't afford not to take my calls. Finally, if I call you, I damned well want to speak to you." Mitch reeled his anger in. "Guess that's it; not quite how I planned to say it."

Samantha burst into tears.

Mitch stared at her, not sure what to do.

Shit, well done! He reached into his jacket for a handkerchief.

"Thanks," Samantha took it and wiped her face.

"It's John's," Mitch shrugged. "He didn't want bleeding in his car. I keep forgetting to give it back."

I'm raving.

"Sam," he reached for her hand.

"Don't do that! Don't sympathize with me; it will make me cry more and I'm already going to regret this later," she sniffed.

Mitch smiled. Samantha caught his expression and laughed.

"Mitch, I hear you loud and clear. I promise to hone my instincts and I guarantee you I will follow orders, especially tonight."

"OK," he looked down at his coffee.

"You can count on me," Samantha added.

Mitch nodded. "Drink your coffee. In the grand scheme of things, there is no one else I'd rather have annoying the hell out of me."

Samantha started to cry again.

Mitch rolled his eyes. *No-win situation.*

———

"This will test you." Nick grinned, watching Adam trying to stay well below the speed limit to remain behind the security guys in the white van.

"Yeah, this car will never get driven at the speed it's meant to be," Adam complained. "What do you drive?"

"A bike."

"What sort?"

"Ducati."

"Yeah?" Adam's interest was aroused. "A Multistrada?"

"Yep, 620."

"Nice." He turned right and followed the driver down Westferry Road and right into Heron Quay.

"I bet they're going down to the Canary Wharf Underground," Nick watched the white van in front. A few minutes later, the van pulled into Nash Court, right near the entrance to the Underground. Nick dialed Mitch.

"Two of Lawrence's security guys are going down into the Underground at Canary Wharf," Nick reported in. "Where are you? Sounds noisy."

"Having a coffee with Sam."

"Geez, nice for some!" He heard Mitch laugh. "Ah, you're giving the pull-your-head-in talk. How's that going?"

"Yeah, real well, one of my strengths. Got to go, keep following them," Mitch said.

"Will do," Nick said.

"I'll let our security guys in the Underground know to look out for them too. What are they wearing?" Mitch asked.

"Um, first one's in black pants, white shirt ..." he looked to Adam.

"Blue sandshoes, red baseball cap with an SG printed on the front in black; silver pen in his shirt pocket. He's got the word Harley written on his pocket; don't know if it's his name or his mode of transport. Second guy's Italian, wearing black jeans, plain black T-shirt, black runners, army-issued green cap and cigarettes in the back pocket of his jeans."

"Did you hear that from smart ass?" Nick smirked.

"Got it," Mitch chuckled. "Nick, turn your microphone on and keep me posted, anything they do now might help us be better prepared later. And don't forget you've got it on," he warned. "Keep the convo on the record; Ellie's listening upstairs."

"Got it," Nick pressed the button on his watch, allowing their commentary to be broadcast.

Mitch grabbed a caramel mocha for Ellen before returning to the apartment. Handing it to her, he briefed her on the two security guards.

"Ellie, take your coffee, head down into the Underground and pretend to be a tourist. Pick up an Underground map, whatever; just watch Lawrence's two guys. Sam, get back to the computer and see if you can hack into SafeGuard Security."

"Done."

Mitch removed his wristwatch and via a small cable, connected the speakers. Nick's wristwatch microphone came through loud and clear. He could hear Nick and Adam breathing as they ran down the stairs at the Canary Wharf Underground entrance.

———

"I'll take left," Nick told Adam as they peeled off in opposite directions.

Nick played the commuter, glancing up at the electronic notice board, checking his watch.

"They're walking the length of the platform," Nick muttered for Mitch's sake. "Harley's looking up. He's checking out the ceiling area. Our officers are watching them. Hang on, Harley's sending the Italian over to my side of the platform."

"OK, lost sight of them both," Nick reported as a train rushed into the station. He rose and walked towards the electronic sign, pretending to read it while he peered through the windows of the train looking for a glimpse of the security guys. The train moved out of the station.

"Ah, Italian guy's arrived on my side, he's doing the full walk of the platform," Nick muttered. "He's looking up and down on the track as well ... Geez, he's blatant. Here we go, our security guy's coming up to him."

Nick listened in.

"He's asking him if everything's alright ... guy's saying he lost his keys. Nice one – accounts for why he's looking down, but not up."

Nick looked over at the other platform.

"Adam and Harley are gone! They've taken a ride."

Mitch's phone rang and Adam's number flashed across the screen. Mitch answered it, his voice cutting out Nick's commentary.

"Mitch," Adam whispered, "we're taking a ride, can you let Nick know? I'll see where this guy gets off."

"Thanks," Mitch hung up and dialed Nick's number.

"Nick, it's Mitch ... Adam's called in. He's tagging Harley, you stay with the Italian."

"Will do."

"I should have got you to wear an earpiece so we could communicate two-way. No chance you've got the car keys if the Italian guy moves?"

"No, damn it! I'd love to drive that Porsche."

"Can you hot-wire it if you need to?"

"Yeah! I can try."

"Do that. I don't want to lose the Italian. Besides, he'll probably pick up Harley."

"OK. Ellie's just come onto the platform," Nick reported. "Hang on ... the Italian's on the move ... I'm onto him."

"Good, keep me posted. Talk it through your mic." Mitch hung up.

Fifteen minutes later, Ellen re-entered the apartment.

"The Italian's gone. He did basic surveillance of the track and above. Nick's following him," she reported.

Mitch nodded reaching for his phone; a call was coming through from Adam.

"Adam?"

"We're getting off at Waterloo," he whispered and hung up.

"Sorry, Ellie," Mitch said. "Anything else?"

"Just one thing. He was counting as he walked from the platform to the stairs."

Mitch thought for a moment. "Nice work. I imagine he's working out how long it will take Lawrence to get out of the station after the handover. That's interesting."

"OK, I'm in their site," Samantha said. "The only thing that's been created since this morning is a timesheet for tonight. I'll print it."

"Excellent, that should tell us how many staff are on," Mitch said, feeling the adrenalin in his body beginning to surge. "Any chance there is a file with pics of their staff on the system? Be nice to recognize them."

Nick's voice cut in again over the speakers.

"The Italian's pulling up outside Waterloo Station, he's staying in the van. Must be picking up Harley. I'll let Adam know I'm here."

Mitch heard Nick dial Adam's phone. The team in the apartment listened in on their conversation.

"Hey, Adam, it's Nick. Don't catch a train back, I'm outside Waterloo."

"OK ... in my car?"

"As luck would have it, yeah! Geez it's beautiful to drive. Hurry, they're pulling out."

"Shit's going to hit the fan over that car-napping!" Ellen smiled.

"Yeah, looking forward to it." Mitch gave her a grin.

Adam bolted up the station stairs, sighting Nick and jumping into the passenger seat of his Porsche.

"Bloody hell," Adam swore. "I paid forty-five thousand pounds for a car with state-of-the-art security and you hot wire it that easily. It's absolute bollocks!"

"What can I say," Nick shrugged, "it's one of my many skills."

Adam looked away disgusted, swearing to himself.

"So?" Nick asked.

"Same thing down there, a bit of station surveillance up and down the track." Adam sulked. He spoke in the direction of Nick's watch microphone. "Mitch, we can probably assume that's where the security team will start from."

Nick followed behind the van at a safe distance, pulling over as it stopped outside the concrete building of SafeGuard Security.

"How long did it take you?"

"What?" Nick asked.

"To hot-wire it."

Nick smiled. "A while, it was pretty tough."

The white van reversed and parked.

"They're back at the office," Nick announced for Mitch's benefit.

Nick's phone rang. "Yeah, Mitch?" he answered.

"Good job, guys. Glad we found where they're starting from. Come back, let's have a think tank," Mitch said.

Nick paused. "Uh, Mitch, we're not coming back."

"What? Why?"

Adam broke in. "Nick and I had a meeting and decided we're not coming back unless you provide food."

"Yeah, we're action guys, we need to eat!" Nick added.

Mitch laughed. "Hang on." His voice came through a few seconds later. "Ellie and Sam are going down to get something healthy."

"Alright, we're on our way, but this better not be a trick."

1430 Thursday, The Apartment, London

"So what do you do after this gig?" Nick asked Adam as he guided the Porsche back into the parking lot at the apartment.

Adam shrugged. "It's anyone's guess. Might do something life changing; new job, new life – who knows."

"Yeah, I get that," Nick parked the car.

"Do you? But you're a tight team."

"I'm the new kid on the block," Nick explained, "the other three have been working together for a long time."

"I thought you and Mitch went way back."

"We do. We've know each other since school, but this is the first job we've worked together since the air force over a decade ago."

Mitch heard Ellen and Samantha return with lunch.

He sighed. *I enjoyed that short-lived solitude.* He came off the balcony and grabbed his phone to update John.

"Sam, pull the plug on that will you?" he said, noticing Adam and Nick's conversation continued to be broadcast over the speakers.

He heard Adam's English accent: "It does get a bit rough some times. Mitch must have seen some action though; those scars on his back are nice trophies."

"Yeah, he's been busy," Nick answered discretely.

Mitch turned to pull the plug as Samantha disconnected it. He dialed Nick's number, feeling Samantha and Ellen looking at him.

Nick glanced down at his ringing phone as he got out of the car. It was Mitch's number. He looked over at Adam and pointing to the microphone in his watch, mouthed the word "shit."

"Turning it off, Mitch," he answered knowing what Mitch was going to say.

1630, Thursday, The Apartment, London

"OK," Mitch started after a mouthful of Coke. "We've got two security guys dressed as Underground rail staff stationed at each entrance to Canary Wharf station. That shouldn't raise any suspicion; the ticket collectors are usually around that area anyway. As soon as Lawrence is identified in the station, these two officers will seal the entrances; people can exit but not enter. They'll stay in place until the job is finished."

"Check," Adam said marking off their locations on an Underground map layout.

"Adam, when you see Lawrence on the platform, you or Ellie are to double-check these guys have sealed the entrances."

"Got it," Adam agreed.

"What if Lawrence is on the train and gets off at Canary Wharf to meet you, or walks through to the last carriage and confronts you there?" Nick asked.

"Yeah, good point," Mitch said. "If that's the case, Nick, you will alert Adam through your headset and Adam or Ellie will call the officers at the entrance and tell them to seal it off. If he's aboard, Nick, you and your two on-board officers will make the arrest, but not until he hands over the briefcase and takes the file out of my hands. It's crucial you don't do it before then."

"Got it. Officers Skinner and Watson will be on board with us," Nick said checking off his notes. "You met them at the run through. I'm hoping we can pick Lawrence's guys early. It's going to be a popular carriage."

"Hopefully, Lawrence will be on the platform; it will give us more control. I'll step off the train to meet him. Nick, you'll stay aboard with Skinner and Watson, monitoring the situation. Adam, once we're on the platform, your team will take over."

"Got it," Adam agreed, "Sam and Officer Kent will be in sniper positions. Ellie, myself and Officer Leath will be on the platform dressed as civilians."

Mitch nodded. "I'll hand Lawrence the folder and he'll hand me the briefcase. Just to make it look real, I'll open it and check the contents."

"You won't have time to count it before the train door closes, if we're going to make this look as real as possible," Adam added.

"I know. It's just a cursory look to ensure there is cash in there before I hand over the file. It's not credible otherwise. Before I step back into the same carriage, the driver will play the announcement 'due to person under train, there will be a delay'. At this point, Lawrence will realize that any plan to follow me home will be delayed. He'll play his hand. This is when we have no idea what he's going to do and there could be a number of scenarios. For example: he hears the announcement and departs leaving his guys on board with us. If he departs, he'll get as far as the stairs where Adam's team will make the arrest as he walks up the stairs with the file. We can expect some action on board and Nick, your guys will move in and pick up Lawrence's guys."

"Got it," Nick said.

"Or, it may be the case that we won't get any action on board, and once Lawrence is arrested, there'll be a stand-down. Highly unlikely, but possible. He could take advantage of the fact that the train's not moving and stick his security guys onto us while we're stationary. If this is the case, Nick, Officers Skinner, Watson and myself will deal with it on board. Adam, you will back us up once you've secured Lawrence's arrest and managed any coinciding outbreak of action on the platform. So, worst case scenarios?" Mitch put it to the group.

Samantha started, "What if he's not worried about the information going to the media or cops? What if he's a sick bastard meeting you for kicks and opens fire at you at point-blank range?"

"In that case," Mitch said calmly, "you'll save my butt, Sam. The snipers will come into their own; you and Officer Kent are well positioned to take him out. It should be a routine exercise if we can isolate Lawrence and his men to that platform and last carriage."

The group nodded.

"Be sure Lawrence doesn't see you, Sam; he'll know the game's up," Mitch reminded her. "Now, Ellie saw the Italian counting the distance from the platform to the exit, so I'm guessing Lawrence's going to bolt and his security team will time their assault to begin on his exit. Finally, on board, what Nick says, goes. On the platform, Adam's in charge. In sniper position, Sam will manage Officer Kent and take the lead from Adam who can see what's going on. Ellie will be the markswoman at close range on the platform and oversee the

Mastermind

guards at the entrances. Adam, Nick and Sam are all connected by intercom, so keep each other posted. Cool?"

"Cool," they agreed.

"Civilians," Mitch pushed on. "Anyone aboard the train will only be coming as far as Canary Wharf as the train will be marked accordingly – so we'll let them exit. The only issue will be if any civilians get off the train and wait for a connecting one. Adam, your team has to get them out ASAP. The lockdown will ensure no trains come in or out on the line, so that should limit commuters, and it is going to be eleven p.m. on a weeknight."

"We haven't had large numbers on our test runs the last few nights," Nick agreed.

Mitch turned to Samantha, "What have you got on SafeGuard?"

"Lawrence's security team has five staff scheduled on according to the time sheet. I couldn't get photos from their website, so we can only identify the two that Adam and Nick followed today."

Mitch looked around. "Anything else?"

No one said anything.

"It's a wrap," he stood and headed for the door, sick of talking.

"Where are you going?" Samantha asked.

"For some air. I'll be back in an hour."

46

Mitch had to get out of the apartment; the walls were closing in on him. He took the stairs, merging on the footpath into the swell of workers heading home. He shivered; walking until he reached the waterline at Fisherman's Walk and sat down away from the coffee-drinking set. He rang Charlotte, she answered right away.

"Charlie!" He felt his heart rate increase when she answered.

"Mitch, are you alright?"

"Fine, I wanted to call, but I haven't had a chance before this."

"I'm glad you called. Where are you?"

Mitch ignored the question. "Is everything OK with you?"

"Everything's fine," she said. "When are you coming home?"

"Hopefully, this weekend. I'm looking forward to having some space, sleeping in my own bed and doing a few other things."

"Uh-huh. Like what?" Charlotte teased.

"Like sleep in your bed!"

"What!" Charlotte laughed surprised. "And where will I be sleeping if you're in my bed?"

"I'm teasing you."

"That's a pity. Is your team with you?"

"Yep."

"Sounds like fun."

"Nah, we're all a bit tired and over it. It's just work. How's Sally?"

"Good. You know Sally."

"Watched any good movies without me?"

"You bet. I've had a huge social life while you've been away … I drop into bed exhausted every night."

Mitch felt an anxious knot in his stomach.

"I'll talk to you before the weekend, and confirm when I'll be home."

"OK. I'm out the next two nights … work functions and a bit of social too, but you can always leave a message."

"Try and remember me," he said.

"Let's see … Mitchell Parker … six-foot something … dark hair, um … blue eyes?"

Mitch bit his tongue. He looked into the distance.

"Hey, I'm joking. I do miss you, hurry home."

"Thanks. See you soon."

"Hope so," Charlotte hung up.

Mitch disconnected and sat staring at the phone, conscious of the ache in his chest and his desire to ring her straight back. He closed his eyes and pictured her amongst the white duvet; her hair tussled, wearing one of her singlet and short sets, eyes sleepy, and smelling of scented talcum powder. He put his head between his hands annoyed at his feelings of needing to see her.

What I really need is a cold shower. I shouldn't have called; made me feel worse.

―――

"I've got to get out of here too," Nick rose. "I'm going for a walk to Jubilee Park. Any takers?"

"I'm in," Ellen grabbed her coat, "I need to expel some energy before tonight."

"Uh, I'm fine here," Adam glanced at Samantha.

"I bet you are," Nick said in a hushed voice.

Adam held the door open for them and Nick punched him on the arm on the way out. Closing it behind them, Adam looked over at Samantha and smiled.

"I've been dying to get you alone," Samantha said her voice frosty.

"Me too, it's been torture."

"Adam! I've wanted to get you alone to kick your butt. How could you say that in front of everyone?"

"What?" he asked surprised.

She imitated his voice. "She can sleep with me, we're all adults."

Adam laughed. "Well, we are."

"You know I'm not in Mitch's good books at the moment. I could hit you."

"Yeah, but you're a girl. I don't think you're fast enough to get me, baby." He grinned.

Samantha rolled her eyes and to his surprise, ran at him, knocking him clean over. When she had him pinned down on the ground, she looked him in the eyes and said, "Take it back."

"Never, you're a girl," he said again with emphasis. He flipped her, rolling her over and rising above her to standing position, he threw Samantha over his shoulder in a fireman pose.

"Not just any girl – my girl," he said to annoy her.

Samantha tried to hit him between laughing, while he carried her straight to the bedroom, closed the door and locked it.

―――

Thursday six p.m. London

Mitch was sitting on the bench at Fisherman's Walk when his phone rang. He looked at the number. Man! Is that guy psychic?

"Hi, John."

"Mitch, I thought I would check up on you. How's things?"

"Good, we're all OK," he said.

"Sure? You sound flat."

"Nah, everything's fine."

"You'd tell me if it wasn't?" John pushed.

"What?" Mitch asked.

"Fine. You'd tell me if something was eating at you?"

"Sure."

There was a silence on the line, while Mitch waited for the conversation to change.

"I have some interesting news," John eventually said. "Maria Diaz has escaped maximum security."

Mitch's instincts went on full alert. "How? When?"

John continued. "Several hours ago. She had a trip to the prison's medical wing and hasn't been seen since."

"Do we know who's involved? Is Johan ..."

John cut him off. "Johan's still under lock and key, and according to the images from the security cameras, Maria's in no danger. The body language from her and her captor on the tape is pretty chummy."

Mitch exhaled. "Hmm, if Nick is somehow involved, I don't want to know."

"Then don't look at his phone records."

Mitch buried his head in his hands again. "Great! Leave it with me."

"Anyway, are you all set for tonight?"

"As ready as we can be."

"Are you confident of the back-up team?"

"Absolutely," Mitch assured him. "Adam's got us some good agents from the SO19 squad, plus our team."

"Who's in sniper positions?"

"One of the SO19 guys and Sam. I'd rather have Ellen there, she's a better shot; but Sam's been seen by Lawrence, so I've got to stick her out of view. Hopefully, her shooting's up to par."

"Now you're scaring me."

"No, it'll be fine."

"Do you need anything?" John asked.

Mitch hesitated.

"Could you book us on return flights on Friday afternoon? We'll be done by then and I'm keen to get home and wind this one up ... we've all got cabin fever."

There was a silence on the line.

Mitch filled the silence. "We've worn a track in the carpet from pacing."

"That's pretty out of character for you, Mitch."

"What do you mean?" Mitch reacted too quickly.

"To be thinking of coming home with all that other pressure on and to be defensive about it."

"I'm not," Mitch took a deep breath realizing he was being defensive. "John, don't analyze me, you know I hate that," he added. "Forget it, forget I mentioned it."

Again there was a silence.

Great! Why did I say anything?

"What's her name?" John asked.

Mitch froze, struggling for something to say. "What do you mean?"

"I'm putting it all together ... your restlessness, short fuse, desire to come home early – must be someone new in your life?"

Mitch laughed uneasily. "Give me a break."

"Mitch, why didn't you tell me this when we talked at the laundromat?"

Shit! I should have known better than to start this.

"There is nothing to tell."

John didn't saying anything.

Damn, damn, damn.

"John, we've all been in the one room for close on five days, day-in and day-out. We're going stir-crazy."

Again the silence.

"Was there really a kid called Anthony Jenkins?"

"Of course, he's real," Mitch snapped. He stood up and walked to the edge of the water. "Come on John, cut me some slack here."

He could hear John laughing on the other end of the line.

"Are you laughing?" Mitch felt the relief running through him. "Do you need to take the piss out of me now, with the pressure already on?"

"Oh, keep your shirt on. I'm just keeping you on your toes. Listen, Mitch, be careful. I've got full confidence in you. As for the flights ..."

Mitch cut him off. "Forget it ... no big deal ... book the flights whenever."

"Don't worry, I'll get you home the minute it's done, Romeo."

John hung up.

Great, Mitch sighed.

47

NINE-THIRTY P.M. THURSDAY, THE APARTMENT, LONDON

MITCH THOUGHT THE HOUR WOULD NEVER COME. HE STOOD IN THE apartment lounge room getting his team—Nick, Adam, Ellen and Samantha—to cross-check their gear. Mitch wore basic civilian clothes; a loose black knitted sweater, jeans and black hiking boots. Underneath, he wore a thin Kevlar vest, bullet-proof and lightweight. Still, he shuffled uncomfortably as a light sweat formed on his skin. His watch microphone was on and the signal diverted to Adam's earphones. Mitch carried a semi-automatic on his belt. He could feel the comforting weight of the gun at his side.

"Start with you, Nick, check off." Mitch worked through each of his team members. When they finished, he reaffirmed the mission.

"No heroes, OK? It's not that important."

They nodded their understanding.

"I mean it. It's not worth life or limb ... everyone got that?"

They answered in the affirmative, Nick and Adam saluting. A smile traced Mitch's lips.

"That applies to you too, Baron," Nick said, "since you're in the front line and all."

"What did you call him?" Ellen looked up at Nick.

Mitch gave Nick a disapproving glance.

Nick grinned back. "Nothing."

"Yes you did," she insisted. "The Baron! Was that your nickname in the air force, Mitch?"

Mitch gave Nick another pained look. "He's just being stupid." He tried to change the subject. "Sam, Adam, head off."

"Oh, admit it," Nick rolled his eyes, "He was nicknamed after Manfred von Richthofen."

Samantha looked at him blankly. "Who's that?"

"The Red Baron!" Nick exclaimed.

"I thought that was just fiction," Samantha said.

"No way. He was the highest-scoring fighter pilot of World War I – and Mitch, the golden boy, did everything perfectly; he was always the highest scorer."

"Yeah, time we headed off, big mouth," Mitch pushed Nick towards the door.

"And what was your nickname, Nick?" Ellen asked.

"Nick," he answered quickly.

"Not as I remember it, Flash." Mitch grinned.

2200 THURSDAY, CANARY WHARF STATION, LONDON

Samantha slid into position, wedged in the ceiling on the outbound side of the Jubilee line at Canary Wharf Station. She grimaced at the dirt and rat droppings around her and with a look to Officer Kent positioned on the inbound side, gave the thumbs-up and received it in return.

They were ready.

As a train pulled out, emptying the station of waiting passengers, Samantha trained her gun to the platform below for a practice run.

A perfect view of where Mitch will be when the train doors open and where Lawrence's back should be when he does the exchange, she thought.

Mitch, you're far too vulnerable this time, stuck out there for anyone to take a crack shot at you.

2215 Thursday, Waterloo Station, London

"This is killing me," Nick said, sipping on a strong black coffee outside the station. He added sugar.

"I've had worse," Mitch said trying his coffee.

"Not the coffee, the waiting."

"Oh, yeah, the waiting is always the hardest part," Mitch agreed. He looked around at the late-nighters going about their normal lives, oblivious to the action about to take place in forty-five minutes.

"What are we going to do after this job?" Nick asked.

"Have a beer."

"I was thinking long-term; but, yeah, that sounds good."

Mitch smiled. "John's already got another few jobs on the boil. But if you need some time off …"

"Why would I?" he asked suspiciously.

Mitch shrugged. "I don't know; to relocate, get an apartment, maybe. You'll have to do the training course as well. I was thinking of having a week off." He looked at his watch again. "Twenty past ten."

"Thanks, got my own watch."

"Sorry. Just a bit time focused."

"I noticed."

They sat in silence. Nick stirred his coffee. Mitch caught himself looking at his watch again and looked away. After a few minutes, he turned his watch microphone off to prevent Adam hearing the conversation and glanced at Nick. Mitch cleared his throat. "I guess you know Maria's people got her out?"

Nick's snapped to look at Mitch. Mitch tried to read Nick's expression.

Are you surprised that she's free or surprised that I know about it, Nick? Mitch thought.

Nick turned away again.

"Why would I know that?" he asked.

They sat in silence.

"Destroy your phone records and text messages, Nick, as soon as you can. It's imperative."

Nick nodded, not looking at him.

Mitch let it go. They continued to sit in silence.

With another glance at his watch, Mitch's foot began tapping. "Will this day never end?"

"Worried?" Nick asked him.

"No."

"It's only me here."

Mitch looked over at him. "Yep ... worried. We're not sure of his game plan, I hate that." He sat up straight, stretching his neck and back.

"You know, I've never seen you so wound up," Nick lit a cigarette. "Not during our flying days or the exams."

"You're going to have to get in line if you want to start psychoanalyzing me."

Nick laughed. "Like that, huh? Oh, well, creates jobs. I just meant you seem more uptight these days."

Mitch looked at him. "I've never had three lives in my hands before."

"OK. Let me ask you then, when we were doing flying missions, why did you do it?"

Mitch shrugged. "I loved it."

"Even when it was dangerous?"

"Especially then."

"So," Nick continued, "you didn't wake up every morning and think, shit, hope the Lieutenant Colonel's thought about this, he's got my life in his hands."

"No. OK, point taken."

"You're here to provide good leadership, not to protect our butts ... except for that incident at Broad Arrow," Nick conceded with a grin. "On the good leadership front, you've got it reasonably covered."

Mitch smirked. "Thanks."

He turned his watch microphone back on and grabbing his phone called Adam for an update.

Hanging up, he briefed Nick.

"None of the officers at the tube have reported any sighting of Lawrence or his men and no one tried to get into the station last night. It all seems too straight forward. Not a good sign."

———

2230 Thursday, Waterloo Station, London

Mitch stopped fidgeting, sat perfectly still, eyes fixed ahead and focused.

Nick watched him. "I remember you doing that before every exam. Still works, huh?"

"Sometimes," Mitch said.

"What part of the job do you like the best?"

"The action," Mitch's eyes lit up. "What we're about to get into is the best part of the job. The prep, surveillance and research is just a means to an end; this is what it's all about."

"I wonder if you'd feel that way if you had a wife and kids."

Mitch shrugged. "I don't, so no use speculating."

"You've got a girl."

Mitch hesitated.

"Obviously that's not general knowledge," Nick read his reaction.

"It's only new. I've known her a long time, but we've just started ..." his voice drifted off.

"What's she like?" Nick asked watching Mitch constantly surveying the scene.

"I'm guessing she's going to be high maintenance."

"Must be love then? Maybe, sooner than you think, you won't get the same rush from being away."

Mitch smiled at him. "This from a man who a few weeks ago was chasing hijack thrills."

Nick shrugged. "My point exactly. I was footloose and carefree, or careless," he conceded.

"I guess it's all in the timing." Mitch glanced at his watch.

"Again with the watch," Nick shook his head.

"Shut up. You check everything all the time, do you know you do that when you're nervous?"

Nick removed his hand from his hip where he had involuntarily checked for his sidearm again. "As if," he said hiding a smile.

2240 Thursday, Canary Wharf Station

Ellen met Adam at the Canary Wharf station entrance, giving him a kiss on the cheek to convincingly play the role of a couple. Adam turned off his microphone.

"You OK?" he asked.

"Fine," she exhaled, "fired up."

"Adrenalin's a good thing," he reminded her. "Now, I might have to kiss you for effect."

"If it's for the good of the mission, we'll both bear it," Ellen teased.

Adam nodded with a smile. "I've had a lot worse missions. Let's go." He turned his microphone back on and linked his arm through hers. They strolled down the stairs to the platform below, making a play of checking the electronic timetable overhead to find out when the next train was due and consulting their watches. They sat on the timber benches. Adam casually looked around. He could see Officers Leath and Kent in place; Samantha was on the opposite side to Kent. He put his headphones on, pretending to listen to music. Now he was connected.

"Come in, Nick?" he whispered.

"Read you loud and clear," Nick returned, "we're in place at Waterloo and ready."

"How you doing, Sam?" Adam asked with affection, looking up towards her position in the ceiling.

"Fine, we're ready," Samantha responded. "Mitch with you, Nick?"

"Got him in sight," Nick assured her.

Adam dropped his eyes from Samantha's position in the ceiling and nodded to Ellen.

"Everyone's where they should be."

2245 Thursday, Waterloo Station, London

Nick glanced at Officers Skinner and Watson dressed in plain clothes and seated nearby on the platform at Waterloo Station. He scanned the area and spotted the Italian from SafeGuard Security, waiting to take the train.

Sloppy, Nick thought with a glance to Mitch, seated three seats away, the folder secure under his arm. He could hear Mitch's accelerated breathing.

"Almost time; train's due in ten minutes," Nick mumbled as though singing along to his headset. "We've got the Italian here, plus a solid guy. Looks ex-military; could be one of their team. There is a possible third – a guy with a Nirvana shirt on. No sign of Harley from SafeGuard."

Adam answered. "Harley's here, waiting for a train. He's got another burly guy sitting a few seats from him with a Jack Daniels T-shirt on – they've exchanged looks; they know each other. Between us, that's four accounted for from their regular staff. One's missing, unless it's Nirvana man."

Nick heard Adam take a sharp breath. "Here we go!" Adam announced. "Lawrence's entered Canary Wharf station alone and he's got the briefcase."

Nick coughed three times as though clearing his throat. He took a bottle of water out of his coat and took a mouthful. It was a sign for Mitch to confirm Lawrence was in place.

Adam came through again on Nick's headset, his voice low and angry. "Andrew and some guy in a red tracksuit have both come in from the right entrance which is supposed to be sealed off. How the hell did they get in? I'm going to check it out."

Nick listened to Adam taking the steps up to the entrance.

"That's all the bodies accounted for at least," Nick said. "Nirvana guy must be public."

He heard Adam running back down the stairs again, saying a few words to Ellen and kissing her for effect. Nick had no choice but to listen in.

"Nice touch," Nick mumbled.

"Yeah, thanks, got to look authentic. Listen, our security guy on the entrance has gone. My guess is Lawrence bought him. I've had to put Officer Leath up there – I'm one down."

Nick glanced towards Mitch who was looking down the tunnel at the Canary Wharf train approaching them at Waterloo Station.

"Our train's coming," Nick said for Adam's benefit. We'll be seeing you at your station shortly."

48

2250 Thursday, Waterloo Station, London

Mitch steadied his breathing as the train pulled into the station. He stood and saw in his peripheral vision that Nick did the same as a handful of people got off the train and less got on. Mitch, Nick and Officer Skinner boarded the last carriage. They made brief eye contact before Mitch looked past them, observing Officer Watson enter the second last train carriage. Mitch took a seat near the door, his eyes taking in everyone on the carriage; the Italian sat at the far end of the carriage; a smattering of other passengers were on board; Nick tapped along to imaginary music through his headset.

He's nervous, Mitch thought watching Nick fidget. He studied Nick's habit of continuously checking gear and instruments and even now, Nick's arm continued to stray to the comfort of his hip where the gun was concealed.

Nick, relax, don't give away the game, Mitch willed him.

He counted it down; the train had four stops before Canary Wharf.

Mitch ran his tongue over his teeth. *My nervous gesture.*

The train halted at London Bridge and three people exited.

That leaves me, Nick, Skinner, the Italian, two girls around eighteen years of age sitting in the corner of the carriage and two heavy-set men – one in a Nirvana T-shirt and the ex-military looking guy from the platform, Mitch summarized. Like to know how many are waiting on the platform at Canary Wharf. Is that Nirvana T-shirt guy one of Lawrence's men?

He glanced towards Nick, hoping he had it under control. Nick looked straight at him, their eyes locked for a few seconds and then Mitch looked away with indifference, but read the fear in Nick's face.

The train pulled in one stop from Canary Wharf and the man in the Nirvana T-shirt stood and exited through the center carriage.

OK, one down. I wonder if we're too prepared for what's going to happen. No, can you ever be too prepared?

As the train moved out of the station on its way to the final stop at Canary Wharf, Mitch saw one of the young girls approaching.

"Have you got the time please?" she flirted.

"No, sorry," he dismissed her, not wanting to take his eyes off the play.

"Are you American?" she asked.

Get the hell out of my line of vision!

"Five to eleven," Officer Skinner said behind the girl.

"Oh, thanks," she turned and smiled at Skinner before walking back to her seat. Mitch heard her friend giggle as she sat down.

The train pulled into Canary Wharf.

Here we go! Mitch scanned the station platform as the train passed along to the end. He counted about half a dozen people including Adam and Ellen. Then he saw Lawrence and recognized Andrew Kenny from the annual report photo. He observed a man in a red tracksuit next to Andrew, and another large man in a Jack Daniels T-shirt sitting several seats apart, trying to appear unconnected.

A tough feat on a station platform at eleven at night.

The train doors opened.

2300 Thursday, Canary Wharf Station, London

Adam watched the platform traffic, studying who was coming in and out. He noted half-a-dozen passengers made their way to the exit and disappeared up the stairs. He saw Mitch at the door of the carriage and two young girls brush past, vying for attention.

Move it girls! Stop flirting and get out of there, he thought watching them. Adam kept Lawrence in sight.

Wearing a baseball cap and scarf, Lawrence moved across the platform towards the last carriage. He was now no more than six feet from the carriage entry, walking purposefully.

Mitch watched him and stepped forward, noting no one else alighted beside him; those left on the carriage were there for a purpose – Nick, Skinner, the Italian, the ex-military man and Watson in the next carriage.

Here we go, thought Mitch with a quick and subtle glance around at his people.

He stepped from the train, the black folder under his arm, not taking his eyes of Lawrence. In two strides he was right in front of him. He felt his team's eyes trained on him. Behind Lawrence, Mitch saw a large man in a red tracksuit stand and stretch. Mitch's eyes found Adam who nodded at him.

It's under control, Mitch assured himself as he stood eye-to-eye with Lawrence.

"Your money," Lawrence said passing him the brief case. Mitch took it from him, still holding the folder.

"Check it if you like," Lawrence offered.

Mitch was about to flip the silver latches open when Lawrence spoke again.

"Before you open it, you might want to consider this," Lawrence was holding his phone and Mitch could see a stopwatch on the face of the phone. A stopwatch counting down! Lawrence wanted him to see it. It was counting minutes and seconds.

With sudden clarity, Mitch realized ... the briefcase was a bomb!

Shit! Mitch felt bile rising in his throat. I didn't see the minutes for long enough ... how long do I have? How many minutes left?

His eyes flicked back to the phone, Lawrence had turned it away and was looking at him, an amused expression on his face.

A thousand thoughts ran through Mitch's mind.

Is everything a sport with this guy?

This is going to blow everyone sky high.

This means Lawrence doesn't care about the file going to the cops or media.

Should I give him the file and get on the train, let Adam's team pick him up?

Should I get everyone off the train?

Drag him on the train with me?

Shit, shit, shit! Must be C-4, or some kind of bomb that can be detonated by a cell phone.

Damn it.

"What's wrong?" Lawrence asked.

The platform was still and silent as Lawrence and Mitch stood facing each other, both in perfect control on the surface.

Mitch smiled at Lawrence. A cool smile.

"Nice touch," he said.

Lawrence smiled, maintaining Mitch's steady glare.

"Thank you, I'm glad it wasn't wasted on you. It's my swansong," Lawrence told him.

"How long do I have?" Mitch asked.

"You missed that, huh? Can't tell you. That would be giving everything away now, wouldn't it?" Lawrence raised an eyebrow.

Mitch's eyes narrowed with fury.

Lawrence snatched the black folder from Mitch's hands. "Thank you, it's been a pleasure."

"The fun's not over yet," Mitch assured him in a controlled voice. He saw the surprise on Lawrence's face as he calmly began to turn and walk back towards the carriage doors, knowing he had a bomb in his hand.

When is this thing going to blow and am I going to get a bullet in the back now as well?

Mitch's body tensed as he waited for the bullet, the burn, the sensation of pain; the expectation was almost paralyzing.

Get a grip, he told himself. Nothing happened. In fact, nothing was happening at all.

Mitch saw Nick's perplexed look. He saw him mouth the words "What the hell is Mitch doing?" to Adam through the headset.

Now, now, now! Make the announcement. What the hell is going on? Mitch's mind was racing ahead. I need that person-under-train announcement as a diversion.

Mitch squinted at Nick hoping he could read his mind, just as the announcement came over the station P.A. system.

"Due to person under train, your service will be delayed. We apologize for the inconvenience."

Mitch turned to see Lawrence looking around quickly, his eyes finding Andrew on the platform.

"Is this a trick?" Lawrence hissed at Andrew.

Mitch grabbed Nick, pulling him close and whispered one word, hoping it would explain his actions.

"Bomb!"

"Got you covered," Nick said.

With split second timing, Nick moved into the doorway not letting anyone out of the carriage. Mitch's mind was in overload as he turned and ran for the stairs taking them two at a time, steadying the briefcase under his arm.

Got to get the bomb out of here.
Where to?
The water. Run the bomb to the water.

Mastermind

He heard Lawrence yell: "Get him!"

The last thing Mitch heard as he left the Underground was the station erupting in noise.

———

Adam picked up Mitch's one word through the watch microphone.

"We've got a bomb situation people, stay alert," Adam announced calmly over their wires as though this was part of a normal day.

He turned to see the ex-military man in the carriage pull his gun and decide to clear Nick out of the way of the door, firing at him at close range.

Adam yelled a warning but it was too late; Nick never saw it coming. One minute he was blocking the entrance to the carriage, the next, he was falling forward with the force of the bullet, hitting the concrete platform hard. He was out cold.

"Take him, Sam," Adam ordered through the headset.

Samantha fired from her sniper's position, taking Lawrence's ex-military man out with one clear shot. He collapsed into the aisle of the train carriage.

Adam could see Nick was breathing but not moving; he was lying right in the doorway of the train, in the open.

Lawrence drew a handgun. Adam saw it and moved in tackling Lawrence to the ground. Within seconds, he had Lawrence's arms back behind his back and cuffed.

Bullets were flying throughout the station, the air rancid and the noise deafening. Shots were fired inside the carriage; the Italian shooting at Officer Skinner.

Adam was within reach of Nick, still lying face down on the concrete. With his foot, Adam pushed Nick over the platform down onto the rails, out of the line of fire.

The man in the Jack Daniel's T-shirt took a shot at Adam from behind a concrete pylon. Adam grabbed his .224 Boz and returned fire. He heard Lawrence laugh through the noise of the gunfire.

413

"What's so bloody funny?" Adam pulled Lawrence's head up from behind, as a bullet whistled past him.

"Your friend, he's never going to make it."

"How long?"

Lawrence smirked. Adam pushed him away. He saw the large guy in the tracksuit draw a gun and head towards him, intent on rescuing Lawrence.

"Stop!" Ellen yelled loud enough to get tracksuit-man's attention.

Good on you, Ellie, Adam thought, relieved.

She had drawn her L85 and had it pointed at Andrew who cowered under a timber bench. The tracksuit-clad man stopped and looked back, debating whether to save Andrew or help Lawrence. The man in the Jack Daniel's T-shirt kept firing at Adam from behind his concrete barrier. Adam was firing back, shielding Lawrence – he wanted him alive. The air was full of smoke making it impossible to see.

"Sam, you and Kent hold off until it's clear. Don't fire unless it's critical," Adam ordered over their headsets.

"Roger," he heard Samantha's confirmation.

Adam saw Skinner and the Italian exchange rapid fire on the carriage. Officer Skinner darting between seats to get closer to the Italian.

"Ellie, report?" Adam requested.

Ellen didn't answer and Adam shot a round at Jack Daniels man before turning to check on her. He saw tracksuit-man's eyes run over Ellen's weapon as she pointed at Andrew's head; weighing up the potential damage. Suddenly, tracksuit-man turned his gun on Ellen. A bullet rang out from the sniper's position. Tracksuit-man collapsed right in front of Ellen, eyes wide open, staring blankly.

"Hesitation kills," Ellen told the dead man, as she dragged Andrew to his feet and cuffed him. "Thanks snipers!" she said looking skywards.

"Sorry, Adam, that was critical," Samantha said via her microphone.

"Agreed," he said.

All of a sudden, Adam noticed the two girls from the train cowering in the corner.

For chrissake! I thought this platform was clear.

Pushing Lawrence aside, he ran towards the screaming girls, firing back at the Jack Daniel's man, as he shielded them to the opposite exit. He pushed them up the stairs.

I don't have time for this shit. I've got to get the timing of the bomb out of Lawrence. Nick, I need you!

Adam turned to find Harley had given up on him and was turning his attention to Ellen, intent on freeing Andrew nearby. Harley tackled Ellen, his fifteen-stone frame knocking her off her feet. The two of them hit the floor.

"Can't risk a shot," Samantha said.

Adam could barely hear her above the roar of gunfire in the carriage. Everything was happening in fast motion.

"Need help back here," he indicated Ellen who didn't stand a chance against the bulk of Harley, unless she could get her gun arm free.

Officer Skinner was still exchanging rounds with the Italian. Officer Watson ran out of the second carriage and with his L85, fired towards the Jack Daniel's guy trying to make his way to Ellen and Harley. Adam looked up in time to see Watson take a bullet and fall off the platform edge.

Damn! I hope that Kevlar vest works.

Adam turned and fired a round at Harley who fell injured and screaming on top of Ellen. Adam raced over, pulled him off and secured his hands with plasticuffs. He ran back to Lawrence.

"OK, enough crap. How long have we got?"

―――

Nick regained consciousness, the blackness lifting. He felt the tracks beneath him and a wave of panic passed over him. He tried to pull himself up and couldn't. He tried again, and got up on his elbows. He looked down to gauge the extent of his injuries. The vest had saved him, but the close range had drawn blood. He struggled up, blinking, trying to clear his vision.

Hell, my head's thumping! He gritted his teeth as his skin burned where the bullet fragments had scraped him.

Nick pulled himself over to the edge of the platform. He could see Adam threatening Lawrence. Behind him, Nick could hear the gunfire in the carriage and Ellen was over on the far side of the platform pushing some huge guy off the top of her. His mind snapped into gear.

Mitch's got the bomb.

"How long?" he yelled at Adam. He saw the look of relief that swept over Adam's face at the sight of him.

"Don't know!" Adam yelled back.

Nick spotted Lawrence's mobile. It had fallen a few feet from Lawrence's body. He grabbed it. "One and half minutes!"

"Go!" Adam shouted.

Nick ran, falling over at the foot of the stairs as the grogginess hit him. He pulled himself up on hands and knees, gripping the rail.

Adam ran across the platform firing at the Jack Daniel's man who returned fire with vengeance. Taking cover, Adam risked a quick look around. Officer Watson was lying on the tracks not moving; Ellen was heading to the carriage where Skinner and the Italian were battling it out; Andrew—Lawrence's right-hand man—had pushed himself, cuffs and all behind the huge deceased bulk of Harley; and Lawrence lay bound on the platform watching it all with a satisfied look. The Jack Daniel's guy was … Adam hit him with a volley of bullets … dead.

Adam turned to see Andrew Kenny, hands bound, reaching for Harley's gun.

Samantha leapt down from her position in the ceiling, calling for Officer Kent to cover her. She landed and raced towards Andrew.

"Drop it!" She yelled.

Andrew froze and Samantha kicked the gun away from him. Adam joined her, pulling Andrew up and yanking him over next to Lawrence. Adam saw Lawrence's eyes widen at the sight of Samantha.

"Sam, get your butt off this platform," Adam glared at her. "Check on Watson and stay down there with him." He indicated Officer Watson lying on the track.

Mitch sprinted as fast as he could.

OK, he thought, Lawrence probably planned the bomb to go off between stations. That gives me about five minutes ... at least two minutes have gone.

The pain from his ribs and ankle made itself known to him. His chest heaved with the effort. The river came into view and he pushed himself harder.

Got to get there in less than two minutes.

His breathing was loud and labored, each step like a knife in his ribs. He clutched the briefcase tightly under one arm and held his ribs with the other.

Unbeknown to Mitch, he had less than a minute left.

The sound of gunshots continued to explode in the carriage as Ellen, Skinner and the Italian exchanged fire. Bullets passed through chairs and struck metal. Adam jumped down onto the rails and pulled himself up on the back of the train and onto the carriage roof. He saw Ellen sidle along to the entrance of the carriage. Skinner was firing from behind the seats. The Italian was surrounded, but still he wouldn't surrender.

Adam needed to speak with Officer Kent in the sniper position, but Samantha had the intercom and had left her position. He looked up from the roof of the carriage, trying to get Kent's attention. He made hand signs asking if Kent could get a clear shot. Kent responded in the negative. Adam looked around.

Too much smoke, fair enough.

Adam moved along the carriage roof. Leaning slightly forward, he got Skinner's attention through the window. He drew his finger across his throat, ordering a ceasefire.

Don't need to be shot by my own team, he thought.

Skinner nodded and Adam watched him pass the message to Ellen. Seconds later, only the sound of the Italian firing could be heard. Instantly, Adam swung in through the broken window, and landed right behind the Italian. With two swift moves, Adam had the Italian around the neck and on the floor. The Italian was bleeding from an arm wound.

"You made contact, but he'll live," Adam told Skinner, handing over the offender.

"It's your lucky day, buddy," Skinner smirked taking the Italian and cuffing him. "All clear in the carriage now," Skinner confirmed.

"Clear on the platform," Ellen added.

Adam strode out of the carriage. He saw Samantha attending to Officer Watson lying on the track injured, but alive.

"OK?"

"Yep, he'll live," Samantha answered.

Adam looked around.

"Looks like a battlefield; blood, bullets, men down and the carriage is a write-off," he muttered.

He put his hands on his hips and did a quick check, securing the area; everyone was dead or accounted for. He looked to the stairs.

Where are you, Mitch? Did you make it?

Suddenly, he heard a sound and froze. He looked from Samantha to Ellen.

"Train!" he exclaimed. "It's supposed to be a secure area. What the hell is happening?"

He turned towards the sound of an engine roaring towards them down the tunnel.

49

ADAM RELOADED.

The train came towards them, pulling up short, so that the last carriage could be seen from either platform. A group of passengers alighted, an elderly couple walked arm in arm towards the stairs.

"What the hell's going on?" Adam looked around. "How did this train get in here?"

Everyone on his team looked equally surprised. The alighting passengers looked across the platform in morbid fascination at the destruction around them.

"Ellie, go through to the driver, check out how this train got in here," Adam directed.

Ellen crossed the platform via the rails and lifting herself up on the other side, ran up the side of the train out of sight.

Adam saw Richard Sinclair, one of Lawrence's directors, step from the last carriage.

"What the hell?"

Richard came up behind the elderly couple and pulled a gun, holding it to the old man's head.

"How the hell did you get in here?" Adam snapped at Richard with a subtle glance to Officer Kent in the ceiling.

Got to get a message to Kent ... buggar, if Sam was up there on intercom. He gritted his teeth.

"Surely", Richard answered, "you've learned by now that money can buy you anything – love, security officers, train drivers," he smiled enjoying the joke. "But you're on a policeman's salary, how would you know? Untie Lawrence now – or else we'll give these two an early departure," he pushed the gun into the neck of the trembling old man.

Lawrence yelled out to his director. "There is one in the carriage still, Richard."

Richard bent to look, not removing the gun from his hostage. Officer Skinner was moving around in the carriage on the opposite track, trying to get an angle on Richard. Pushing the elderly couple in front of him as a shield, Richard stood on the edge of the platform and yelled, "Drop your weapon and get out here now!"

Good, he doesn't know about Kent in the ceiling, Adam thought.

Skinner emerged with his hands in the air. Richard ordered him to move next to Samantha and Adam.

Stay at the front of the train, Ellie, Adam willed her in his thoughts.

"Release Lawrence," Richard ordered Adam.

Adam swore. No bloody way. This is my show. His mind was clicking over looking for a solution.

"Hurry up!" Richard snapped.

Adam pulled Lawrence to his feet and pushed him into a sitting position on a platform bench.

"Richard, I didn't know you had it in you," Lawrence beamed.

"Me either," Richard agreed.

"Please ..." the old man begged.

"Shut up," Richard ordered.

I need a distraction, a miracle. Adam's eyes searched the station and the faces of Samantha and Skinner.

Then, it came in the form of the elderly hostage. His heart gave out with shock and he collapsed to the floor.

Nick could see Mitch was almost at the water's edge near the South Dock. It was under a minute away. Nick sprinted faster than he thought himself capable of doing. He had almost caught up; the stopwatch told him twenty seconds remained.

Mitch was limping, not moving fast enough.

Twenty seconds before the bomb blows!

"Throw it!" Nick yelled, struggling to catch up.

Seventeen seconds.

Charging at full speed, Nick yelled again from behind Mitch, "Throw it, Mitch." He groaned as his shirt rubbed the burnt skin with every movement.

Fifteen seconds.

Mitch glanced back.

"Get away, Nick!" he gasped.

"Mitch, it's going to blow, throw it, now!" Nick yelled panting, his words escaping him. "Now!"

Nick could almost touch him. Panic was overpowering him. In ten seconds the bomb would go off in Mitchell Parker's hands.

"Get ... off ... Nick ... get ... back!"

Nick had him.

Five seconds.

He grabbed the brief case from Mitch's hand and cast it high into the air towards the river.

Three seconds.

Hurling himself at Mitch in a side tackle, they went sprawling down onto the concrete pavement. The bomb exploded in mid-air, hitting the water in a huge fireball. They stayed covered while the explosion peaked, feeling the heat above and random bits of debris hitting them. For a few seconds, neither of them moved. When the debris stopped flying, they raised their heads and exchanged looks.

"You had a little less time than you calculated," Nick gasped.

Mitch, breathing erratically, looked shocked.

"That stupid bastard," Mitch spat.

"You OK?"

Mitch nodded. "That was close."

"Too close," Nick agreed.

They pushed themselves up and began running back to the station.

"Help him," the elderly woman screamed as her husband gripped his heart and gasped for oxygen.

"I said shut up!" Richard pushed the gun against her temple.

The elderly man lay on the platform, clutching his chest.

Adam glanced towards the ceiling at his last remaining sniper.

Take him, Kent! He thought. Then he saw Ellen rise inside the carriage. One shot rang out, the elderly lady screamed – beside them, Richard fell backwards, dead.

"Beautiful work, Ellie." Adam looked over to Lawrence. "Any other directors you want to pull out of a hat?" he demanded reaching for his phone to call an ambulance.

"Carriages are clear," Ellen advised him.

Adam saw Samantha run across the platform to help the couple.

"Sam, I needed you in sniper then."

"Adam ..."

"Save it," he said angrily. "We're done people, stand down." He looked back at Samantha. "That was the only order that should have seen you leave sniper position."

He watched as Officer Kent lowered himself from the ceiling.

"There is an ambulance on the way," Adam told Ellen as she moved to assist the elderly man. He looked down at the Italian who moaned loudly, holding his bleeding arm. "Shut up, you'll be the last to get treatment."

On the platform, three of Lawrence's security men lay dead.

Mitch vomited; the pain from his chest restricting his breathing and movement.

"Feels like a knife's been wedged in my ribs," he wiped his mouth.

Nick stopped with him and waited. Mitch looked up, noticing the blood on Nick's shirt.

"You've been hit!"

"The vest stopped it, knocked me out with the force. I think I've got a slight concussion, I feel a bit groggy."

"I think you broke the land speed record catching up to me," Mitch told him with an attempt at a smile.

"Helps that you're a slow runner," Nick ribbed him.

Mitch gave him a wry glance as the pair kept moving, hurrying to the Underground entrance. An ambulance could be heard coming down the street. Mitch's heart caught in his throat and he quickened his pace.

God, no!

The officer at the Underground entrance let them through. Mitch and Nick raced down the stairs, clinging to the outer walls until they surveyed the scene. It was clear; the battle was over. Samantha, seeing him at the entrance, called out his name in relief. Mitch looked around; everyone was alive. He looked to Adam.

"OK?" he asked bending over to catch his breath, relief coursing through him.

"We're all done here," Adam patted him on the back. "Glad to see you though."

"See, we needn't have come back," Nick joked to Mitch, his hands on his hips, taking deep breaths.

"No dramas?"

"A few, but nothing we couldn't handle," Adam answered.

Mitch had stopped listening; he was staring straight ahead, recognizing Andrew Kenny. He bolted across the platform and dragged Andrew up from the bench, knocking him to the ground with a powerful punch. Andrew, his hands tied behind his back, was screaming when Adam pulled Mitch away from him. Blood poured out of Andrew's broken nose.

"That's for Anthony Jenkins," Mitch spat a mixture of blood and saliva at Andrew's feet.

Pulling away from Adam's grip, Mitch massaged his hand. "Before you start thinking I'm out of control, I want you to know that I planned that," he glanced back to Andrew lying on the ground.

"Fine by me," Adam assured him, "he had it coming."

Mitch walked past Nick. "Don't say it."

"What?" Nick turned to follow him.

"I don't want to hear it."

Nick grinned. "I wasn't going to say anything about you being wound too tightly or being too tense."

"Good."

"Seriously, though, I wonder how you survived this long without me," Nick joked.

"One of life's great mysteries," Mitch agreed.

The Chief of Police, William Irwin, entered followed by a number of uniformed officers. Mitch went over to meet him. The two stood in the corner debriefing.

———

Lawrence watched the events unfolding from where he sat, propped up on a bench, his hands cuffed. He passed his cuffed hands under his backside, and succeeded in pulling his arms in front, his cuffed hands now on his lap. He looked down at his Armani suit covered in dirt and frowned.

Time to play another card. The thought made him smile.

———

Mitch watched Lawrence from a distance as one of Irwin's officers began to lead Lawrence away. He heard Irwin order the trains to be moved out of the station to clear the debris. Mitch walked over to Adam. He turned, hearing someone yell behind him and saw

Lawrence break away from the police and bolt towards the tunnel. At the same time, the two trains began to slowly move out.

Mitch watched amazed.

What's he doing? Shit! He's going to ... Samantha's near the tunnel!

Mitch ran down the track in pursuit, Adam beside him.

"Sam!" Mitch yelled.

Before Samantha could react, Lawrence leapt, knocking her over and pulling her in front, restraining her around the throat with his cuffed hands.

"Nice to see you again, that's one point for your team," Mitch heard Lawrence say. "I didn't see that one coming."

Samantha fought to breathe. Mitch's gut instincts about Samantha being at risk came back to haunt him.

"Stay back," Lawrence jeered, pulling himself and Samantha to standing position and keeping her firmly in front of him, as she gasped for air.

"He's not armed," one of the officers said, charging at Lawrence.

"No!" Mitch yelled as Lawrence, leaping to avoid the officer, fell over the edge of the platform, taking Samantha with him, directly in front of the train gathering speed along the line.

Mitch leapt from the platform, slamming into Samantha and wrenching her from Lawrence's grips. His body engulfed Samantha as they cleared the track, and he felt the rush of air from the carriages passing within inches of them.

Lawrence fell onto the rails directly under the front wheels of the train. Mitch reached for him, missing him and feeling the fabric of Lawrence's suit brush his fingertips.

Mitch and Samantha lying level on the parallel tracks, watched as Lawrence met his death.

50

No one moved, and then everything happened at once. The train screamed to a halt further up the tunnel, paramedics jumped onto the tracks, officers began to photograph the area. Samantha and Mitch gingerly raised themselves from the tracks. Mitch was up first, offering her a hand.

"You saved my life," Samantha said as he pulled her up.

"Again," he teased, dusting her off.

"I was seconds away from death. That could be me now," she said, her eyes fixed on Lawrence. The tone of her voice made Mitch take notice.

"Sam," Mitch turned her to face him. Her eyes were darting around the scene, her face was ashen. "Hey, look at me." He held her shoulders. "Samantha!"

Mitch motioned to one of the paramedics.

"I think we might have shock here," he indicated Samantha who refused to let go of his arm.

"Can you bring her up?" the paramedic asked with a nod to the stretcher on the platform.

Mitch agreed, then just as suddenly Samantha snapped out of it.

"I'm OK," she struggled out of his grip.

"Samantha let the paramedics ..." Mitch started.

"I'm OK," she blinked rapidly. "I was blown away seeing Lawrence sliced and diced."

Mitch winced at her turn of phrase. He was still holding her arms.

"Go over there and let them check you out. It's an order!" Mitch pushed her towards the edge of the platform.

Adam leaned down, extending his arm and pulled her back up on the platform.

———

Mitch was in a discussion with the Chief of Police, William Irwin, when John rang. He handed the phone to Ellen with a promise to call back.

As he talked with Irwin, Mitch watched the paramedics treat his team; Nick lay on a bench as the paramedic stripped off the Kevlar vest to clean and bandage the wound and treat him for a mild concussion. The skin was burnt around the area where the bullet fragments had penetrated the vest and Nick gritted his teeth as the area was disinfected.

Lying next to Nick was Officer Watson undergoing the same treatment and next to him, Samantha was being treated for shock. Mitch glanced to Adam as he collected weapons and debriefed the remaining officers on duty.

Irwin departed to supervise the clean up and Mitch returned to his team, noticing only the medics, Underground cleaning staff and his team remained on the platform.

"Great job guys, thank you." His tone conveyed how grateful he felt.

"You're welcome and your shout," Adam said.

Mitch laughed. "Since I'm alive, that's probably a fair call."

"You need to get those ribs seen to first," Nick told him.

"They'll heal, they're not broken, just bruised," Mitch said.

"You can share my painkillers," Nick said. Turning to Ellen, he smiled. "That was some crack shooting."

"I'll second that," Adam agreed, "she's a hotshot."

Ellen shrugged off their praise. "Thanks."

She handed Mitch back his phone. "John wants you to call back later with a full report. I gave him a brief overview. He also said to tell you to get the medic to check you out."

Mitch gave her an exasperated look.

"I swear he's got me chipped."

———

When they were thrown out of the local pub at two in the morning, closing time, they took supplies and headed back to the apartment. Everyone was far too wired to sleep. They sat around unwinding, eating takeaway pizza and drinking beer and wine. When Nick went outside for a cigarette, Mitch got up, stretched and followed him onto the balcony.

Mitch took a mouthful of beer and leaned back against the wall. He looked over at Nick. "Nick, hey, thanks for saving my butt tonight."

"Don't mention it. You'd do the same for me, I think," Nick said with an amused look on his face. Anyway, now we're even – you got me onto your team, after all."

"Hardly lifesaving stuff. Pretty much the opposite given the injuries you've scored already."

"Don't be so sure about that," Nick looked away.

"I confess it was somewhat self-motivated. I wanted to keep an eye on you."

"And I'm supposed to be the eldest."

"By twenty days," Mitch shook his head. "Heard that line a few thousand times."

Nick lit a cigarette.

"Your hands are shaking. Are you OK?"

"Yeah, I'm good," Nick put his hand in his pocket, out of Mitch's line of vision.

"How are you really feeling?" Mitch prodded.

Nick exhaled.

"On fire. I'm not sure how I ended up down on that track. I can't remember."

"That'd be the concussion," Mitch said. "You know, it's pretty normal to have the shakes after these sort of things. It's not every day you get shot or get a gun stuck in your face."

Nick nodded. "How about you?"

"It only hurts when I breathe. Nothing that a few beers and some painkillers won't fix."

Five minutes later they went inside to rejoin the group. They were still sitting around at three in the morning when John called. Mitch left the team and sought the quietness of Nick's assigned room to fill John in. His own bed, the sofa, was occupied.

At three-thirty they were finally spent; the surge of adrenalin had been replaced by exhaustion.

"Where's Mitch?" Adam asked. "He can't still be on that call."

"I'll check it out," Nick rose and went into the room.

Mitch was fast asleep on the bed, phone still in his hands, fully dressed.

Nick removed Mitch's boots and manoeuvred the phone out of his hand. Tossing the bed cover over him, he grabbed a spare pillow and departed, the sofa in sight.

51

The next morning across the U.K, radio broadcasts and the second edition of the Evening Standard were breaking the news of Mastermind, Lawrence Hackett and his untimely death. The story read like a movie in the making. It featured the heroism of the U.K. team, a bit about the American contingent, photos of the wrecked carriages and witness accounts from passengers who spotted the team or heard gunfire.

"Check this out – you guys barely rate a mention," Adam read from the article. "A crack team of the U.K.'s finest supported by FBI agents … blah, blah, blah."

Mitch grinned. "Yeah, just autograph that copy for us and we'll take it home and frame it."

Adam laughed and read on. "Being an only child, Lawrence Hackett has left his entire personal fortune to charity."

"Touching," Nick sipped on a strong coffee and rubbed his lower back.

"Sore back?" Ellen asked.

"Hmm, that sofa wasn't the best."

"I slept great," Mitch glanced at Nick.

"Yeah, you're welcome. I would have woken you up and sent you packing if I'd known how uncomfortable the sofa was."

Adam continued. "Goes on to tell us he was a poor little rich kid whose father never had time for him; money can't buy happiness – it's lonely at the top," Adam sighed dramatically, "don't we know it."

Mitch rose and stood by the glass doors of the apartment, looking over at Lawrence's building as he finished his coffee.

"What are you thinking?" Samantha asked.

Mitch shrugged. "I'm guessing Lawrence never expected to walk away alive, nor had he intended for us or anyone on that train to either. It was, as he said, his swansong."

"That's fine for him, but he's left behind a train wreck – the families of the directors and Anthony Jenkins's will never recover," Ellen leaned over and read over Adam's shoulder. "They've already charged Andrew and they're looking for the remaining directors."

"You wait," Adam handed the paper over to Ellen. "The paternity claims will be next. Women by the hundred claiming their child is a legitimate Lawrence offspring to get a bit of that fortune."

"Damn! I should have slept with him," Samantha shook her head and smiled as Mitch grimaced at her. "For the good of the mission."

"Of course," he nodded.

At Heathrow Airport, Mitch shook Adam's hand firmly.

"Thanks for everything, Adam," Mitch said. "We couldn't have done it without you. I'm glad you were on our side."

"Thank you, Mitch. The pleasure was all mine, really."

"Look us up when you next come over."

"I will," Adam assured him. "Might get another gig together."

"Yeah, we'll show you around our turf."

Nick followed Mitch, extending his hand to Adam.

"Listen buddy, don't be too concerned about the Porsche's security ... it was hard to hotwire," Nick said tongue in cheek.

"How hard?" Adam asked shaking Nick's hand, a grin on his face.

"Took me a good two minutes."

Adam shook his head. "Go catch your plane, leave me in pain." He gave Ellen a quick hug and saluted the three as they boarded. Samantha stayed behind to say her goodbye.

Halfway down the boarding tunnel, Mitch waited for her. Samantha fell into stride beside him.

"Did Adam debrief you on what happened on the platform?"

"Yep."

Samantha swallowed. "What did he say about my performance?"

"Nothing in particular, he said it all went fairly smoothly."

She nodded. Mitch noticed Samantha looked relieved.

"Why, did something happen?"

"No! I just wanted some feedback."

"You survived! That was top of my agenda," Mitch said. They followed Nick and Ellen on board the plane. "You sure nothing happened I should know about?"

Samantha rolled her eyes. "If it did, I'm not telling."

52

Mitch walked through the office. With a glance to the left, he saw John talking on the phone. He continued to his own office, throwing his luggage on the floor and sizing up the pile of paperwork that had amassed in his absence. Mitch ignored it, reaching for the phone. He called Charlotte and got her voice mail.

Great! He left a message, hung up and began to log into his computer. John appeared at the door.

"Mitch!"

"Hey, John!" Mitch's phone began to ring. "Sorry, won't be a minute, I'll just get this."

"Mitchell Parker," he answered.

"Charlotte Curtis" he heard her voice and smiled. His eyes flickered to John and he reddened.

"Uh, just a minute …" Mitch stammered.

"Come and see me later," John pre-empted him as he reached to close Mitch's door.

He nodded and waited until he heard the door click close.

"Hey, Charlie."

"Hello, when did you get back?"

"An hour ago."

"And you went straight to the office? That's keen."

"To tie up loose ends."

"So, how are you, Mitch?"

"I'm great. How about you?"

"I'm totally distracted and unable to concentrate; otherwise I'm well."

"That sounds terrible. Is there anything you can take for that?" he teased her, lowering his voice, despite the closed office door.

"Did you ring up for any particular purpose or just to embarrass me?"

"I rang to hear your voice. I need to see you," Mitch sighed.

There was a silence on the line.

"Are you there?" Mitch asked.

"Yes, sorry. I think that's such a lovely thing to say, you surprised me."

"By being honest?"

"By being open."

"See, I am capable of it!"

Charlotte laughed. "Touché. By the way, Mitch, you never did tell me what happened to library girl. I hope you haven't broken her heart."

Mitch stopped to think.

"Ah, library girl. No, her heart's still intact, I imagine. That seems like a lifetime ago."

"It was two weeks ago. So, it wasn't a successful date?"

"To be perfectly honest, it was going pretty well until I called her Charlie."

"Oh, my God," Charlotte laughed, "that's terrible".

"Yes, you sound so sincere. Naturally, that was the end of the date, so I paid the bill and we called it a night."

Mitch could hear Charlotte laughing.

"Anyway," Mitch continued, "I thought I'd try out my dating technique again. I rang to ask if you might be available for a date tomorrow night? I should be awake by then."

"Let me see," Charlotte said. He heard her rustle the pages in her diary. "As luck would have it, I have an opening."

Mitch laughed. "Great. Well, shall I pick you up at say, seven-thirty, at your room?"

"That would be fine. What do I wear?"

"Something dressy," he assured her.

"OK."

That sat in silence for a few seconds.

"Well, I'll be seeing you," Mitch said.

"Tonight?"

"Tonight, for sure," he confirmed.

Mitch hung up and sat back in his chair. He had an idea. With a smile on his face, he leaned forward and dialed a number. Giving his pilot registration number, Mitch booked a light plane for the next evening.

This is one night we are not going to forget!

THE END

Dear reader,

We hope you enjoyed reading *Mastermind*. Please take a moment to leave a review, even if it's a short one. Your opinion is important to us.

Discover more books by Helen Goltz at https://www.nextchapter.pub/authors/helen-goltz

Want to know when one of our books is free or discounted for Kindle? Join the newsletter at http://eepurl.com/bqqB3H

Best regards,

Helen Goltz and the Next Chapter Team

The story continues in:

Graveyard Of The Atlantic by Helen Goltz

To read the first chapter for free, head to:
https://www.nextchapter.pub/books/graveyard-of-the-atlantic

ACKNOWLEDGMENTS

My sincere thanks to:

Francis Price for his great ideas and endless network of contacts that provided information, clarity and credibility to the research element of this book;

Author Anita Bell—made available via the Queensland Writers' Centre—my mentor throughout the process;

Assistant Commissioner Clem O'Regan who generously gave his time to answer my police procedural questions;

Family and friends who proof read the manuscript and gave me feedback –Merle Goltz, Michael, Craig Williams and Chris Adams;

Chairman of the Australian Book Group, Catharine Retter for championing this novel;

And most importantly Atlas B. Goltz – my writing partner.

ABOUT THE AUTHOR

Helen Goltz has worked as a print journalist; television and radio producer; and editor for community newspapers and lifestyle publications. Helen is the author of twelve books across a range of genres and is postgraduate qualified with majors in English Literature and Communications. Helen lives in Queensland, Australia with her husband and boxer dog.

Connect with Helen at:
Website: helengoltz.com
Facebook: www.facebook.com/HelenGoltz.Author
Twitter: @helengoltz

NEXT IN THE MITCHELL PARKER SERIES (CRIME THRILLER):

Graveyard of the Atlantic

Below the surface of the ocean, off the shores of Cape Hatteras, lie the bodies of many ships that never made it to shore and something more ... silent and sinister.

Two sets of fresh fingerprints on a pair of binoculars left on the beach are cause for concern for FBI special agent Mitchell Parker and his team, Nick Everett, Ellen Beetson and Samantha Moore. The prints belong to a criminal that is currently not listed as in the country and a foreign diplomat who disappeared a year ago.

And are the six Beijing police officers that are guests of the USA to study, the same six officers that left Beijing?

It's a rough and violent ride for Mitchell Parker and his team against the ocean and the clock.

———

"Every time you think you have it figured out, something else happens ... and a big surprise at the end. A fast read because you can't put it down."
Lorraine Montgomery, Ms M's Bookshelf

Next in the Mitchell Parker series (crime thriller):

"The interactions between these characters, and the way that the whole team works is undoubtedly one of the great strengths." Karen, Aust Crime Fiction Reviews

"This book makes for compelling reading." Michael Swensson, Aussie Readers, Goodreads

MORE IN THE MITCHELL PARKER SERIES
...

The Fourth Reich (Mitchell Parker series)

The stilted footage of Holocaust survivors marching through the gates of Auschwitz projects behind Benjamin Hoefer at the book launch of his father, Eli's biography. As it comes to the end and closes in on Eli Hoefer's gaunt face, four red words are scratched across the last frame— Nazi, Jew hater, fake!

FBI Special Agent Mitchell Parker is frustrated to be called in on what he believes is a police matter, but digging soon reveals a threat that has far-reaching implications.

Parker and his team, Nick Everett, Ellen Beetson and Adam Forster find themselves in the middle of a neo-Nazi plot that spans two continents and threatens to bring one of the worst atrocities of history back to life.

―――――

"Well-written and full of suspense and interesting characters, these books keep me on the edge of my seat waiting for the next installment."

More in the Mitchell Parker series …

— Lorraine Montgomery, Ms M's Bookshelf

"Starts out at breakneck pace, and that doesn't give up at any point."

— Karen, AustCrimeFiction

"A great read with incredible twists; gripping and intense."

— Brenda Telford, Aussie Readers.

"Another fine instalment in what is fast becoming an action lovers' dream."

— Michael, Goodreads.